I0729759

VANGUARD
ANNIHILATION

BOOKS BY JAROM STRONG

Paragon Space

Vanguard Strike

Vanguard Nemesis

VANGUARD ANNIHILATION

JAROM STRONG

SECOND SKY

Published by Second Sky in 2025

An imprint of Storyfire Ltd.
Carmelite House
50 Victoria Embankment
London EC4Y 0DZ

www.secondskybooks.com

The authorised representative in the EEA is Hachette Ireland
8 Castlecourt Centre
Dublin 15 D15 XTP3
Ireland
(email: info@hbgi.ie)

Copyright © Jarom Strong, 2025

Jarom Strong has asserted his right to be identified
as the author of this work.

All rights reserved. No part of this publication may be reproduced, stored in any
retrieval system, or transmitted, in any form or by any means, electronic,
mechanical, photocopying, recording or otherwise, without the prior written
permission of the publishers.

ISBN: 978-1-83618-317-4
eBook ISBN: 978-1-83618-316-7

This book is a work of fiction. Names, characters, businesses, organizations,
places and events other than those clearly in the public domain are either the
product of the author's imagination or are used fictitiously. Any resemblance to
actual persons, living or dead, events or locales is entirely coincidental.

To Ryan, for teaching me to love storytelling—and for teaching me to believe that my stories were worth telling.

ONE

I floated, and the universe sank slowly beneath me.

I don't know how to describe the sensation besides that. It wasn't like floating in water or like being suspended in mid-air without gravity. I felt distinctly that I was untouched by the forces of the universe, that I *was* the force, looking down upon the countless arms of creation as they spun in their wild, decadent, self-cannibalizing vortex.

I saw it all. Stars without number. Planets of every kind. Moons locked in faithful orbits around the objects of their devotion. Black holes straining at the fabric of reality. A thousand different types of celestial debris flung heedlessly across the black canvas of space—and, crawling ant-like between the pieces of heavenly wreckage, people. Humanity, claiming the cold, indifferent void for themselves.

I saw all of it, spread out beneath me like a child's diorama.

And I *hated* it.

———

My eyes snapped open.

I was home.

Kessa's stars swirled across the ceiling of my room on the *Orpheus* above me—bright and yellow and warm where the ones in my dream had been distant and cold. I sat up slowly, massaging my temple. That dream. I'd always been a vivid dreamer, but that had felt... different, somehow. Usually my dreams were just terrifying combinations of my worst memories. I awoke from them panicked, my heart racing and my sheets soaked through with sweat. Now, though, I just felt... confused. Disoriented. As if I'd been asleep for centuries instead of hours. The images were blurred, but one thing remained, seared into my brain.

Hate.

"This is your pilot speaking." Rose's voice crackled over the intercom, her cadence cheery and clipped as if she were speaking to the crew of a passenger shuttle about to land for a holiday. *"Just a quick update that we are about half an hour from dropping out of nullspace."*

Half an hour. I inhaled, held it, and then exhaled through my nostrils, hoping the oxygen would help to clear my head. I didn't have time for dissecting whatever bizarre dreams my head had decided to thrust upon me. Right now, I had to focus.

"And a reminder before you all disembark," Rose's voice continued, *"that tipping your pilot is always both welcome and appreciated."*

Chipper as ever. But then, she always was right before we were about to do something that should have terrified her. Crazy girl.

A gentle knock at my door.

"One sec," I said. "I'm on my—"

The door slid open and Sev stepped through. The words caught in my throat, and for a moment all I could do was blink at her. She was wearing her old pilot's outfit, a dark-red leather jacket with white stripes down the sides, and a pistol on her belt. Without the world-weary crows' feet beside her vivid-green eyes, I'd have thought that everything I'd been through the past nine years had been a bad dream. That I was back with my old crew on the *Orpheus*, making our way to one last job. Always one last job.

In that respect, at least, nothing had changed.

Sev leaned against my doorframe, raising an eyebrow. "You alright? Look like you've seen a ghost."

"I'm looking at one right now," I said, shaking myself. My memories still felt jumbled and foggy, as if they'd been torn out of my brain and then dumped back in.

She glanced down at her jacket and flushed slightly. "I—well, figured it wouldn't do to be dressed in one of my pantsuits when we go aboard. I'll blend in better like this."

"Makes sense." I looked around groggily. Sev followed my eyes, studying my sweat-soaked sheets.

"More nightmares?" Sev asked quietly.

"No. Yes. Sort of." I reached for my shirt and pulled it on. "Felt... different from my usual ones. Couldn't really say why."

She nodded slowly, studying me. "Are you... are you *sure* you're ready for this?"

I frowned. "Ready?"

She said nothing. I realized Sev was staring at me—no, not at me. At my left hand. I frowned down at it.

The memories all came rushing back.

The *Aboena*. The ultrarippers. Nadus. The Shapers. The desperate fight against the Paragon. My final, brutal struggle with Cairn. I remembered his bloody, leering face twisting suddenly into fear as I hurled him into the churning machinery of the *Aboena*'s powercore. I remembered the burning, twisting, searing pain lancing up my arm as my left hand was taken with him.

I turned my hand over. Stretched the palm out. Wiggled my fingers.

"I can't quite believe it, either," Sev said. Her voice was almost reverent. "I thought for sure that we'd have to get you a prosthetic. But now, it looks…"

"Like it never happened," I muttered.

She nodded.

I didn't remember much of what had happened after I'd killed Cairn. Hours, days, weeks had blurred together. I'd felt a floating sensation, not dissimilar from what I'd felt just now in my dream. I'd been in the Stranger's quarters—the ones I'd been brought to earlier, before the battle. Only this time I hadn't seen the same man clad in an exo. I'd seen hands. White, elongated, inhuman looking. Radiating with a distant, starlike light. Then I'd awoken in the Shaper's grove.

That had been a little under a week ago.

I lowered my hand and took a deep breath, grounding myself. The confusion was gone. In its place was a growing resolve.

"Are you *sure*," Sev asked again, "that you're ready for this?"

I reached beneath my bed, fingers grasping.

Are you ready?

I'd spent my entire life since the Last War avoiding the fight, lurking in the corners of space and living off the scraps of humanity. Watching the destructive force I had helped spread across the stars consume humanity. Trying to convince myself that there was nothing I could do about any of it.

My fingers closed around Peacebreaker's familiar weight.

No more.

"You're damn right I'm ready," I growled.

"Little busier up here than I remember," Sev said.

I nodded grimly. The *Orpheus* was by no means a large ship. It was built to be just big enough for a crew, a handful of passengers, and a generous amount of cargo. She was a stealth flyer, after all, not a warship. But by the amount of armed men and women waiting in the *Orpheus*'s bridge as I climbed the hatch, you'd never have guessed.

Rid turned and fixed his eyes on me with a relieved look as I entered. He pushed uncomfortably between two particularly mean looking men and halted by my side. "We're almost there," he said quietly. "But I think they're getting... restless."

"Can't blame them," I said, Rid following behind me alongside Sev as I cleared a way to the bridge. "They've all been cooped up in this tin can together for, what... two days now?"

"Thirty-seven hours and forty-two minutes," Rose said from the pilot's seat without looking up. I didn't miss the wave of motherly pride that washed over Sevani's face as she set eyes on her daughter. Rose continued. "Which means we now have just over three minutes until we drop into position."

"They're used to it," I said. "Tight quarters. Long trips. All of 'em."

I stared through the *Orpheus*'s window into the deep, impenetrable darkness of nullspace. Not a celestial object in sight. I thought, with some discomfort, back to the strange dream before dismissing it. More important matters at hand.

I turned my attention to the mass of humanity that crowded the *Orpheus*'s bridge. They were divided roughly into three groups. My crew was mostly gathered around me. Sev stood resolutely by my side, her presence granting me clarity and courage. Rid waited nervously on my other flank, while Rose was in her pilot's seat. Bentley was sitting at the communication console. Shell was standing near the second group: Roamers.

There were four of them here, all clad in sleek gray composite armor still bearing scars from our desperate battle with the *Leonidas*. They stood at loose attention, but I could see the skepticism in their eyes as they studied me. I recognized them only vaguely as faces I'd passed at one point or another during my nightmarish stay aboard the *Aboena*. Their leader was tall and muscular—by human standards, at least. He carried himself with the vigor of a man much younger than his bald pate and gray-white beard suggested. Tetra had introduced the man to me as Winter.

Winter's eyes moved cautiously from me to the third and final group. On the other side of the bridge were several men and women dressed in ragged combat gear that looked as if it had been salvaged or stolen from a dozen different military units from across the Paragon. They were as unruly and brutal in their appearance as Winter's Roamers were calm and disciplined. Renault's followers, each one of them looking increasingly eager at the prospect of combat—or, more likely, the possibility of loot. Their leader was a burly Vanguard with a badly burned face named Flint. He returned Winter's cool, measuring gaze with a bloodthirsty grin that highlighted the gnarled scar tissue spread across his face, then turned his focus to me. I realized with a start that all eyes were fixed on me, waiting with waning patience for me to say... something.

For the thousandth time since I'd impulsively decided to propose this bizarre little coalition, I cursed myself for a fool. I could've just flown away, leaving the *Aboena* to the Paragon. Could have found Sevani and ran off and hid somewhere far, far away from all this. But I'd just *had* to play the hero. And look where it had gotten me.

I cleared my throat.

"We're just a minute or so from dropping," I said. "We don't know exactly what we're gonna find on the other side, so just hold tight for now while we figure it out."

Winter frowned. "It is true, then. We have no plan."

"We have a plan to make a plan," I said irritably.

"Screw that." Flint cracked his knuckles. "I say we go in guns blazing. Last we heard, they ain't got no Paragon support—it's just a handful of mercs. They'll fold right away once we give 'em a taste of what we're packin'.'"

Winter scoffed. "That would be unwise. It could be a trap."

"Sure," Flint said. "But sometimes the best way to disarm a trap is to kick it. *Hard.*"

"Winter's right," I said reluctantly. There was a part of me that agreed with Flint, but that was the old me. The version of myself that figured the best solution to every problem was a bullet—and if that didn't work, a few more bullets. I was trying to be better than that now. "Our intel is old. They may have been reinforced since Sev escaped the station. We need to figure out what's going on first."

Sev folded her arms. "Plus, we may not need to fight at all. I know the man Vatheson left in charge. He's a greedy bastard, but he values his own skin above all else, so I might be able to talk some reason into him."

Winter nodded, but I was surprised to see some of the pirates grumbling among themselves. Flint cleared his throat. "Pardon me, ma'am, but the boys came all this way looking for a scrap. Some loot, at least. If there ain't nobody to fight, there ain't nobody to loot."

"Maybe we pay some of the locals a visit," one of his followers muttered. "See what they're sitting on."

Sev glowered. "Absolutely not. The residents are *not* a hostile population. You are not here to murder, loot, and destroy, whatever your instincts might be. You're here to liberate. The civilians are on your side. Any reports that come through of mistreatment afterwards will be taken seriously, I promise you. So make sure your men are on their best behavior."

More grumbling. Flint listened to one of them whisper something in his ear, then straightened. "No disrespect intended, ma'am, but the boys, they want to know... can we at least loot the mercs? They understand that there'll be pay for all after the battle and whatnot, it's just... well, with the war going on, credits ain't hardly worth much these days."

I saw no problem with that. I opened my mouth to say as

much only to shut it abruptly as Winter spoke up. "If there *is* to be loot," he said, "we must ensure that it is equally distributed. The Roamers have needs as well."

Flint scoffed. "Then I guess they'd better do their fair share of the killing. Cause I ain't rescuing your sorry hides again for a fistful of worthless digital credits."

Winter's eyes flashed with anger. I cut him off before he could make his retort—likely a warmly delivered reminder of the hundreds of Aboenians who had died defending their home-ship. "Look," I growled. "Credits ain't the point here. Neither is loot. The point is that once we've secured the station, we have a foothold for all three of our groups—Roamer, pirate, and, uh…" I blinked at Sev. What were we? "Smuggler, I suppose. We need to be able to use the infrastructure Sevani's built on that station."

Winter relaxed, nodding his head. The pirates looked unconvinced, though, continuing to mutter among themselves while Flint scowled.

I sighed. "Point is that we've all got to learn how to think about the big picture now. The galaxy is falling apart. And all our groups will fall apart with it unless we can band together and combine our resources. And right now, there's a hell of a lot of resources on that station that we need. So: *no* looting. No slowing down the fight to pick corpses clean. No running off on your own to see what valuables you can pilfer from unarmed civilians." I made eye contact with Flint, hoping his old Vanguard training—the training I knew all too well—would kick in. "We're soldiers now, whether we like it or not. Except this time we ain't fighting for rich bastards a million lightyears away who couldn't care less whether we live or die. We're fighting for ourselves—for our own futures. And I figure that's a hell of a lot better than an armful of loot."

Flint held my gaze for a few moments, then nodded slowly.

Rose's voice boomed across the bridge. "Dropping in ten... nine... eight..."

"Not bad, as far as speeches go," Sev muttered to me. "Didn't know you had it in you."

"Four... three..."

"Me neither," I muttered, turning my gaze to the *Orpheus's* cockpit window.

"Two... one..."

There was no flash of light or rush of sound. Just a slightly nauseating twisted sensation in my gut as the *Orpheus's* null-breacher tore a hole in the fabric of reality and shoved us through it. The darkness out the window was still infinite—except now it was punctuated by the occasional speck of cold, distant light. A golden-red gas planet loomed before us.

My mind stirred uncomfortably back to my dream. A vast, cold, dark universe spread out beneath me, empty save for the tiny specks of light and the infinitesimally smaller humans who dared to venture between them.

I focused on one particular point of light, closer and less cold than the others, locked in orbit around the gas planet. A set of blinking flashes. Albeni 7, a massive, overpopulated citysta-tion that served as a population center for the nearby mining facilities. The home base of Sevani's smuggling empire—or, at least, it had been before Vatheson had swooped in on it.

"Home sweet home," Sev muttered.

TWO

"Scans show five warships surrounding Albeni," Rose said. "Not Paragon, though. Looks like a PMC."

"Where's everyone else?" Rid asked.

"A few minutes behind us," Sev said. She turned to Bentley. "Hail Kenton. Let's get this party started."

While we waited, I glanced down at the holomap in the center of the bridge. Five dots—marked red by Rose to designate them as hostiles—flanked a blue dot labeled ALBENI 7. They must have detected the energy surge of the *Orpheus* breaching from nullspace, because one of them began to pivot to face us.

Bentley raised his hand, attracting all eyes to where he sat at the comms station. He flushed, lowering his hand. "Kenton is on, Sev." Sev nodded and moved towards the communication console, standing in front of the camera. She took a deep breath, calming herself.

That calmness shattered immediately into a simmering glare as Kenton's image appeared in the holoprojector.

Rasfel Kenton had become the station manager of Albeni 7 around the same time Sev had started her smuggling enterprise. Her careful bribery of the man was a cornerstone of her success—she had managed to tie his success to her own in a way his greed simply couldn't resist. Not until Vatheson had come around, at least. We still weren't sure exactly what deal they'd struck, but it had been lucrative enough to make Kenton turn completely on Sev, allowing Vatheson's mercenaries aboard and giving them free reign to tear apart her entire organization.

I'd never met the man and had never had any desire to, so this was my first chance to get a good look at him. His sharp, thin features reminded me of the furtive feline creatures I'd often spotted roaming the ancient corridors of the *Aboena*.

"Kenton," Sev growled. "We need to talk."

Kenton's face split into a wide, leering grin. "*Ah, Maren,*" he crooned. "*I'd been hoping we would have a chance to speak again. I'm ever so glad you managed to survive that awful mess. Why don't you come aboard and we—*"

"I'm giving you this one chance, Kenton," Sev said. "Just one. Work with me now and maybe, just maybe, you walk away from this."

His grin faded for a moment as he studied her cold, deadly fury. Even through the fuzzy holographic image I saw doubt flicker through his eyes. Then it was gone, shaken off like rain from a dog's fur as he giggled. "*Why, Maren, disgrace hasn't changed you one bit. If we'd been having this conversation a few weeks ago, I think I might've soiled myself just now. But that was then, and this is now, and in case you hadn't noticed, there is a vast, vast difference between the two. Most notably you are now out there, alone and powerless, while I am in here, quite safe and surrounded by a large number of heavily armed mercenaries.*" He waved to someone out of my view. "*Werrel, why don't you be a dear and say hello?*"

Another figure stepped into view. Tall, middle-aged, and wearing an old officer's uniform of an origin I didn't recognize. He bore an expression of distinct annoyance.

"*This,*" Kenton said proudly, "*is Major Katen Werrel, proud leader of the—*"

Werrel coughed. "*Sir, probably best not to tip our hand any more than we have to.*"

"*It's called a show of force,*" Kenton said irritably.

Something about the way he said it—the crestfallen bitterness in his voice at being cut short in the middle of his power fantasy—shifted my perspective of Kenton. I might not have ever met him before, but I suddenly knew exactly what type of man he was. I'd dealt with dozens of commanding officers like him in the Vanguard. He was the type of man SkyCom attracted: small of mind and large of ego; so desperate for power that when they got even the smallest amount of it, they flailed it about like it was some sort of weapon, using it to beat down everybody they had any sort of authority over just so they felt more important. Getting him to flip on Sev had probably been easy. All it took to sway a man like Kenton was a few empty promises of grandeur.

Werrel gritted his teeth, shook his head, and vanished from my view. Kenton straightened, recovering his smile. "*I propose a different deal. Why don't you surrender, and I'll put in a good word with Vatheson on your behalf? It would save us all so much trouble.*"

Sev watched him for a few seconds, then gave a heavy, disappointed sigh. "Whatever he offered you, Kenton, it's not worth it."

"*Oh?*" Kenton raised his eyebrow. "*Back to trying to scare me? Didn't you hear a word I said? You're finished, Maren. Beaten, irrelevant, and alone. There's not a single thing you can...*"

He trailed off as Werrel appeared again, muttering something in his ear.

"They're here," Rose said.

The holomap in the center of the bridge sounded an alert as

a green blinking dot appeared on it, a comfortable distance to our right. Then another on our left. More and more, following each other with increasing speed until there were eleven green dots surrounding us. Renault's fleet.

One final alert sounded. A larger dot appeared behind us. I glanced over my shoulder, through the *Orpheus*'s rear viewport. Even at this great distance, I could make out the *Aboena*'s massive, ancient form.

The five red dots on the holomap slowed their approach.

Rose grinned. "Heh."

It was hard to tell through the holograph, but it looked like Kenton's face had gone pale as he stared down at something. Probably a handcomputer.

"You still feel *safe*, Kenton?" Sev asked.

Several long, empty seconds passed as the station manager stared down at his screen. The uncertainty in his face continued to grow. Just when I was sure he was about to break down and surrender, though, he suddenly straightened, a malicious glint in his eyes.

"*Well played, Sevani,*" he said. "*I suppose I shouldn't be surprised you found allies. But you see, I've still got the stronger position.*"

"Sure doesn't look that way," Sev said. "I'm no general, Kenton, but then again, neither are you. And it doesn't take a tactical mastermind to see that we've got you outgunned."

"*Outgunned, yes.*" Kenton gave a particularly nasty grin. "*But you see, guns aren't all that matter in a fight. I've got bodies. Several million of them, in fact.*"

Sev scoffed. "If you think they've got any loyalty at all to you, Kenton, you're an even bigger idiot than I thought. There's not a soul aboard Albeni 7 station that wouldn't jump at the chance to see you hang."

"*You're right, of course.*" Kenton's grin widened. "*But you see, that's my secret weapon. I don't give a single solitary damn about those disloyal souls, Maren. Which is fortunate, because I can only imagine how many of them are going to be caught in the crossfire of the epic battle that seems to be upon us."* He leaned forward, leering into the camera. *"Can you picture it, Maren? The bullets piercing those paper-thin walls. Grenades tearing through overcrowded rooms. Wounded children crawling into the smoke-choked hallways, desperate to escape, only to be trodden underfoot by exo-clad soldiers rushing to take the fight to the enemy. The panic, spreading through the station like a virus."*

He paused a moment, giving Sev a chance to respond. She didn't. I felt my gut tighten as I glanced at her. Her knuckles were white, her eyes burning with hatred.

We'd underestimated Kenton. Drastically.

"You see, Sev," Kenton continued triumphantly, *"you may have more ships than I do, but I control the station. And we both know you're far, far too soft to do what's necessary to take it from me. So, if you want my advice, it's to take your little fleet and run away, before—"*

Sev terminated the link. Kenton's face vanished, leaving a heavy silence in his wake.

"Well," Bentley finally said. "Bastard can talk, that's for sure."

"We're not going to just... give up, are we?" Shell's voice was low and worried.

Sev's eyes had narrowed as she stared into the empty space where Kenton's face had been a moment ago. I watched as the thoughts churned away in her head.

"Um..." Bentley cleared his throat nervously. "The others are calling."

"Put 'em through," I said.

Several faces appeared where Kenton's had been. The first of the faces spoke. *"Looks like we all made it in one piece,"* Tetra said, her face as stoic as ever. She was clad in her usual Aboenian Marshal's armor—except that now she bore a white pauldron on her left shoulder. I assumed it was a reflection of her status as the *Aboena*'s newly appointed Warmaster. "*How are the scans looking?*"

"*They're looking like victory is merely a matter of reaching out and taking it!*" Renault said from the other half of Bentley's screen. His face beamed with excitement. "*There's only five of them. If they've got the guts to fight at all, we'll make short work of them. Then we can move on to the station.*"

I glanced at Sev. She had backed away from the holoprojector and was staring through the window at the distant speck of light that was the station.

"It's... not that simple," I said.

I quickly summed up our conversation with Kenton. They listened impassively. By the time I finished, I'd expected to see their lips curl in horror at the thought of spreading war through the station's densely populated halls. Or at least for them to seem mildly disturbed.

They didn't.

Renault shrugged. "*That seems to be a fair assessment. No matter how careful I tell my lads to be, there are bound to be casualties. This is war, Lax. You know how it goes.*"

I did. All too well.

"*You didn't hesitate to turn the Aboena into a battlefield,*" Tetra said, her voice cold. "*We're still counting the dead, and the damage to the ship itself will take decades to fully repair.*"

"That was different," I said, maybe a tad too harshly. "We had time to prepare. To relocate civilians."

"*Regardless,*" Renault said, "*We've already determined that the station is a vital strategic asset. Once we have Albeni 7, we'll be in a position of power to bargain with the other stations in the system. We'll be a legitimate power rather than a fleet of scruffy ne'er-do-wells. We—*" He scowled suddenly. "*I shouldn't be explaining all this to you. It was your idea in the first place! You*" *simply need to decide if you're willing to pay the price of victory."*

I gritted my teeth, staring through Renault's translucent head and out the window into space as I worked through the brutal, bloody arithmetic.

Renault was right. So was Tetra. We *needed* the station. This wasn't some salvage job where I was just looking to make some money. Thousands of lives depended on us being able to take Albeni 7. Millions, when you counted those who were already aboard the station. We had the advantage. We *would* win. We'd pay for it dearly, but dammit, we *would* win. And at the end of the day, wasn't that all that mattered?

Like Renault had said—this was war. Collateral damage was inevitable. It would be messy and brutal, but in the long run it would be worth it, because once we had the station, we'd be able to...

Memories assailed me.

Once lively city streets, now choked with ash and blood and corpses. A young boy, face gray and red, standing distraught amid the rubble that had once been his life. Terrified, helpless screams as rippers tore through windows into homes.

No.

This was the Paragon's way. To insist that so long as you believed your goal was worthy, the means were justified, no matter how extreme. The whole reason I'd let myself get dragged into this mess was to give people a fighting chance at being *free* from bastards like them. I'd be damned before I let myself become one of them.

"No," I said.

Renault frowned. "*No what?*"

"If the price of victory is the massacre of innocents," I said, feeling more confident with each word, "then it's not worth paying. Not in this battle, anyway." I turned to Sev. "There's *got* to be another way. Any ideas?"

She pivoted to face the camera. "Yes. We need just a few hours before you engage. That's all I ask for."

"*And what will you do with these few hours?*" Tetra asked.

"We're thinking about this like soldiers," Sev said. "But that was never how I controlled the station in the first place. We should be thinking like smugglers. I can sneak a small group of us into the station. There is a place I can tap into the station's communication array. I'll be able to send out a message to all civilians to clear the way for our forces and minimize the casualties."

Renault frowned. "*A few hours' delay could be disastrous for us. We have the advantage now. With your plan the risks are far greater and the chances of success far slimmer. Tactically, I'm afraid it simply doesn't add up.*"

"There's more than tactics to consider here, though." I stepped up next to Sev. "And we need to do more than simply *beat* Vatheson. If we're really fixing to be a new power, we need the people of this station on our side. And if we tear through the station like a bunch of rippers, they'll never see us as anything other than invaders—even with Sev's reputation. They need to know that we're *not* like Vatheson, and Kenton, and the rest of the Paragon. So, if there's even a chance that Sev's plan might work, we need to take it. Because if we *are* willing to trade their lives for our goals... well, then maybe we ain't any better than the bastards we're fighting. And then I just don't see the point in any of this."

That seemed to get through to them. There was a moment of silence as they mulled over what we'd said.

Renault sighed. "*Fine. I don't like it, but... you raise a good point about the locals. Three hours' delay—then we begin the attack in earnest. Because it doesn't matter how moral our high ground is if we die on it, and trust you me, if we're here long enough for a Paragon fleet to arrive, we will die.*"

Tetra nodded. "*Go. Quickly. We can hold their attention in the meanwhile.*"

The two faces vanished. Rose broke the silence that followed. "So... should I start moving in?"

I turned to Sev. "You sure about this?" I asked softly.

She grimaced. "No. But... it's the best option we have."

I glanced around at the rest of the room and the dozens of faces watching me expectantly. Winter's face was as unreadable as a slab of concrete. Flint looked skeptical, as if he was certain I wouldn't have the balls to follow through. Rose's expression was eager, one hand already perched atop the *Orpheus*'s throttle, while Shell and Bentley both seemed... calm. Confident. They'd been through worse than this.

But it was Rid's face that suddenly gave me the confidence I was looking for. Standing tall and confident next to Rose, the edge of his glowing Scorcher tattoo behind the popped collar of his jacket. So different from the terrified, furtive kid who'd been shoved into my cell almost two years ago. I remembered the desperate cries he'd made as the Scorchers had beaten him. The plea in his eyes as he'd begged me for help. To abandon the apathy I'd clung so desperately to in the wake of Kessa's death.

Those eyes—that plea—had been what had finally given me the jolt I needed to reclaim myself. To escape both the literal and figurative prison I'd been bound in. To step out of my miserable self for long enough to realize that I *could* make a difference—and that the world needed me to.

Rid grinned, as if reading my thoughts, and nodded.

I turned to Rose.

"Take us in," I said.

THREE

"Just a few minutes till we make contact," Rose's voice said over the intercom as I descended into the cargo bay. *"Doesn't look like they see us coming—they're all focused on Renault's fleet."*

That took at least some of the burden off of my mind. Renault had been right about one thing at least: it wouldn't matter how noble we were being if we got ourselves killed. The *Orpheus*'s stealth systems were advanced enough that nobody should be able to spot us unless they were very carefully and deliberately looking for us in the right spot. Given that a fleet of pirates—accompanied by a massive Exodus class Roamer homeship—had just appeared on their doorstep, the mercenaries couldn't be blamed if they were slightly distracted.

The cargo bay was bustling with activity as Winter and Flint's squads prepared themselves for battle. I was still hopeful that we wouldn't need to use them, but... well, hope had never gotten me very far in life. Sev and I didn't even know what we'd find on the other side of her secret docking bay. Having a few dozen heavily armed fighters behind us made me feel slightly better about our chances.

Slightly.

A hulking figure was standing in front of the Icarus, hands on his hips as if he were admiring a painting hanging in a gallery. For just a moment my brain convinced me that it was Nadus standing there, alive and well.

"Hell of a piece of hardware."

My heart sank. It wasn't Nadus, of course. It was Flint. The grotesque burn-mark across his face stretched as he grinned at me. "Where'd you find this thing? Looks like Paragon tech, but I never saw nothing like this in the field."

"Experimental prototype. Stole it." I pushed past him, hoping he'd leave it at that. The circle of people who knew about what had happened on the *Revelation* was already a lot wider than I was comfortable with.

"Thermal blades," he said admiringly. "Bet you could cut up a lot of rippers with those."

"Not just rippers."

"Good. Cause we're gonna have to kill a lot more than just rippers."

I paused, glancing over my shoulder at him. His expression had turned grim as he regarded the exosuit. His voice quieted. "You know this one is gonna be a whole lot worse than last time, right?"

I didn't have to ask what he meant by that. We were Vanguards. There was only one *last time* we had in common. We might have been in different squads or even different campaigns, but when you were a Vanguard, it was all the same. The Last War was more than some shared experience. It was a deep and visceral piece of who we were. A part of our DNA, just as much as the Divinity gene the Paragon had used to create us. I didn't need to know Flint to know who he was—or at least what he'd been through.

"That's why Sev and I are going first," I said. "To give ourselves a shot at avoiding that."

He shook his head. "That ain't what I mean. This is a *battle*. I'm talking about the *war*."

That gave me pause. I'd been trying not to think about that. About the larger implications of what we were doing here. The Paragon was falling to pieces all around us. It was hard to know what was true and what was just rumor, but the last we'd heard was that rebels had successfully pushed the Paragon out of the Redhawk system, and that several other systems were now embroiled in their own struggles for independence. A struggle that would be made much harder by the increasingly strong blockade the Paragon had set up in the gate system.

We *might* have been able to get away with fighting off the *Leonidas*. Slink off into the darkness and keep our heads down, hope that the big players would ignore us while they focused on each other. But after this—claiming our own territory—we were essentially dealing ourselves into the game.

And something told me it was going to be a long, grueling, bloody game.

"Sure," I finally said. "Except we ain't got anyone's strings on us this time. We're fighting for *ourselves*."

He gave a sharp snort of a laugh. "Maybe, for now. But it's a dangerous game you're playing, VanDunn."

I raised an eyebrow. "What game is that?"

"Playin' at being heroes." He gave me a darkly amused look. "I heard that conversation in the bridge. Bein' better than our enemies and all that crap. But there are no heroes. Just puppets." His scarred face twisted into a malicious grin. "We're always dancing to somebody's tune. Even when we don't hear it. And pretending otherwise'll just get you killed."

I had no response to that. So I left him, his grinning leer still following me and his words echoing in my head as I made my way towards Sev.

She was leaning against the wall near the airlock's control panel, waiting for the pressurization process to complete so we could disembark. I leaned against the other side of the hatch. We waited in the comfortable, familiar silence of friends who knew they'd already said everything they needed to say to each other.

Except that wasn't true. My mind was pulled irresistibly back to the battle on the *Aboena*. In what I'd suspected would be my final moments, all I had been able think of was how sorry I was that I wouldn't see Sev again.

I'd known I was attracted to Sev for a while now. The idea scared me, though. So I repressed it. Shoved it back into my subconscious every time it worked its way back into my thoughts.

I wanted to say something. I opened my mouth, only to snap it shut again.

Stupid. We were about to sneak aboard a ship full of people who wanted us dead. Now was *not* the time. And even if it was, why the hell should I expect she would feel the same way? I felt a sudden rush of guilt. She was better off keeping her distance from me anyways. If I said anything I'd only make a fool of myself and throw away the only friendship I had left.

"What?"

I blinked. *Dammit.* I'd been staring at Sev for who knew how long. She raised an inquisitive eyebrow at me.

I shook my head, feeling flustered. "Nothing."

She studied me a moment longer, then looked down at the floor.

The control panel beeped. PRESSURIZATION COMPLETE.

Sev took a deep breath. "Ready?"

I nodded grimly, my frustration melting away as I directed my thoughts back to the task in front of us. Relationships were confusing. War, though—now that was something I understood.

The interior of Sev's secret docking bay was lit only by a single throbbing red emergency light. It was a small space filled almost entirely with stacks of crates. Sev began opening one crate after another, muttering under her breath as she dug through them.

"Stay tight," I said into the ship's intercom right before we left. "And stay dark. We'll keep in touch via quantcom. If you haven't heard back from us by the time Renault's deadline is up, contact him securely and co-ordinate. Otherwise, stand by for orders."

Sev finally found what she was apparently looking for—a tangled mass of black wires attached to a small black box, making it look like a mutated, long-legged spider. She shoved the device into a small backpack and slung it over one shoulder. She peered briefly at a dingy monitor on the wall showing an empty maintenance corridor I assumed was just outside the docking bay. Satisfied the way was clear, she opened a hidden door that led us out, then struck off down the hallway. I followed behind.

"Alright," I said, habitually keeping my voice low despite the fact that we were alone. "Please tell me you've got more of a plan than you let on back there."

"Slightly." She kept her pace brisk. "There's a point not too terribly far from here where I should be able to access some of the station's communication systems." She hefted her backpack higher on her shoulders. "That's what this is for."

I glanced backward. "Maybe we shoulda brought Bentley."

Sev scoffed. "Please. He's not the only one around here who knows how to run a computer. I had to manage on my own for years after the *Panama*. Besides, we'll look suspicious enough as it is with just the two of us wandering around here."

"You worried about anyone recognizing you?"

"Not particularly," she said. "It's not as if I personally delivered my smuggled goods to everybody aboard the station. And even those who've seen me before—which is a tiny percentage of the millions living here—probably won't recognize me in casual clothing."

I nodded along. The thought of walking freely through the hallways made me uncomfortable, but covering our faces would likely have only drawn more attention to us.

"Once I've accessed the communication channels," Sev continued, "we'll have all kinds of options open up to us. I'll see if we can get a look at where the mercenaries are concentrated. Maybe even see if we can reach out directly to their commander and work out a deal of our own."

Made sense. Sev might not be able to pay them more than Vatheson could, but even in her disenfranchised state, she had enough emergency assets sitting around that she might be able to sway them. After all, it didn't matter how much you were paid if you were dead, and Kenton's all or nothing gambit had to be making the mercenaries uneasy.

"Plus," I said, "even if that doesn't work, we should be able to wreak some havoc internally."

She nodded as we left the maintenance corridors and entered a much longer hallway with graffiti-covered concrete walls. It reminded me of the one where I'd been ambushed by hitmen a little over a year ago. I remembered vaguely how Artemis had nearly had me believing that Sev had been the one to put out the hit. And now here I was working alongside the man who had actually done it, even if indirectly. I shook my head to myself. Strange allies for strange times, I suppose.

It was hard not to compare Albeni 7's endless corridors to those I'd traversed on the *Aboena*, but other than basic shape, they shared little in common. Where the *Aboena*'s cold innards were defined by their ancient, otherworldly qualities—growths of alien tendrils spider-webbing across the walls, strange crea-tures roaming the darkness—these were defined by their mundane, ever-changing *aliveness*. Graffiti, not lichen, covered the walls. Rats fought over scraps in the hallways. Lights flickered overhead, silhouetting drug addicts huddling in the corners and thugs muttering sullenly among themselves as they watched us pass their alleyways.

A child, not much more than skin and bones, peered at us through an ajar doorway on our right. A moment later, a man who didn't look like he was in much better shape pulled the child back and shut the door abruptly. I got a good look at the graffiti scrawled across it in brutal red lettering: REPENT, FOR THE END OF ALL THINGS IS UPON YOU.

If the *Aboena* had been a corpse now hosting strange new life, Albeni 7 was a man thrashing as he was dragged to his grave.

I cocked my head to the side as a distant, muffled sound met my ears. No, not *a* sound. Hundreds of them, all mingling together. Voices. Sev heard it too. She frowned down the hallway the commotion was coming from.

"They don't sound happy," I said cautiously.

"No." She hesitated, then turned and started towards them.

I cursed as I caught up to her. "Sev. We're trying to *avoid* people. And we're on the clock."

"I know," she said, quickening her pace. "But I *need* to see. We're here to learn the situation, aren't we? Well, *this* is the situation."

The noise grew louder. Shouts. Hundreds of them, swelling together in a cacophony of anger, fear, and confusion. Sev took us on a side route that led up a flight of stairs and to a heavy door. She tried the handle. Locked.

The noise pulsed from the other side of it.

She turned to me. "Lax?"

I eyed it. It was resting on a heavy set of hinges rather than a pneumatic sliding system. "Let me see." I took a few steps back, then charged forward and kicked the door near the handle.

It crashed open. I winced, anticipating drawing the attention of every nearby set of eyes, but the noise was almost imperceptible over the roaring voices that rushed in through the empty doorway.

Sev crept through. I followed. We found ourselves standing in an alcove overlooking a large, open atrium. I recognized it—a market hex, similar to the one I'd been attacked in by thugs a year ago. This was where residents of the station block gathered to purchase supplies, interact with each other, and take care of errands.

Normally.

Today, the press of humanity was so tight that I couldn't see an inch of open space. The object of their ire seemed to be the commissary, which had its doors barred shut. A group of men and women wearing tattered mining uniforms and wielding power tools were cutting away at the doors. As we watched, the doors fell inward with a crash. The shouting escalated as the crowd surged forward, only to condense into a strangled mass in the commissary entryway.

I had to hold back a surge of guilt as I watched the chaos. These people were desperate. Would bringing war into their station help them? Did we truly have their best interests in mind? Or were we just as bad as Vatheson—trying to claw out a place for ourselves in whatever new pantheon of power took the Paragon's place?

A figure was ejected from the commissary. Then two more. I craned my head to get a better look. They were wearing white uniforms that marked them as the commissary managers. Those white uniforms were starting to look awfully red.

Sev paled. She leaned forward, looking like she was about to scream down at the crowd. I pulled her back. "*Hey*. It's too late. And even if they could hear you, they're in no mood to listen to reason."

She gritted her teeth, not taking her eyes from the three

figures as they were dragged through the crowd. I looked upwards, across the atrium. There were several other alcoves, some of them occupied. One of them in particular drew my attention. It had only a single occupant—an old man wearing a grimy technician's uniform, leaning against the railing and staring at us. We locked eyes.

More commotion from below. I glanced down to see a tall, metallic figure press into the room. A Jericho, painted black. Dammit. Must be one of Vatheson's mercenaries. The mercenary's visored head swept across the crowd.

"*HEY!*" His voice boomed over their heads, amplified by his exo. "Everybody, stand the hell down, before I have to get violent."

"We'll stand down when we have *food!*" somebody shouted.

"There's pirates coming for the station!" somebody else wailed. "Kenton said it himself! What the hell are any of you doing to help us?"

The merc's gaze lifted up, towards us.

I pulled Sev back. "We've *really* gotta go," I said. "Best way we can help them now is taking the station back from Vatheson—and we ain't gonna do that here."

The three managers vanished beneath a sea of flailing fists, thrashing feet, and furious shouts. Sev turned away without a word. I spared one last glance across the atrium. The man who'd been watching us was gone. The Jericho watched us a moment longer, then turned his attention to the crowd, wading into them and swatting them brutally out of his way. Several smaller combat exos appeared behind him.

"It's worse than I thought," Sev muttered when we had traveled a safe distance away.

I nodded. "This entire station is an unstable ultracell, waiting to blow. If we make a wrong move..."

"There won't be a station to rule afterwards," Sev agreed. Her face turned from angry to thoughtful. "We need to organize them. I don't know what Kenton's been doing to them—or *not* doing—but they're all desperate. I've never seen riots like this before. Not since..." She paled slightly. "Not since the neurovirus, anyway."

I thought back to the graffiti I'd seen scrawled across the door earlier. *The end of all things is upon you.* "Poor bastards are terrified. And Kenton's probably feeding 'em full of lies about the fleet. I mean, they aren't wrong: there *is* a fleet of pirates gearing up to attack the station."

Sev nodded, her face growing resolute. "Not if I can help it. Let's get to that access point."

We quickened our pace. I was glad I'd uploaded a map of the station to my handcomputer before we'd boarded, or I'd have quickly lost track of where we were. Sev guided us confidently through the concrete labyrinth while I kept a wary eye on our surroundings. I found myself growing more nervous with each step we took. I was almost certain that mercenary had seen us, but whether he'd recognized us was a different story altogether. Either way, all I could do was hope that we'd put enough distance between us.

Finally, Sev paused in front of a heavy doorway sealed shut by a simple combination lock. She muttered to herself as she tried to remember the combination. "One sec..."

I glanced over my shoulder. A tall, lanky man with gaunt features and hollow eyes was standing in an empty doorway, watching us through a sheet of sickly looking yellow smoke emanating from an inhaler device in his hand. I returned his dead-eyed gaze with what I hoped was an intimidating glare. He blinked slowly, then retreated into his room and shut the door behind him.

"Got it," Sev said triumphantly.

I went through the doorway first, moving slowly and cautiously. I'm not sure exactly what I'd been expecting, but it wasn't this. The large room on the other side looked like a condemned kitchen complex. Where once, cooks might have bustled through a maze of countertops, ovens, shelves of tools, and sets of cooking ware hanging from the ceiling, now rats and insects skittered for cover. Every surface was coated in grime. The entire place reeked of... well, it was hard to say where one foul odor ended and the next began.

"Nice place," I said flatly. "I was expecting something more..."

"Technical?" Sev stepped around me, letting the doors swing shut behind her. "This space was a datacenter, a long time ago, before it got repurposed during some sort of reconstruction. Then it became a kitchen, and then... this."

"Seems an awful waste of space to leave it in this condition," I said, watching idly as a cockroach skittered past my feet. "Especially considering how cramped everyone on this station already is."

Sev scoffed as she crossed the disgusting floor and headed towards a counter near the middle of the room. "Yes, but of course, why would a bastard like Kenton let it get put to use if nobody's paying to rent it? Still—it's to our benefit. Nobody's moved in to seal up the old wirings." She extended a hand towards me. "Be a gentleman?"

I moved closer and proffered my hand. She grabbed it tight and I felt a slight rush of warmth in my cheeks. If she saw it, though, she ignored it, using my strength to climb onto the counter while avoiding touching the grime as best she could. She handed her bag to me, then craned her head upwards and began fiddling with a panel in the ceiling.

I let her work, studying the room again to identify exits. Besides the door we'd come through there was only one other way out—an identical set of heavy doors on the opposite side of the room. Judging by the debris piled around those doors, I guessed they were locked. I thought I could hear footsteps echoing from behind them.

"There we are." Sev gave a satisfied grunt as the ceiling panel fell open. She reached upwards into the darkness, then cursed irritably under her breath as she brushed aside what looked like a dead rat. "Hand me the... thingamajig."

I reached into her bag, only to pause as my eyes were drawn to the doors. The footsteps had stopped. But I swore I could hear metallic clinking now. Like a lock being tampered with.

"Hey." Sev waved her hand. "The thing? It's not exactly—"

"*Shh.*"

There was a sharp metallic clang from the other side of the doors.

I already had my weapon up by the time they burst through the doors on the far side of the kitchen.

I recognized them immediately—not personally, but conceptually. Five of them, wearing tactical armor too uniform to belong to a gang of thugs or pirates, but too mismatched to be enforcers or military. No, these were the awkward middle ground between lawless bandits and state-backed soldiers: mercenaries. Dogs of war, going wherever the fight led them—so long as the pay was good.

Today, it seemed it was.

The first one raised an assault rifle. "Drop your weapons!" he shouted through a tactical visor that concealed his face. "This doesn't—"

I pulled the trigger and the merc's visor exploded in a spray of blood, glass, and bone.

I was moving before his body hit the ground, grabbing Sev's legs in a bear hug and pulling her down behind the counter she'd been standing atop of. Her shocked cry was drowned out in a deafening volley of gunfire as the remaining four mercenaries opened fire. Bullets zipped through the air above us, tore into the countertops, and slammed into the concrete walls behind us, sending explosions of debris showering in every direction.

"How'd they find us?" I shouted in Sev's ear.

She shook her head. "Don't know!"

I looked back towards the door we'd come through. Too far. We'd be shot to ribbons by the time we reached it.

The gunfire slowed, then stopped. Somebody shouted, "We've got you pinned down and outnumbered! Make this easy on yourselves!"

I reached into my jacket. My fingers closed around a small, cylindrical device.

If there was one lesson I'd learned from the *Aboena*, it was to never go anywhere without a few tricks up my sleeve. I pulled the pin from the top of the grenade, then met Sev's eyes and jerked my head towards the door. She nodded.

"Alright," I said. "We're coming out!"

I tossed the grenade over the countertop and dove for the door, Sev right behind me.

There was a panicked shout. Desperate scuffling as the mercenaries scrambled for cover. A concussive boom. Pots hanging from the ceiling shook and fell to the floor as the explosion rocked them. I used my shoulder as a battering ram and burst through the doors into the hallway beyond, then pivoted to—

A gunshot thundered. Something slammed into—no, *through*—my back. I staggered forward, blinking.

"*LAX!*"

It didn't hurt. My body was going into shock. I tried to reach back and assess the damage, but my hands wouldn't obey me. I sagged forward. My nose snapped as my face slammed into the floor.

I was dimly aware that Sev was screaming. Dimly aware that somebody was standing over me, their combat boots the only thing I could see. Dimly aware that a pool of warm, red liquid was gathering around me.

Something cold and metallic pressed against my head.

A way out. There was always a way out. Sev was in trouble. I needed to get to her. Needed to help her. To see my crew again.

Green dots, flashing—
A flash of light.
Nothing.

FOUR

I blinked.

It changed nothing. Everything was dark.

I couldn't see my hands. Couldn't feel them, either. I saw nothing. *Was* nothing.

I turned—maybe. I thought I was turning, at least. But with no reference point, and no bodily sensation, it might just have been my imagination. I was floating, drifting alone in a dark, infinite void. The only comparable thing I've ever seen was nullspace.

A point of light appeared.

I focused on it. It grew larger. It was rushing towards me. If I'd had lungs or a mouth, I'd have screamed.

The light overtook me. I frowned around myself. The void was gone. I was inside a room—or I thought I was, at least. It was a room unlike any I'd ever been in before.

Scratch that. It was unlike any I'd ever been in before—except one.

Every surface of the room was covered in long, twisting tendrils, similar to the ones I'd seen in the Stranger's chamber. But where those had been green and earthy like thick vines, these were... celestial, almost. They were transparent, radiating white light as they pulsated. I followed their swirling tangle from the floor, along the walls, across the ceiling, and down to their central convergence point.

A tall figure loomed in the center of the room. The tendrils were connected to it, extending from its back and its limbs. I stared, trying to comprehend what I was seeing.

Then the room shuddered. The light pulsating through the tendrils flickered. The figure in the center of the room turned its head sharply to the side. In the flashing light, its profile was obscured. But I could see what it was looking at.

The tendrils on the wall had bled transparent to become a window into space. I saw tiny pinpoints of light. Stars.

One in particular loomed large. A ship of some kind. It surged larger, closer.

A flash of light and I was blind again.

Pain—deep and piercing—throbbed like a frenzied heartbeat in my brain.

I blinked.

I was lying face-down on cold concrete in a pool of something warm and wet. My mouth tasted like copper. Voices were shouting somewhere far away. Shadows danced back and forth on the walls in an ethereal struggle.

Something clinked onto the floor next to me. My vision focused on it. I frowned. It was a bullet. Misshapen, coated in blood and tiny bits of flesh. It rolled to a halt in a pool of red liquid.

Blood. I was lying in a pool of my own blood.

The piercing pain in my skull faded from a cacophony to a roar. I squinted the blurriness out of my eyes, raising my head from the floor. I was lying in an Albeni 7 hallway. I stared at the bullet on the floor, then held a hand up to my temple. My fingers ran over the surface of a jagged abrasion in my skin. A moment later it was gone, the skin knitting itself back together until there was nothing left of the wound.

That bullet had been *in my head.*

The memories started to reform; a scattered puzzle being pieced back together. There must've been soldiers waiting for us behind the door I'd barged through. I wasn't sure how the mercenaries had tracked down our location, but they'd trapped us like rats in a cage. There'd been no way out. I'd been gunned down before I could resist, and Sev...

Sev.

I sat up, looking around. I didn't see Sev. I didn't see anybody. The hallway I was in was empty, save for me, the puddle of my own blood I was sitting in, and the bullet that had been in my head. My weapon was nowhere in sight, either.

They must've taken her. But not far. I could hear voices echoing from the condemned kitchen. One of them was Sev's. She was shouting, her voice laced with fury, grief, and shock. The sound of her anguish tore through my foggy confusion, grounding me with razor-sharp focus.

I climbed to my feet.

They'd dragged her into the kitchen—or what was left of it after the concussion grenade I'd thrown. I counted seven mercenaries surrounding Sev. One of them, a Vanguard, was holding her arms behind her back while she struggled. A man who looked like their leader was standing in front of her, speaking into a radio, while the other five sat idly by, their weapons lowered, seemingly persuaded the danger had passed.

"We're securing the subject now," the officer was saying. "She's not talking right now, but the description matches Sevani. No, I don't know how they got on board. I—"

Sev spat at him. "Go to hell, you piece of—"

The officer struck her with a short, brutal punch to the

mouth. Her head snapped sideways, blood flicking from her torn lip.

"Quiet, bitch," he growled.

The pain in my head vanished, engulfed in a wave of cold, bloody fury stronger than any ignicerin could have given me.

The merc grinned, staring at the trickle of blood running down Sev's chin. "You know, I can't believe I get paid for this."

Sev's eyes flickered up to me. Then widened.

I started forward through the doorway.

"Alright. Let's try this again." The officer grabbed Sev's chin, wrenching her face back towards him, but her eyes stayed fixed on me, unbelieving. "HEY. Don't look over there. Look at me. Your big dead friend can't help you now. The only way you can help yourself is by calling that fleet off. I don't..."

He finally turned his head in my direction. He blinked in confusion.

I'm not sure why they all just stared at me as I strode closer. Might've been that they were simply having a hard time making sense of what they were seeing. I must've been quite a gruesome sight, after all. I could feel the blood, still warm and sticky, caked thick on the side of my face and all across my chest and back. Maybe they'd simply let their guard down, figuring the fight was over. Or maybe they were just slow.

Made no difference to me. By the time the officer had opened his mouth—and well before any of them could raise their weapons—I was vaulting over the ruined countertop, landing spryly right in the middle of the group.

My fist struck the officer square on the mouth, right where he'd hit Sev. His jawbone caved inward with a gut-wrenching crunch, and his upper teeth scraped along the back of my hand. He took a staggering step backward, eyes bulging.

I was already on to the next one. My elbow slammed into the side of another merc's head, hurling him into a countertop like a ragdoll. One of his buddies gave a startled shout of visceral fear and raised a shotgun towards me. I grabbed the barrel and turned it. The gun went off, sending its load of buckshot straight into the chest of his buddy. I jerked the weapon free, drew it back, and slammed it into the chest of my assailant, sending him flying backward.

Three down; four to go. The Vanguard was still holding Sev tight, backing slowly away, while the other three were finally raising their weapons towards me. I kept my momentum up, charging into them and swinging the shotgun like a club to sweep their rifles off target. I felt a sharp pain in my arm as one of them managed to get a shot off.

I swung the shotgun again, downward, sending the butt into the side of a mercenary's knee. Bones snapped and flesh tore. He went down screaming. The other two didn't fare much better. I disabled one of them with a knee to the gut that lifted him from the floor, then fired the shotgun into the torso of the last one.

"Look out!" Sev called.

Movement below me. I looked down to see the mercenary whose leg I'd broken drawing a pistol and aiming it up at me. A gunshot echoed through the room as I grabbed his wrist and yanked him up towards me, then drove the barrel of the shotgun down into the visor of his helmet with all of my strength.

It punched through the front of his helmet and out the back like a ripper's tailspike. The mercenary spasmed, then went limp.

I looked up.

The fight had lasted no more than a few seconds. Four of the mercenaries were dead or close enough to it; the officer was on his hands and knees, hands trembling violently as he tried to stop the blood gushing from the shattered remains of his lower jaw, while the two who'd been hit with the shotgun were twitching slightly as they bled out. I was still holding up the corpse of the one I'd skewered. Two others were clearly out of the fight, moaning as they clutched at their injuries.

That left the Vanguard.

He was backing slowly towards the far exit, dragging Sev along with him, holding the barrel of Peacebreaker against her head. Seeing Sev's face drove the battle rage out of my mind. The time for recklessness was past. One wrong move and Sev was a dead woman.

"Let's talk this through," I panted.

The Vanguard took another step backward. "There's nothing to talk about, brother. Drop the gun before I splatter her brains on the wall."

I eyed Sev. Her hand crept downwards, towards her belt.

"Alright." I lifted my hands, letting go of the shotgun. The mercenary I'd skewered with it sagged to the floor. "But if you hurt her..."

"I wouldn't worry about that." The Vanguard's pistol moved away from Sev and towards me.

There was a flash of metal as Sev drew a hidden knife from her belt and jammed it between two plates of armor on the Vanguard's thigh. He grunted in pain—but he didn't let go. The distraction gave me enough time to charge him, though. Peacebreaker went off with a thunderous boom as I slapped it from his hands.

I shot a fist towards his face, forcing him to duck. Sev took advantage of the change in posture to slip out of his grip, leaving her knife embedded in the man's thigh. The Vanguard lashed out at me with a fist but I evaded it easily, stepping to the side and then kicking the handle of Sev's knife.

The dagger disappeared completely into the Vanguard's leg. He screamed in pain, dropping to one knee.

I drew a haggard breath, then coughed. Blood dribbled from my lips. I frowned down at my chest. It was hard to tell given the copious amount of gore I was covered in, but there was a bullet hole in my chest. The mercenary with the pistol must've managed to hit me before I could finish him off.

The Vanguard stared as the wound in my chest slowly closed itself. I heard Sev gasp. Hell, I was staring too.

"What... *are* you?" the Vanguard growled.

"I..." I frowned at him. "I don't know."

He growled, tensing to charge. A gunshot boomed and his head jolted to the side. He sagged and went still.

I turned to see Sev kneeling on the floor and panting, holding Peacebreaker. She dropped it to the floor with a clatter, then sprang to her feet, staring wide-eyed at me. "Are you..."

"Yeah." I looked down at myself. I was completely covered in blood—most of it mine. There were no holes where the bullets had struck me, though—just raw, pink-looking scar tissue. "I... I think so. Are you?"

"Yeah." She nodded, still unable to take her eyes off of me. She looked like she was fighting back a sob. "You were... I mean, they... I thought they'd killed you."

I held a hand up to my head, carefully probing where the wound had been. I couldn't feel anything there now but congealed blood. "I... I think they did."

Sev stared a moment longer, then shook herself. She kicked Peacebreaker towards me, then grabbed one of the mercenary's assault rifles, cursing under her breath. "We need to move. This is my fault—they must have ID'd us at the commissary, then somehow tracked us to here."

I remembered the stoned man who'd watched us as we'd entered the kitchen. "Locals probably helped them," I said as I scooped up my pistol.

"Back to the *Orpheus*." Sev stumbled past me, towards the door. "Before we get cut off. We need to get there before—"

Footsteps, pounding rapidly towards the door. I raised Peacebreaker, but I knew even before the newcomer emerged that it wasn't a mercenary. The steps were too light, too quick, and there were only two sets of them. Mercs would have been in greater numbers, and they'd have been moving cautiously.

With that in mind, I forced myself to lower my weapon as the footsteps slowed at the door. A face emerged a moment later, peering carefully around the corner. It was a young woman, appearing to be about Rose's age, with dark hair and serious brown eyes. Those eyes widened as she took in the gory sight before her.

"It's alright," Sev said, lowering the barrel of her rifle and raising one hand with palm outstretched. "We won't hurt you."

The girl's eyes moved from the wreckage of the mercenaries I'd dispatched to the blood coating my head and torso and finally to Sev, where they lingered. She let out a low whistle. "You were right, Mikah. It *is* her."

Another figure appeared beside her. Mikah was a burly, gray-haired man wearing a grime-coated technician's uniform. It took a few seconds for me to pinpoint why he looked so familiar to me. I'd seen him just a short while ago, in the commissary. He was the man I'd locked eyes with, standing in the alcove opposite from us. I wondered briefly if he'd been the one who'd put the mercs onto our tail, before dismissing the idea. There'd be no reason for him to approach us himself if that were the case; besides, we'd been sloppy. The mercenary in the black Jericho had probably gotten a good look at us before we left.

The old man let out a low whistle, scratching his head as he studied us. "You, ah, really let 'em have it, eh?"

Shouts echoed down the hall. Several sets of heavy footsteps. I tensed. *That* was what a group of soldiers sounded like.

Sev straightened. "We need to get out of here," she said urgently. "*Now.* I don't know who you are, but you clearly know me. Can you help us?"

To my surprise, the man looked to the girl for confirmation. She folded her arms, eyes narrowing as she stared Sev down. With each passing second my heart beat faster. Just before I was about to brush them out of our way and start sprinting, she gave a curt nod.

"Follow us." She turned to Mikah. "Stay here, see if you can throw them off our trail. Meet up at Vivia's as soon as you can."

Mikah nodded. "Be careful, Jala."

"You too." Jala turned away. "Come on. Hurry."

She didn't have to tell us twice.

FIVE

Jala moved quickly, only occasionally checking to see if we were still behind her. We followed her for maybe ten minutes, winding through the filthy hallways, tensing at every sound or flash of movement along the way. I'd expected that the hallways would be full of bystanders crowding to see the source of all the commotion—after all, our fight had hardly been a quiet one— but was relieved to see that the doors lining the corridors stayed mercifully shut. Most likely the locals had learned a long time ago that the best response to the sounds of violence was to mind your own business.

That didn't explain Jala and Mikah, though. I resisted the temptation to question her as we walked; there would be time for that later. Besides, I had other questions on my mind right now.

I couldn't shake the mental image of that bullet rolling on the floor, misshapen and gore-covered from its trip through my own skull. Or the empty blackness that I'd floated through after I'd been shot.

Some part of me knew that I should have been expecting something like this to happen. According to Ramar, I'd received the same "gift" that Cairn had. The image of Cairn rising from his own bloody wreckage, his flattened face rebuilding itself before my eyes, was burned into my memory forever. Beyond that, my miraculously regrown hand was a testament to the Stranger's work. Still, experiencing it firsthand was unnerving.

I clearly wasn't the only one feeling that way, either. Sev kept shooting worried glances at me as we walked. I could tell she was fighting an impulse to stop and look me over. But we'd both been in enough tight places to know that the time for worry comes *after* you've gotten away from the thing you're worried about.

"Wait." Jala stopped right before an intersection, holding up a hand. I heard it a moment later. Footsteps coming from a hallway on the left. A lot of them.

Heavy footsteps.

I cursed viciously. "Exos. We need to get out of here."

Jala looked around us, eyes calm, then strode towards a door and knocked on it. It opened just a crack a moment later. She whispered something to the person on the other side.

Sev glanced over her shoulder at the corner, raising her rifle. The footsteps were growing louder by the second. They were sprinting at full speed—which is pretty damn fast in a powered combat exo.

The door opened. I made sure Sev and Jala went in first. The doorway was almost too small for me to fit through, and I brushed against the frame as I passed it. Jala shut the door firmly behind us.

It was darker inside than it had been in the hallway. It took my eyes a moment to adjust. We were standing in a small, cramped living room. A long, ragged couch was pressed up against one wall, while a projector on the ceiling vomited a flickering children's show onto the wall opposite it. Five children huddled on the floor, staring at us with wide, innocent eyes. I felt a rush of panic as I considered what might happen to them if those mercenaries caught us here.

An elderly woman—evidently the one who had opened the door—shrunk into the corner.

"*Shhh*." Jala held up a finger to her lips.

I leaned against the wall next to the door, Peacebreaker ready in my hand. Footsteps thundered outside. One particularly heavy set of footfall caught my attention. Sounded like a Jericho.

My eyes drifted back to the children. They were staring at me in particular.

"Are you a zombie?" one of them asked.

I looked down at the mostly dried gore coating my chest with a grimace. I sure as hell looked like it. Just about every bit of me was red, except for a short streak across my chest where I'd...

The footsteps drew nearer. Then slowed.

... where I'd brushed against the doorway in my haste to enter.

Dread flooded my body like ice-cold water. I tightened my grip on Peacebreaker as if it were some kind of life preserver and held my breath. I heard muffled voices from the other side of the door.

"Set up here. Security system is bugged as hell but it hasn't picked them up at the next intersection yet, so they probably haven't come through here."

Jala glanced over at me. Her eyes narrowed as she saw my chest, the same realization I'd had evidently dawning on her.

"I told you to let me handle it," a second voice growled. "I saw 'em in the commissary. If I'd gone, they'd already be dead."

"We don't want them *dead*, you daft idiot," the first voice said, irritated. It sounded familiar. "And we needed exos on hand dealing with the riots."

Somebody stopped outside the door. I gritted my teeth. If

they really were planning on posting up here, it was only a matter of time before they saw the blood.

"I thought they said they killed the Vanguard. There's no way the woman could've done all that."

"Well, I didn't see their bodies, did you?" The voice drifted closer, pausing in front of the door. "And the old man claimed he didn't know anything. Wherever they went, it can't be—"

Jala took a deep breath, then opened the door slightly and slipped through, shutting it tight behind her. I restrained a curse and stepped back. I locked eyes with Sev, unsure of what to do. She only clenched her teeth.

"I know where they went," I heard Jala say.

Dammit. I glanced over my shoulder at the huddled children, waving at them to get away from the door, then at the older woman. They just stared.

"Alright, then." The mercenary sounded amused. "Where?"

"Is there a reward?"

I moved closer to the door. The gap between the door and the frame was just wide enough for me to peep out of it. A Vanguard clad in a Jericho exosuit was standing outside. It was the same one I'd seen in the commissary, painted all in menacing black. There was something attached to the underbarrel of his Jackhammer rifle, but I couldn't quite make out what it was.

I aimed Peacebreaker at the mercenary through the door, only to lower it with a silent curse. Might as well be threatening him with a toy for all the damage I'd do. Jala, however, seemed much less intimidated. She folded her arms and stared defiantly up at the hulking metal monstrosity.

"Yeah, there's a reward." The Vanguard stepped closer to her, his voice now cold and ruthless through the exo's filter. "The reward is I don't bust down that door and shoot everyone inside while you watch."

Jala was either a very good actor, or she suddenly realized

her mistake. She tensed, creeping back towards the door. The merc growled and grabbed her arm, holding her in place. "Or, we could always start with breaking things. Usually I start with fingers. But you've gotta understand, these exos, they ain't cut out for precision work. So I think we'll start with something bigger."

Jala cried out in pain as the Jericho's gauntlet began to slowly squeeze her around her slender arm.

I put a hand on the doorknob, ready to burst out and take the offensive as soon as the game was up. I didn't know what the hell I would do against the Jericho, but anything was better than nothing. I paused as I realized that Jala had positioned herself directly in front of the smear of blood I'd left on the doorframe. *Dammit.*

"Easy." Another mercenary approached, clad in a smaller exo. This one had lifted his visor, revealing a face with unkempt facial hair and tired-looking eyes. I realized with a start that I knew him. Werrel, the mercenary commander Kenton had introduced to us. "Nothing bad needs to happen here today, love. Just tell us where the big man and the lady went, huh?"

"I heard them say something about the resupply chute," she whimpered.

"Good girl." The second mercenary turned to his companion. "Come on, then, let her go. No point in hurting people when we're not paid to."

The Vanguard showed no sign of loosening his grip. "How do we know she ain't lying?"

"What reason would she have?" Werrel sounded bored as he turned away, a change in his tone suggesting he was speaking into his comms. "This is Commander Werrel. Possible lead. We're heading to investigate. Keep frosty—they're dangerous, wherever they are. Let's not lose anyone else today." He pointed towards somebody I couldn't see. "Reinforce the boys at point seven on the map. Assuming they haven't somehow slipped past already, we've got the area locked down now." He gave a heavy sigh. "If we're lucky enough to catch Sevani, maybe we can avoid this whole stupid, bloody mess. I doubt the rest of her fleet will want to attack while we're holding her hostage."

He strode away. The rest of the squad followed him. The mercenary holding Jala's arm shoved her towards the door. She struck it with a whimper.

Jala watched until his heavy mechanical footsteps had receded, then quickly opened the door, scrubbed away the bit of dried blood with her sleeve, then slipped through and shut it behind herself. The fear in her face vanished instantly, replaced by cold concentration.

Sev eyed her. "You're quick."

"And you're lucky," Jala said. "Wait here." She brushed past us, taking the older woman with her. They disappeared behind a curtain lining the back of the room. I could vaguely see their shadows speaking in hushed but animated tones.

I let out a heavy breath, sagging against the wall. "That was way too damn close," I whispered to Sev. "You have any idea who these people are?"

Sev shook her head, looking around. "No. But we can't stay here. We're putting them all in danger."

"Where do we go?" I asked. "Sounds like they've got the place locked down. You know any ways we could sneak through?"

She grimaced. "Maybe. But even if we did... we've only got a half-hour before Renault's deadline. And I'm more convinced than ever that a direct assault will lead to a bloodbath."

I nodded somberly. The station was on the verge of having a collective panic attack. Pirates and Roamers attacking would only throw fuel onto the fire.

Jala emerged from behind the curtain. She beckoned for us to follow her. There was a kitchen on the other side of it, small and cramped like everything here was, but what held my attention was a wall panel on the far side that came loose as Jala tugged on it.

"Come on," Jala said, gesturing to the other occupants of the room. "The others are gathering."

"Wait." Sev caught Jala's arm. "Who are you? Why are you helping us?"

"We're the people who *live* on this tin can," Jala said stiffly, shaking Sev loose and proceeding through the hidden door. "And we've got some questions for you."

SIX

The opening led us into another kitchenette. Somebody else's apartment, then. This one was significantly busier than the other had been. By the time the five children who'd been in the first apartment shuffled through the secret door, there were almost a dozen kids crammed into the living room. Three adults —another young woman, looking to be in her early twenties, as well as two middle-aged women—watched us as we entered.

"I'll be damned," one of the older women said. "It's really her. I thought for sure Mikah was seein' things. Where is Mikah, anyways?"

"On his way," Jala said. "He ran interference. I'm so sorry to bring this on you. I'd been hoping to make it to Vivia's, but we got cut off."

Sev cleared her throat. "I can't thank you all enough for helping us. They would have—"

"You!" The other middle-aged woman pointed a finger at me. "This way. Quick. I'll not have you getting your filth all over my home."

The bathroom the lady led me to was—predictably—small, cramped, and messy. I shoved a pile of dirty children's clothes to the side to avoid getting blood on them, then stripped off my tattered shirt and studied myself in the mirror for a moment.

I looked... fine. My entire torso was coated in dried blood. But other than that and a few white scars, there was no indication that I'd been shot multiple times in the back, chest, and head just a few minutes ago.

What the hell had the Stranger done to me?

I grabbed a rag hanging from the sink and began scrubbing myself clean. No time for a full wash—we were still being hunted. I just need to look... well, less like a *zombie*, to quote a local child.

I wiped blood off of my left hand. The one the Stranger had somehow regrown.

You are Chosen, now.

A chill crept down my spine as I remembered the words. The Shaper had sounded reverent and yet cautious as he'd said them. Like he was bestowing an honor upon me that he didn't think I deserved. What did it mean, though? The Shapers had referred to Cairn as the Stranger's champion—and yet, the relationship between them had never seemed more than a loose alliance.

The bathroom door opened. Sev poked her head in.

"You alright?" I asked, wringing bloody water from the rag into the sink.

She raised an eyebrow at the swirl of red vanishing down the drain. "I came to ask *you* that. Here." She opened the door wider so she could enter the room. "Move."

I stepped to the side, making just enough room for her to squeeze into the bathroom with me. She stood on her toes. "Head. Down."

I stooped and craned my head so that the temple I'd been shot in was facing her. She studied it, thumbing through my short hair.

"I don't understand," she said. "Did it... miss?"

"No." I turned around in response to a gentle push, turning my back to her. "When I woke up the bullet was on the floor next to me. It might have hit some Vanguard hardware that kept it from penetrating too deeply. But still, there should be..."

"Something." She ran her fingers down my back, where the shotgun blast had struck me. "What about these ones? Did the shrapnel come out?"

"I don't know."

At her urging I turned again—this time to face her. She scrutinized my chest. Three pale scars. "And these ones?"

"I don't know." I looked down at her. Her lip was still bleeding from being struck by the mercenaries. "I was distracted. Here."

I moved to wipe her face clean, but she snatched the bloody rag from my hand and tossed it into the sink. "Lax! Ew." She grabbed a clean one and pressed it into my hand. "Use this one."

I began gingerly wiping the blood from her face. It had settled into some of the lines around her mouth. She looked so much older than she had back in the good old days we'd flown the *Orpheus* together. I did too. So far as years went, the nine that had passed since then had been particularly hard ones—on both of us. And it seemed like they'd only get harder going forward.

"Now what?" Sev asked, voice soft and uncertain.

"I was gonna ask you the same thing," I said. I thought about what we'd overheard Werrel say in the hallway about wanting to capture Sevani and felt a chill at how close we'd been to disaster. "First plan kinda went to hell, didn't it?"

"Yeah." She winced as the rag brushed against her split lip. "But... we can't just give up. You saw the commissary. The situation is even worse than we thought. If Renault launches a full-on assault, the chaos will be... well, there might not even be a station left to control by the time all is said and done."

I glanced towards the door. "Might be that our second plan

found *us*. Jala made it sound like this is some sort of organization. Clearly they've got a good system for communicating—they spotted us in the commissary. Maybe they can help us." I shrugged. "If we really believe we're fighting for them, then we may as well let them help."

She nodded. Her eyes lifted once again to my head, and the place where the bullet had struck me. "So are you just... unkillable now?"

"Probably not. I reckon if that headshot had penetrated a little further it wouldn't matter how much magical healing power the Stranger gave me. Dead is dead, right?"

"Shame. I'm just about mad enough to shoot you myself over the scare you gave me."

I chuckled softly. "Well, for what it's worth, I'd have preferred to have skipped all that too."

I realized she was looking into my eyes. I blinked. Lowered the rag slowly. We might have been standing in a cramped bathroom full of dirty clothes, bloodied rags and a toilet, but this was the closest we'd ever been to each other. Her lips were no more than a foot from mine.

"I don't know if I could handle losing you again," she said. A slightly guilty flush crept over her face. "Not that... before... I mean..."

"I know," I said.

Sev's lips parted ever so slightly.

The door crept open. A little girl peered through the crack.

"I need to pee," she said.

Even more people had gathered in the living room. The children had all been ushered into the back. I was relieved to see that Mikah was there, safe and sound.

"I *knew* I wasn't crazy," he was saying as we entered. "Her, I wasn't too sure about, but that Vanguard is hard to miss."

"Looks that way," Jala muttered, eyeing my blood-stained, bullet-hole ridden shirt. I'd soaked it and wringed it dry as best I could, but, well... there was only so much you could do. I was starting to wonder why I even bothered to wear shirts anymore, given how frequently they were ruined when I got stabbed, shot, exploded, or some combination of the three.

Sev cleared her throat. "Thank you again, for helping us. I recognize the amount of risk you're putting yourselves in. Now: can I ask who exactly you are?"

Mikah spoke up. "We call ourselves the Citizens' Watch," he said. "Jala started the group, only a few months back. At first the idea was to have somebody advocate for residents' rights to the station administration. And... well, that hasn't gone too well. So we mostly just try to keep order in the residential zones— ours, at least—and help spread news and whatnot." He shrugged. "It's hard to know what's *really* going on, what with Kenton controlling the station communication systems and the Paragon controlling everything else."

Jala nodded, face hard. "What we *don't* know is what's going on outside of the station. First those mercenaries appear and you disappear. Then we start hearing talk of civil war all across the Paragon. Then the food shipments stop coming in. And now Kenton has everybody convinced that a fleet of pirates is about to raid us. He's been putting talk of wanton pillaging and destruction over the station broadcasts."

Sev's face grew tighter with each sentence the young woman spoke. The other civilians nodded along, though some of them exchanged nervous glances between Jala and Sev, as if uncomfortable with how brazenly she was addressing the former Smuggler Queen of Albeni 7.

"And *now*, with a horde of pirates apparently getting ready to kill us all, *you* show up again," Jala continued. "You're lucky Mikah spotted you in the commissary, or Kenton's thugs would have caught you by now."

Sev glanced at me. I glanced down at my handcomputer. We were running out of time.

"Tell 'em," I said. "Fast."

Sev started speaking, explaining the basics of the situation. Meanwhile, I took out my quantcom and quickly read through several messages I'd been too busy getting shot to see. To my relief, it sounded like we were still in the clear. Nobody had attacked the *Orpheus* and no reinforcements had arrived to threaten our fleet. We were running out of time, though—and fast. Our window of opportunity was already almost closed. We'd have to pry it back open—and somehow find a way to do it without damaging the frame. Being here with these people, a cross section of normal Albeni civilians, made me feel even more guilty about the prospect of unleashing a full-blown war on the station.

"And *now*," Sev finished, "we're here to kick Kenton's ass. As soon as we can figure out a way to do it without destroying the station."

Mikah and the others gave approving nods. Jala, however, only narrowed her eyes. "And then what? You and your people rob us instead?"

One of the older women gave a shocked gasp. "Jala!"

"What?" Jala looked indignant. "We *all* know that people like her don't give a damn about people like us. Everybody's the same. They just want to rule, without caring what happens so long as they make a profit. That's the whole reason we organized this group—to watch out for people down here when nobody else would. Why should we believe she's any different? She's a smuggler!"

I hoped my face didn't show how hard the words hit me. It was as if Jala had pulled my worst fears right from my brain—not about Sev specifically, but about our endeavor in general. Would these people *actually* be better off for having us in charge?

"It's alright." Sev raised a hand. She kept her eyes fixed on Jala. I thought I recognized a sense of begrudging admiration in Sev's expression. "It's a fair question—I'd be asking it too."

Jala's hard expression softened in surprise, looking like she'd expected a more confrontational answer. So had I, frankly. Sev hadn't become the Smuggler Queen by letting people question her authority. Now, though, her eyes were soft as she spoke.

"The Paragon is currently in the process of falling apart," Sev said, settling into an open seat with a weary groan. I remained standing by her side. "I'm not going to pretend that I know how everything is going to work out. Nobody does. But no matter what happens, nothing is going to be the same after. Powerful people everywhere are jumping at the chance to seize even more power. The Albeni system is one of the biggest mineral exporters in the Paragon, which means that somebody is always going to want to control it—and so long as whoever controls it is from outside of the system, they're not gonna give a damn about the people who actually live here."

Mikah nodded. "Damn right."

"Kenton works for a man named Vatheson," Sev continued. "All he cares about is securing this station—and about hurting me, specifically." Sev took a deep breath. "I know you might not believe it—what with my running Odyssey Logistics for the past few years—but I'm one of you. I lost my husband to the neurovirus. Nearly lost my daughter, too. I had to fight and scrape to get to where I was. Yeah, I made my money with a smuggling operation. Made quite a bit. I'm not gonna pretend I'm some kind of saint. I *am* one of the powerful people scrambling for more power in the chaos. But I want that power because I believe I'm the only one who actually wants to make this system and this station a better place. And I don't think it's *ever* going to be better until we—until *you*—have something nobody else is going to give you: independence."

A silence fell as the citizens exchanged looks with each

other. Jala didn't look entirely convinced, but she did look thoughtful. The others were nodding approvingly. I felt a surge of pride. Sev hadn't gotten where she had by accident—but she hadn't gotten there by being evil, either. She cared about people, and it showed.

"Do you..." Mikah's voice caught in his throat, his eyes brimming with emotion. "Do you really mean that? Independence?"

"Yes," Sev said firmly.

One of the women placed a hand solemnly over her heart as if to calm herself. Another wiped away a tear. Mikah clenched his teeth as if trying to harness his excitement into determination. Hell—I was caught up in it too. It was impossible *not* to believe Sev.

And standing there, in the middle of that dirty, cramped living room, coated in my own blood and gore, I suddenly realized why we were fighting. Why all of the risk, and the death, was worth it.

These people had been puppets their whole lives, every bit as much as I had. Their strings weren't the chemical ones the Paragon—and, by extension, Divinity—had used on me. They were more mundane, but no less restrictive. Poverty, debt, crime, all of it enforced by Kenton and his oppressive station regulations and fines. The Paragon had made a prison of this place.

And now—for the first time in their lives—these people were facing the prospect of freedom. *Real* freedom. Not the illusory promises the Paragon perpetually made.

I had always wondered what made people willing to go to war. It had always seemed like a futile exercise in death, where only the rich bastards in charge profited and everybody else simply bled and died. Even when I'd been with Tekka and his rebels, I couldn't help but scoff at their enthusiasm for their cause.

But now, staring at this room full of normal, everyday

people whose eyes were suddenly filled with fire and hope, I understood.

I glanced down at my quantcom again as it buzzed. Renault was getting antsy—as was the crew of the *Orpheus*. I cleared my throat. "This is nice and all, but... if we're gonna get out of here alive, much less take the station back, we're running out of time."

The members of the Citizens' Watch exchanged glances. Some skeptical. Some excited. Some worried. In the end, I found them turning to Jala. It was an odd sight, to see so many experienced people looking to such a young woman for leadership. I found myself wondering just what she had done to earn so much of their respect.

"I want a guarantee," she said. "That once you've taken control of the station, you'll install a democratic government. A *real* one. Fair elections. Representation for everybody aboard the station, no matter how poor."

Sev didn't so much as hesitate. She nodded resolutely. "You have my word. I can't promise that you'll get everything you want right away. We'll need to organize ourselves. But I'll see to it that this station gets its independence."

Jala looked around at her followers. She took a deep breath. "Then, in that case, we'll do whatever we can to help. But... those mercenaries are everywhere. Even with your fleet, you'll have a hard time fighting through them all. What can we possibly do?"

Sev turned to me.

An idea had started forming in my head as they'd been speaking. My mind kept getting pulled back to what I'd overheard Werrel saying in the corridor about capturing Sevani. *If we capture Sevani, we can avoid this whole stupid, bloody mess. Her fleet won't want to attack while we're holding her hostage.*

"Can you get us to the administrative offices?" I asked, turning to the citizens.

"I know some folks who run the maintenance elevator system," Mikah said. "They could get you closer, at least." He hesitated. "Well. They *could*, if we could get you to them. But the halls are swarming with mercenaries right now. There ain't a saint's chance in hell they won't collar you."

I nodded thoughtfully. "How quickly could you evacuate this zone?"

"There's an emergency shelter a few blocks away," Jala said. "Designed to keep people alive if there's a catastrophic life-support system failure. It's not maintained, but the walls should be thick enough to stop bullets, and it should be able to fit a lot of us. I don't know if I can make everyone listen, but I'll do my best." She hesitated. "Can't say how long it will take, though."

"How far does your influence go beyond this zone?" I asked.

"I have contacts all across the station," Jala said. "But not strong ones. Not like these people. But I could probably get a message passed around."

Sev raised an eyebrow. "I have to say, I wish I'd found you before this mess started. Could have used someone like you." Her face turned dark. "Then again, maybe it's for the best, considering Vatheson and Kenton killed most of my former employees."

"Alright." I straightened as the pieces of my plan started to come together in my mind. "Here's what I need you to do. Start the evacuation. And pass the word across the station that Sevani is coming back. The attackers are working for her. They will not hurt the civilians, but they need to get out of their way."

Jala nodded.

I turned to Sev. "I'll signal Flint and Winter to move out and engage the mercenaries who are looking for us in this zone. Between that and the chaos of the evacuation, we should be able to slip past the mercs and get to the elevator, then start working our way towards the administrative offices—where we'll find Kenton."

Mikah's expression was excited and bloodthirsty. "And when you find him?"

Sev's eyes were hard. "Then we finish our conversation."

They worked fast.

I was increasingly impressed with Jala's organization as I listened to the flow of footsteps passing through the hall on the other side of the door. A river of humanity, flowing in one direction. I'd been worried the evacuation would be chaotic, but I heard no shouting or panic. Not yet, anyway.

"Winter and Flint are ready to engage," I said, glancing down at my quantcom.

Sev checked the magazine of her stolen assault rifle. "Good."

I glanced at her and hesitated. "Are you sure you want to come with me? It's gonna be intense."

"I know the station better than you," she said, sounding annoyed at me for even suggesting she stay behind. "And you'll need backup."

I nodded reluctantly. Much as I wished I could have gotten her out of the way, there was no denying she was right. "Bentley and Rid will be meeting up with us too."

"Do we have time to get exos from the ship?" she asked.

I sighed. "I wish. That would make this a hell of a lot easier. But the minute Winter and his team engage, every merc in the zone is gonna head towards them to form a perimeter and try to box them in. Their job will be to keep them engaged for as long as possible and keep the pressure off of us while we try to get to Kenton."

"Are you sure they'll actually surrender when we capture him?" Sev asked. "They don't seem particularly loyal to him."

I hesitated. "No. I'm not. But my hunch is that Werrel is looking for an out. Kenton—and Vatheson by extension—has put him in an impossible situation here. He knows as well as we do that the fight for the station will be grueling and bloody, and the bloodier it is, the less profitable any of this will be for him. Right now, Kenton's orders seem like the only thing keeping him from just retreating. If we take Kenton out of the picture..."

Sev nodded. "It might be just the excuse he's looking for."

"Might be." I grimaced. "Hopefully. But hey, if nothing else, we'll have the administrative offices. That'll let us control the station's systems, which will be a big advantage for the fight."

My quantcom beeped. It was Rose.

NOW?

I glanced at Sev. "You ready?"

She nodded. "You?"

I grinned, Sev's little speech still buzzing in my head. Freedom. A cause worth dying for.

Worth killing for.

"Yeah," I said.

NOW, I typed to Rose.

Sev and I burst through the doorway. The corridor beyond was still bustling, filled with civilians all flowing in the same direction—the opposite of the direction we were going. I'd heard no message on the overhead PA system. Whatever method Jala and the others had of spreading the word, it was damn effective.

I opened a general comms channel to Renault, Rose, Winter, Flint, and Tetra on my wrist computer. Using comms would make it easier to detect the *Orpheus* if the mercs didn't already know where it was, but with the civilians on the move, the time for stealth was over already. "Alright, everyone, it's go time. We've evacuated civilians from zone, uh..."

"V13, Subsection 8S11," Sev said briskly.

"Uh... our zone," I said. "Sev and I are on our way to the meeting point."

Movement ahead caught my eye. A group of three mercenaries, not wearing exos, were standing in the hallway, shouting at the flow of civilians. "Where the hell do you all think you're going?"

Before I could get there, there was a panicked shout as somebody tried to grab a weapon from one of the mercs. A gunshot went off, echoing thunderously in the busy hallway.

"Here we go," I growled.

Screams erupted around us. Somebody was bleeding on the floor. There was another gunshot as the three mercenaries were dragged down and buried beneath a pile of angry civilians. I saw a vibroknife flash as one of the civilians started stabbing.

Two more mercenaries appeared at the end of the hallway.

I drew Peacebreaker.

It wasn't ideal—but nothing about war was. The three mercenaries on the floor spasmed and screamed as they were strangled, kicked, and stabbed. Their allies started shouting, sprinting towards them and raising their rifles. I knew they wouldn't hesitate to mow down this entire corridor of civilians—unless I put them down first.

"All units," I said into the comms. "*Engage.*"

Then I opened fire.

SEVEN

I've fought a lot of different types of battles over my life. They're all a pain in the ass. But I harbor a special hatred for intramegastructural combat, as some bright-eyed academic who wasn't bullied enough as a child deigned to name warfare aboard a space station. You combine all the claustrophobia of something like salvage work and combine it with the sheer chaos of a battlefield, except that it's all funneled into a maze that you never know as well as you think you do. Just when you thought you'd stopped the enemy at a chokepoint, *bam*. Turns out there was some bull-crap maintenance tunnel or something that let some of them sneak around behind you. Just one giant, never-ending headache.

"Flint!" I snapped the word into my wrist computer's radio as I ejected an empty magazine from an assault rifle I'd taken from a fallen mercenary. "Status!"

"*We're having a good ol' time in here,*" the pirate's voice crackled in my ear. Or maybe that crackling was just the gunshots echoing down the corridor. I withdrew a fresh magazine from my plundered tactical belt and slammed it home as

Flint continued. *"We've got 'em running scared. Whatever they were expecting, it weren't us."*

"Good." I glanced at my wrist computer's minimap. Three green dots showed the locations of Flint, Winter, and me, respectively. Winter's green dot had been stationary for several minutes now, while Flint's had pushed far ahead. Mine was somewhere in the middle. We were almost to the place we'd agreed to meet up with Bentley and Rid, but there were more mercenaries than we'd thought, and Sev and I had been forced to engage some of them. It had been about fifteen minutes since the first shots had been fired. "Don't overextend yourself. There's no backup on the way."

"Overextend? Hah!" Flint's voice shook as he fired his Jackhammer. *"It'll be a cold day in hell before these bastards can pin us down."*

Damn pirates. Out of habit, I tried to use my neurointerface to switch the channel, only to remember that I wasn't in my exo. I gritted my teeth and switched the channel manually on my wrist computer.

Sev ducked back into cover beside me, panting as bullets zipped through the air around her and slammed into the walls. "There's a lot of them," she gasped, tossing aside her empty mag and reloading. "We can't keep pushing like this. We'll never get to that maintenance elevator with this many of them in the way."

I glanced at the map again. "Hang on. I might have a better idea." I triggered the radio. "Winter! What's your status?"

"They've assumed a strong defensive position," Winter replied. His thick accent combined with the static made his voice barely intelligible. *"We have hurt them, but they have hurt us back. We are in a stalemate."*

"Alright. Keep them distracted." I mentally mapped out the route on the minimap. "We're coming to you."

I took off jogging down the corridor, stepping over several

bodies. They were mostly mercenaries, some killed by Sev and me, while others had been dispatched by the angry mobs of civilians. The only civilians I saw now, though, were a few corpses—those who'd confronted the mercenaries and paid the price. Jala had done an excellent job ushering everybody else towards the shelter. Just in the nick of time, too—the residential zone was now a warzone. The graffiti-covered walls were riddled with bullet-holes. The floor glinted with spent brass scattered among fallen corpses. Gunshots echoed down the hallways from every direction. Like I said—a headache.

Sometimes, though, that headache played to your advantage —as it did to ours right now.

A squad of mercenaries had taken up positions around several intersections, preventing Winter's men from pushing up their corridors and instead relegating them to hiding behind their corners, occasionally popping out to take shots at each other.

But the Roamers had forced the mercenaries to spread themselves too thinly. Which gave us a chance to take them from behind.

"Alright." I crouched next to a corner, watching as several mercenaries down the corridor from us fired at a target we couldn't see, blissfully unaware of our presence. "We'll creep forward as far as possible to maximize our advantage. I'll take the ones on the left, you target the ones on the right. As soon as they realize we're here, I'll press the assault. You hang back."

She made a face like she wanted to protest, but nodded. She was smart enough to see the value in letting the apparently invincible meatshield take point on an assault. Not that I was eager to test the limits of that invincibility. Getting shot in the head earlier had knocked me out—I'd been lucky they'd taken my death for granted and hadn't decided to do anything more drastic to me. If I got hit by an explosive round, I had to assume it would kill me as surely as it would kill a ripper.

I spoke into my wrist computer. "Winter, we're assaulting junction TC34-Z4. Tell your men to watch their fire for friendlies and push our position on my mark. As soon as we've broken their lines here, we'll have a brief window to use the chaos and take out as many of them as we can. Got it?"

"*Understood.*"

"Good." I took a deep breath, lined up my target, and exhaled. "Mark."

Sev and I fired at the same time. Two mercenaries jolted and fell. I kept firing, taking down two more before several Roamers clad in gray armor swarmed the hallway. Ever efficient, they finished off the wounded mercenaries with their knives rather than waste ammo.

The sounds of combat cascaded down the corridors as the mercenary position collapsed in on itself, one junction at a time. I turned to Sev. "Nice shooting."

She gave a casual shrug. "Thanks. You did okay too."

I chuckled, then looked up to see a gray-clad figure approaching us. Winter, blood splattered across his armor. "That accounts for them," he said, pulling off his helmet and wiping sweat from his brow. "It was a good push. We have established a foothold."

"More like the beginnings of a toehold." Sev held up her own wristwatch and zoomed out on the minimap. Winter and I grimaced simultaneously. If anything, Sev was being generous. Compared to the rest of the station, the ground we'd covered was essentially irrelevant—especially considering that only the *Orpheus* could dock here. Renault's ships were currently making their approach to the station, exchanging torpedoes and long-range cannon fire with the defending mercenary fleet. They'd attempt to board the station via the docking bays, where the invasion would begin in earnest. If my plan worked, though, they might not need to bother.

Flint's voice crackled in my ear. "*We've pushed 'em up a few levels, but they've got reinforcements pouring in. We're gonna have to fall back soon."*

"Understood." I switched the channel to contact Renault. "Renault—what's the situation?"

"They're putting up a fight," Renault admitted a moment later. *"But they know it's a losing one. They're clearly trying to buy themselves time. Not that there's any amount of time in the universe that would save them from—"*

"Push them harder," I said. "Don't hold back. We're going full power ahead." I switched channels again. "Rose. Have Bentley and Rid left yet?"

"They're on their way," Rose responded. *"What about me and Shell?"*

"Stay put. We've taken enough ground that the *Orpheus* should be secure for now, but I want you there just in case."

I expected some sort of protest—Rose's usual indignance at being put anywhere other than the hottest part of the action. Instead, she just gave a crisp, *"Affirmative."*

I shared a glance with Sev, who raised an eyebrow. "You're *sure* that's Rose on the other end?"

I grinned. "They grow so fast, huh?"

"Certainly doesn't *feel* fast."

I radioed Flint again, making eye contact with Winter as I spoke. "Flint, we're going up. Pull back. You and Winter have one job: keep the mercs busy. And watch each other's backs."

"That's two jobs," he growled.

"You have two jobs, then. If you absolutely can't hold your ground, retreat onto the *Orpheus*. Rose'll get you out of there."

"Oh, we can hold it, alright." Flint sounded amused.

"Just make sure you don't let them get behind you," I said. "Use the detailed schematics Sevani sent you. All it'll take is a few guys shooting at your backs to cripple your entire position."

"I know how to fight on a space station," Flint said irritably.

"Do not lecture me on ship combat," Winter growled at the same time.

"Fine." I spotted two exo-clad figures sprinting towards us—Rid and Bentley. Their exos weren't built for combat, but they'd still offer them at least some protection from small arms fire. I found myself wishing desperately that I had time to run back to the *Orpheus* and gear up in my own exosuit, but we couldn't afford any more delays. A few more minutes and the mercenaries would have the area completely locked down.

Bentley and Rid came skidding to a halt in front of us, raising their visors. Bentley's face paled slightly as he looked at the bullet-ridden corpses of the mercenaries. Rid, meanwhile, was staring at me. "What the hell happened?"

"I got shot," I said. "I'll fill you in later. We need to move before the enemy can re-establish a perimeter around us. I'll explain while we go. Sev—lead the way."

The sounds of gunfire became gradually muffled as Sev led the way through the snaking passages. I kept my assault rifle up and ready all the same.

"You know," Bentley muttered, looking around us at the endless concrete walls, layered in graffiti and punctuated occasionally by rickety-looking doors, "one of these days, maybe we should go risk our lives somewhere with a view. A nice sunset, you know. Some trees. Or at least something better than a never-ending maze of concrete. Be a nice change of pace, right?"

"Not much salvage work to be done planetside," I said absentmindedly, keeping my focus on the corridor ahead of us. After spending enough time around Bentley, you learned to tune out his never-ending stream of sarcasm.

"Oh!" Bentley was unfazed. "Salvage work. Is *that* what we're doing here?"

"Here." Sev stopped in front of a set of sealed blast doors.

Bold, faded lettering across the top of the doorway read: DO NOT ENTER.

"So," Bentley said. "I assume we're gonna enter?"

Rid flicked his arm, unfolding the plasma cutter from the wrist of his exosuit. "Hell yeah we are."

"We are," Sev said. "But not in the usual way."

Rid frowned, lowering his tool. "Then how?"

Sev grinned, then stepped forward, raised one hand, and knocked on the door.

It opened a few moments later. A group of weary-looking maintenance technicians wearing dirty green uniforms peered at us from the other side.

The foremost one—a woman with wrinkles that made it hard to guess her age, wearing her wispy brunette hair in a bun behind her head—sucked on a cigarette, blew out a puff of smoke, and looked at us through it. Her flat, bored gaze settled on Sev.

"You're Sevani?" she asked in a raspy voice.

Sev pushed me gently aside. "Yes."

"And you're here to take the station?" The woman cocked an eyebrow. "For real this time?"

Sev's face hardened. "You're damn right."

The stranger rolled her cigarette between her lips, then nodded and stepped aside, gesturing for her followers to make way. "Well, it's about damn time, I says. Mikah told us you'd be coming. You better get up there. We can get you most of the way. After that you're on your own. Come on through."

The maintenance workers led us through several rooms full of machinery and then into a large elevator car. The woman leading them hit a few buttons on the control panel.

"This'll take you to about as close to the administrative offices as I can get you," she rasped. But you're still gonna have a bit of a ways to go. And let me tell you, there are a *lot* of bastards up there. Seems like the only part of the station Kenton really cared about protecting was his own ass." She eyed us curiously. "I'm assuming you've got a plan to make it through them?"

"Yep." I grimaced. I'd been hoping that more of them would be drawn away by the fighting happening in other parts of the ship. "Shoot them until they go away."

The woman took a long, tired drag on her cigarette, then stepped away from the door as it began to shut. "Well, in that case, if they take any of you alive, just do me a favor and don't mention we let you through, huh?"

The doors clicked shut. The elevator began to move upwards—slowly at first, then faster and faster. Albeni was a big station.

"We've, uh..." Bentley grimaced. "We've got more of a plan than that, right? I mean, these aren't street thugs. They're professional soldiers. From what I saw back there, our entire little army is having a hard time getting through them."

"Nope." I twisted my back, stretching. "But we're out of other options."

"Just as long as you don't walk in the way of any more bullets," Sev said.

Rid raised an eyebrow at my bloodied shirt.

After several minutes, the elevator finally began to slow. I took a long, deep breath. The mercs should be spread thin by now, with most of them on their way to counter Winter and Flint, while others were probably rallying at the docks in preparation for Renault's assault. With any luck at all, there'd only be a few guards at the offices.

I stared at the control panel screen, watching the green dot that represented our elevator car move closer to the top. My reflection stared dully back at me, haggard and still spotted with dried blood.

I grinned wryly. *Luckiest man in the universe.*

The elevator groaned to a halt. The doors slid open.

We walked through several rooms full of machinery, similar

to the ones we'd passed through below, until we reached a set of heavy doors. I readied my gun, then nodded to Sev, who pressed a button on the control panel to set them grinding open.

The hallway we found ourselves in was significantly nicer than the bleak, barren corridors I'd come to associate with Albeni 7. The floor was made of artificial wood with a deep red carpet running down the middle. The ceiling was much higher and the walls wider apart. Rather than graffiti, the walls were marked by occasional paintings or pieces of furniture. I saw no sign of mercenaries, though. In fact, I saw no sign of anyone.

"Seems clear." I frowned, stepping out into the hallway. I half expected the doors to burst open and mercs to pour out into the halls. They didn't.

"What the hell?" Rid muttered. "Where is everyone?"

"Welcome to the ghost town," Sev said, a faint sense of disgust lining her voice. "The area around the offices is too expensive for just about anyone who actually lives on the station—and anybody who can afford it wouldn't be caught dead living in a poverty-ridden tin can like this, even if they are sealed away from it all." She stepped through the doorway and started down the hall, her assault rifle tucked into her shoulder. "So they sit empty, mostly."

I walked beside her, thinking about how many people had been crowded into Jala's apartment. I didn't think about it for long, though. After a few minutes of creeping through the empty hallways, Sev came to a halt next to a heavy set of locked doors.

"There's an open area through here," she whispered. "A sort of waiting room. The entrance to the offices is on the other side of that."

I put my ear against the doors. I heard voices. Sounded like orders being shouted. I stepped back, gesturing for Rid to begin his work. "I think we found the rest of the hired guns," I muttered. "There's no other way through?"

"Not that I know of." Sev glanced at Rid and Bentley. "The office doors are locked from the inside, and I don't think they'll open as easy as the last one. Once we're in there, our first priority will be finding Kenton."

"What about the defensive batteries?" Bentley asked.

"Once we've got Kenton, we'll get you to the control center," I said. "The faster you can get them down, the better. But none of that matters if we can't get to the door."

Bentley raised his Jackhammer rifle in trembling armored hands. It suddenly occurred to me that I wasn't sure Bentley had ever killed another human being. He'd mowed down plenty of rippers, but that didn't feel the same.

"Just focus on suppressing them," I said. "They're lightly armored. As soon as they see a Jackhammer, they'll duck for cover."

Bentley nodded, exhaling slowly.

I held up my wrist computer. "Status reports, everyone."

Renault's voice sounded in my ear. *"Their fleet has retreated to the station. If we want to continue the engagement, we'll have to move within firing range of the defensive batteries."*

Flint spoke up a moment later. *"We've circled the wagons, but they're pushing us. Hard. They've got exos."*

Dammit. We were running out of time. Rid stepped back, put away his lockbreaking kit, and held up his Jackhammer. "It's unlocked. You just need to hit the enter button."

I glanced at Sev. She nodded, tightening her grip on a stolen assault rifle.

"Alright," I said into the radio. "Hold tight. We're making our move now."

I hit the button. The doors slid open.

The waiting room had a simple, pleasant design. Couches, tables, and chairs lined the outer edges of the room, while the center was open. Several pillars divided the two spaces, while a large, rounded desk sat helpfully next to the door into the offices. I imagine that whoever designed the room had pictured it full of well-dressed men and women, chatting amiably and waiting to do rich-people business.

The waiting part was right. The people waiting just had more guns than the designer probably had intended.

A *lot* more guns.

I counted roughly two dozen mercenaries, scattered in small clusters across the room. They all had weapons nearby, but none of them looked as if they were expecting an imminent attack. Instead, most of them were sitting. I spotted a few drinking. Some, sitting at a table directly to my right, were even playing a card game.

"Damn you." One of the men playing cards tossed his hand onto the table. His back was to me so I couldn't see his expression. "Not gonna make a damn credit on this job at this rate."

His companion grinned, spreading his own cards out. "Hey, don't sweat it. It's just my lucky day."

He looked up and saw us. The grin faded. He blinked in confusion.

Not so lucky after all.

Peacebreaker jumped in my hands. The mercenary's head snapped backward as the bullet tore straight through his skull and into the wall behind him.

All hell broke loose.

EIGHT

I fired several times in rapid succession, blasting away each man at the table before they could so much as reach for their weapons. Their blood splattered across the cards. Behind me, Sev's assault rifle was drowned out by the thundering of Rid and Bentley's Jackhammers.

Mercenaries across the room cursed, reached for weapons, scrambled for cover, or screamed in pain as bullets struck them. Sev was careful and deliberate, firing controlled bursts that took down several targets. Rid and Bentley were less disciplined, holding down their triggers and spraying explosive rounds across the room. Most of the bullets missed their targets, instead slamming into the walls behind them and sending bursts of shrapnel spraying through the air.

As for the rounds that *did* hit... well. Explosive rounds against soft targets are never a pretty sight. But there ain't much pretty about war.

"The entrance!" I barked the words as I turned Peacebreaker from the mercenaries at the table to the rest of the room. "Go! I'll cover!"

Rid started sprinting. Sev followed right on his heels.

Bentley either hadn't heard me or was too filled with adrenaline to listen. He continued firing until his gun went empty, then stared down at it as if he couldn't figure out why it wasn't shooting anymore.

Dammit. Bentley was an experienced vulture by now, but he was rarely doing the shooting himself. Beyond him I saw mercenaries poking out of the various bits of cover they'd found, aiming weapons in our direction. We'd had our chance to deal damage—now it was their turn.

"Move!" I grabbed Bentley by the shoulder plate of his exo and grunted as I pulled him along with me towards the nearest pillar, firing Peacebreaker as I did so. One merc grunted and ducked back behind his own pillar as my bullet grazed his arm. The others opened fire. Bullets whistled past my head. There was a metallic ringing sound as one glanced off of Bentley's armor. Lucky. Rid and Bentley's exos wouldn't hold up under sustained fire. Oh, to be wearing a Jericho right now. Or, better yet, the Icarus.

Bentley grunted as I slammed him against the pillar. Bullets chewed into it from the other side but didn't penetrate. Must've been a steel beam in the center. I reloaded Peacebreaker and glanced towards the office entrance, assessing our position. Rid was already posting up next to the door, his plasma cutter out and working, but he was dangerously exposed to the mercenaries. A shot slammed into the heavy door next to him and he flinched, but kept working. Sev had taken cover behind the desk, keeping low as bullets shot through it and into the wall behind her.

I assessed our position.

In a word: bad.

A way out. I looked around. We'd made it this far—we just needed to buy enough time for Rid to unlock the door. My eyes settled on the corpse of the first mercenary I'd shot at the table— more specifically, on his belt.

"Reload," I growled to Bentley, pulling a Jackhammer mag from his own belt and handing it to him.

He stared at it for a moment, then snatched it. Muscle memory fostered over hundreds of hours of training I'd forced into the crew kicked in as he dropped the spent magazine and slammed the new one home with perfect form.

I judged the distance between myself and the fallen mercenary I'd been eyeing. "Now cover me."

We both moved at the same time. He stepped out to the right of our protective pillar, opening fire, while I dove to the left, towards the dead mercs who'd been playing poker. I threw the table onto its side, scattering stacks of credit chips and blood-soaked playing cards across the floor, fired a few quick shots at the enemy, and then took cover behind the overturned piece of furniture. A bullet would pass right through it without even slowing down, but at least it concealed my position a bit.

"Now what?" Bentley yelled.

"Keep 'em busy!" I reached out and grabbed the boot of the first mercenary I'd shot, dragging his corpse closer.

A gunshot—loud enough to rise above the already deafening cacophony of the firefight—caught my ear. Bentley gave a sharp cry and staggered back behind the pillar. A shock of cold horror ran through me as I saw blood running down his side. A bullet must've pierced a weak point in his armor. I looked across the room to see a mercenary holding an armor-piercing rifle. He'd moved up and flanked us while we were focused on the others. He took aim at Bentley, preparing to fire a second shot. Bentley was too focused on his wound to notice the threat.

"Bentley!" I lifted Peacebreaker, knowing damn well I wouldn't be able to fire in time. "Move!"

Bentley looked up and froze. I saw a satisfied grin spread across the mercenary's face as his finger tensed on the trigger.

Then a spray of blood as a bullet tore through his neck. He

spasmed, the rifle firing into the floor with a concussive crack, then fell.

At the back of the room, Sev fired a few more shots from her rifle before diving back into cover. "Rid! How close?"

"Almost—dammit!" He grunted as a bullet slammed into the back of his exo, the force of the blow interrupting his work. I heard one of the mercenaries give a shout. "Focus fire! Exo by the door!"

I gritted my teeth and reached down to the belt of the corpse I'd dragged closer—and the three grenades clipped to its belt. I grabbed a grenade and pulled the pin.

I tossed it overhand—then the second, then the third, throwing each towards a different area. The gunfire in the room was already deafening, but the three explosions were apocalyptic. The floor shuddered. Debris tore through the air. A thick haze settled over the room. By the time the third one went off I was up and moving towards the enemy.

I skirted the edge of the room. A merc stumbled out of cover, bloodied and dazed. I put him down with a bullet through the chest and kept moving. Another was crawling on the floor, his legs shredded by the blast. I kicked his weapon away and fired at several shapes in the haze as they moved backward—towards the far exit.

"They're clearing out," I said into the comms.

"About damn time," Sev said. "Rid?"

"Almost," he growled. "Just need to take care of... one more..."

I frowned. A shape appeared in the haze. Larger than the others had been, and moving closer. I aimed Peacebreaker at its center mass and fired three times.

The shape didn't so much as slow down. A moment later it materialized into an all-too familiar sight as it stepped through the smoke. A hulking mass of armor painted black.

Ah, *hell*.

I dove behind the nearest pillar. The familiar sound of a Jackhammer rifle tore apart the near silence that had followed the explosions. Chunks of plaster and concrete burst into dust as the explosive rounds slammed into the pillar I was hunkering behind.

"They've got a Jericho!" I yelled into the comms.

"Door's open!" Rid shouted.

"Go!" I dashed towards the next pillar. I barely made it, sliding to safety as bullets tore the air apart over my head. The enemy Jericho continued to advance towards me. From the bullet marks on its armor, it looked like it had already seen its fair share of fighting. The Vanguard must have abandoned his companions in the heat of the battle to come protect the offices. I noticed again that his Jackhammer rifle had something attached to the underbarrel, but I was too busy avoiding getting torn to shreds to figure out what it was.

"Rid!" Sev shouted as she dashed through the doorway. "Cover him!"

Next to the doorway, Rid raised his own Jackhammer and opened fire. The mercenary staggered backward as the volley struck him. I took advantage of the reprieve to make another dash to the next pillar. Bentley was still standing where I'd left him, one hand over his wound.

"We gotta go." I pushed him towards the entrance. "Move!"

He breathed in sharply but started moving, even going so far as to raise his own weapon and fire a few wild shots at the Jericho. The enemy exo had stabilized, though, as the mercenary set his feet like a man fighting against a heavy wind. There was a thumping sound as his shoulder-mounted grenade-launcher fired. A moment later Rid cried out as a concussion grenade slammed into his chest, sending him flying backward through the office doors.

"Rid!" I thumbed Peacebreaker's dial to maximum bullet density and aimed at the Jericho's head. The Vanguard turned his Jackhammer towards me just as I fired. The bullet didn't pierce the armored visor but it sure as hell rattled it. His rifle swerved to the side, sending its stream of bullets off to my left to destroy a portion of the wall rather than straight into my chest to turn me into a fine red mist.

What was it I'd told my crew, way back when I was first prepping them to fight rippers? *Can't heal what's not there.*

I kept moving. *Almost to safety.*

Not almost enough, though. The mercenary recovered quickly. I shoved Bentley behind the last pillar, then ducked behind it myself.

"Can't hide forever." The mercenary's familiar voice was cold and metallic through the Jericho's visor. His heavy footsteps drew nearer as he moved to flank us, speaking while he reloaded. "It true what they're saying? You walked away from a bullet to the head?"

I ignored him and dragged Bentley behind me, keeping the pillar between us and the threat. More explosive rounds thundered into it.

"Now what?" Bentley groaned.

I gritted my teeth. The Vanguard had all the cards. If I could reach the armor-piercing rifle, I *might* be able to make him back off, but it was on the other side of the room. We were fighting, basically unarmed, against a mobile weapon platform that had conquered all humanity. Nobody knew the terrifying, unstoppable power of a Jericho better than I did.

The thought gave me pause. That was it. The closest thing to an advantage I had here. I knew a Jericho just about as well as anyone in the universe. I furrowed my brow. What would I be doing in that mercenary's situation?

No sightline to the target. No point in repositioning to give the enemy a chance to maneuver away. Jackhammer rounds wouldn't penetrate the cover.

The Vanguard stopped firing. "Well," he growled. "Let's see you walk away from *this*."

Obvious option: grenades.

I dove from cover, sliding across the floor on my side and aiming Peacebreaker just above the Jericho's right shoulder. Sure enough, I saw the telltale sign of the grenade-launcher unfolding from the armor plating, barrel pointed right towards me.

I heard the thump of the grenade firing just as I pulled the trigger. There was a flash of light as the grenade detonated, still partially inside the launcher. The Jericho was flung backward.

"GO!" I leaped to my feet and sprinted towards the office entrance, Bentley right behind me. Rid was still climbing to his feet on the other side. Sev was standing next to the door, blood streaked across the side of her face.

I darted through and pulled Bentley in beside me. "Close it!"

Sev slammed her fist on a glowing red button on the control panel. The heavy doors began to grind shut. Before they could close, I caught a glimpse of the Vanguard stumbling to his feet, smoke rising from the misshapen mass of torn metal that had been his shoulder-mounted grenade-launcher. He reached for his Jackhammer and raised it with one hand, aiming directly at me.

Then the doors slammed together. There was a mechanical whirring sound as the locking mechanism closed, intermingled with the thudding of explosive rounds striking the other side of the heavy plating.

"Won't he be able to just... open it?" Sev panted.

Rid climbed to his feet with a groan, then staggered over to the doorway. He tinkered with the control panel for a moment. There was a flash of sparks and the glowing buttons went dark.

"Not anytime soon," he panted.

I turned, inspecting our new location. A long hallway, with

several doors on each side. After the cacophony of the battle outside, it felt eerily silent. No sign of opposition, though.

I glanced around at my crew. I wanted to ask if everybody was alright, but that seemed a laughably stupid question. Somehow—for what was probably the first time ever—I'd been the only one to come out of a fight unscathed. Rid's exo appeared to be compromised, his movements slow and awkward. Sev was bleeding from a nasty cut just below her left ear—looked like she'd caught a chunk of shrapnel, probably from the desk she'd taken cover behind. Bentley worried me most, though. He had sagged against the wall and was holding a hand over his injured side.

"Let me see." I reached towards the injury.

"I'm fine." He groaned, pulling his hands away. His exo's self-sealing technology had kicked in, automatically compressing the wound. "At least... I think so. Doesn't matter anyways. We're running out of time."

True that.

"The administrator's office is at the end of the hall." Sev wiped blood from her face and began striding briskly down the corridor, towards a set of huge, ornate doors. "We just need to hope he didn't make a run for it during all the commotion."

"I thought you said that was the only way in," Rid panted as we followed her.

"Only one I know of." Sev grimaced.

"Do we even"—Bentley staggered along, panting—"know he was here in the first place?"

"No," Sev admitted. "Not for certain. But the amount of mercs we had to fight through to get in here seems like a good sign."

We passed by a door with a window in it. I peered through into a wide office space and caught a glimpse of several people dressed in business wear cowering behind furniture. One of them was wearing a Paragon enforcer's uniform. He paled as my face became visible, then vanished behind a desk.

"Seems like it was just another day in the office until we showed up," I said, moving along. "And the local security doesn't seem too keen on trying their luck against us."

We came to a halt in front of Kenton's office. I tried the open button on the control panel out of a distant hope it would be unlocked. It wasn't, of course.

Sev rapped on the door with a closed fist. "*Kenton!* Open up! Your security can't help you."

There was no answer.

A loud clang filled the hallway—coming from behind us. I frowned and looked back over my shoulder.

A voice spoke from overhead—smug and nasal. Kenton, speaking into the office PA system from within his office. "Oh, can't they?"

CLANG. The doors we'd come through shuddered.

Sev narrowed her eyes. "He can't make it through, can he?"

CLANG. One of the doors folded slightly inward, creating a tiny gap between the two.

Dammit. I turned to Rid. "Hurry!"

Rid groaned and got down on his knees. The mechanism on his plasma cutting tool appeared to have been damaged, so he had to unfold the tool himself. There was a flash of light as he started cutting.

CLANG. The gap between the other doors widened slightly.

Bentley turned slowly towards the wall next to Rid. He groaned and sagged against it, his Jackhammer falling with a loud clatter to the floor. "I think I'll just... sit down for a moment..."

I wanted to ask Rid how long we had—but I knew the answer was "not long enough."

CLANG. The doors shuddered violently. I saw a set of

armored fingers begin to worm their way through the gap between the doors.

Within a few seconds the Jericho and the mercenary Vanguard wearing it would be on us. This hallway gave us absolutely no cover. His Jackhammer would tear us to shreds.

I held up Peacebreaker like some sort of futile ward against evil. The best it could do would be to temporarily distract him. I glanced down at Bentley's discarded Jackhammer. The massive autorifle stared back at me. Too heavy to be used effectively without the assistance of an exo—even by a Vanguard.

One of the doors began to slide open, inch by dreadful inch, grating metallically as the Jericho's power fought against the locking mechanisms.

Screw it. I holstered Peacebreaker and hefted Bentley's Jackhammer from the floor. It felt lighter than I'd expected.

Too heavy for use without an exo—even by a Vanguard. But then again, I was no regular Vanguard. Not anymore. I aimed it at the doorway and pulled the stock tight into my shoulder, settling into a rifle-shooting stance with my torso angled slightly forward, leaning into the gun, with one leg positioned as an anchor behind me.

The locking mechanism finally gave way. The door thundered open. The Jericho stepped forward, raising its weapon.

I pulled the trigger and the Jackhammer roared to life, driving itself back against my shoulder like—well, like a jackhammer. My stance held firm, the enormous force of the recoil transferring from the gun, through my shoulder, down my torso and leg, and into the floor. Shells shot out in a steady stream, clinking noiselessly on the floor as they were drowned out by the deafening sound of the rifle.

The Jericho staggered sideways, trying to avoid the bullets, only to be slammed backward against the closed portion of the doorway. The explosive rounds burst in flashes of light against its armor. I fought against the Jackhammer's upwards force to pull my aim down, towards the one part of the Jericho I thought I might actually have a chance at damaging.

My opponent's weapon rattled as my bullets struck it. Jackhammers were durable weapons, but they weren't invincible. I aimed for the trigger well, slowing my rate of fire to make sure I was accurate. I couldn't tell if I'd hit my target or not.

The deafening crescendo next to my ear came to an abrupt end, leaving an aching throb in my shoulder. Out of ammo—unsurprising, since Bentley had already emptied most of the magazine. I lowered the weapon, holding my breath.

The Vanguard straightened, shaking himself. He stepped into the center of the hall. I couldn't see his face through his visor, but from the sound of his voice, I imagined he was grinning.

"*My turn,*" he growled, and raised his weapon again.

Nothing happened. I breathed a sigh of relief. I'd shot true—his trigger well had been destroyed, rendering the weapon temporarily useless.

"Almost... there..." Rid muttered.

The Jericho stared down at his damaged weapon for a moment, then chuckled. "Alright, then. We'll do this the fun way."

"This guy doesn't give up, does he?" Sev muttered.

He reached down to the attachment on the end of his Jericho and hit a button. A length of shiny, jet-black metal folded into place at the end of his rifle. A bayonet—fashioned from what appeared to be a ripper's biosteel talon.

Well. Maybe not *completely* useless.

The Vanguard charged.

And I, dammit all to hell and back again, threw aside my empty Jackhammer and charged right back at him.

Look. I do a lot of stupid things. Charging a fully armored Jericho barehanded and barely dressed is certainly up there among them. But I promise, on all things I hold sacred, that I never do them because I want to. Life just frequently seems to put me into impossible, stupid situations where impossible, stupid actions seem to be the only chance I have at getting out.

The Vanguard didn't expect me to charge him any more than I did. That was probably the only thing that saved me from getting skewered on the end of his bayonet. His reaction was just a tad too slow, and I managed to shove the weapon aside. That didn't save me from the sheer momentum of his Jericho, though. Pain lanced through my body as the mass of hardened steel, wrapped around an already considerable mass of flesh, slammed into me and sent me flying backward. I rolled on the ground with a grunt, landing on my back.

He loomed over me, raising his bayonet. I managed to roll out of the way just before it came down and stabbed deep into the floor. I leaped to my feet and drew back a fist to punch, only to falter awkwardly. What the hell was I doing? I'd turn my fists into a mush before I so much as rattled him.

Instead, I braced myself against the wall behind me and shoved him with one foot. He was already unbalanced and the force was just enough to send him staggering sideways.

"I'm in!" Rid yelled. I heard a pneumatic whoosh as the doors to Kenton's office opened. "Let's—"

Gunfire.

Rid staggered away from the door, sparks flying as bullets slammed into his armor. I caught a glimpse of two enforcers with rifles just inside Kenton's doorway, standing like they'd been waiting for the door to be breached. One of them took careful aim at Rid, lining his sights up with a weak spot on his exo.

"NO!" I turned and started to run towards them—only to feel something grab me by the arm from behind. The Jericho's armored fingers wrapped around my elbow and jerked me backward, flinging me into the opposite wall.

Plaster crumbled and concrete crunched beneath me. My

vision flashed and my skull rang. Sharp, vivid pain lanced through my arm as my elbow snapped.

More gunshots. Screams of pain. I couldn't turn my head to see what was happening, though. The Vanguard was pinning my arm to the wall with one huge mechanical hand while the other careened towards my head like a comet towards a doomed planet. I jerked my head sideways. The Vanguard gave a frustrated grunt as his fist plunged through the already compromised wall.

I tried to wriggle free. No luck there—only pain as my mutilated arm wriggled in the Jericho's vise grip. Nowhere to go.

Almost nowhere to go. I felt the wall behind me give slightly as the Vanguard wrenched his fist free from the hole he'd made, drawing it back once again for a blow that would without doubt turn whatever part of my body it struck into a fine paste. I grabbed his fist with my free hand, pushing back.

Flesh against machine. Even enhanced as I was, it was a battle I was bound to lose. Unless something else lost first.

The wall behind me finally gave way to the enormous pressure. The Vanguard grunted in surprise as we both tumbled through it. He let go of my arm as he tried to steady himself and I managed to stumble away, nearly tripping over a desk. Screams filled the air as dozens of terrified office employees scrambled for the far wall.

My right arm was still hanging limp and useless, but I could feel the flesh around my ruined joint pulsating as my body drew energy from some unknown source to knit itself back together. I ignored the strange sensation, focusing on my enemy—and, perhaps more urgently, the sounds of conflict echoing from the hallway beyond. My friends were in danger. They needed me.

The Vanguard took a step towards me. I feinted for the door, then darted the other way, trying to get around him. He took the bait, stepping to the right as I dashed left.

Jerichos might be big and bulky, but they sure as hell aren't sluggish. The Vanguard activated his lateral thrusters, giving him an extra boost of speed as he shot towards me. His fist slammed into my side, and I grunted as I was hurled sideways, into and through yet another wall.

I rolled to a halt in a pile of debris in the next room over. Groaned. Clambered to my feet. I'd definitely broken a few ribs that time. I ignored the pain and slammed my fist on a control panel next to the door, staggering back into the hallway.

I caught a glimpse of Sev struggling with somebody in Kenton's office before the Vanguard stepped into my line of sight. He chuckled as he put his armored fists up. "You're looking a little roughed up, there."

I felt *more* than a little roughed up. My entire body hurt. My shirt was hanging by a few tattered threads. My arm no longer felt quite so limp, but it certainly didn't feel like it was ready to punch anyone—especially not a walking mountain of armor.

I put it up anyways, though. Like my old man always said— no point in starting something if you don't intend to finish it.

The Vanguard cried out and stumbled forward.

Behind him, Bentley staggered backward, wrenching the modified Jackhammer free. The biosteel bayonet made a metallic *shink* sound as it pulled free from a hole in the Jericho armor right behind the kneecap.

The Vanguard whirled towards him.

"Throw it!" I yelled.

Bentley tossed the weapon overhead as the Vanguard charged him. I caught it from the air, charged forward, and slammed my shoulder into the Jericho's back, managing to knock him down. He activated one of his thrusters as he rolled onto his back—just in time for me to throw my full weight onto the bayonet, plunging it towards his chest.

Biosteel is one of the most terrifying materials I know of. With it, rippers can cut through just about anything like it's butter. But there's a reason that biosteel isn't commonly used for weapons and armor. It has to be attached to a living ripper in order to maintain its impossibly sharp edge.

The bayonet glanced off of his chest plate with a spray of sparks.

That said, even once you cut it free, it's still incredibly tough stuff. With enough force behind it, it's more than capable of punching through armor. You just need to put it in the right place.

The point slid upwards towards the Vanguard's neck, trailing sparks all the way, then vanished into the weaker armor right between the neck guard and the helmet.

The Jericho suit spasmed, kicked, thrashed, and went still.

I didn't take the time to make sure he was dead. I left the bayonet and the attached Jackhammer embedded in his throat and staggered towards the office, drawing Peacebreaker. I burst through the doorway.

Three corpses littered the floor—all of them wearing enforcer uniforms. As I watched, Sev wrenched a knife free from the throat of a fourth and final one. He fell to his knees, blood gushing from the wound as he stared blankly at me, then collapsed onto his face with a crunch.

Rid was on the floor, leaning against the wall and panting heavily. One of his exo's fists was coated in blood. It looked like the power to his legs had shut off at some point in the fight.

Sev, Rid, Bentley and I all turned our attention to the large desk at the end of the room. A small, weaselly man slowly peered over the edge of it at us, eyes wide.

"Kenton," Sevani said, as if she were greeting a neighbor while on a stroll.

"Sevani," the man behind the desk said slowly.

Sev wiped blood from her face. Not that there was much point to it, as her hand was covered in blood too.

"We need to talk," she growled.

NINE

There's no good side to war. But as a soldier, if there was any part of it I *did* enjoy, it was the break that came after: when the terms were settled or the enemy was obliterated, the ground was secured, and the orders came in to set up camp. The simple knowledge that for now, your work was done and you were still alive, always felt like a gift.

The aftermath of the battle turned out to be *significantly* less relaxing if you had any measure of leadership responsibility. And, as it happened, I currently had too damn much of it.

"Commander! Many congratulations upon your most glorious victory." Renault beamed as he strode down the cargo ramp of his ship, now safely docked to one of Albeni 7's ports. His ridiculously flamboyant blood-red coat fluttered behind him as he set foot upon the floor of the docking bay and extended a hand towards me.

"Congratulations yourself," I said, wearily shaking his hand with my now fully functional arm. "And don't call me commander."

"Why not? You take well to it! Your plan turned out brilliantly. The battle would have been *significantly* more costly had we simply pressed on as I wanted."

I wasn't sure what to say to that. Part of me wanted to point out that Sevani had been more responsible for the plan than I had. Another part of me was still dwelling on how close the plan had come to ending in disaster on multiple occasions. But knowing that Renault would turn whatever response I gave into a long, meandering conversation, I simply nodded and said nothing.

He let go of my grip to put his hands on his hips and survey the interior of the docking bay. "So—this is what it was all for, eh?"

"Partially." I nodded to one of his officers as they walked down the ramp behind him. Similar ramps were being extended all along the length of the terminal as more ships docked and unloaded the passengers they had ferried from the larger ships. One group in particular caught my eye—a group of gray-clad Aboenian Marshals, led by Tetra.

Renault raised an eyebrow as he turned his attention to me and, more specifically, the blood coating... well, pretty much all of me. I hadn't had time to clean myself up since the fight in the offices. I was still wearing the tatters of my shirt and was coated in blood. "You, ah, look like you took the lion's share of the fight yourself."

"I kept busy. Your men did themselves proud."

Renault beamed with pride. "Flint says it was a hard battle, but they held the line." He turned to face Tetra as she drew near. "As did your soldiers, I hear."

"They served their homeship loyally." Tetra came to a brisk halt, eyeing me skeptically. "You look—"

"I know," I said irritably. "How's Command doing?"

"They're still uncertain of this entire endeavor. But they're happy the battle ended in victory, with significantly less harm to our ship or people than your last one."

I grimaced. "They're still holding a grudge about that, huh?"

Tetra's eyes held no humor. "I'm sure I don't need to remind you that the damage will haunt my people for generations. Command accepts what has occurred, but they're not convinced it was the only way out—or the best way."

"Are *you* convinced?" I asked.

"Mostly," she said.

Renault cleared his throat. "Well, fortunately, *this* battle seems to have gone considerably smoother. Minimum casualties, in the grand scheme of things, though I understand the boarding crews suffered not inconsiderable losses."

"No loss of life is inconsiderable." Tetra folded her arms, treating the pirate to a glare. "But yes—all things seen together, I believe that this fight went about as well as could be hoped."

I nodded wearily. Truth be told, it was a miracle how well it had all turned out. The nightmare scenarios I had so feared— residential zones turned into bullet-ridden hellscapes, hallways carpeted with civilian corpses, massive structural damage inflicted by Renault's gunships—had been averted. The damage had been incredibly limited. The site where Flint and Winter had made their stand had been pretty chewed up by the fight, but Jala and her friends had evacuated the vast majority of the civilians from the zone before things got too hot. Despite our best efforts, there had still been a handful of civilian casualties, but they had mostly been sustained by enraged locals throwing themselves at the mercenaries. The offices were pretty much destroyed, but that didn't worry me too much.

The battle was over—and now the work began.

"Oi! Captain! VanDunn!" I turned to see Flint approaching us, alongside Winter and a familiar-looking man clad in a tattered mercenary's uniform. Flint's Jericho was scarred and splattered with blood, but he wore a wide-toothed grin. "Brought him in safe and sound, just like you ordered."

I turned my attention to the mercenary, finally recognizing

him as he drew closer. Werrel, the mercenary commander. He was out of his exo and appeared to be disarmed, but wore no manacles. If he was intimidated by his escorts, he didn't let it show.

They came to a halt in front of me.

"Werrel, right?" I asked. "I believe we met. Briefly."

The man straightened slightly. "Aye. And you must be the one and only Lackan VanDunn."

I frowned at that but chose to press on. "You're in charge of this outfit?"

"That's right."

I studied him, trying to decide how best to proceed. We'd beaten back his forces pretty soundly—both on the station and in space—but they were far from depleted. After we'd captured Kenton, the mercenaries had retreated and dug in at the old enforcer headquarters, while the damaged starships had withdrawn out of firing range. Our victory had been much more bloodless than I'd feared it would be, but it wouldn't be complete until Vatheson's forces had been completely ejected from the system. Now, then, the only question was what it would take to get them out.

"What are your latest orders?" I finally asked. "From your employer, I mean."

He raised an eyebrow. "I'm assuming you don't mean Kenton." He made no attempt to conceal the disdain in his voice. "Please tell me you've put a bullet in that lazy bastard's head already."

We hadn't. After taking him hostage and using him as leverage to get the mercenaries to stand down, Sev had ordered the station manager thrown into a cell. Interrogating him was high on my priority list, but first I needed to make sure that we had control of the station. If Vatheson *did* launch a counterattack, I didn't want us to get caught with our pants down.

"You know who I mean," I said. "You might've temporarily

been taking orders from Kenton, but he wasn't the one paying you."

He nodded, looking almost relieved that I already knew. "Last orders we received from Vatheson were to hold the station and assist Kenton."

Renault folded his arms. "No update to those orders when the attack began?"

Werrel eyed us. "Truth be told... we haven't heard from him in three days."

Renault and I exchanged a confused look. "What do you mean?" I asked.

The mercenary shrugged, almost apologetically. "I mean that one day we were in regular contact with him, and the next he was nowhere to be found. When you and your fleet showed up I did everything I could to raise him, get him to send in reinforcements. Never got so much as a word in response. Truth be told, you're damn lucky, because that was the real reason I agreed to a ceasefire. With no word from Vatheson, I'm increasingly certain that there's no pay coming, so..." He shrugged. "What's the point?"

I tried to make sense of it. Maybe Vatheson was simply distracted by other problems. After all, war was raging across the entire Paragon now. He probably had bigger problems than us on his hands. Still—I didn't like it. It felt too much like a trap. He had devoted considerable resources to his crusade of retribution against us. Abruptly giving up like this the moment we made our counter-attack made no sense.

"Anyways..." Werrel glanced around at the numerous troops pouring off of the dropships. "You've clearly won this round. Beat us fair and square. And I'm increasingly doubtful that we'll get any kind of reward for causing any more problems for you, so how's about we call it a day, I round up my boys, and we get out of your hair so you can enjoy the fruits of your victory?"

He gave me a tired grin, which I returned with a flat stare.

"That sounds nice," I said. "Except for the fact that I've got no reason to believe you won't go running right back to Vatheson, and then we'll have to fight you all over again. You'd say anything if it got you out of here."

The mercenary shrugged. "Sure. Won't deny that. I'd sell you my own grandma if I thought it might save my sorry hide. But let me put it to you another way. Let's suppose I *am* lying. Let's suppose that this is some ploy of mine to get out of here and back to Vatheson's frigid embrace. Even if it *were*, wouldn't you rather I was out there than in here?"

It was a solid point. If Vatheson did attack again, we'd be dealing with a fight on two fronts. This way, we were at least guaranteed control of the station.

"You already handed our asses to us once," Werrel continued. "And I'm far too old and greedy to care about revenge. Letting us leave peacefully will be a hell of a lot easier for everyone involved than trying to take us by force."

I gave it another moment's consideration, then nodded. "Seems fair. We'll make the arrangements. Your ships are pretty beat up, but they should still be able to get you wherever you need to go. After that, I'd recommend you find an easier job for a change."

Werrel smiled wryly. "I'd call that a good piece of advice right there. Guarding a mining station or breaking up a union sounds pretty nice after the fight you put us through." He raised an eyebrow. "Unless, of course, you happen to be hiring..."

I couldn't help but chuckle at the audacity. "Get him out of here."

Werrel held his hands up apologetically. "Can't blame a fellow for trying."

"I like him," Renault said thoughtfully as the mercenary commander was led away.

"Like him all you want," I said, turning as I noticed another ship docking. The *Orpheus*. "But don't trust him. Something's off about all this. Can't think of any reason Vatheson would just ignore Werrel's calls for help and let us have the station back—not after all the effort he went through to take it."

"I would hardly say he *let* us have it," Renault said. "Though I will admit that it's odd he cut off communications."

"For now, just keep a damn close eye on those mercs. I'll rest a lot easier when we've got the station to ourselves."

Renault nodded thoughtfully. "We shouldn't be too hasty in driving them away. If there's any truth at all to his tale, Werrel might be a valuable tool to exploit against Vatheson. The perfect disgruntled ex-employee."

I scoffed. "You're not *seriously* suggesting we take him up on his offer to hire him."

"Not for mercenary work, per se. But he might at least have some information he'd be willing to barter."

I grimaced. Much as I hated the idea of working with someone I'd just fought a battle against, Renault had a point. "Fine. You can see what he's willing to tell you. But take it all with a grain of salt."

My eyes locked on a welcome sight. The *Orpheus* had docked, and I could see Rose emerging from the cargo bay. As our eyes locked, she broke into a sprint towards me, Shell following behind her.

"Where are they?" Rose asked urgently.

"They're both in the medbay," I said. "Bentley is fine. Well—not *fine*, he got shot, but he's gonna be alright. Just stiff for a while."

Rose sighed in relief. She moved as if she were about to hug me, then stopped as she noticed just how much red was staining my shirt.

"Are *you* alright?" she asked. "You look—"

"I know how I look. I'm fine." I squeezed her shoulder. "How're you? Can't have been easy waiting on the ship while everyone was in danger."

She frowned at me. "Are you being sarcastic?"

"Not at all." I shook my head. "Because I know if you'd had your way, you'd have been in the thick of it all with us."

She nodded slowly. "It... it wasn't. I was worried sick the whole time. But I knew that was where I was needed."

"You did a hell of a good job getting there, too." I glanced at the *Orpheus*. "Old girl's never had a better pilot."

"If you don't have anything going on after this is all over," Renault said, "I might have a job waiting for you. Can always use a skilled pilot."

Rose got an intrigued look on her face. I didn't like that at all. I glowered at the pirate. "Stop trying to poach my crew and start getting your troops disembarked. The more firepower we have to bear, the less chance of things going sideways while the mercenaries are on their way out."

He clicked his heels together and gave a ludicrously exaggerated salute. "Aye aye, sir. Twill be done post haste." He winked at Rose before turning away. "*Think about it*," he mouthed.

"*Don't* think about it," I growled as I watched him go.

She gave me a mischievous smirk. "Why not? He's on our side, isn't he?"

"He's on his own side," I said, watching the pirate as he disappeared into his entourage.

"Glad to see you have so much trust in this coalition you've built."

"Everybody's got their own agenda," I said wearily. "We're just lucky ours are all aligned right now."

Rose shook her head at me. "You're starting to sound like Artemis."

She strode off before I could respond, walking in the direction of the transport that would carry her to the main portion of the station. I assumed she would proceed to find Bentley and Rid from there.

"Stick with her, will ya?" I said to Shell. "Station is still a mess. Don't know who might be lurking around here."

Shell nodded, breaking off her conversation with Tetra and following Rose. I watched them go, feeling more miserable with each step they took. I wished desperately that I was going with them. That we were all going to gather at Tyrell's Bar, celebrate our victory, and put the misadventures of the day behind us before planning our next simple job.

But something told me those days were over, now. For good. If I'd still held any illusions about myself being a simple vulture, they vanished as I watched Shell and Rose vanish into the crowd of disembarking pirates and Roamers.

I lost track of time after that. It seemed that everywhere I turned there were decisions to make, arguments to settle, needs to fulfil. It was impossible to solve most of them immediately, but I did what I could, delegating to Tetra and Renault when appropriate. With each passing moment my exhaustion grew heavier. Somehow all of this administrative stuff wore me out more than fighting. At least in combat I knew what I was doing. When it came to all of this—leadership, administration—I was woefully out of my depth.

It didn't help that Vatheson never left the back of my mind. I wanted to feel triumphant. We'd won, hadn't we? We'd captured Kenton, Werrel and his troops were preparing to depart, and the station was all in one piece. The civilians were safe and our own losses were minimal. Everything had gone far better than we'd had any right to expect.

Maybe that was what was bothering me. I'd been in the salvage business way too long to trust a good thing to stay good. Vatheson wasn't done with us. And now that we'd made our move, it was his turn again.

My mood grew even fouler as I spotted a familiar figure: Ramar Vent, looking out of place in a set of oversized Aboenian work clothes.

He seemed like an entirely different man than the calm, controlling mastermind I'd met aboard the *Revelation* at the end of his long self-imposed exile. His ordeal aboard the *Aboena* had changed him. The marks of Cairn's torturers were easy to spot. One of his ears was mangled where the Wolves had taken a blade to it, and I could see the top half of a nasty burn scar on the side of his neck. His limp had improved since the last time I'd seen him, but it was definitely still there.

Blatant as those physical scars were, however, they didn't stand out to me nearly as much as the psychological ones. Before the *Aboena*, Ramar had carried himself with an air of cold, resolute arrogance. He *knew* what he was doing was right, and everybody else was simply too slow or too weak to admit it. That was all gone now. He looked... lost. Listless.

Seeing him in his pitiable state drove away some of the burning resentment I still held for the man. Yes, it was his fault that Nadus was dead. I didn't think I'd ever find it in me to forgive him for that. But after the hell he'd gone through... well, maybe he'd suffered enough. I sure as hell wouldn't say I *trusted* Ramar, but I at least believed in his sincerity.

When he spotted me, he straightened. It looked like it took effort to banish the uncertainty from his face, but he did it anyways. By the time we were within speaking distance, he was almost back to his old, confident self.

Almost.

"Limp seems to be getting better," I said, pushing away the dozens of traumatic memories Ramar's face brought flooding to my mind.

He nodded, doing his best to stand tall. "Recovery is slow, but every day is an improvement. I find myself wishing that the Stranger would heal me as they healed you."

The memory of my hand vanishing into the bowels of the *Aboena*'s engine flashed through my mind. Then the flash of white light that had come as that mercenary fired his pistol into my head at point-blank range.

I lowered my voice. "It did a hell of a lot more than just heal me. Whatever the Stranger did to me, it's... well, I don't even know how to describe it. But I've survived things today that *nobody* should be able to survive."

Ramar nodded. "I was curious about that. Cairn was much the same, as you recall. My understanding is that the Stranger has given you the same 'gifts' they gave to him. However, since you already had small amounts of the Divinity gene embedded within you, the... *enhancements* may have taken to you even more strongly."

Huh. That was news to me. "Have you been able to see them yet? The Stranger?" I asked, lowering my voice further still. Despite his trauma, Ramar had opted to stay aboard the *Aboena* with the Shapers during the nullspace journey to learn as much as he could. "Or at least figured out anything helpful?"

"Disappointingly little," he said, his false confidence faltering slightly. "The only thing that is clear to me is that the Stranger has a highly specific goal. The Shapers talk frequently of some great purpose. I just... don't know what it is."

I wanted to ask more questions, but another figure approaching from behind Ramar caught my eye. A woman, veiled completely behind an unarmored, matte-black exosuit. My mood immediately soured even further.

"You prove yourself more worthy of the Stranger's gift with each passing hour," Zeka said. Her tone carried none of the warmth her words suggested, though. I felt more as if I was being chided than praised. "This station will be an invaluable asset in the days to come."

"Yeah." I made no effort to hide the skepticism in my voice. Her words gave me the uncomfortable impression that she thought of the station as merely another tool in the Stranger's hands. "Thanks, I guess. Look—the situation is bad here on

Albeni 7. Even with the resources Kenton was stashing, people are gonna run out of food soon. I know you can't feed everyone, but the sooner we can get whitefruit production running on the station, the better. Could save a lot of lives."

She nodded stiffly. "The process has already begun. There are technical details that need to be discussed, but now is not the time."

I let out a quiet sigh of relief—both at the fact that the Shapers intended to follow through on their part of the deal, and that I didn't have to work through the specifics of it right now. Zeka wasn't done, though.

"The Stranger is pleased with the results of the battle," she said. "There is much work to be done. We will require access to a shipyard, and some time."

Made sense. The *Aboena* had been pretty banged up in the earlier battle. It seemed odd that Zeka would be the one making the request, rather than the Roamers' actual leaders, but I didn't give that too much thought. "We'll get you what you need," I said, adding it to the rapidly growing to-do list in my head. "Somehow."

She watched me, face invisible through the black visor of her exo. "You too must be prepared, Lackan VanDunn. It is no small thing to be the Chosen of the Stranger. If we are to be victorious in the end, your part will be essential."

Ramar watched me, eyes holding a subtle warning. This must be that mysterious purpose he'd mentioned. But I was way too exhausted for subtlety.

"*My* part," I said, "is taking care of my people. Which somehow includes you and the Roamers, now. So, forgive me if I don't have much time or patience for playing your Stranger's little games."

"Games?" She sounded... not indignant. Disappointed. Like she was chiding a wayward student who should know better. "You should not trivialize a thing simply because you do not understand it. You, better than most, should understand that the Stranger's work is not to be taken lightly." She tilted her head towards my regrown hand. "After all, you would not be here without it."

"Well, if you want to explain what that work *is*," I said, "then I'll be happy to listen. But until then, I've got a station to stabilize."

"The Stranger alone knows their full purpose," Zeka said. "It is not given to us to understand; merely to serve the purposes we have been given. Your purpose will become clear when you are ready to accept it." She turned away. "Until then, recover. There is much, *much* work yet to be done."

Ramar lingered with me as we watched her stride away. "I should stay close to her. But I wanted to let you know that I've reconnected with some of my contacts to gather intelligence about the war. I can brief you on what I've learned later."

I nodded sullenly, Zeka's final words echoing in the increasingly noisy confines of my skull. *Much*, much *work yet to be done*. The last vestiges of triumph I'd been feeling over our victory were crushed as my mind was drawn beyond Albeni 7 and into the rest of the galaxy, where—so far as I knew—the Paragon was waging a brutal war against the rebel forces that had finally risen up against them. Thousands, if not millions, of soldiers were probably fighting and dying across the stars at this very moment.

My guts twisted into a knot as I watched Zeka and Ramar disappear into the crowd. Damn that woman. Damn the Stranger. Damn the Paragon. Damn Vatheson and Cairn and Ramar and most of all, damn *me* for letting myself get caught up in all of their twisted, tangled, bloody schemes.

I should run. That was the first thought that came to mind. Round up my crew, load up the *Orpheus*, and fly far, far away. I was already in over my head. All I could accomplish now was to get everyone I cared about killed.

My heart started beating faster. My breath quickened. My legs felt heavy and sluggish. I saw a group of Renault's pirates moving a crate full of plundered Vanguard equipment and suddenly found myself itching for a can. Just a hit. Something to take the edge...

A familiar face caught my eye.

Sevani. Still clad in her pilot's uniform, but trailed by an entourage of what appeared to be station locals. It was a strange marriage of the two versions of Sev I'd known over the years: the roguish pilot and the commanding smuggler queen. She spoke briskly as she walked, addressing one follower after another. Exhausted as I was, the words were static, but I recognized some of the faces behind her. All the great and the good of the station. Important business owners, administrators, community leaders. I even recognized the young woman who had helped us after being ambushed just a few hours ago.

Sev's eyes settled on mine. She smiled.

My foul mood crumpled. The exhaustion retreated. Thoughts of Vatheson and the Paragon and the Stranger faded away and I felt a big, stupid grin spread across my face.

Sev came to a halt in front of me, dismissing her entourage with a nod. They melted away into the chaos surrounding us.

"Well," Sev said, "we've still got a hell of a lot more work to do, but it's a start. Kenton just about ran the station into the ground in my absence, but I've done what I can to set things right again. For now, at least, I think things are stable. What's the story on the mercenaries?"

"I've agreed to let them retreat," I said. "Renault is arranging for their ships to come back and pick them up. But he wants to ask Werrel some questions first."

"Makes sense." She nodded wearily, looking around. I followed her gaze. Roamers, freshly disembarked from their boarding vessels, stared around in awe as they stepped aboard a non-Roamer space structure for the first time in their lives.

Pirates laughed among themselves and studied their surroundings like wolves scanning the horizon for prey. Station dockworkers watched all of them with skeptical, guarded expressions.

Thousands of lives. *Millions*, by the time you counted the population of Albeni 7, the *Aboena*, and Renault's fleet. And all of them now depended on us. I felt panic rising again. I wasn't cut out for this. I wasn't supposed to be a leader—not on this scale, at least. Hell, I'd barely ever felt like I was able to care for my small crews with the attention they deserved. How was I going to take charge of all *this*?

I realized suddenly Sev was watching me. "Hey." She put a hand on my arm, and her touch felt like a rush of heavenly warmth. "You alright?"

I shook myself. No time for self-pity now. "Yeah. What next?"

She looked around thoughtfully, then turned her gaze towards a familiar door towards the very back of the terminal.

She grinned. "How about a drink?"

TEN

The doors to Tyrell's Bar swung open with a lethargic creak. Broken glass crunched beneath my combat boots as I stepped through the doorway.

"Somebody really did a number on the old place," I muttered, looking around. The tables and chairs had all been overturned, and many of them were broken. The windows at the front had been smashed in. The only lighting in the room came from the remains of the blue neon sign hanging haphazardly behind the bar. The Y and the R had been broken, so now it read: TELL's.

Sev stepped in behind me. I watched her as she surveyed the damage. I'd expected to see despair or grief on her face as she confronted the wreckage of her husband's old bar. Instead, she just looked tired. And vaguely annoyed.

"Not the first time it's happened," she said, kicking a broken bottle out of her way as she walked through the wreckage towards the bar. "And compared to everything else on our plates, rebuilding a bar is a pleasant pastime. Shut that door behind you. I need some peace and quiet."

I glanced back. The docking bay was loud and chaotic,

bustling with problems and responsibilities. I closed the door. The cacophony faded into a pleasantly distant murmur.

"Much better." Sev bent over and righted two fallen stools, shoving them against the bar.

I frowned at the back bar. It was woefully empty—looked like somebody had helped themselves during Sevani's absence. "Whoever came through here, doesn't seem like they left much behind."

Sev scoffed, walking around the bar. "Come now, Lax. You know me better than that." She reached below the bar top. I heard a metallic clicking sound as she triggered some hidden cabinet. A moment later, she lifted a tall bottle of blue liquid and waggled it enticingly at me. "You really think I wouldn't have an ace or two hidden away?"

I chuckled, then joined her at the bar as she took a seat. As the stool groaned beneath me I realized it was the first time I'd sat down since leaving the *Orpheus* before the battle. Sev unstopped the bottle with a pop, looked around briefly for an unbroken glass, then gave up and took a long swig directly from the bottle. Then she handed it to me, wiping her mouth.

I closed my eyes and took a drink. A long one. The alcohol hit hard and sweet and just the way I'd hoped it would.

I opened my eyes. Lowered the bottle. Set it gently on the countertop. Looked at Sev. She was leaning wearily on one elbow against the bar, watching me with thoughtful, serious eyes.

Dammit all, but she was beautiful. Even with her hair a frayed mess and tired lines under her eyes. Even with dried blood clinging to the side of her face where she'd been nicked by shrapnel and a nasty split in her lip where the mercenary had struck her. Or hell, maybe because of it. Sev had gone through the thick of it all with me without falling behind once—and she'd given as good as she'd got.

At some point, our eyes locked. Her expression was unreadable for a moment. Then a slight smirk crept across her face. I felt an unrestrainable grin growing on my own. I chuckled. Then we both burst out into laughter.

I don't know what we were laughing at, or how long we laughed for. Maybe it was just the sheer relief of knowing that we'd survived—and more than that, we'd *won*. Maybe it was in acknowledgement of the irony of finding ourselves exactly where we'd begun this bizarre journey. Maybe it was just at the sheer absurdity of it all: sitting together, exhausted, covered in blood, drinking as if there wasn't an entire station full of people outside this bar that now relied upon us for leadership. All I know for sure is that by the time our laughter had finally settled down, my bad mood was gone.

Sev took another drink, then passed the bottle back to me, shaking her head. "What're we doing here, Lax?"

"Damned if I know." I took the bottle. "Seems like not that long ago we were just a crew of vultures, trying to keep the *Orpheus* running for a few weeks. Didn't have to worry about war, or prisoners, or alliances, or managing an entire damn station." I chuckled softly, staring into the bottle. "Funny how you never realize that you're in the simple times until they're over. I was so desperate to get out of the salvage game. Now I'd give anything for life to be that simple again."

"Yeah." Sev's eyes drifted over the damaged neon sign. TELL's. "Too late for that, though. We're locked into this now, for better or worse."

We fell silent. I watched her. The profile of her face lit a soft blue in the dim light.

"I've never really been good with words," I said slowly. "But I just want you to know... I'm really glad I found you again."

Sev turned sharply towards me, her eyes unreadable in the darkness.

"After the *Panama*, I got used to being alone. Even came to rely on it. Going into harm's way was a lot easier knowing that there was nothing holding me to this life." I turned my gaze away from Sev, staring down at the bar and hoping that the darkness would hide how hot my face was growing. "But... on the *Aboena*, when I thought Cairn was gonna kill me... well. I thought about you. And it was the first time since Kess died that I've felt like I had a reason to live. A real one."

I didn't dare look up from the counter. She was probably trying to hold back laughter. But when I finally worked up the courage to glance at her, I found that she was just staring into the bottle, thoughtfully running her thumb along its surface.

"When you came back," she said, "it was like you brought back some part of me that had died with the rest of the crew. With Tyrell. And that scared me at first, because I thought that was the part of me that got them all killed. But every time you left on a run, that part of me would go with you." She looked over at me, the half of her face that wasn't hidden in shadow searching mine. "And each time, I found I missed it more. I missed you."

There was a long silence, deep enough to contain universes, while we stared at each other. The space between us seemed to compress.

"We shouldn't," Sev said, so softly I could barely hear her.

"I know."

We stared at each other a moment longer.

I'm not sure who moved first. Maybe it was simultaneous. All I know is that the tension suddenly broke like lightning in a storm. We crossed the distance in a flash and our mouths pressed together and she winced slightly as I brushed against her split lip, but when I tried to pull away she wrapped her hands around the back of my head, locking us together.

"Mom! Lax! Are you—"

I caught just a glimpse from the corner of my eye of Rose peering through the doorway at us. Her eyes widened. Sev waved her away and she retreated without so much as a word, the door swinging shut behind her.

I broke briefly apart from Sev, gasping. "Should we—"

She pulled me back. I didn't resist. I shoved her back against the bar, not taking my lips from hers. Her body was warm and it fit perfectly against mine, moving in sync, our breath mingling together. We kissed hungrily, greedily, desperately, pushing back and forth against each other in a passionate, single-minded struggle until I broke away with a growl, then lifted her and swung her body onto the counter, sweeping aside the bottle and sending it tumbling to the floor with a hollow thud. She gripped my tattered shirt by the collar and tugged, and I followed her up onto the counter, kneeling over her and burying my face in her neck, listening to her moan as she writhed, feeling her hands pressed against my chest. A sharp pain bit into my palm as I pressed it into a shard of broken glass on the counter but I ignored it, no room for anything but her in my mind.

Sev grabbed my face and pulled it back to hers. There was a cracking sound and the bar suddenly tilted sideways, breaking beneath our weight—well, mine, really—and sending us rolling onto the floor. I grabbed Sev tightly, making sure that I landed flat on my back, and shielded her from the fall. Glass crunched beneath me. Sev landed on top of me with a grunt, straddling me.

We stared at each other, panting. Her breasts heaved up and down with her breath—and mine. Her eyes glowed blue in the refracted light of the shattered glass littering the floor beneath me. She gave a short gasp of a laugh.

I pulled her back down. And then—

You know what?

It's none of your damn business.

"How... long has it been?"

I groaned, rubbing my temple. I stretched my legs out, brushing aside dozens of tiny shards of broken glass on the floor. A few of them were red with blood—mine—but I could tell any little cuts I'd sustained had already healed.

"Well, since Kess," I said. "Unless you mean—"

"No, you numbskull." Sev kicked my leg, grinning. She was sitting on the floor among the wreckage, resting against the ruined backbar, while I was leaning against the destroyed bar top opposite her. She raised the bottle of blue liquor we'd been drinking, carefully pouring some into her open mouth. The top part of it had broken when it fell, leaving a jagged edge, but there was still some booze in it. "I mean how long were we out?"

"Oh." I took the bottle from her. "Damned if I know. Can't have been more than an hour or two." I glanced over my shoulder at the wreckage. That we'd fallen asleep in all of this was a testament to how truly exhausted we'd been, by the exertions of both the battle and what had come after. "Sorry about your bar."

"Well, you know." She looked around at the twinkling sea of broken glass surrounding us. "We were due for a renovation." She gingerly picked up a blood-stained shard, inspecting it. "Are you alright? I didn't intend for things to get so..."

I chuckled. "I'm invincible now, remember?" I held up the hand that I'd cut on the counter top. The wound had healed, but I frowned as I noticed a slight bulge beneath the skin. "Aw, *hell.*" I reached down for my belt and knife but I'd lost both at some point. Instead I took the jagged edge of the bottle, drank briefly, and then winced as I dug it into my palm.

"*Very* romantic," Sev said, raising an eyebrow as the offending piece of glass fell to the floor with a soft *tink.*

"Sorry." I absentmindedly rubbed the blood off the bottle on my pants. "Guess magical healing comes with its own problems."

"Yeah." Sev watched with wary eyes as my torn palm pulled

itself back together, fleshy fibers weaving back into place as if nothing had ever happened. "Does it feel... weird?"

"Not really." I hesitated. "Well... the first time it happened —when I got shot, I mean—I had the strangest dream." I frowned as I remembered it. "I was in a room like the one the Stranger fixed me up in. If *that* was even real. Except different. And there was a ship coming towards me. About to run me down."

Sev studied me for a few moments. "I'm worried about all this, Lax. I'm glad that you're alive, don't get me wrong—and that's two times now that you'd be dead without whatever it is the Stranger did to you. But I can't help but feel like we missed something. That there's some hidden price you're gonna have to pay down the road."

I nodded slowly, staring at my hand. Finally, I lowered it with a sigh. "Yeah. Me too. I just... don't know what to do about it. Can't very well give it back. And the Stranger's mostly left me alone. Sure, there's all that 'Chosen' nonsense, but they haven't asked anything in return."

"Haven't asked anything *yet*," Sev said.

I grimaced. "Yeah."

A beam of light suddenly pierced the darkness above us. Somebody had opened the door.

"Hello?" It was Rid's voice.

"Time's up," I grumbled. I vaguely remembered Rose barging in on us. Any hopes of keeping this little tryst a secret were long, *long* gone.

Sev grinned and reached for the bottle. I handed it to her. She drank the last few swallows, then wiped her mouth on her arm. "Just a minute," she called, adjusting a few articles of disheveled clothing. I felt around in the darkness until I found my shirt. It was down to a few pathetic, blood-soaked rags at this point, so I tossed it aside and instead settled for strapping my belt and holster back on.

"It's just that…" Rid cleared his throat, clearly uncomfortable. I thought I heard somebody stifling a giggle. I was willing to bet that he was bringing this message as the result of a lost bet. "They've called a meeting."

"Who?" Sev asked, shrugging into her jacket.

"Everybody," Rid said. "Pirates, Roamers, locals from the station. Everyone wants to know what's happening next."

"That's a damn good question," I muttered. I started to climb to my feet. "Coming—"

I cut off as Sev suddenly leaned forward and planted a quick kiss on my lips. Something in my brain short-circuited. I could only stare stupidly at her as she grinned mischievously and then stood up.

"Had to get one more in while I could," she said. "I have a feeling it's gonna be a long, *long* day." She turned back towards the door. "We're on our way."

I heard Rid cough awkwardly and excuse himself. Sev spared one last glance at me as she strode away. "Put some clothes on. We've important business to attend to. We should talk to Kenton before we meet with everyone else."

She winked at me and vanished. I watched her go.

Luckiest man in the universe.

ELEVEN

Rasfel Kenton looked up with a start as the doors of his cramped cell opened.

Sev let out a low whistle as she stepped into his narrow confines. "Gotta say, Kenton, it's quite a step down, isn't it?"

He sat up straight, shoulders tense and hands grabbing tightly at the edge of the small bed he was perched on. His eyes flicked towards the door, desperately searching for an escape, only to widen as they fixed on my enormous frame blocking the way. I was no longer coated in gore—I'd found time to shower and change before coming here with Sev—but, judging by the fear in his eyes, I must still have been an intimidating sight.

I wasn't the one he should be afraid of here, though.

He took a breath, composing himself, then—much to my amazement—managed to plaster a warm smile across his face. "Why, Maren. And friend. So good of you to come visit me. And so soon, too. I'm sure you're very busy. Running a station is a *lot* of work."

Sev snorted. "You've never worked a day in your life, Kenton. As far as you were concerned, the station could rot as long as the credits kept flowing to you."

"Why, I'll have you know it took a *lot* of work to spend all of those credits." His smile only broadened. "But, alas, all for nothing now, it appears. So, tell me then: to what do I owe this great honor?"

"When was the last time you heard from Vatheson?" I asked.

His eyes shifted slyly towards me. "Vatheson? I'm afraid I'm not sure who you're referring to."

Sev and I exchanged a glance.

Kenton sighed, then tilted his head so his cheek was facing me. "There you go, good sir. I'm assuming that's what you brought him for. Though if you'll take my advice, starting out with more *gentle* tactics will leave you the option of greater escalation further down the—"

Sev punched him, fast and hard, straight in the nose. He gave a startled cry of pain, flailing back against the wall, as blood gushed down the front of his shirt.

"Come now, Kenton." Sev reached forward and grabbed him by the hair, yanking him back towards her. "I thought you knew me better than that. You think I'd turn down the chance to beat the hell out of you myself?"

He spluttered. "I—"

She hit him again, in the exact same spot. He shouted again.

"I've only been waiting sixteen years for this," she growled, drawing her fist back again. "Sixteen years of watching your greed sap this station for everything it was worth. Sixteen years of watching you turn crisis after crisis into your own profit. That's all over now, you bastard. But you get to decide how painful the end is for you."

She shoved him back against the wall, then looked down at the blood on her hand. She let out a heavy breath.

"Now," she said, wiping her knuckle clean on Kenton's bedsheets. "Answer the nice man's question."

Kenton's eyes flicked back and forth between the two of us.

"It's been three days," he finally groaned, his voice pinched as he held one hand over his bleeding nose. "You can check my records. I didn't even bother clearing them."

Sev's eyes narrowed. "Why did he stop communicating with you? Werrel said the same thing."

"If I *knew*," Kenton growled, "I probably wouldn't be *here* right now."

I gritted my teeth. Made no damn sense. Was Vatheson trying to set some kind of trap? Had he *wanted* us to take the station?

"What were the terms of your deal with him?" Sev's voice was icy cold.

Kenton cursed as several drops of blood spilled from between his fingers. "The deal? What do you think it was for, you stupid bitch? Hugs and handshakes? *Money!*"

Sev's hand balled into a fist again, causing Kenton's eyes to widen. "I already paid you a *ridiculous* amount to operate out of your station," she growled.

"And yet he offered more." He held up an outstretched palm, as if to ward off her fury. "Look. I'm sorry. But it wasn't personal. Just practicality. He gave me a better deal. And one that would last. I knew that you two were fighting. And I knew he'd win. So I sided with him."

"Personal?" Sev took a sharp step towards him. "Do you have *any idea* how many close friends of mine were killed when you let Vatheson's mercenaries aboard?"

He stared at her, then slowly lowered his hand. A sneer broke out across his face. "Look at you. Pretending you're so high and mighty here. *Aw, I'm Maren Sevani. I'm gonna profit off of poor desperate people for years and then act like I'm their savior.*" He spat blood at Sev. "Screw yourself, Sevani. You're no better than I am. You're just stupid enough to trick yourself into thinking you are."

I eyed Sev, genuinely worried she would simply draw her

pistol and execute Kenton where he sat. But she didn't. If anything, his words seemed to calm her.

"You think you can *save* this station?" He gave a harsh bark of a laugh, sending blood spraying from his nose. "*I* was the one trying to save it! You've doomed it! You've *personally* signed a death warrant for every single bastard living here. Vatheson ain't done with you. I may not know all his plans, but he made it *very* clear that if there was one thing he cared about, it was taking you out. He tried to do it surgically. That didn't work. So now he'll do it with a sledgehammer. He's got blackmail on every general in the Paragon. He's got all their plans and schemes tucked away. And he'll do everything he can to point all of them at you."

He pointed towards me with one bloody finger. "Next time it won't be mercenaries. It'll be ten thousand of *him*. And about a million rippers. You and everybody on this station are rebels now, and you know damn well how the Paragon feels about rebels. They're gonna kill every single person on this station." He leaned forward, leering at her. "And I just hope I live long enough to see the look on your face when it happens."

She stared into his eyes for a long, icy moment.

Her hand inched slowly towards the holster I knew she kept concealed in the small of her back.

Kenton saw it too. His lip quivered for just a moment, then steadied. He clenched his teeth.

Sev paused.

Then sighed and turned towards the door. I made room for her to pass.

"I'm currently doing my best to set up a representative government," she said, her voice weary. "I don't know how long it will take. And I'm not really in charge of it. But I'll see to it that when they're ready, and the time comes, you'll receive a proper trial for your crimes. And whatever punishment the people of this station see fit."

The fight bled out of Kenton. His shoulders drooped, and his eyes went hollow as he stared after Sev. His eyes flicked to mine as she left the room.

"Just... kill me," he whimpered.

I hit the button on the control panel. The door to his cell slid shut with a resounding thud.

Sev sagged against the wall, massaging her temple. "That... was not as helpful as I'd hoped it would be."

"Well, at least we know Vatheson ain't done with us."

"We already knew that."

"Yeah, but now we *really* know it."

She gave me a dry, questioning look.

I shrugged. "Hey, I'm in a good mood for once. Just trying to find the positive."

She gave a humorless laugh, shaking her head and staring off into space.

"Hey." I craned my head until I was looking into her eyes. "You know he was just trying to get in your head, right? With all that *we're not so different, you and I* stuff? Not a word of it was true. You *care* about these people. And we're gonna do right by them."

She sighed. "Yeah. I know. But... I have a hard time believing that they're better off getting eaten by rippers than simply living under the Paragon."

That took my mood down a peg. I fell silent, watching Sev. Finally, she shook herself and straightened.

"Well," she said as she straightened her jacket and strode past me down the corridor. "Let's make sure we don't prove him right. Come on. And bring that good mood with you. I have a feeling we're gonna need it."

I did my best.

I really did. Despite everything going on, we'd *won*. To be honest, I wasn't sure if that was the source of my good mood or if it was my little rendezvous with Sev that had come after, but either way, I was determined to hold on to it. We'd *accomplished* something, dammit. We were making progress. Making a difference, like Nadus had always wanted to. And nothing was gonna make me feel any different. I even found myself whistling a jaunty little tune as Sev and I strode through the bullet-ridden atrium and the hallway with the suspiciously *me*-shaped hole in the wall.

It vanished like smoke in the wind the moment I walked into the spacious conference room and saw every set of eyes contained therein turn towards us.

No. Not us. *Me.*

For a few, blissful hours, I'd almost managed to make myself forget that I'd somehow—for some reason—made myself the de facto leader of this bunch of renegades. I still don't know where I'd gotten the nerve to throw myself into the position, much less why they'd so much as considered me. Dammit, why couldn't they have just laughed me down like any normal, sane people would've?

Then again, nobody at this table was particularly normal.

Renault leaned back in his seat and thudded his fancy boots onto the table. Flint and two other captains I didn't recognize were sitting next to him. "Why, there he is!" The self-proclaimed King of the Buccaneers gave one of his trademark grins. "The man of the hour!"

"The *late* hour." The speaker was a distinguished-looking Roamer in a white officer's-style coat. His gray brows furrowed as he regarded me. That was Everest, the senior member of the Aboenian Command. Everest was flanked by several other distinguished-looking Roamers I recognized as the Command council. They didn't look particularly impressed with me either. Which, to my mind at least, was hardly fair, given that I was the reason their precious homeship wasn't currently in the hands of the Paragon.

Thankfully, however, I had at least one ally among them. Tetra held up a calming hand, and to my amazement, the captain seemed to heed it, settling back into his chair. "Peace," Tetra said. "He's a busy man."

The next group was a set of civilians from Albeni 7. I was surprised to see that Jala, the young woman who had saved Sev and me yesterday, was among them. Judging by the lines beneath Jala's eyes, she hadn't gotten much more sleep than I had since last we'd met. Still, though, she had enough energy to treat everybody around her to distrustful looks—myself in particular. She gave a scoff at Tetra's words. "We're *all* busy. And there'll be no peace for anybody until we've fixed the problems aboard this station."

"Then there's no point in wasting any more time." Sev's voice was firm, commanding, as she took a seat. She'd changed her clothes too. Her new outfit looked like a compromise between her old and new styles—a clean white dress shirt worn beneath her leather pilot's jacket.

Ramar and Zeka were next. At least, I *thought* it was Zeka. Hard to tell behind the exosuit. Still, regardless of who was hiding beneath that matte black visor, the presence of a Shaper meant that the Stranger wanted to know what we discussed today—and maybe to offer input.

Ramar had swapped his oversized Roamer jumpsuit for a long gray coat with a high collar that concealed the scars on his neck. Even with the outfit change, though, he seemed a shadow of his former self. He gave me a brief nod as our eyes met.

I moved across the room, feeling more awkward with each step, and finally settled into a seat next to Sev. It took several more seconds of agonizing silence for me to realize that nobody else was going to start the meeting. This was *my* war council.

"I..." I cleared my throat. Dammit, why was this so hard? I

thought desperately of the smartest people I'd known over the years. What would Artemis say? What would Sev or Renault say? "Well. Thanks to everybody for being here."

Excruciating silence. Two of the Roamers exchanged a whisper. I caught a snicker from one of Renault's lieutenants. I felt my face growing hot as I searched for what to say next.

I felt a surge of relief as Sev rose abruptly beside me. "Lax has asked that I lead this meeting," she said, nodding to me as if we'd prearranged this. "We're all very busy and under enormous pressure, so I won't waste time with any more pleasantries. Let's get into it, shall we?"

I hate meetings.

I think it's fair to assume that you do too. So I'm not gonna bother giving you every single excruciating detail of the seemingly endless hours we spent around that conference table. Here are the broad strokes, though.

Sev started by summarizing our current position.

So far as positions go: not great.

First, there was the situation on Albeni 7, which Sev had Jala explain. Sev had appointed her to a position they were calling the People's Advocate, putting her in charge of establishing outreach programs to instill some sense of order among the station's panicking, desperate populace. I'd been dubious of that choice at first, given how young Jala was, but the longer I listened to her talk, the more impressed I was. I just wished she'd had better news to deliver.

The general mood among the populace *was* improving. It sounded like the riots had mostly stopped. At Sev's orders, the food reserves that Kenton had been hoarding and selling at a premium had been opened and were in the process of being rationed out, which would hopefully hold us over until the Shapers' whitefruit production was up and running. People found a renewed sense of hope and energy in Sev's return and her promise of independence. But that hope brought with it a new sense of dread, too.

I couldn't help but think of what Kenton had said as Jala described those fears. Vanguard troopers blasting through our defenses. Rippers, tearing through the station and its inhabitants. I wished I could have told Jala that those fears were unrealistic. But they weren't. They were the simple reality of what would happen if the Paragon attacked us in force.

From there we launched into a discussion of the state of our own forces. Our casualties during the battle for Albeni 7 had been shockingly light, but that didn't quite make up for how staggeringly heavy they'd been during our last battle. The Roamers, of course, had suffered the worst. The *Aboena* was still in tatters, and thousands of Roamers were dead, wounded, or still missing. Several of Renault's ships had sustained heavy damage from the *Leonidas*'s weapon arrays.

"None of our ships are beyond repair, of course," Renault said, "but... well, I wouldn't want to risk another battle before getting repairs." He scratched at his jaw. "Repairs more extensive than we can get at Albeni 7, I'm afraid. We'll need a proper shipyard."

"There's one in the Karak system," Sev said. "I've worked with them several times. I believe I can get them to agree to work with us." She turned to the Roamers. "I'm assuming you'll need access to the shipyards as well?"

Everest scoffed. "We are capable of making repairs without such luxuries. We shall—"

"A shipyard will be necessary for us as well." Zeka spoke up over the Roamer leader. "The damage is extremely extensive."

I glanced at Everest in surprise, expecting him to fight back. Instead, he simply shut his mouth, sagging slightly in his seat. The other Roamers shifted uncomfortably but made no more effort of resistance than he did. Even Tetra said nothing, though

I noticed a look of sharp anger in her eyes as she stared at the black-clad Shaper. It seemed that the Stranger's influence had only grown since the last time I'd been aboard the *Aboena*.

"If all of your ships are off getting repaired, though," Jala said, "who'll defend the station if the Paragon attacks?"

Renault grimaced. "I hate to say it, but... I don't think we *can* defend the station."

Jala frowned, looking sharply between Renault and Sev. "I thought that was the entire point of this alliance. We provide a home base, and you help protect us."

"It is. And you're welcome, by the way, for the liberation." Renault fixed the young woman with a reproachful look. "But the simple reality is that there's a vast difference between fighting a handful of mercenaries, or ambushing a single battle-cruiser, and defending against a sustained assault, even if we have a foldgate to use as a chokepoint. My fleet is built for quick, targeted strikes. Piracy, may I remind you, not wars of attrition. Obviously, we will wield it however necessary against whatever comes our way. But, if we're being realistic, we must face the cold, hard truth that the moment the Paragon turns its attention from the rebels to us, it won't matter how well repaired my ships are."

There was a long moment of silence as we were forced to finally consider the most daunting of all our problems: the situation *outside* of our system.

"Ramar," I said. "You mentioned you've gathered some intel about what's going on out there."

"Yes—I have." Ramar rose to his feet, wincing slightly as he did so. He pulled his jacket tighter around him as he began speaking, as if worried we could see his still-healing wounds beneath his shirt.

"*Accurate* intel?" Renault raised an eyebrow. "I've heard rumors of just about everything. The rebels have already defeated the Paragon. The Paragon has already defeated the rebels. The Paragon has collapsed completely, and the prime speaker has jettisoned himself into space."

"Well, certainly more accurate than those," Ramar said. "And certainly more accurate than anything you'll hear from an official Paragon news broadcast."

I nodded sullenly. I'd forced myself to listen to a few minutes of one of those earlier today before shutting it off. It had been full of the same old contradictory claims the Paragon always made: that their enemies were evil beyond redemption and posed the most dire threat to all the decent values the Paragon stood for, while at the same time, they were cowardly miscreants who were being rapidly crushed beneath a barrage of highly militarized justice.

"Since emerging from nullspace," Ramar said, "I've re-established links with several old contacts, many of whom happen to have aligned themselves with various rebel factions." His eyes drifted guiltily to me. "Including one Denatus Carston, who is currently putting his considerable skills to work on their behalf."

I felt a slight rush of anger at the name, the memory of Artemis's lifeless body on that Brahmian street flashing through my mind, but repressed it. I couldn't say I'd completely healed from that wound, but at least it wasn't raw and bleeding anymore. Carston had been trying to save humanity from the ultrarippers. It was hard to blame him for using whatever means necessary.

I still did, though. After all, it hadn't just been Artemis he'd killed. As far as I knew, both of the Khendars had died in the chaotic Paragon assault, and with them, their dream of an independent Brahma. And then, to make matters worse, I'd put the nail in that dream's coffin by killing Tekka to keep him from getting his hands on the ultrarippers.

I forced my mind, and the guilt now flooding it, back to the matter at hand as Ramar continued. "The rebel factions have formed a coalition in order to make a united stand against the

Paragon. I don't know much about their leadership, but I do know that they seem to have an impressive amount of money behind them, thanks to an anonymous benefactor. The eleven systems that have banded together have named themselves the Sovereign Systems, or simply the Sovereigns for shorthand."

"Anonymous?" One of the Roamers demanded, voice laden with skepticism.

"Secret, at least," Sev said thoughtfully. "It makes sense. Whoever is backing the Sovereigns is betting against both the Paragon and Divinity. If the rebels lose, this anonymity will protect them from the fallout. Maybe."

Ramar plugged his handcomputer into the large conference table we were all seated around, activating a holoprojector in the center of it. A few moments later, a star chart of the entire foldgate network—simplified to be readable—appeared.

The sight was nothing new to me, but I still found myself leaning forward as I studied it with a new appreciation for the situation we were in. The map before us didn't illustrate the actual space between systems or their positions within the galaxy; instead, it simply showed which systems were connected to which via foldgate. It looked like a disheveled spiderweb, with fewer lines connecting dots on the outside of the web and a congested mass of lines coalescing at the center. That would be Alpha Centauri, of course—or, as it was more casually referred to, the gate system. While some systems had multiple foldgates, most had just one, connecting them directly to the gate system.

An eerie, familiar sensation tugged at the back of my brain as I looked at the sprawling mass of humanity's achievements floating phantasmal before me. Thin white lines cutting through the dark ether of space. A child's diorama. I realized suddenly what the star chart reminded me of. Those strange dreams I'd been having, where I floated alone in the void. That visceral, consumptive feeling that came with them.

Hate.

I shook myself. While I'd been lost in thought, Ramar had highlighted several of the dots on the star chart. The first one to catch my eye was highlighted in green—our own home sweet home, the Karak sector. It was composed of two solar systems, Albeni and Karak, and a single foldgate leading directly to the gate system. The sector boasted a plentiful harvest of minerals, but no habitable planets, putting us in a precarious economic position.

Next, Ramar highlighted eleven different sectors in blue. I was familiar with most of them—they were home to systems that had been particularly stubborn during the Last War. I also noted, guiltily, that Brahma was not among them.

"These," Ramar said, "are the Sovereign Systems. You'll notice that many of them have their own foldgates connecting them to each other." He pointed at one in particular, more isolated than the others were. "This is the Redhawk system. Just over three standard earth weeks ago, the Sovereigns began their revolt by launching a joint assault on the Paragon's shipyards in Redhawk. The attack was enormously successful, and not only did they destroy much of the Paragon's reserves and cripple their production capabilities, they also managed to completely drive their forces from the system. The rest of the systems highlighted here capitalized on the chaos of that fallout to declare their own independence."

He highlighted the central point of the star chart, where the vast majority of the lines converged, in harsh red. "The Paragon's response has been to divide their fleet into three portions. The first is concentrated on suppressing the Sovereign forces in the Redhawk sector." He zoomed in on the center of the map, pointing towards the Redhawk gate and drawing a red squiggle outside of it to signify the Paragon's presence. "Meanwhile, the second portion of the fleet is spread throughout the rest of the gate system, forming a blockade. They've ground trade nearly to a halt throughout the entire foldgate network.

"The third portion of their fleet, in the meantime, is going on the offensive." He zoomed back out, then focused on one of the systems highlighted in blue. "Currently, they are focused on the Ebisu system. It seems that their strategy is to isolate the rebelling systems and retake them one at a time, while leveraging the blockade to keep the Sovereigns from supporting each other."

"And how are the rebels holding up against this strategy?" Renault asked.

Ramar grimaced. "Not well. My reports indicate that the Sovereigns consider Ebisu to be a lost cause. Even if they wanted to support it, there's nothing they can do. The Paragon's blockade has effectively cut off the Sovereign systems from each other, with a few exceptions."

I frowned down at the map, but I didn't see dots and lines anymore. I saw cities burning. Families screaming as they were chased down by hordes of rippers. "I don't get it. What's the Sovereign's endgame?"

"Well, independence, obviously," Sev said.

I shook my head. "I don't mean politically. I mean strategically. I'm no admiral, but I have a hard time seeing how they expect to win this fight. Do the Sovereigns have some kind of ace up their sleeve?"

Renault wagged a finger at me. "You forget—they're *idealists*." He pronounced the word as if it were some sort of rare, untreatable medical condition. "They subscribe to the quite dangerous notion that their cause is a noble one, and therefore worth pursuing regardless of its realism."

Sev raised an eyebrow at him. "I don't recall hearing any of that when you agreed to help us attack the *Leonidas*."

"That was a premeditated tactical decision." Renault waved her words away. "And I still stand by the logic of it. Even if the

Paragon's downfall is looking, ah, slightly less certain than it did then."

Ramar stared down at the map. He looked exhausted. "Nothing is certain," he said softly. "I don't know the Sovereigns' next move. For our sake, though, I hope that Lax is right. I hope the rebels *do* have some trick they have yet to play. Because if they don't, it seems inevitable that the Paragon will reclaim each revolting system one by one. And eventually, it will be our turn."

"Eventually might be sooner than we think," Sev said. She glanced at me. "We can't forget about Vatheson. He'll be using every ounce of his influence to throw as many Paragon ships in our direction as he can."

I nodded grimly, the memory of his rabid tirade all too fresh in my mind. As long as Vatheson was still on the playing board, he'd be doing everything in his power to ensure that the Paragon crushed us as soon as possible. Hell—for all we knew, a fleet was on its way right now. I shifted my gaze towards the tiny dot that was Albeni 7. I pictured the narrow, crowded hallways we'd just fought the mercenaries through, now overrun by an endlessly hungry wall of flesh and claws.

"Even if the rebels *do* somehow win, and the Paragon grants them their independence," Tetra said, "that doesn't guarantee *our* security. The Paragon will be hurting, looking for any way they can recover lost territories."

"Perhaps we negotiate." One of the Roamers spoke up. "Agree to terms with the Paragon. Peace is cheaper than war, for both sides. Surely we can find an arrangement."

Renault scoffed. "We're *far* beyond that point."

"You might be, perhaps." The Roamer held her head high. "*We* were attacked and merely defended ourselves."

Jala folded her arms, treating the Roamers to an indignant glare. "We will *not* go back to living beneath the Paragon's oppression. If we have a chance at winning out independence, we *have* to take it."

"Independence will do *nothing* for us if we're all dead!" the Roamer retorted.

"Alright, alright." I held up my hands. "Three things are clear. First, we can't simply wait for the Paragon to attack us. If we do, we'll lose. Second, we need to find a way to deal with Vatheson." I grimaced as I thought, once again, of Kenton's furious rant. "The sooner he's off the playing board, the sooner we can breathe easy."

"Sure," Renault said. "But how exactly are we going to deal with him?"

I took a deep breath. "That brings me to our third point. We need allies." I looked around. "We need to join the Sovereign Systems."

Silence.

"Can we just... *do* that?" Tetra asked.

"I can arrange a meeting," Ramar said cautiously. "But my suspicion is that they won't let us in without a show of good faith."

"What kind of show?" Sev asked.

Ramar shrugged. "Something to prove that we're serious. That we can add significant value to their coalition."

I nodded. "Right. That's where Vatheson comes in. Kenton claimed that Vatheson has the Paragon's battle plans. If we can get those from him, somehow, I'm sure they'd be more than willing to allow us into their little club."

"I'm still a little lost on how exactly we'll manage that part," Tetra said. "Given that... well. Given a *lot* of reasons."

I turned to Renault. "You're the pirate. Offense is your area of expertise. Any ideas?"

He hesitated. "One that might work. But I doubt you'll like it."

"I'd already counted on that," I said. "All I care is that we can do it."

He furrowed his brow in thought for a few moments. "I'll need to arrange a few things. And I'll need money. Lots of it."

"*That*," Sev said with a sigh, "is something we do not have."

I gave Ramar a meaningful look. "Unless... we happen to align ourselves with a group of rebels who, apparently, have a very generous sponsor backing them."

Ramar nodded thoughtfully.

One of the Roamers scowled. "I do not like this plan. We are gambling on too many unknowns. What reason do we have to trust these Sovereigns? What reason do they have to trust us?"

"The same reason we have to trust each other," Sev said, looking grimly around the ring of skeptical faces staring back at her. "Because we don't have a single other good option."

Silence fell. What else was there to say? I didn't like this plan anymore than the rest of them. But Sev was right. Every other option I came up with ended in certain catastrophe—for everyone. Yeah, the odds were against us here. Yeah, there were a lot of unknown variables to account for. Yeah, it would probably all fall apart one way or another. But a plan that would probably end in failure was a hell of a lot better than a plan that was certain to end in failure.

"Arrange the meeting," I said to Ramar.

He nodded.

TWELVE

The rest of the day passed in a blur.

The meeting itself dragged on for several more hours even after we finally committed to going on the offensive and teaming up with the rebels. Not that it was a sure thing, yet. Ramar was still working on arranging a meeting with them. In the meantime, though, it seemed like our list of other problems knew no end. The Shapers needed space to set up their food production on Albeni 7, and thousands of displaced Roamers needed living quarters on the station while the *Aboena* was repaired. Jala needed help distributing resources and enforcing order among the frightened, desperate masses already living aboard Albeni 7. There were deals to arrange with neighboring stations, especially the shipyard in Karak. And on, and on, and on...

And on, because *that* had just been the meeting itself. I had hoped that the meeting would make our list of things to do shorter. It did the opposite. And once we got out of the meeting, it seemed that for every task I completed, every decision I made, every argument I settled, two more popped up.

Fortunately, I didn't have to do it alone. I relied perpetually on Sev's significantly more developed leadership skills. I could handle a crew alright, but with each passing hour, I found myself increasingly aware of just how out of my depth I was trying to lead an entire... well, *nation*, I suppose. A small, malformed, half-baked, prenatal excuse of a nation that was probably doomed to die a wretched and ignominious death only moments after being born, but still. A nation nonetheless.

Now *that* was a daunting thought. One I certainly hadn't considered back when I'd first proposed Renault, Sevani, and the Roamers team up. All I'd been after was survival. Not... whatever it was I'd become.

Run. Despite my best efforts, I couldn't banish the thought from my head. *Run. You've got no business being here, doing any of this. You're just a puppet. You'll only get everybody killed.*

I gritted my teeth, quickening my pace as if I could leave the traitorous thoughts behind, then wrenched my mind back to the task at hand. Which was.... Damn. What *was* I doing again? It all blurred together.

A sign on the wall ahead of me caught my attention. MEDBAY.

A surge of relief filled me. Right. I'd finally carved out just enough time to come and check in on my crew. My steps felt lighter as I passed through the security checkpoint and was pointed to the room my crew was in by a staff member.

The medbay was like everything on Albeni 7: cramped and poorly maintained. There wasn't an empty cot in any of the rooms I passed. I was sure that other medbays in the station had their fair share of guests, too. After a few moments of searching, I found a large room, one corner of which was occupied by my crew.

"There he is!" Rid grinned at me as I walked in. "We were starting to think you were too important for us lowly vultures now."

"I know where I belong." I glanced around. Rid, Rose, and Shell were all gathered around Bentley, who was stretched out across his own cot. I was gratified to see that he was already looking much better than the last time I'd seen him. Rose pushed an empty chair towards me and I sank into it with a sigh.

Rid's voice cut through my weariness. "Long day?"

"Yeah." I shook myself, looking up. I was surprised to see another figure sitting with my crew—a familiar one. Shepherd, the young boy who had guided us through the *Aboena*. I blinked at him in dull surprise. He only briefly met my eyes before looking down at the floor.

"Oh, yeah!" Bentley gestured towards the Roamer boy. "Shepherd here's been hanging out with us."

I gave Shell an inquisitive look.

"He never had many friends on the *Aboena*," she said, her voice grim. "And many of those he did have died in the battle. So he's trying to make a new start. After what he did for us on the homeship, I thought that letting him join us was the least we could do."

"I thought Roamers would rather die than leave their home-ship," I said, studying him. Something about his furtive pose reminded me of Rid, back when we'd first met.

"Times are changing," Shell said. "A lot of the Roamers I've talked to feel like they hardly recognize the *Aboena* anymore. The Stranger's changed things too much. That, plus how many of them were displaced by the battle, well... Shepherd is *far* from the only one seeking a new home."

I nodded, guilt growing heavier in my chest by the second as I studied the Roamer boy. Logically, I knew that what I had done on the *Aboena* had been the best option. That if I *hadn't* taken charge, the Paragon would simply have killed all the Roamers and taken what they wanted. But that rationality did little to assuage the guilt blooming in my gut. The fact remained that I'd made the calls. I'd given the orders. And now, hundreds of Roamers were dead.

Hell—not just Roamers. A quick survey of my surroundings showed a young, too-skinny girl with her arm in a cast, a pirate with both legs ending in carefully bandaged stumps just below the knees, and an elderly man covered in bruises with a bandaged head. It looked as if he'd been trampled underfoot by a panicked crowd. Not to mention Bentley, though he looked better than most of the others in here.

And these were the lucky ones. I'd seen cargo trucks carrying telltale black body bags through the hallways on my way here. A trail of bodies, following me everywhere I went, stretching out longer and wider and bloodier the more I tried to—

"Hey." Rid slapped my arm, jarring me. "You alright?"

"Yeah." I wrenched my thoughts into order as best I could, slapping a tired grin onto my face. "Sorry. Just... lots to think about." I turned my attention to Bentley. "How you holding up?"

Bentley lifted his blanket, exposing a white bandage wrapped tight around his midsection. "Haven't bothered trying to move much, but whatever drugs they have me on feel *amazing.*"

I chuckled. "Well, you sure as hell earned a rest. All of you did. Did your parts perfectly."

"You deserve a rest too," Rose said. "Seems like you've been running around pretty much nonstop since the fight."

"And it seems like you didn't get any rest last night," Rid said, raising an eyebrow at me.

I felt my face grow hot. "I, uh... look." I scratched my head. Dammit, why was this so awkward? I'd been too wrapped up in the moment to give much thought to how getting together with Sev might affect my relationship with everyone else—especially

Rose. It didn't escape me that while the others chuckled at Rid's jab, she looked down at the floor, expression unreadable.

"I'd appreciate it if you didn't spread that around too far," I finally managed. "Gotta at least try to look professional for our allies."

"Right," Bentley said. "You know, that's always been what I've thought about you. Lackan VanDunn. A true professional. Running head first into every bad situation he comes across out of sheer professionalism. Throwing aside entire fortunes. Starting wars. Breaking—"

"I get it, I get it." I waved his words away, still focused on Rose. She was smiling again, but when our eyes met, I could tell there was something hiding there beneath the surface. A distance I'd never felt from her before. It was enough to send a ripple of alarm through me.

"What's going on out there?" Shell asked. "We got any sort of plan for what we're doing next?"

"Yeah." I nodded, grateful for the change in subject. I didn't want to confront Rose in front of the whole crew, so I made a mental note to find some time to catch her alone later.

Because I had *so* much free time these days.

I lowered my voice. "Keep this between us. No point in spreading rumors around. But after talking it over, we've decided that it's not enough to just mind our business on the station." I grimaced. "We're gonna try to throw in our lot with the rebels. See if we can help them take down the Paragon."

Rose perked up at that, the coldness in her eyes replaced by vivid excitement. Shell nodded somberly, then muttered something in Aboenian to Shepherd, whose eyes widened. Rid and Bentley exchanged a slightly worried glance.

"Forgive me for retreading ground I'm sure has already been trampled to death," Bentley said, "but... how exactly are we going to do that? It seems like we're barely hanging on by a thread here as it is."

"We'll see." I shrugged. "We've got the beginnings of a plan, but I don't want to say too much here."

"Should we be getting ready to move?" Rose asked.

I leaned back wearily in my seat. "Maybe. But don't get too excited. I want to keep you guys out of this to whatever extent I can."

Rose frowned. "Why? We've proven over and over again that we can handle ourselves!" Her eyes narrowed suspiciously. "Is this about—"

"*Stop.*" I held up a hand. "I just... look. You have my word that if we have a need for you, we'll use you. But we aren't running salvage jobs anymore. This is *war*. And it's only gonna get messier from here on out." I gestured towards Bentley. "We're lucky that this is the worst we suffered yesterday. And we're gonna run out of luck eventually. I just... I couldn't live with myself if I lost any of you guys. Not after all we've been through together." I looked down at my hands. "Not after losing Nadus."

That shut down the protests. There was a moment of somber silence.

"Sure would've been nice to have had him here yesterday, huh?" Bentley smiled wanly. "Maybe he could've been shot instead of me."

I chuckled. "You make a pretty good meatshield. Honestly, though, you did pretty damn well for your first time in a warzone." I turned to Rid. "Both of you did."

"I was scared out of my mind the entire time." Bentley's eyes widened slightly as he stared into blank space. "Even more scared than when we go up against rippers, to be honest. I barely even remember getting hit. But, then again"— he shook himself—"what's new? I'm scared just about all the time with you lot." He chuckled weakly. "Guess that's what happens when you stick a cowardly tech guy into a combat suit."

I raised an eyebrow. "Bentley, if you're a coward, I'd have to say you're just about the bravest coward I've ever met."

Bentley blinked at me. "I... uh... thanks." He wiped suddenly at the corner of his eye. Rid grinned and squeezed his shoulder.

I turned my attention to Rose, clearing my throat. She looked down at the floor again. Better to get it out of the way sooner than later. I hesitated. "Rose. Can I talk with you in—"

My pocket computer pinged. I pulled it out to see a message from Ramar.

MEETING WITH SOVEREIGNS SCHEDULED. MEET ME AT THE CONFERENCE ROOM ASAP.

Dammit. Just when I'd thought I could slow down for a few minutes. I was shocked to see that, according to the clock on my computer, a full eight hours had passed since Ramar had initially promised he would contact the rebels.

"Somewhere to be?" Rose asked flatly.

I winced. "Yeah. I'll be back, though, as soon as I can. Stick together. And don't get too comfortable. Like I said—I'm gonna try my best to keep you guys out of it. But there's a pretty good chance we'll need you."

"Well, you'll know where to find me, at least," Bentley said with a weak chuckle.

I forced myself to stand and made my way to the exit, my mind heavier with each step as I contemplated what came next. What the hell would I even say to the Sovereigns? Maybe I should just have Sev and Ramar handle the entire thing.

I paused in the doorway. Well. Maybe less *paused*, than simply ground to a halt, like an exo with a damaged power supply.

What was I doing here? I'd only screw everything up. Like I always did. The trail of bodies in my wake was growing bigger by the day. Shouldn't I just quit now? Stop pretending like I could make any sort of difference for good? *Before* I got everyone I loved killed in this reckless, futile crusade?

A burst of laughter made me turn, shooting one final glance over my shoulder. Rid was showing something on his handcomputer to Shepherd, who was smiling for what I believed to be the first time since I'd met him. Even Rose was laughing again, though I thought I caught her glancing in my direction.

A small part of me was irritated they had the energy to be amused. Didn't they know what was at stake? What was going on around us? But the larger part of me—the part of me I chose to listen to—was simply glad that *somebody* could be laughing. And that somebody happened to be them.

Seeing them like that made me stand a little straighter. They were still here, despite everything. Still following me. Under my leadership they'd gone from a helpless group of misfit rookies into as good of a salvage crew as any I'd met, and all in the space of just over one year. This wasn't the first time I'd felt like I was at the end of my rope. I'd felt the same way before the *Revelation*. And on the *Aboena*.

I *could* do this. I *would* do it. For them.

I took a deep breath. Then turned and found the energy to stride down the hall.

"Hey, you."

Sev grinned as she fell into step beside me, striding down the long hallway towards the conference room. I felt a smile tug involuntarily at the corner of my mouth just at the sight of her.

"Hey. How did it go with Jala?"

"Good. She seems determined to solve every problem on this station."

"Hell of a long list," I grumbled. I side-eyed Sevani. "I've got to ask, though... she seems awful young, and we literally *just* met her. That's an awful lot of responsibility you've thrown onto her plate, all that considered. So... why her?"

"Honestly?" Sev grimaced. "She was there. And she was willing. If I took the time to scour the station, I'm sure I could find somebody with more experience and qualifications to do what she's doing. But I'm not sure that would be the right move anyways."

"Why not?"

"Because I don't want to find someone who's set on doing things the old way," Sev said. "If this *works*—if the Karak sector does gain independence—I don't want this station to go back to being run by people like Kenton." She hesitated. "Or even people like me."

"Like you?" I frowned. "Seems like you've done a good enough job so far. People practically worship you."

She scoffed. "Only because they've got no better options. But an entire citystation shouldn't have to depend on a rogue smuggler's operation to live. I only ever did it because it didn't seem like anybody else could—or would. I started smuggling because people needed help and I needed money. But one thing led to another, until people started depending on me. But I was never really much of a leader. Just somebody with a solution to a problem." Her eyes went distant. "All of the problems we're dealing with right now—the wars, the poverty—are due to greedy people with too much power. I don't want that to be the future of Albeni 7. And my gut tells me that means that I should be paving the way for people like Jala to take the lead instead of grabbing as much power as I can for myself."

I raised an eyebrow at her. "I think that Renault would say you're sounding dangerously idealistic there."

She snorted. "I'll choose to take that as a compliment. But it's like you said on the *Orpheus*, before we made our attack. If we go through all of this just to end up no better than the people we're fighting, then I just don't see any point to it. The way I see it, a leader's real job is to make themselves redundant. To build a better future for everybody else, even if they're not in it." She glanced coyly at me. "Besides, I don't *want* to stay in charge forever. I'm thinking that buried treasure of ours is sounding awful nice."

That conversation felt like a lifetime ago. *Maybe peace is out there somewhere. Hidden away like a pirate's buried treasure.* Dammit all, but it did sound nice. I'd have grabbed Sev's hand, taken the *Orpheus* and run as far as we could if it had been an option. But it wasn't. We were in too deep—the only way out was through.

"Gotta find it, first," I said, pausing in front of the conference room door. I reached to open it, only to pause as Sev grabbed my hand. She stood on her toes to kiss me gently on the lips.

"We will," she said. "Eventually."

And for some reason, I believed her.

Inside the conference room, Ramar—with the assistance of a few office technicians—was in the middle of configuring several holoprojectors that were built into the long table. "Good," he said, not looking up from his computer. "You're here."

I looked around. Other than him and his assistants, the room was empty. "Where's everybody else?"

"I spoke to them," Sev said, sidling past me and into the room. "We agreed that having our entire council present would be too chaotic. The two of us will represent the needs of our alliance."

I grimaced. "Weren't you the one just saying my diplomacy needed work?"

"And what better place to work on it?" Sev grinned mischievously. Upon seeing my discomfort, she pulled out a chair. "Come on. I've got your back. But we're here to talk war. That's *your* area of expertise."

"Plus, the Sovereigns specifically requested to see you,"

Ramar said, finally looking up over his computer screen at us. "You're no longer an anonymous figure, I'm sorry to say. Word's gotten out about the rogue Vanguard and his exploits."

I growled, settling into the chair and remembering just how exhausted I was. "And just how heavy of a hand have you had in spreading these words?"

"None, actually." Ramar waved a dismissive hand to the techs, who promptly left the room. "But people talk. Carston tells me that there have been rumors about you since the *Revelation*. And nobody could ignore what happened with the *Leonidas*. And after the last few days, well—I couldn't have kept any of it a secret if I'd wanted to."

I stared gloomily into a camera that had risen from the surface of the table. All that effort to stay under the radar—wasted. It was all my fault, of course. I could've given in to my instincts and run away from it all at any point. Maybe I should've done that. I could have slipped away right after Nadus and Artemis busted me out and found some quiet work mining somewhere. I almost wished that I had.

Sev's hand on my shoulder as she slipped into her own seat next to me made the feeling evaporate.

"Don't worry, though," Ramar said. "I highly doubt they know anything too sensitive. I've made sure to keep the Stranger a secret, as well as the, ah, *enhancements* you've received."

I nodded. The thought of the rebels trying to weaponize the Stranger's control over the Divinity gene was not a pleasant one. That was why I'd killed Tekka and his men in the first place. They'd wanted to take the Paragon's weapons and use them—to turn the ultrarippers against their masters. I wouldn't stand for any of that.

I glanced around the room, making sure we were alone and the doors shut. "You learned anything else since our last talk?"

Ramar shifted uncomfortably in his chair. "I... no. Not particularly, I'm afraid. Zeka continues to speak of a great crusade. And I know that she's eager to get the *Aboena* to the shipyards."

"I *did* think that was strange," Sev said. "Roamers are pretty famous for their self-sufficiency. And you saw the exchange in the meeting earlier—the Roamer leaders were pretty certain they could repair the damage on their own. Why is Zeka so insistent on getting to the shipyard?"

I shrugged. "I mean, they sustained a *lot* of damage. Multiple hull breaches, and entire sectors of the ship that got devastated by the fighting. But it is odd that they let Zeka talk over them like that."

Ramar nodded. "That's happened more and more, lately. Before the battle, the Shapers got their way through quiet manipulation. Now, they simply give Command orders and are obeyed. The shift in the general mood aboard the ship cannot be understated. The ranks of the Shapers are swelling, while the Roamers are leaving the ship in droves—mostly due to logistical reasons, since so many of their homes were destroyed. But I've heard many of them stating that they have no intention of returning. I've heard others say that the Shapers have overstayed their welcome, and that something needs to be done about them to return the *Aboena* to its natural state."

I thought back to Shepherd, sitting forlornly in the medbay with the rest of my crew. "Well, as long as we can make room for them on the station, I don't much mind."

"I've been shocked at just how much extra room we've been able to make," Sev said. "Remember that empty floor we passed through during the battle? There are dozens of areas like that throughout the station, all of them sitting empty because nobody could afford to pay the premiums. When you're trying to maximize efficiency rather than profits, all kinds of new housing solutions present themselves." Her face turned serious. "Food is a different problem, though. We really do need that fruit production up and running. Just to tide us over until we can work out some trade deals."

I had to pinch my arm to keep my eyes from drifting shut. I desperately needed to sleep. *After*, I promised myself.

I noticed Ramar studying me, his eyes holding just a glint of his old intensity. I perked up. "What?"

"How have *you* been feeling?" he asked. "I've hardly been able to speak with you since the battle. And since your enhancements."

"Oh. Right." I glanced at Sev. "Good. Whatever the Stranger did to me, it sure as hell worked. I shrugged off a bullet to the head."

Ramar's brow furrowed. "The *head*?"

"Yep." I tapped the side of my skull where the bullet had struck me. "Knocked me out for... what, Sev, a minute or two? Then I was back up like nothing ever happened."

Ramar stared at me, brows furrowed. "Would you be opposed," he asked, finally, "to allowing me to perform some tests on you? Nothing extreme. But I don't understand what the Stranger has done to you. And the Shapers don't seem very eager to explain it to us."

I glanced at Sevani again. She looked hesitant. I didn't blame her. I still couldn't say that I fully trusted Ramar. But compared to the Stranger, he was an open book.

Before I could respond, Ramar's computer chimed. He glanced down at it. "They're ready," he said. "Are you?"

I took a deep breath. Another day, another meeting with important people I wanted nothing to do with. "I'm ready."

"Remember," Sev said. "The fact that they've even agreed to meet with us means they need our help as badly as we do theirs. We're in a position of strength here. Let's act like it." She squeezed my hand. "I'll handle the diplomacy, then let you handle the strategy. Got it?"

That made me feel better. I straightened myself in my seat and nodded.

Ramar hit a key on his computer. A few moments later, several images flickered to life around the conference table, hovering above the holoprojectors. I felt as if I were meeting with a council of ghosts. The projections were of varying quality—some looked almost lifelike, others were grainy, and one wasn't a hologram at all—just a floating message with the words: NO VIDEO FEED.

I studied them one by one. By the look of things, they were studying us right back. There were eight of them in total. There was little by way of similarity between them. Some wore military style uniforms. Others were dressed more stylishly, and one was wearing what looked like a stained set of overalls. Of the ones visible, two were women while the rest were male. Most of them were middle-aged, with one looking to be in his twenties and the oldest appearing to be at least in her sixties.

If there was one thing they all had in common, it was a serious, fatigued expression. I knew without them saying so much as a word that they'd all been fighting this battle for a long time—long before things had started escalating a few weeks ago. If I'd felt inadequate at the meeting we'd held earlier, I felt positively preposterous now. Each of the individuals now studying me from across the stars was a grizzled veteran at rebellion. They had dedicated their lives to fighting against the Paragon in whatever desperate, scrappy ways they could. These were the most wanted fugitives in the galaxy. And now here I was—a Vanguard, a man who'd spent the Last War butchering rebels like animals—showing up and demanding that they let me into their inner circle.

A square-jawed man wearing a crisp uniform leaned forward, clasping his hands together in front of him. His eyes were locked straight forward into his own camera, putting the gaze of his projection straight into the wall beside me, but I got the idea nonetheless. "Lackan VanDunn," he said. His voice was deep and authoritative. "And Maren Sevani. Thank you for arranging this meeting."

Sev leaned forward. "We appreciate you agreeing to meet with us—especially considering how short the notice was. We hope you can appreciate the common position we're all in."

"We can." The rebel nodded gravely. "Our coalition realized long ago that our only hope of victory comes through unity. We're happy to see others realizing the same."

I had to resist the temptation to chuckle at the irony of that. *Unity* had been the rallying cry of the Paragon as they had gone from world to world leaving destruction in their wake. I remembered the statue in the Gharseva city square, back on Brahma. *Forever United.*

The rebel's gaze grew somehow more serious than it had already been. "That said, you can understand if we're not immediately ready to welcome you with open arms. Some of us have ample reason to be wary of you."

Sev raised an eyebrow. "I wouldn't have thought that a group of rebels the Paragon has deemed '*terrorists*' for years now would be so reluctant to work alongside a smuggler. I distinctly recall helping several of you obtain supplies in the past, in fact."

"It's not you we distrust." A woman's voice—coming from the projection with the NO VIDEO FEED message. I furrowed my brow. I could swear that I recognized the voice's cold cadence as it continued speaking. "It's the Vanguard."

I froze.

The hovering message vanished, replaced by the translucent image of a well-dressed, stone-faced woman. She looked to be roughly in her sixties. Despite her finely tailored clothes, however, there was an air of stark, brutal utilitarianism about her.

"Aw, *hell*," I muttered.

Sev glanced sharply at me. "What's wrong?" she whispered.

I didn't reply. There was no quick way to sum up the problem. And even if there was, I was too focused on the hologram to spit it out.

The woman's phantasmal eyes narrowed as she came into focus. Her tone was as cold as deep space and sharp as a ripper's claws. "Hello, VanDunn. What a pleasure to see you again."

The rebel who had been speaking earlier cleared his throat. "VanDunn, Sevani—this is Nalis Khendar of Brahma. Leader of our little coalition."

Looked like I wasn't the only one capable of rising from the dead.

THIRTEEN

If you asked me to sum up Nalis Khendar in one word, that word would be dignity. When I met her in Gharseva she carried herself like a queen. Even the insults she'd rained down upon me had carried a sort of nobility to them—like arrows shot from an ivory tower. No matter what happened, she—along with her husband—existed on a higher plane of being, untouchable in any meaningful way by us mortals.

It would be wrong to say that the Nalis Khendar I saw before me now had no dignity. But it was a different kind. The ivory tower had crumbled and the fallen queen had exchanged her arrows for a sledgehammer. Her face was marred only by time, but she looked battle-scarred nonetheless.

It must have been a hell of a year for her since the Paragon had assaulted her Gharseva mansion.

I was suddenly glad that there were lightyears separating us. Even over the great distance, I could feel the hatred burning behind her eyes.

It took every ounce of willpower I had not to burst into a fit of vile cursing. Our task had just become *significantly* more complicated. If there was one person in the world who had good reason to hate me, well, it was this woman. Her—and her husband.

Why—*how*—was she here? Tekka had said that the Khendars were dead. And Brahma was not among the Sovereign Systems. Had Ramar known about her? I glared sharply at him but got only a grimace and shrug in response.

I cleared my throat, trying to wrench my face into an expression that didn't convey how utterly daunted I felt. "Khendar. It's been a while. Our last meeting was, uh, cut short."

"Indeed." She hardly moved, looking for all the world like a snake waiting for the right moment to strike. Dangerous silence filled the air.

I searched desperately for something else to say. What came out was, "Tekka told us you didn't make it out of Gharseva."

I knew the moment Tekka's name left my mouth that I'd stepped right into the snake's biting range. Her eyes flashed with anger. "Tekka was only half correct. My husband did not survive the ambush. I did. I was forced underground, where I fought to salvage what little I could of the operation my husband and I had built over so many years. Years of planning. Years of sacrifice by loyal Brahmians. All turned to dust over the course of a few hours. All for *nothing*."

I clenched my teeth. Not much I could say to refute that.

She continued. "Afterwards, when I had the opportunity, I tried to understand what had gone so horribly wrong. Artemis's corpse was found in a safehouse. Tekka vanished into the void, along with his team and your crew. I waited for him to return for a long time, knowing he never would. Waited for him to tell us that this gambit that he and Artemis had hatched—incurring so much risk for such a small chance of success—had paid off. But of course, all I heard was silence."

I glanced towards Sev. She'd clearly worked out what was happening by now. She was doing a good job keeping her face passive—far better than I was—but I could tell that she was just as shaken by this as I was.

"I took that to mean that the operation had ended in tragedy," Nalis continued. "That you had found the *Revelation*, only to be overwhelmed by the dangers aboard. After all, if you had found *nothing*, Tekka would have returned—empty-handed, but alive, and ready to continue serving his home planet. And if you had been successful, he would have returned a hero, bearing the technology we needed to defeat our enemy for good. You *all* would have been heroes."

I shifted uncomfortably. It was obvious where she was going. And yet I could think of no valid response.

"And so imagine my surprise," she continued, her voice growing harsher with each word, "when—a full year later, after I have fought tooth and nail to rebuild what I can, in the middle of the final, ultimate fight against the Paragon—I hear that Lackan VanDunn, vulture of no small renown, is, inexplicably, alive. And not only alive; he's advanced from a desperate salvager into the leader of a not insignificant coalition of rogues. And now he comes crawling to *us*—we who have sacrificed everything they have in the name of independence. And he wants our help."

Sev leaned forward. "I understand that there is a complicated history here, but we would be fools to let that—"

"I'm not addressing you, smuggler." Nalis's voice held a deep contempt. "I want to hear the puppet speak for himself—if he even has a voice of his own."

Sev settled back into her seat, eyes narrowed.

A cold anger gripped me. Not at being called a puppet—I'd gotten used to that long ago. But Nalis addressing Sevani like she was some common, lowlife criminal pissed me off. Just enough to drive my uncertainty away.

I'd been so focused on wondering what other people would do. How Artemis, or Sev, would talk their way through these touchy diplomatic situations. With a sudden rush of cold clarity, I realized that was the entirely wrong approach. I was no good at diplomacy. So there was no point in acting diplomatic.

"I didn't hear a question," I said.

Nalis gave a malicious smile. "I see your loquaciousness has not improved since our last meeting. Very well. I'll say this as simply as possible. What happened to Tekka?"

I studied her for a moment, considering my options. I could lie. I could tell her that the mission had gone bad—which was true—and that I'd barely made it out alive, unable to save Tekka and his team. But it was a thin story and I knew it. And it would still leave an unanswered question in her mind, along with any of the other rebels she'd told: what had I discovered aboard the *Revelation*?

I squared my shoulders. Sev tensed.

The truth, then.

"I killed him," I said.

Sev let out a barely perceptible groan. If Nalis's gaze had been cold before, it was terminally so now. But I wasn't looking at her anymore. I let my gaze slide over each of the other leaders, gauging their reactions. They didn't look happy. But they were sure as hell listening.

"I'm not sure how much Nalis here has told you about our little expedition," I said. "But let me fill in some of the blanks, just in case. We boarded the *Revelation* with a goal: to find what we believed were stolen Divinity secrets. Ultracell blueprints, to be specific. I don't need to tell you what that would've done for the prospects of your rebel forces."

Slow, careful nods around the room. I spotted multiple people flickering in and out of existence as they leaned out of frame, muttering with invisible companions. Nalis didn't look any less pissed, but she stayed silent. At the edge of my vision I saw Ramar tensing. I took a deep breath and continued.

"Well, that's not what we found. We found death. The

Revelation wasn't on its way to Brahma to build a new ultracell factory. It was on its way to Brahma to test out an experimental new breed of ripper. Smarter, deadlier, able to adapt to whatever environment they found themselves in. They'd make all the other ripper attacks look like a pleasant memory. And Tekka wanted to use these new rippers against the Paragon."

I let that sink in for a few moments. I got exactly the reaction I'd been expecting. Some of the rebels looked impassive, as if they were waiting for a punchline, but I was relieved to see that a decent amount of them—at least half—looked perturbed. Even for hardened rebels, the idea of using rippers was bound to be controversial. They'd spent their lives fighting the Paragon's evil—far too long to be casual about the notion of using it themselves.

"I tried to dissuade him," I said. "He didn't listen. So we fought." I met Nalis's eyes. "And I won."

A heavy silence filled the room.

When Nalis didn't speak, one of the other rebels did. "Do you have proof of any of this?"

I glanced hesitantly at Ramar. Between Ramar and the Stranger, I was sure we could come up with some sort of evidence. But that would mean admitting that if we really wanted to, we could probably make a whole lot worse than rippers. Ramar must've been in agreement, because he carefully shook his head.

"Nope," I said.

"Then you can understand that we're... *reluctant* to take your word for it," one of the other rebels said.

"Sure," I said. "But I don't particularly care. Because what happened on the *Revelation* doesn't matter. What matters is that right now, the Paragon is kicking your asses. And once they're done kicking yours, they'll come kick ours."

A few of them looked positively angry at that. Others remained impassive. Nalis looked... well, about the same.

"So if you want to talk about Tekka and the *Revelation*," I continued, "then sure. Let's talk. But if you want to get around to solving the problem you've spent the last twenty years fighting, then I've got a fleet of pirates and an army of pissed-off Roamers ready to go. I just need to know where to put 'em."

Nalis scowled. "And how do we know you won't simply stab us in the back? *Again?*"

"Cause there's not a single damn reason that would benefit me," I said. "We're just as screwed as the rest of you if the Paragon wins. I'm not asking you to like me. I'm not even asking you to trust me. But I am telling you that if things keep on going the way they are right now, you're screwed. I might not know all the details, but I know you're in a tight spot. I know you're boxed in on your own systems while the Paragon takes you out one at a time. So unless you've got some sort of secret ace up your sleeves, I'd recommend hearing me out."

They exchanged glances through their cameras. Nalis gave a subtle smirk that made me wonder if they did have an ace or two. Still, she let me carry on.

"The way I see it," I said, "the more of us there are rebelling, the broader the Paragon has to stretch their forces. The easier it'll be to break them. Now, we've got our eyes on a prime target. Boadicea 1."

That got their interest. I continued. "I'm sure I don't need to tell you how important Boadicea is. Taking it would be a hell of a way to put some dirt in their eye. But even more important is the system overseer who lives there, Adrian Vatheson."

Nods around the table showed that they were well aware of his reputation. I continued. "Vatheson knows what the Paragon is planning. He knows their next move. If you want to break this stalemate you're in, that's your key to doing it right there."

One of the rebels—the square-jawed man who had started the meeting—spoke up. "And you can take the station? You have a way through the blockade?"

I nodded with more confidence than I felt. I still didn't fully understand this plan of Renault's, but at this point, I was too deep in to do anything but trust him. "Yep. Only need one thing from you."

Nalis's face turned darkly amused. "Oh? And that is?"

Despite myself, I felt a flush of embarrassment. I'd never been much for begging. But, then again, I'd never been much for leading rebellions, either.

"Money," I said. "Lots of it."

Nalis scoffed. "Ah. There it is."

"It's not for me," I said, irritated. "Taking Boadicea ain't gonna be easy. And nobody knows better than you that war ain't cheap. If we're gonna pull this off, we'll need funding." I studied Nalis carefully. "Something I hear you suddenly have an abundance of."

There was a long silence as Nalis returned my gaze. Judging by the curious looks the other rebels were giving her, I figured I'd struck a nerve of some kind. Maybe she was the only one who knew the true identity of this benefactor of theirs. At the very least, it was clear that they were just as curious about her response as I was.

"Give us a moment, if you please," Nalis said.

The images froze.

I leaned towards Sev. "How's that for diplomacy?" I asked.

"That was diplomacy in the same way putting your head through a door counts as knocking," she said, grinning wryly. "But it seems to be working. Maybe I should have brought you on as a partner a long time ago."

"Telling them about the *Revelation* was unnecessarily risky," Ramar said. "We need to remember that if we lose, these people will be quick to turn on us and each other, selling secrets back to the Paragon for whatever scraps of dignity they can. And if we win, they'll be our neighbors—and rivals. If they find out about the Stranger..."

I shrugged. "All true. But I sure as hell ain't a good enough liar to spin any kind of other yarn they'd believe. Best I can do is give the truth watered down with a few falsehoods."

"They're coming back," Ramar said.

The images resumed moving. Nalis locked her icy gaze onto me once again. I straightened, anticipation building within me. If she said no, I'd... well. I wasn't sure what there *would* be to do, other than wait for the Paragon to come and finish us off.

"Let me be clear on one matter, VanDunn," Nalis said. "I do *not* trust you."

I deflated.

She sighed. "But it is clear that, for now, at least, our goals our aligned. The information you claim Vatheson possesses would be of great benefit to our plans. We will fund this operation of yours. And, if it is successful, we will discuss terms for allowing you and your allies to become full members of the Sovereign Systems."

I tried not to show how relieved I was. It was a strange feeling, being grateful to work with a woman who so clearly hated me, but these were strange times.

"Rest assured, however," she continued, "that this changes nothing of what I think of you. I still think you are a treacherous leech. I still think you deserve a fate worse than death for the crimes you have committed against Brahma and her people. I will be watching you, Vanguard. And if I detect so much as a whiff of betrayal, you'll wish you'd died on the *Revelation*."

"Well, I hate to say *I told you so*, but..." Renault chuckled. "Well. No I don't."

"I wouldn't be too smug about it," I said, not slowing my pace as we strode down the corridor towards the station transit system. "All the problems we discussed before still stand. Taking Boadicea will be a hell of a lot harder than taking back Albeni 7 was. And that's if we can even get there."

Movement on the left. Rose fell into step beside us, panting. "Mom said you needed me. Are we going?"

"Soon," I said.

"And you want the *Orpheus*?"

I clenched my teeth. "Most likely. We're going after Boadicea 1. And we're gonna need every edge we can get if we're gonna pull it off."

Rose tried—unsuccessfully—to repress a wide, excited grin. "I'll get the crew ready." She darted off.

I shook my head, turning back to Renault. "Plus," I said, "we'll have fewer numbers than last time. I don't want to leave Albeni 7 unprotected."

"A noble thought," Renault said. We stepped into the railcar that would transport us from the main portion of Albeni 7 to the outer docking ring. "But it might not matter. If the Paragon does decide to attack, it likely wouldn't matter if all five of my ships were here. So what's the point in taking half measures on what is likely our only chance at survival?"

Hard to argue with that. Still, the thought of leaving Sevani behind again without at least a semblance of protection made my stomach sour. I held myself steady with a handrail as the car began accelerating. Well—decelerating, actually, since the whole point of the system was to transition from the spinning central portion of Albeni 7 to the stationary outer docking ring. "Even if we did bring your whole fleet," I said, "how do we get past the blockade?"

"Actually," Renault said, giving me an odd sideways look, "I have a solution for that particular problem."

The car came to a halt. I let Renault go through the door first, raising an eyebrow at the jauntiness in his step. "I don't think your ol' mineral hauler trick is gonna work this time."

He chuckled. "Oh, it's not that. In fact, I think you'll like this plan even less than you liked that one."

I followed him out of the car and into the loading bay terminal. I came to a halt when I saw Renault's target.

Then muttered a curse.

Katen Werrel, sitting on a stack of cargo crates surrounded by armed pirates, didn't look any more pleased to see me than I was to see him. He sighed, rose to his feet, flicked a cigarette away, and gave me a lazy salute.

"VanDunn," he drawled.

I put my hands on my hips, looking from him to Renault. Truth be told, I'd thought the mercenaries were gone already. But looking past Katen I saw dozens of them, milling about the portion of the docking bay that had been allotted to them. I was relieved to see that there was at least some semblance of an armed guard keeping watch over them—a combination of pirates and gray-armored Roamers were nearby, weapons close at hand.

"I thought we made arrangements for you to get out of here," I said, looking back to Werrel.

"You did," the mercenary said. "There have been a few logistical, uh..." He eyed Renault. "Delays."

Renault held up a finger as I turned an irate eye on him. "They're ready to go and will be gone at the drop of a hat if you wish it so. But before we banish them, I want to make you see that we could potentially be throwing away an invaluable tool."

"Invaluable?" I raised an eyebrow. "Mercenaries are the *opposite* of invaluable. Hell, he'll tell me his value right now if I ask him."

"That's true," Werrel admitted, reaching two fingers into his shirt pocket. They emerged a moment later with another cigarette pinched between them.

"See, that's not what I'm referring to, though," Renault said. "We don't need them for their fighting capacities. We need them because they're a known element to Vatheson and the Paragon."

"That's also true." Werrel tore the self-lighting cap off of his cigarette, let it flare, and then perched it between his teeth.

I studied the mercenary for a moment. A known element. The Paragon blockade would more than likely let his fleet through. Hell, we might even be able to take Vatheson completely by surprise.

Might.

"Have you communicated with Vatheson since the attack?" I asked.

Werrel sucked at the cigarette. "Nope."

"And you're willing to go along with this?" I asked.

Werrel shrugged. "I mean, you gotta pay me. A lot. I don't work for cheap—especially not to betray an employer. But sure, I'll play along."

So *that* was why Renault had needed more money for his plan. I narrowed my eyes. "I don't like it. If we can pay him to betray Vatheson, Vatheson can pay him to betray us. What's to stop him from just taking us right into a trap?"

"That's where things get slightly less clever," Renault admitted. "But simplicity is sometimes best. You see, we'll just make sure that Werrel here knows there's a gun pointed at the back of his head the whole time. If he's true to his word—his word to *us*, that is, not the word he's breaking with Vatheson—and we are victorious, then he lives to get paid another day. If he betrays us, he dies."

The mercenary rolled his cigarette. "Listen, you do what you need to do to feel secure. But I ain't got any particular reason to like Vatheson. Far as I'm concerned he already screwed us by leaving us high and dry here. Now, if he makes a better offer, sure, I'll take it. But a good offer's about a whole lot more than money."

I looked back and forth between the two of them. Renault raised an eyebrow.

I still didn't like it. But I didn't like any of our other options, either. Damned if I did—and even more damned if I didn't. Besides—I'd already told the Sovereigns that we would go through with the operation. We had the money. We had the means. Now we just had to make it happen. I sighed, turning away. "Fine. Co-ordinate with Winter and Tetra. Make it secure. And I mean airtight."

Renault threw up a salute. "Your wish is my—"

"Stop it." I held up a hand as I walked away. "Just get it done. Aim for departing in twelve hours."

"Where are you going?" Renault called after me.

"None of your damn business."

"That," I panted, "was *much* nicer than last time."

Sev laughed, nestling into my side and pulling the blanket over us. "I don't know. I miss the broken glass."

I wrapped an arm around her, relishing the feeling of her warm body pressing against mine and looking around at our surroundings—I hadn't exactly had much time to study them when we'd first come into the room. All things considered, Sevani's living quarters were shockingly modest. Better than the stark, depressingly utilitarian apartments most of Albeni 7's residents lived in, but a far cry smaller than the decadent housing we'd passed through near the administrative offices. It reminded me of her old room aboard the *Orpheus*. In fact, I recognized several items. Knick-knacks plundered from various ships we'd worked. Mementos of our old crew mates. One of Kessa's paintings hung on her wall—an image of our old crew gathered around a table in the *Orpheus*'s galley, featuring everyone but Rawlins, who hadn't joined at the time. I vaguely remembered when Kessa had painted it. I'd pointed out that the lighting in the mess was better than that, and we hardly ever ate potatoes. She'd said it was an homage. I'd left it at that.

What drew my eyes most, though, was a small photograph on Sev's nightstand. A portrait with Sev, a *very* young Rose, and a tall, handsome man with a well-trimmed beard and mustache. They looked happy.

Sev followed my gaze, then blushed. "Sorry. Maybe I should've..."

"No." I shook my head. "It's alright."

I'd expected that being reminded of Kessa would make me feel guilty. Sev and Kess had been best friends back in the day. The three of us had been the very first to start the crew. Being with Sev had seemed wrong. Now, though, it just felt natural.

Kessa would've wanted me to be happy. I knew it. I recalled that dream I'd had with her on the *Aboena*. *You have to move on, Lax.*

I turned back to Sev, giving a deep, contented sigh. "You know, I think this is the nicest bed I've ever been in."

Sev chuckled. "As much as I find myself missing the adventuring life sometimes, being stationside *does* have its perks."

"Yeah. I just wish I could stay."

She adjusted her position, lying on top of me and looking me in the eyes. She opened her mouth only to hesitate. I knew exactly what she wanted to say. And she knew exactly what my response would be. And we both knew that I was right.

Stay here.

They need me there.

Let me come.

They need you here.

She sighed and settled back into me. "I hate this," she said quietly.

"Me too."

"Every time we used to leave on a job, Ty would be so nervous. I remember resenting it, the pressure it placed on me," she said. "But I get it now. Even this last year, each time you'd go out with Rose and the crew, all I could think about was everything that could go wrong. I thought it was just because Rose was with you. But now it's worse." She grimaced. "I miss being the one going out into the danger."

I nodded. "After the *Panama*, I kinda stopped being afraid of death. My own, at least. All I really cared about was keeping my crew safe. My own safety was an afterthought. But now..."

I trailed off, thinking about what the journey ahead of me might bring. Like I'd told Rid and Bentley—salvage was one thing. War was another entirely. Brutal, uncontrollable, and random. And I knew better than to think that I could stay lucky forever.

"Now what?" Sev asked.

"And now," I said, "for the first time in about as long as I can remember, I'm afraid." I looked at her. "Because for the first time in about as long as I can remember, I've got something to lose."

She dug a finger into my rib, making me flinch. "Asshole. Now if something happens to you, I'll blame myself."

I winced. "Sorry. I didn't mean—"

"I know." She ran a finger along the side of my face. "Look. We're both too old to pretend that there's no chance this goes wrong. I'm not going to ask you to make any promises about whether or not you'll come back. But I want you to know that no matter what happens—to either of us—I'm glad that we had this time."

"Me too."

"That said..." She kissed me gently, then reached over and flipped off the light switch, plunging us into darkness. "You *better* come back."

She rested her head on my chest. I held her close. Felt the fear and anxiety bleed slowly away from me.

"We've got buried treasure to find," she murmured.

FOURTEEN

"There's still no word from Vatheson," Renault said, standing over the holoprojector in the bridge of Werrel's flagship. "Which is both good and bad."

Werrel stood next to him, arms crossed and a cigarette dangling from his lips. One of his captains was at his side, treating me to an untrusting scowl. Flint and Winter flanked me on the other side of the holodisplay, shooting watchful, threatening gazes of their own at the mercenaries.

For my part, I was having a hard time keeping my attention focused on the projector and the blueprints of Vatheson's station it was currently displaying. I was too busy staring towards the tiny dot that was Albeni 7 as it faded into the black of space.

You better come back.

"Good," Renault continued, "because that means that he hasn't attempted to co-ordinate any kind of further attack against us with Werrel's mercenaries. And bad, because, well... it means we don't know *what* he's doing."

"There's a lot of things you can say about that bastard," Werrel said, scratching his stubbled chin. "But not that he's careless. There's a reason he went silent. Just don't know what it is yet."

"Long as you remember that if we find out you're lying," Flint growled, "I've called dibs on hanging your head from my Jericho."

Werrel didn't look particularly perturbed by the threat, but his companion stirred angrily. I'd made sure the mercenaries were disarmed while on the bridge with us, but I also had no doubt in my mind that the entire ship was brimming with hidden weapons. But it was also brimming with angry pirates and Roamers. One wrong move and the entire ship would turn into a battleground.

With that in mind, I held up a calming hand. Flint and Winter had the task of making sure that Werrel didn't attempt to stab us in the back, and they were taking to it with an over-abundance of enthusiasm. "He knows," I said. "But point is we've got no intel. Fine. Let's focus on what we do know."

What we knew didn't turn out to be much.

Werrel walked us through the station's layout, pointing out the docking stations, the location of Vatheson's office complex, and the checkpoints we'd be most likely to face resistance at. He claimed not to know much beyond that, and I didn't press him on it. There was no reason he should—he was a mercenary for hire, paid to take and hold Albeni 7, not a member of Vatheson's inner circle. Unlike somebody else we'd been fortunate enough to capture.

"Sevani and I took the time to ask Kenton a few questions," I said. "He doesn't know why Vatheson cut off contact. But he does know quite a bit more about the station itself." I pointed towards a spot the terrified man had indicated to us on the blue-prints. "He has a getaway ship ready to launch hidden here. A stealth interceptor, like the *Orpheus*. So we'll need to make sure that we have an eye on it before we make our move so he doesn't slip away. If that ship is out of sight for more than a few seconds, it'll be lost in the black."

"I can attest to that," Renault muttered.

I restrained a chuckle. Seemed like a lifetime ago that Renault had ambushed us outside of Vatheson's Lifeblood stash. "Exactly. So we'll want to get the hunter drones out *fast*. Remember that the whole point of this is to take him alive. We need to know what the Paragon is planning next."

"Do you truly think he'll talk?" Winter asked.

Flint snorted. "Oh yeah. He'll talk. They all do, with enough encouragement."

"Fortunately, we might not need him to," I said. "Kenton says he's got some kind of computer implant." I tapped the back of my head. "Right in the base of his skull. Stores his memories and whatnot in it, I guess."

"Can we hack it?" Winter asked. "Your man seems good enough."

Renault shook his head. "I'd bet astronomical, unfathomable odds against it being hackable without a direct connection. And even then it might not be. A careful fellow like Vatheson would never choose to compromise himself like that."

I nodded along. There was a reason most Vanguards got their regulators removed when they got out. The idea of having a part of your brain wired so that somebody could reach in and mess around was damnably violating.

"Why don't we just kill him, then?" Flint asked. "All we need is the implant, right?"

"It's not that simple, unfortunately," Renault said. "I dealt with a similar situation once. The computer's function is very much integrated with the subject's brain; it can't simply be unplugged and transferred like a hard drive. The only way to transfer data from the device to an external source is for the wearer to willingly do so."

"Like a neurointerface," Flint said thoughtfully.

"Precisely," Renault said. "Well. I assume so. Never had one myself. But, the point stands: if Vatheson dies, our chance at getting any information from him dies along with him, implant or not."

"Then we keep him alive." I turned back to the blueprints. "But none of that matters if we can't catch him—alive. So: how the hell do we do that?"

"You're off your sleep cycle."

I looked up sharply. Winter stood in the doorway of the *Orpheus*'s mess hall, studying me. He looked older out of his armor, but no less warrior-like. His short gray beard and bushy eyebrows perfectly complemented his cold blue eyes as he watched me. I couldn't help but tense as I noticed the long knife at his side.

"And you aren't?" I asked, turning back to the schematics I'd been reviewing on my handcomputer while keeping him in the corner of my vision. Winter had been a faithful soldier so far, there was no doubting. But there was also no forgetting that he'd been a Wolf, even if he had forsaken Cairn before he'd attempted his coup.

"I just finished my shift," he said. "It would be foolish to come all this way only to be murdered by mercenaries in our sleep."

I nodded. The *Orpheus* was docked to Werrel's flagship. The proverbial scorpion on the back of the frog. It was far from an ideal situation, but it seemed to have been working so far. Werrel had easily talked his way past the Paragon blockade, and so far no fights had broken out between the pirates or Roamers and our semi-captive host. There was plenty of reason for resentment, but the mercenaries stood to be paid if everything went well, and that seemed to be enough to keep their tempers in check.

"Get some sleep, then," I said. "You'll need it."

"So will you."

I grimaced. I'd sure as hell tried. But each time sleep took me, I found myself back in that void. Floating. Finally, I'd given up and decided that if I wasn't gonna get any shut-eye I may as well get some work done. We'd spent hours in the bridge huddled around the blueprints of Vatheson's station making and modifying a dozen different possible plans, but they still seemed woefully insufficient. We just didn't know enough about what we'd find when we got there.

"I'm fine," I said.

Winter didn't move. Something in the way he was watching me reminded me of Cairn: cautious, opportunistic, predatory.

Under the table, I loosened Peacebreaker in its holster.

"You're seeing them, aren't you?" Winter said softly.

I frowned over at him. "Seeing what?"

"The visions."

I froze for a moment, then shut off my handcomputer, turning my seat to face him. "How did you know?"

He moved into the room, sliding out a seat at the far end of the table and settling into it. "Because Cairn started having them. Not long after he got back from his... pilgrimage."

I stared at him. "He told you about them?"

Winter nodded, eyes not leaving mine. "He did. We were close, back then. I taught him how to fight. Taught him how to lead. Thought he might be the future, for a while." He pinched his tongue between his teeth. "Until the Stranger got him."

I wanted to punch him. I'd realized Winter was involved with the Wolves, but not to such an extent. But on the other hand, I desperately needed to hear what he had to say.

"These visions," I said. "What did Cairn see?"

"Stars, mostly," Winter said. "And the Stranger." He frowned. "He said he saw a tree of blood, sprouting from the

Stranger's chest, with roots spreading between the stars across all of Paragon space."

That last one didn't sound familiar. But the stars and the Stranger sure as hell did.

"How much do you know about the Stranger?" I asked.

"Less than you do, I imagine. I know they brought madness to my ship and told us it was aid. I know they give gifts that poison the receiver. I know I don't trust them."

I grimaced. Not exactly the words of comfort I'd secretly been hoping to hear. "What did they *want* from Cairn, though? If he was their Chosen, like I kept on hearing, surely they had a specific task in mind for him."

"I believe that they did." His eyes darkened slightly, still fixed to mine. "But we never found out what it was. Somebody killed him."

A long, cold silence.

Winter's hand shifted slowly towards his knife.

"Cairn murdered my friend," I said. "And tried to murder my crew. So I ain't gonna apologize for putting him down. But if that's what this is all about, then you're welcome to try to finish what he started."

Winter's eyes narrowed. I could see resentment smoldering there. For a moment I thought he might actually go for it—draw his knife and lunge across the table at me.

Instead, he took a long, ragged breath in through his nose, then released it through his mouth. The fight bled out of him all at once, his shoulders sagging and the bitterness clearing from his eyes. His hand relaxed, moving away from the handle of his blade. He looked as if he'd aged twenty years over the course of a few seconds.

"I am no fool," he said, sounding exhausted. "What you did was necessary. The Stranger's gift had consumed him like a cancer. It would have spread further still had you not removed it, and him with it. Still. I regret that he could not be saved."

I nodded slowly. Seemed to me Cairn had already been a bloodthirsty bastard well before we'd arrived on the *Aboena,* and well before he'd been Chosen. But sometimes we're all blind to the faults of those closest to us.

Winter groaned as he climbed to his feet. "This will be my last raid, Vanguard. I have grown too old for all of this nonsense. But heed my warning before I go. Do not trust the Stranger. Despise the gifts you have been given. Reject utterly the Stranger's commands. They have no regard for you—or for any of us."

"What do they have regard for, then?"

"The Crusade," he said. Something in the way he said it sent a chill down my spine.

He gave me a malignant grin and walked out.

I sat there for a long while, letting his words drift around in my head, before I finally sighed, rose, and headed for my room. I'd just moved my thumb to open my door when I saw a movement on my right.

Rose flinched as I pivoted towards her, one hand reached down for my pistol. I winced the moment I realized what had happened.

"Sorry," I said, feeling an embarrassed flush in my cheeks. "Just... a bit jumpy these days."

She sighed, letting her shoulders droop as she relaxed. "I get that."

We stood in awkward silence for a moment.

"About your mom," I said finally.

"About my mom," she said at the same time.

I winced again. "I'm sorry. Look, I... I see how this whole situation might be awkward for you. And listen, if you don't like it, I can—"

"No." She shook her head adamantly. "That's not what I wanted to say. If anything, I'm happy you guys are together.

Really. I am. You deserve each other. And I mean that in the best possible way."

"Oh." I blinked. I'd been expecting... well. I don't know what I'd been expecting. Biting sarcasm. An accusation of some sort. Not... *this*.

"But." She raised a finger. Any awkwardness was gone, replaced by deadly seriousness. "I wanted to make something very clear to you. Every single person in my mother's life has abandoned her. My dad. Her old crew. *You*. And when Vatheson took Albeni 7, she even lost the few friends she'd made there." She took a menacing step towards me, pointing with one finger to punctuate each word. "So what I'm saying is don't you leave her, Lax. Don't. You. Dare."

I wasn't sure what to say to that. Rose didn't seem to mind, though, because she turned sharply and retreated, vanishing into her own room. I could only stare after her.

Don't you leave her.

Sev and I were both too experienced to pretend that was something within our control. But Rose's words—threat, really— made me suddenly begin spiraling through all of the horrible possibilities of what could happen to Sev if I did finally bite the bullet before this mess was over. What if we failed to grab Vatheson and he captured her? What if the Paragon sent assassins and I wasn't there to protect her? What if Divinity found out about her involvement in Vatheson's Lifeblood dealings and went after her?

I knew Sev could handle herself. She probably already had plans in place for each of those possibilities. She'd gotten along just fine before I'd come back from the dead. She'd managed to make it out of Vatheson's surprise attack on Albeni 7. She could survive whatever the universe threw at her next, with or without me.

Still, though. I couldn't help but worry.

I finally sighed and entered my room. The worries followed me, all the way into a restless sleep.

———

Alpha Centauri is the closest system to Earth, which is why it was chosen to become the gatehub. There are seventy-six systems that humanity has colonized and connected via foldgate, and three-quarters of them are linked directly to Alpha Centauri. Like I've said before—if you wanna go anywhere in Paragon space, chances are you're going through the hub.

Which means that if you control Alpha Centauri, you control just about everything.

In the vast, open emptiness of space, the hub system is the closest you're ever likely to get to feeling claustrophobic. Between the foldgates, the massive queues of vessels moving ponderously between them, and the stations that serve all this traffic, it's usually positively crowded.

Not today, though.

Today, as we passed through the Albeni foldgate and into the Alpha Centauri system, I felt... naked. Exposed and vulnerable. The long lines of ships were gone, the space between the foldgates eerily empty. Instead, visible only as distant specks against the black of space, a vast Paragon fleet waited, watching us as we approached.

"That's a lot of firepower," Flint mused as we studied the holoprojector. "I count eleven battlecruisers. And twice as many destroyers."

Renault pointed towards a particularly large cluster of red dots on the holoprojector's map. "Looks like the bulk of their forces are gathered around the Redhawk gate, but you can tell they're being careful not to get too close."

Werrel nodded. "I've got some buddies on both sides of that fight. Rebels have been holding the line a hell of a lot better than the Paragon expected them to. The entire Redhawk system is still in rebel hands. Other rebel systems don't have the same strength, though. Paragon will snuff them out one by one."

Flint grunted. "This Lifeblood stuff better be worth it."

One of Werrel's adjutants cleared her throat. "The Paragon flagship is hailing us, sir."

All eyes turned to Werrel. He sighed, moving towards the comms station. "I'll handle them."

Flint followed close behind him. "Just remember," the Vanguard growled, "one word out of place, and..."

"You'll turn my head inside out or something," Werrel snapped. "I get it. Your concern is understandable, but if the Paragon catches wind of what's going on, they'll probably launch a hailstorm of torpedoes at us and incinerate my entire fleet. So believe me when I say that I'm *quite* motivated to get us safely to Boadicea."

Flint glanced towards Renault, who nodded his confirmation. Flint finally stepped back, giving the mercenary room to work. Werrel took a deep breath and began speaking. "This is Katen Werrel, captain of the *Adamant Will* and commander of Voidkiller Security Solutions. We are a licensed private military unit under contract with System Overseer Adrian Vatheson. We're en route to Boadicea 1. Requesting permission to pass through."

The silence that followed grew more painful with each second it stretched out. My mind raced through the possibilities. Had Vatheson foreseen this possibility and disavowed Werrel? Had somebody else gotten word to the Paragon of the battle on Albeni? I half expected to hear alarms sound as the *Adamant Will*'s scanners detected a hundred missiles firing towards us.

Instead, I heard a voice crackle to life. *"This is the Paragon Battlecruiser* Harmony. *Your request is denied. Boadicea station is under quarantine."*

Werrel looked sharply at me. "Uhm... may I ask why? This is the first I'm hearing of it."

The officer sounded vaguely annoyed. *"You think they tell me? All I know is the orders. Nobody goes through to Boadicea."*

Werrel pursed his lips. "Shame. Here I am with all these credits, then, and nowhere to spend them..."

There was a long pause.

The voice spoke again. *"Please provide the license identification sequence for your company charter as well as the authorization code for your active contract."* A brief hesitation. *"And... stand by for an incoming direct text communication."*

"Certainly." Werrel confidently listed two long sequences of letters and numbers.

When he was done, the Paragon official said flatly, *"Power down your engines. Do not advance further until verification has been completed."*

This silence was even worse than the last one. I found myself wondering if I could sprint down to the *Orpheus* quickly enough if we were attacked, rather than cramming myself into an escape pod. I stared out across the empty void towards a distant speck I thought was the *Harmony*. I turned to a nearby foldgate, catching the glimmer of a planet on the other side, untold lightyears away. Several Paragon ships were flying through the gate. I glanced down at the map on the holoprojector. Looked like that was the Ebisu system. No rebels and no blockade there, it seemed.

In the meantime, Werrel was busy opening his communication computer. Flint watched carefully over his shoulder as he made the bribe.

"My fee," the mercenary muttered, "just went up. Substantially."

"Fortunately," Renault said, winking at me, "we've got friends in high places."

I grimaced. That was, apparently, true. The Sovereign

Systems had been able to handily cover Werrel's steep price. But I still wasn't comfortable with the prospect of not knowing whose money we were taking.

"*You're authorized to proceed.*" The Paragon official's voice startled me. "*Go directly to your destination. Any deviation from your course will be interpreted as a threat.*"

"Thanks. Moving." Werrel moved his finger to close the communication channel, only to hesitate. "And, uh, just to put on your records, we'll likely be coming back this way again soon."

"*As long as it's on contract.*" The voice hesitated. "*And... as long as it's on the same terms.*"

"Then we'll be back soon." Werrel shut off the communication, then leaned back in his seat and treated Renault and I to two raised eyebrows.

"*Very* high places," Renault said.

"Three minutes from nullspace drop," Werrel's pilot said. "I'm putting us as close as we can safely get to Boadicea."

"That'll still be well outside of the station's firing range," Werrel said. "So we'll have time to make a decision before we fully commit ourselves."

"Good." I stared out the front window into the eerie darkness of nullspace.

"*We're all set down here, Lax.*" Rose's voice sounded in my earpiece. "*Ready when you are.*"

"On my way." I turned to Renault. "You've got things handled up here?"

He nodded, gesturing towards the handful of well-armed pirates with him. "We'll make sure no funny business happens up here while you're away."

Werrel raised his hands defensively. "Like I said—I've got

no incentive to stab you in the back. If this goes to hell, I'll be going along with it."

"Damn right," I said. "Cause you're coming with me."

Werrel blinked. "What—onto the station?"

"Yep." I turned towards the bridge exit. "We'll need somebody who actually knows their way around."

He looked helplessly from my face to Renault's, but found no aid. Finally, he gave a heavy sigh and followed me. "I've only been on the station a few times. I'm hardly an expert, if that's what you're looking for."

"Don't need an expert," I said. "Just need someone to point us in the right direction."

On the *Orpheus*, Winter and Flint were both hard at work prepping their assault teams. Flint was halfway through strapping into his Jericho, but he made time to shoot Werrel a nasty grin as the mercenary walked into the cargo bay behind me. "There he is!" Flint crowed. "I was so worried I wouldn't see you again."

I ignored him, walking up to where Shell, Rid, and Bentley stood, already in their exosuits. "You guys ready?"

Rid nodded, looking around at the chaos filling the cargo bay. "Kinda miss how quiet it used to be in here before a job."

I chuckled. "Yeah, me too."

A murmur passed through the cargo bay as we all felt the brief, telltale sense of dissociation that came with nullbreaching. I pulled out my pocket computer and gestured Werrel over. "What're we looking at up there, Renault?"

"*Uhm...*" He sounded puzzled. "*Nothing.*"

I frowned at Werrel. "What do you mean, *nothing?*"

"*I mean, we see the station. It seems to be functioning like normal. But there's no sign of any external traffic.*"

"No fleet?" I asked.

"*Nothing but empty space between us and the station.*" He paused. "*They did say it was under quarantine, after all.*"

Bentley looked from me to Werrel. "That's a good thing, right? No resistance?"

"Typically," Werrel said. "But when you expect heavy resistance, and see none at all..."

"... then you have to wonder if you're walking into a trap," I said. "You're confident none of your men could have contacted Vatheson?"

"Could have? Sure. Would have?" He hesitated. "I don't think any of them are *that* stupid."

"Maybe it was someone back on Albeni," Rid mused.

I felt a brief spike of panic at the thought of the station getting attacked again. There was some validity to the idea that Vatheson had wanted to lure us away. I withdrew the quantcom Sevani had given me and sent a short message appraising her of the situation, along with a code phrase we'd selected together. She responded within seconds, using the correct response phrase. "Everything's looking fine on the home front," I said.

"*I don't like it,*" Renault admitted. "*But I like just sitting here less. We need to move, one direction or the other.*"

I didn't like it either. Not one bit. But we'd come a hell of a long ways just to get cold feet now.

"Then let's move," I said.

The plan wasn't perfect, but it was simple.

A set of hunter drones went out first, scouting for any hidden threats and taking a position so they could make sure Vatheson didn't slip away. It also gave us a chance to prove the defensive batteries. When they didn't open fire on the hunters, we launched the transports.

I held my breath as the *Orpheus* moved through the darkness towards the station docking bays. We wouldn't appear on any scanners, but a particularly sharp-eyed turret gunner might be able to hit us. My worry was in vain, though; we crossed the space without incident.

"*I'm not detecting so much as a radio signal from inside the station,*" Rose said. "*It's completely silent. But I do see a lot of ships docked.*"

"Maybe Vatheson's out for groceries," Bentley mused. "Should we leave a note on the door?"

"Or he's trying—*ugh*—to lure us in." A shiver ran down my spine as the Icarus's neurointerface plugged into my neck port, causing my vision to briefly flicker. "Odds are there'll be a dozen heavy machine guns pointed at these doors when we walk through."

"It's possible," Werrel said. "But... if he was going to go through all the hassle, why not simply blow us up in our ships?"

It was a good question. One I didn't have an answer to. I stepped off of the Icarus's mounting platform, twisting in it, making sure everything was working properly. I'd really put it through the ringer during the battle on the *Aboena*. I'd spent damn near half the return journey getting it fixed back up. It seemed to be operating just fine now. As much as I hated not knowing what we would find on Boadicea 1, the Icarus's protective shell made me feel a hell of a lot more confident.

"*Initiating forced docking procedures,*" Rose said, trying—and failing—to keep the excitement out of her voice. Usually on our salvage jobs we would have to brute-force our way into the ship through an escape pod port or personnel airlock, then hack into the ship to allow the *Orpheus* to dock so we could load our ill-gotten gains. Not today, though. Renault had graciously agreed to fit the *Orpheus* with a "can-opener" docking system that would allow us to cut through the airlock and create our own entrance. They were extremely illegal and extremely difficult to conceal. Before, that had been enough to keep me from even attempting to get one. Now it was laughably low down on my list of problems.

The *Orpheus* rumbled as it slid into place. A muffled grinding sound vibrated through the ship as the can-opener did its work.

One by one, the other crews called out their statuses. We had five transports deploying, with a simple plan: push. Aggressively. The closer we could get to Vatheson the greater the chance he'd attempt to bolt—only for Renault to catch him when he tried to vanish into the black.

I took a long, steady breath.

I didn't like this. Any part of it. The fact that the Paragon had dubbed the station quarantined told me that Vatheson was trying to limit who came here—likely to protect himself. Or to draw us into a trap. But... dammit, we *needed* that information. Not only because we needed it to help the Sovereigns win, but because if we *didn't* get it, the Sovereigns would likely leave us to be consumed by the Paragon.

There was a loud metallic crash outside the airlock.

"*And, we're good to go,*" Rose said.

I lifted my Jackhammer and pointed it at the doors.

They slid open, and I stepped out.

FIFTEEN

I immediately noticed two things.

First was that I'd *never* been on a station like Boadicea 1. Even tense as I was, I couldn't help but be distracted by the sheer grandeur of it. You get used to finding a rugged practicality to space station architecture. Sure, there are variations, but they're mostly just in the layout and the amount of rust. See one and you've seen 'em all.

But I sure as hell had never seen this one.

The docking bay was smaller than most, designed for boarding passengers rather than loading cargo. The walls and floor were all a shade of white so pristine they seemed radiant. Lush green potted trees dotted the walkways to each docking port. Two gentle streams of water fell from the ceiling above to feed a pool of clear water in the center of the room—wait, no, that wasn't right. One of the streams was falling. The other was *rising*, defying gravity as it flowed upwards to feed into an identical pool on the ceiling. In fact, the entire ceiling was identical to the floor. Trees hanging upside down, their branches swaying slightly in an artificial breeze. Roamers and pirates were pouring through the loading ramps and into the terminal. It took me a few seconds to realize it wasn't a mirror.

"Fancy, ain't it?" Werrel shook his head slowly as he looked upwards. "Some clever gravity work. They've got stuff like it all through the station."

I couldn't help but agree. A moment later, though, I shook myself out of my stupor. "We're not here to sightsee," I growled, finally managing to convince my brain that no, I was *not* about to fall upwards. I tore my attention from the decadence surrounding me. "We're here to..."

I frowned.

That was the second thing: the emptiness. The silence. There was not a soul in sight. The only sounds were the gentle rippling of water and the mechanical movements of my invading force.

"Where is everyone?" Shell muttered beside me. "We know they're here. There were dozens of ships docked."

Werrel cautiously eyed Flint's Jackhammer. "I'd imagine they're in one of the checkpoints, waiting for us to walk into a firing zone."

I narrowed my eyes, studying the doors ahead of us. It just didn't make sense. No opposition as we approached the station. Not so much as an automated docking validation. And now no resistance on board.

"We keep moving," I said, striding forward.

I took point. Flint went behind me along with several other ex-Vanguard pirates clad in Jerichos. When I stepped through the terminal exit and into the security checkpoint I fully expected to be met by a hail of gunfire. But there was nothing.

I moved cautiously down a long, wide hallway. The walls were the same brilliant white as the docking bay. Shallow grooves were carved into them, through which rivulets of water flowed. On a whim, I reached out and touched one, assuming it was an illusion. It wasn't.

The ultra precise control of gravity was an astounding technical feat in and of itself, but it was the water that impressed me. On any other station, water was more precious than gold. Every ounce of it was carefully recycled and reused, coveted and hoarded. Here, it was a part of the decor.

The hallway ended in an open atrium. It was green and vibrant. Streams of water snaked through the air like constellations. The entire space was lit by a bright, wholesome light that felt almost like sunshine.

Bentley let out a low whistle. "You know, this is the first time I've actively wanted to move someplace we're raiding."

"Hell of a lot nicer than Albeni," Rid agreed, his tone awed.

I shut out their voices, lifting my Jackhammer and scanning for threats. We should have been under heavy fire right about then. But the only movement came from the impossible streams of suspended water.

"Werrel," I said, "what's going on?"

"I'm wondering the same thing," he said. For the first time since I'd met the mercenary, I detected a hint of worry in his voice. "Last time I was here—which, admittedly, was a while ago—this whole place was bustling with activity. Full of the fanciest-dressed bastards you've ever laid eyes on."

"Other teams aren't finding anyone either," Winter said.

"What's the call, boss?" Flint asked.

At the edges of the atrium, several hallways led in different directions. There was also what appeared to be a railcar system built into the wall on the right. I hesitated. This was a trap of some kind. It had to be. It was a dumb trap—there was no tactical advantage to be gained from letting us this far into the station unopposed—but a trap nonetheless. Maybe they wanted to split us up. But it seemed like an awful lot of effort to evacuate an entire sector of a citystation—especially a citystation populated by some of the richest people in the galaxy.

"Set up a chokepoint," I said. "Make sure we've got the

terminal secure. We move deeper in. Flint and Winter, I want each of you to take a combat team and start searching. See what you can find out and don't get too far away from each other. If you run into any resistance, retreat and regroup before engaging." I turned, pointing out two Jericho-clad pirates, one wielding an APMP-17 and the other a Jackhammer, as well as four Roamers in soft tactical exos and Werrel. I'd agreed to let the mercenary wear his armored exo for protection—he'd be no use to us dead, after all—but had refused to allow him to carry a weapon. "You all," I said. "With me and my crew."

"Where are we going?" Werrel asked.

I glanced towards the transit system. "You said that goes all the way to the administrative offices, right?"

Werrel grimaced. "I suppose I did."

I started towards it. "Then we're taking a ride."

The transit system was perfectly operational. Bentley seemed almost disappointed at how easily he was able to get it running.

"Literally just a press of a button," he said, settling awkwardly into one of the transit car seats. The sight of nearly a dozen men and women clad in armor stuffed into this elegant vehicle was vaguely amusing. Like we were embarking on the universe's most violent daily commute.

I pulled up my minimap on the Icarus's wrist computer, watching as the clusters of green dots gradually separated from each other. Seemed like every op I ran there were more and more green dots to keep track of. "Anything yet?" I asked into the comms.

"*Nothing,*" Winter reported.

"*Same here.*" Flint sounded vaguely annoyed, as if he'd been looking forward to a bloodbath. "*Plenty of loot, though. We're in some sort of fancy shopping center. Shelves are still stocked and everything.*"

I glanced out the transit car window. On Albeni 7, and every other station I'd visited, the transit systems operated in long, dark tunnels—focused simply on getting you to where you needed to go. This transit system seemed to take the long way around, giving us a tour of the station's dazzling architecture—and it was one hell of a tour. The room we were looking down into now was even bigger than the others we'd seen, and combined all of their features into one breathtaking space. Verdant plant life and cool blue water offered a pleasant contrast to the faintly luminescent white walls, ceiling, and floors. A large lake pooled out in the center of the room, before narrowing into a long channel, wrapping up the wall, and then spreading out around the transit car rail system. I found myself wondering what would happen if someone stepped out of the transit car right now. Would gravity pull them down to the floor? Or would they cling to the wall like the water?

Focus. I shook myself. We weren't here to gawk; we had a job to do. I tried my best to ignore the features of the room and scanned the floor far below for signs of life. Nothing. I felt as if we were traveling through some architect's concept video rather than an actual, lived-in station. It was all too pristine.

"Renault," I said into the comms. "What's the view from out there?"

"*Nothing out of the ordinary,*" he said a moment later. "*And still no traffic. Guess they're really enforcing that quarantine.*"

"We're not gonna get sick, are we?" Rid muttered.

"Not so long as you stay in your exos," I replied. "Besides—I doubt it's a sickness that led Vatheson to do this. I just... don't know what did."

"Once we're in the offices," Bentley said, "I'll be able to access the security feeds. That should give us at least *some* idea of where everyone went."

The transit car came to a gentle stop. I nearly jumped as a

pleasant, artificial voice gently announced, "*Now arriving at the administrative offices.*"

"Sounds good," I said to Bentley. I stepped up to the door, readying my Jackhammer. When it slid open, I was confronted by a long, empty waiting area. It was about the same size as the one I had battled through on Albeni 7, but the sheer elegance of this one put Albeni's to shame.

I stepped off of the transit car, cleared the corner, and then lowered my weapon as the rest of the team followed me. "Vatheson's office is just ahead," Werrel said. "I doubt we'll find him at this point, but we might at least—"

Movement.

A white rectangular cube, perhaps a meter across each way, moved silently into the room from a doorway, gliding effortlessly across the floor. A dozen weapons were raised at once, all pointing in its direction.

"Hold your fire!" I shouted.

Too late. A Jackhammer barked a single time. The shot missed, exploding against the wall behind the cube. The sound of the report was strangely muffled—something in the architecture of the room, probably. There was a metallic clinking sound as the ejected shell bounced across the floor.

The cube paused, then turned and started gliding towards us.

Dammit.

"What the hell is that thing?" one of the pirates hissed.

"Some kinda combat drone," his companion snarled.

"Get back." I waved them backward, stepping aside as the cube approached. "And hold your fire."

The cube moved silently into the center of the group, not seeming to be focused on any one person. I held my breath as I watched it come to a halt next to the ejected shell.

I took a step backward, bracing myself.

I half expected the cube to explode. Instead, it simply rolled over the shell, then continued moving silently through the room, taking the shell with it.

"It's a vacuum," Bentley said, voice drooping with relief. "A cleaning robot."

One of the pirates chuckled, lowering his weapon. "Well. That was a lot of worry over nothing."

"Don't stop worrying yet." I gestured for Werrel to lead us onward. He complied, keeping a wary eye on the cleaning robot as it happily scooted away. We pressed past it and into the larger office complex, clearing each corner of threats before proceeding.

"Looks like the security center is down this way," Bentley said as we reached an intersection. "If we want a chance of finding out what happened, that'll be it."

I hesitated, not liking the idea of splitting up any more than we already had, but finally nodded my consent. I pointed towards the four Vanguards who had come with us. "Go with Bentley. You too, Rid. Stay in touch. You feel anything's off at all, let me know."

They set out. Werrel continued leading the rest of us towards Vatheson's office.

"*Still no signs of life,*" Flint's voice said in the comms. "*Unless you count the cleaning robots. Damn things are everywhere.*"

Werrel finally stopped in front of a set of heavy black doors. "This is it."

I tried the access panel. Locked. Out of habit, I stepped back to make room for Rid, only to remember he'd gone off with Bentley.

"Your skeleton key's not here," said Shell, amused.

"He's not the only one who can get through a lock," I said.

She raised an eyebrow at me. "What's your technique?"

I activated one of my thermal blades. "The messy way."

A few minutes of cutting later, there was a heavy metallic thud as a chunk of Vatheson's door slammed to the ground, spraying drops of molten steel across the floor as it fell. I deactivated my blade, raised my Jackhammer, and stepped through the hole I'd made.

Vatheson's office was spacious, with a clean, minimalist design. In the center of the office was a wide, black marble desk with streaks of gold, with several guest chairs in front of it.

Behind it sat Adrian Vatheson.

It was a strange feeling, finally coming face to face with the man who had been the source of so many of my problems. The man who'd hunted me from Albeni 7 to the *Aboena*. The man who had blockaded the Albeni system foldgate and driven Sevani from her home. Since we'd stumbled into Vatheson's hidden Lifeblood stash he had been constantly in the back of my mind.

And now here he was.

Dead.

He looked like he'd been here for a while. His head was draped unceremoniously over the back of his seat, his hands sloughed at his sides. He didn't look like the unnaturally youthful man I'd seen in the video message he had sent to Sevani. He seemed ghoulish now, deflated, as if his body were trying to catch up to its age.

There was a small black hole in the center of his forehead.

"Looks like somebody beat us to it," Shell said, lowering her weapon.

"Yeah." I stepped around the table, getting a closer look at the corpse. There was another one of those cubic cleaning robots calmly moving back and forth over the space beneath the deceased system overseer. I was just glad the Icarus protected me from the smell. "Question is *who* beat us to it? Bentley—are you in the security center yet?"

"Yep. Just getting my bearings in here."

I looked up, inspecting the ceiling corners. I saw no sign of security cameras. "See if there's a video feed for this office."

"Yeah. One sec."

Shell stared sourly at the corpse. "I don't like this."

"Me neither." I glanced down at my wrist computer. The green dots that represented our fledgling army were getting wider and wider apart. "All units," I said into the general channel. "Pull in. I don't want us spread all over the damn station."

"Look at that." Shell pointed at something on the floor. I squinted down at it. Some object had been smashed on the floor, scattering hundreds of tiny fragments of itself. Looked like a wristwatch.

"Hang on," Flint said. *"I think I'm finally onto something. Check this out."*

My wrist computer dinged as the pirate sent me an image. I frowned. It looked like a massive pile of garbage. "What am I looking at?"

"Disposal center of some kind. This is where all the cleaning robots seem to be reporting to. Look closer."

Bentley's voice crackled in my ear. *"Hey. Um. We have a problem."*

I squinted closer at Flint's image. It didn't look like typical garbage. It was hard to make out what any of it was. As I watched, though, one of the cleaning robots approached the pile. One side of its cube opened, shoving out a pile of refuse it had gathered during its patrol. Most of it seemed to be clothing. Stained red.

Ripped.

My eyes widened. The entire massive pile of garbage was torn, bloody clothing mixed with discarded personal belongings. No sign of bodies. Which could only mean one thing.

Ah, *hell.*

"RIPPERS!" Rid spoke over Bentley, his voice loud and

urgent. *"There are rippers in the powercores! And now they're on the move!"*

I dismissed the image Flint had sent, resummoning the map of the station. I quickly identified the powercores, near the center of the station. Several green dots were in that area.

"All units," I said into the general channel. "Back to the ship. *Now.* There are rippers inbound from the—"

"WE'VE GOT RIPPERS!" a voice yelled in my ear. *"RIPPERS IN THE—"*

A green dot flashed red.

SIXTEEN

It was no more than a moment between moments, but for a split second I was tempted to panic. I felt all of the old fear rush back in an instant, clawing at me, fighting desperately to pull me back into that pit of dread and apathy I'd been climbing out of since the *Panama*. *You led them all here. Now they're all going to die. Because of you. Because of you. Because of—*

NO.

A way out. There's always a way out. I zoomed out on the holomap. More dots were already flashing red, spreading out from the first casualty like a disease in a crowd. I quickly assessed the terrain around them. If they stayed there, they'd get surrounded. And if they ran, they'd simply be chased down.

Only if they were alone, though.

"Flint!" I said. "Get your men out of there. Winter—create a chokepoint at the main docking bay we entered at. Hold the area so that Flint and his teams can come through."

"*On it,*" Flint's voice said, panting as he sprinted.

"What about us?" Shell asked.

"We'll take Vatheson's getaway ship," I said. "That'll be

safer than taking the transit system all the way to the docks. Bentley! Rid! Meet back up with us so we can get out of here."

"*Way ahead of you,*" Bentley gasped.

"Let's go!" Shell turned, ushering the rest of our team out the door. I didn't follow, though. Instead I found myself staring angrily at Vatheson's corpse.

All of this for nothing. The strings we'd pulled to get across the blockade. The casualties we were suffering right now as rippers harassed Flint's retreating troops. All rendered pointless because Vatheson couldn't even do us the decency of being alive. Without those warplans I'd have nothing to report to Nalis. Albeni 7 would be on its own. And then we'd all be screwed.

But dead men tell no tales, as they say. And Vatheson looked just about as dead as it was possible to be.

Base of the skull.

I grimaced, hesitated a moment longer, and then sighed and activated a thermal blade.

The implant might not work while Vatheson was dead, but I'd be damned before I walked away from this operation empty handed.

"*We're taking heavy casualties.*" There was an edge of panic in Flint's voice I'd never heard before. "*These rippers—they ain't normal rippers.*"

I frowned as I skidded to a halt with the rest of my group in the office complex atrium. "What do you mean? What's wrong with them?" A terrifying thought struck me. "Do they have wings?"

"*Wings? What? No. They just—UGH—they're armored. Biosteel coating their heads and torsos. Jackhammers only slow 'em down!*"

Bentley stared at the round object I was clutching in my hand. "I, uh, thought Renault said it didn't work if he was dead."

"We'll find out," I growled as I tossed Vatheson's decapitated head to him. "Catch. I'm gonna need my hands."

Bentley scrambled to catch the grotesque souvenir. He looked down at it, disgusted, and I couldn't blame him. But that implant was the reason we were in this mess. No way I was leaving it behind.

"You sure you don't want me to have a weapon?" Werrel asked.

"Just get us to that ship," I growled.

I tried to work through it all in my head as Werrel led us towards Vatheson's getaway ship. Enhanced rippers—but not ultrarippers. Clearly they were the reason that the station was empty—they'd cleared the entire place out. Except that there'd been none of the signs of forced entry to the station you'd expect to see in a structure that had been hit by ripper drop pods.

"Rose! Do the scans show—"

"*They don't show anything,*" she said.

Another sign these weren't the Paragon's usual rippers. And this was an important Paragon station, anyways. There'd be no reason for them to hit their own. Had the rebels set us up somehow? This hadn't been a random attack, after all. Vatheson's body was the only one we'd been able to find. Had the Paragon taken out Vatheson? They were the only other ones who—

A chill ran down my spine.

No. They *weren't* the only other ones who could want Vatheson dead.

"Almost there!" Shell's voice pulled me back into the present moment. I shook myself, quickening my pace to catch up to the rest of the group. Right now it didn't matter who'd done this. What mattered was getting off of the station. I glanced down at my wrist computer's map, forcing myself to ignore the blinking red dots and focus on the way out. Once we got to the getaway ship, we could circle around to the docks and help repel the flood of rippers. The entrance to Vatheson's secret docking port looked like it was just around the corner. One of the exo-clad mercenaries pressed ahead of Werrel in desperation to escape.

Something *yanked* on my brain.

Look, I know that doesn't make sense. But it's the best way I can think of to describe it. It felt like some sort of tiny, psychic hook got lodged into my brain and tugged—gently, at first, and then more insistently with each passing moment. It wasn't an emotional feeling, like back in the Vanguard when SkyCom would activate our regulators and deliver a rush of ignicerin or frigicerin. It felt more like using my neurointerface. An extra sense, pointing me towards... what?

I tried to ignore it as we ran. Tried to push the bizarre sense to the back of my mind. But it only grew stronger. As if I was being reeled in by that increasingly strong psychic hook—or whatever was on the other end of it.

The yank grew stronger. It was hard to focus. I almost stopped running to try to orient myself, certain I was having some sort of psychological breakdown. Damn inconvenient timing, that was for sure. Before I could, though, I heard a terrified shout from ahead of me.

"RIPPERS! THEY'RE—"

Gunfire. A cry of pain. The exo-clad pirate who'd been at the head of our group staggered backward, flailing at the blur of movement clinging to his back. Werrel scrambled backwards, eyes wide. The pirate reached back and grabbed at the thing on his back to pull it off of him. There was a flash of black steel and a spray of sparks. The pirate's forearm thudded to the floor.

He froze, facing us, blood shooting in rhythmic pulses from his severed arm. His body jolted as the points of three claws emerged through the front of his visor. He stood in place for one long, terrible moment, then sagged forward and landed face first on the floor with a metallic thud.

The ripper that had killed him was still crouched on his back, looking up at us. Flint had been right. This wasn't any regular ripper. Its chest, shoulders, head, and legs were covered by a thick, carapace-like layer of jet-black biosteel. The biosteel had a strangely liquid appearance, as though it rippled when the ripper moved. Or was I imagining it?

The yank on my brain intensified. I realized with a start that it was linked to the ripper. A psychic thread stretched between us. I could sense the ripper's perception scanning my team as it decided which target to leap at first. Could feel the deep, insatiable hunger that drove every action it took. The never-ending desire to consume.

Its focus latched on to Shell, near the front of the group. It leaped at her, claws outstretched.

I lifted my Jackhammer and fired. I wasn't the only one, either. The hail of bullets struck the ripper hard enough to fling it backward against the wall.

"It's not dead!" a pirate shouted. "Keep shooting!"

The ripper braced itself against the gunfire. My eyes widened as I saw bullet after bullet slam into its carapace and bounce harmlessly off. The biosteel shimmered and rippled with each blow.

I felt the yank again. The ripper's simple intent.

Wait.

Feed.

The yank split. No, not split—I could still feel the psychic pull towards the lone ripper curled up against the wall. There were just *more* of them now. Dozens of tiny little pulls on my psyche coming from the same direction the first ripper had come from. Towards where we were trying to go.

"Stop!" I yelled. "*Stop!* Conserve ammo!"

"How's it still moving?" growled a pirate, reloading his Jackhammer.

"Back." I gestured down the hallway the way we'd come from. "To the transit. This way's blocked."

Bentley stared at me. "How can you tell?"

I grimaced towards the lone ripper, stepping closer. It was uncurling now, studying us. I could feel its hunger slowly overwhelming its patience. How the hell was I supposed to explain what was happening to me? I hadn't even had time to process it myself. And the other rippers were getting closer. Hundreds of tiny little yanks on my brain. A rolling tide of endless hunger.

"Just do it," I growled.

"Come on." Shell carefully backed up, keeping her gun trained on the ripper, then turned and broke into a sprint once she was past me. The others followed suit.

"You're coming with us, right?" Rid asked.

"Yeah." I didn't take my eyes from the ripper. It crept slowly forward, eyeless gaze locked on me. I wondered if it could feel the pull. Did it know what I was thinking too?

No time to figure it out. I could sense the horde approaching. I backed up a few steps, then turned and broke into a run.

"Flint! Winter!" I panted. "Status!"

"*Our position is established,*" Winter said. "*We have not yet seen the enemy.*"

"*Well, get ready, cause we're bringing them with us.*" Flint sounded winded, his voice rattled by Jackhammer fire. "*I've lost half my boys. These things are damn near unkillable.*"

I glanced over my shoulder at the lone ripper I'd left behind. It hadn't moved, just sat there watching us go. Tendrils of smoke drifted upward from where the explosive rounds had struck its armor.

Wait.

Feed.

"Weren't there any signs?" Shell panted. "Usually rippers

leave a whole lot of mess. Blood and shredded clothing at least. The place was spotless."

Bentley pointed at one of the cubic cleaning robots as we sprinted past it. "That's why. We saw them. In the security footage. Cleaning up."

A grim thought. The same servants who constantly silently tidied up after you would mop up your blood and shredded belongings as if they were any other regular piece of waste. They weren't made of organic material, so the rippers would have ignored them during their feeding frenzy.

The yank grew stronger. It was pulling to the side, now. Fear gripped at me. They were trying to cut us off. I saw the atrium up ahead. Which meant that the transit station was just beyond it. Once we were safely aboard we could assess the best destination. I burst out of the hallway into the atrium, pivoting to the right towards the station.

The yank was stronger. Closer. They were almost on us.

I skidded to a halt.

"Go!" I waved my team past me. "Get it started!"

Movement. A ripper burst into view at the far end of the atrium, tearing towards us.

Feed.

I aimed at its legs and fired a burst. There was a flash of sparks as rounds struck biosteel—then a spray of black blood as one hit home. The ripper buckled, tumbled in a swirling mass of razor-sharp claws, but then it was back on its remaining feet and charging at me again within less than a second.

Feed.

The ripper tensed to leap—then there was an echoing boom and chunks of flesh sprayed out behind it. The ripper's twitching form skidded on the floor until it thudded into my leg. I glanced over my shoulder to see a pirate lowering a smoking APMP-17. He nodded to me.

I looked down at the ripper. I could see the gaping wound in the back of its head already started to pull itself back together. The APMP-17 was designed for piercing armor—the bullet had passed right through the ripper without transferring nearly as much energy as a Jackhammer round would have. I took aim and fired a single Jackhammer shot directly into the bullet hole.

"Heal from *that*," I growled.

Feed.

I looked up.

Feed. Feed.

More rippers. A trickle at first, one at a time charging through the doorway. Then a flood, with each one tugging at my mind.

Feed. Feed. Feed.

I fired a concussion grenade into the middle of the biggest group I could see, staggering them, then turned and sprinted. Bullets cracked the air around me as my crew laid down suppressive fire.

"Where are we going?" Bentley asked frantically as he started manipulating the transit system control panel.

"Anywhere but here!" I shouted, sprinting towards him. There was a rush of heat and a whoosh as a pirate fired an incendiary grenade then retreated with me. We scrambled onto the train.

"Close the doors!" I shouted.

"I'm trying!" Bentley squeaked. "They're too damn *safe!*"

A ripper leaped through the flames enshrouding the doorway, fire clinging to it as it charged towards us. It staggered as rounds struck it but carried on.

The transit doors started to close. Slowly. So. Damn. Slowly.

The ripper leaped. I leaned back and kicked it in the face, sending it spinning away. A pirate at my side fired several Jackhammer rounds into its exposed back as it tried to recover.

Feed. Feed. Feed. Feed. Feed.

More rippers burst through the flames, ignoring the heat, rushing towards us, their minds full of one thing only.

Feed. Feed. FEED. FEED. FEED. FEEDFEED-FEEDFEED—

The doors clicked shut. I staggered backward, my mind reeling. I felt as if my psyche were being torn into tiny pieces.

"Dammit!"

I looked up, clenching my teeth through the pain in my head, to see three claws punch through the door. They started tearing downward, leaving a set of long, jagged grooves in their wake.

"Bentley!" I yelled. "We need to—"

The transit started to move. Again, slowly. So. Damn. Slowly.

Another set of claws punched into the carriage from the ceiling. Then another, through the wall. A window shattered as a ripper smashed its head through. A pirate slammed the butt of his Jackhammer into its head, repelling it, only to scream as a tailspike shot through the window a moment later, piercing his chest and dragging him forward.

The train moved a little faster. A long arm reached through the rapidly growing hole in the doorway, clawing at us, only to vanish in a spray of blood and a hail of Jackhammer rounds. I heard a screeching sound as rippers clinging to the side of the transit were thrown off. One managed to keep its grip, hacking furiously at the door—until the transit passed into the narrow tunnel. There was a sickening crunch as the creature was caught between the vehicle and the wall. The pirate who'd been stabbed in the chest slumped to the ground as the tail that had skewered him was torn off by the tunnel entrance.

FEEDFEED... FEED. FEED. Feed. Feed...

I breathed a sigh of relief.

Rid looked down at me. "Hey. You alright?"

"Yeah." I panted, staring at the broken windows. "I... something is..."

I trailed off.

Feed. FEED. FEEDFEEDFEED—

The yank pulled my brain back the direction we'd come—to the cars in the back of the train.

"They're on the train!" I yelled.

The door sealing our compartment from the next thudded, bending inward. There was a metallic shrieking sound as claws began to tear through it.

"Cover the door!" Shell yelled.

Gunfire. Bursts of sparks. A shape surged through the doorway, leaping onto a pirate who'd been kneeling over his fallen comrade. He threw it to the floor and began pummeling it, screaming, only for another ripper to sink its claws deep into his back.

Green dots, flashing red...

There was a deafening boom as somebody fired a concussion grenade through the doorway into the next car.

FEEDFEEDFEEDFEED

I gritted my teeth and shook my head. *Come on, Lax. Pull yourself together. Your team needs you.*

Another scream as one of the Roamers was skewered by a tailspike. Shell bellowed and chopped down on the tail with her knife, severing it. The ripper the tail had been attached to focused its attention on Shell.

FEED.

I pushed myself to my feet, discarding my Jackhammer.

Your CREW needs you.

The ripper leaped. I charged forward, intercepting it and slamming my shoulder into its midsection. Sparks flew as the Icarus's conduction armor repelled the creature's claws. It spun through the air and crashed into the horde behind it.

I activated my thermal blades and waded into the mass of

carapace and claws, bellowing, hacking. These rippers were resistant to the blades but not invincible. Their shells boiled into steaming, fizzing black goo as the white sheets of energy cut through to the flesh beyond.

"How"—I sliced off a ripper's head, sending its body twitching to the floor—"far"—I grabbed another ripper by its arm and flung it like a club, knocking back several of its siblings—"are"—a ripper scurried past me, anxious to get at my companions behind me and I hacked through its unarmored back—"we?"

"Just a few minutes!" Bentley called.

FEEDFEEDFEED.

A ripper leaped onto my back, sparks flying as it tried to dig through my armor. It jolted and fell as explosive rounds struck it. I finished it off with a downward slice, then turned, grabbed another offending ripper by the arm. I flung it through the nearest window. The glass shattered and the ripper was sucked into the tunnel beyond, making a squelching sound as it was crushed against the wall.

FEEDFEED... Feed...

Wait.

I held up a blade, ready for the next attack, but it didn't come. The remaining rippers began to slowly retreat, crawling backward through the ruined doorway to the carriage they'd attacked from.

"What the *hell?*" One of the pirates lowered his APMP, staring at them. "These rippers ain't right."

It was easy to forget that most people had never so much as heard of a nonstandard ripper.

"They're not ultrarippers, though," Rid said.

"The hell's an ultraripper?" the pirate asked.

"I'll explain later," I said. "Bentley, where are you taking us?"

"I figured we wouldn't want to fight through the horde that

Flint and Winter have attracted," he said. "And we don't want to bring *our* horde to them, either. So we're going to a different terminal. I've already radioed Rose with instructions on where to meet us."

"Good work," I said, not taking my eyes from the doorway. I could feel the rippers lurking just out of sight beyond it.

Wait... wait...

The tug pulled at me from the other direction. Faintly, but growing stronger. I glanced back over my shoulder. I could see a glimmer of light through the tunnel, brightening by the second.

"Ambush," I said quietly. "As soon as we're out of the tunnel."

Shell looked sharply at me, but said nothing. Instead, she aimed her Jackhammer towards one of the windows. The pirates exchanged confused glances then followed suit. I squared up against the doorway, moving closer to it so none of the rippers would be able to slip around me.

Wait... wait...

The yank intensified again, pulling my brain in all directions. Light burst through the windows as the train shot out of the tunnel. We were traveling around the edge of another one of those massive spaces. Water wrapped up around the length of the wall beneath us in a bizarrely beautiful, gravity-defying lake.

FEEDFEEDFEEDFEED

The light was blotted out as dozens of rippers slammed into the windows. Seemed like they'd been waiting above the tunnel exit. Most of them fell off, vanishing from sight, but others managed to hold on to the side of the speeding train, their claws puncturing its sides.

Gunfire erupted throughout the car, blasting away the rippers that were trying to force themselves through the windows. The rippers who'd been waiting in the car behind us made another attack, rushing me all at once. I fired an incendiary grenade into the middle of them. They pushed through the flames, but I could hear their flesh sizzling as they threw themselves at me. The chokepoint meant that they could only attack me a few at a time, while the rest were forced to wait and melt.

"We're almost to another tunnel," Bentley called out. "Just a few more—"

"*Stopping*," said a pleasant robotic voice overhead.

The train came smoothly to a halt.

"Bentley!" shouted Shell. "What did you do?"

"I didn't do anything!" Bentley screamed. He gave a groan. "You have *got* to be kidding me. It's the automatic safety brake. It stopped for a ripper on the track..." He trailed off, then gulped. "A *lot* of rippers."

FEEDFEEDFEED

"Can you get it going again?"

"I'm trying," he growled. "Not sure it's going to matter. There's a *lot* of them."

I could tell. The incessant pulling on my brain had become a raging storm, tearing me apart from the inside. They were coming by the hundreds from every direction.

Every direction except one.

"We *need* a plan!" Werrel screamed as he desperately kicked a ripper away from him.

I punched a ripper in the face, flinging it backward into the roaring flames, then turned and glanced out the window and over the edge of the massive drop below us. A ripper tried to leap through, only to be thrown back over the precipice by a barrage of explosive rounds. It didn't fall like I'd expected it to, though. Instead of going straight out and over, gravity pulled it sideways, into the water clinging to the wall below us, where it tumbled to a splashing halt.

I looked back up and around. We were moments from being overwhelmed here unless the train started moving again.

"Bentley, hurry up," I growled. "I'll see if I can distract them."

"*How?*" Rid yelled, his voice jolting as he fired a Jackhammer into the horde with minimal effect.

I took a deep breath, then charged forward through the flames engulfing the next car. I dispatched a few rippers with ease as I strode towards my target—the door.

"Where's he going?" one of the pirates shouted in confusion.

The door was locked—which made sense, seeing as it was currently hanging over a wide precipice. I made a quick cut through the lock, kicked it open, and then stepped out.

"LAX!" Shell screamed.

Gravity took me. My stomach dropped. For a sickening moment, the only comforting thought I could conjure was that falling to my death would still be better than being eaten alive by rippers.

But then gravity changed.

Down became sideways. My momentum kept me going and I skipped once on the surface of the water like a stone before splashing to a halt. Steam shot into the air around me as my thermal blades boiled the water. I groaned and pushed myself to my feet. The stream was about a meter deep, coming up to the shins of the Icarus. As I straightened I wobbled—I could feel another source of gravity tugging my head towards the floor far below. The gravity generators keeping me bound to the wall had a very limited reach. I held myself at a slight crouch to avoid being pulled off balance.

I turned, trying to orient myself. From my perspective, the wall that the tracks had led us along was now the floor, while the train itself was sitting on its side, embedded in a groove in the now-floor—along with the swarm of rippers attacking it. I turned towards it.

FEEDFEEDFEED

"Please clear the tracks," the transit system PA called in a cheerful voice, barely audible over the sounds of gunfire.

I took aim at a cluster of rippers gathered in front of the train and fired a concussion grenade from my shoulder-launcher. Any glass that hadn't been broken in the front of the train exploded into tiny shards of light. Rippers were flung in all directions—some violently against the wall, while others went sailing over my head to the lake far below us. Others were caught by the gravity generators, splashing into the water next to me.

I felt the intent of the rippers swarming the train shift from my team to me as they realized that I'd be the easier target. Alone and exposed.

FEED.

"Come on, you bastards," I growled.

One of them carefully reached over the side of the precipice, realized that gravity would hold it, then grew emboldened and lurched over the edge, charging towards me. The rest of the rippers followed suit, splashing through the water.

FEEDFEEDFEEDFEED

Awareness of them filled my brain. Overwhelmed me. I wanted to scream.

I took a deep breath. Stood my ground, letting the rippers do the work of crossing the ground towards me. The water slowed them down significantly.

Breathe.

Focus.

Think.

None of the other Vanguards with us seemed to be experiencing the strange sensation. Which meant that it wasn't the rippers that were strange. It was me. This was being caused by what the Stranger had done to me. Was this how Cairn had controlled the ultrarippers? Had being "Chosen" made us like them?

The rippers splashed closer. I fell into a low crouch, blades held at the ready, steam rising all around.

Instead of trying to push away the hundreds of tiny threads yanking on my brain, I focused on them. Felt them. Listened to them.

The first ripper came within tail-striking distance. I felt its raging, endless hunger focus on me. But the hunger was more complex than that. It wanted to feed. But before it could feed it needed to kill. And at this distance the quickest way to kill was—

Its tailspike leaped at me, aimed straight at my head. But I was already ducking, flicking my wrist upwards. The biosteel spike whistled through the empty air above my head, then fell thrashing into the water as my thermal blade sliced cleanly through the tail.

The ripper surged forward, unfazed. It tried to leap at me only to flounder in the water. I took a long stride forward and lashed out with my other blade, striking it just below the neck and hacking its head off.

It sagged beneath the water's surface, black ichor mixing with the clear liquid.

The rest of the horde surged just behind it.

I grinned and charged.

We danced through the water, the rippers and I, until its surface was coated black with their blood.

With so many rippers attacking at once I couldn't possibly make sense of every string pulling at my brain. But I learned how to single them out. How to prioritize them. In ordinary circumstances they'd have killed me long before I had time to work out the brutal patterns. But I had both the Icarus and the water to protect me. Normally, fighting rippers in an open space like this would have been suicide. They'd have attacked from not only every side but from above—leaping, striking with their tails. But they clearly had no idea how to handle the water. They floundered constantly. Each time one of them tried to leap it would stumble. When they turned too quickly they'd slip beneath the surface. I wasn't sure if they could drown or not, but so long as they were beneath the water, they weren't fighting me.

I felt none of the battle joy that usually filled me in moments such as these. All of my focus was on those tiny, invisible psychic threads, connecting me to the rippers. Listening. Responding. I knew when a ripper behind me was about to strike with its tail. Knew when one was about to dive at my legs. I knew when and where each strike was coming, and I responded to all of them before they could happen, intercepting them rapidly and precisely.

Well—I tried to, anyways. The water might've worked to my advantage, but I wasn't much more used to fighting in it than they were. More than once I struggled to stay on my feet as I sidestepped an attack. The floor beneath the surface quickly became cluttered with writhing bodies, nearly tripping me multiple times.

Two rippers attacked at once from opposite sides. I killed one but missed the other and it managed to crawl onto my back. Gravity pulled sideways at it, threatening to topple both of us into the water. Before I could reach up to pluck it off, I heard a gunshot. The ripper went limp and fell sideways, too high for the gravity generators to grab it. I glanced towards the train to see Werrel leaning out of the window, aiming an APMP he'd probably taken from one of the fallen pirates down at us. For just a moment, I worried he'd turn the weapon on me. Instead, he fired again and another ripper twitched and fell.

"I've figured out how to override the emergency brake system," Bentley said in my ear. *"But it might take me a few more minutes."*

"Do what you've gotta do," I growled. Another tailspike shot at me. I twisted out of the way, caught it in one gauntleted fist, then *yanked* on it, pulling the ripper into the air. Its trajectory suddenly changed as it left the range of the gravity generators, spinning through the air towards the lake far below us. I didn't have time to watch it land, though, several more rippers already assailing me. I killed the first few. Another ripper managed to score a strike on my side, sparks flying as the Icarus repelled the attack. The ripper staggered and toppled into the water as a hail of Jackhammer rounds struck it a moment later.

I had a quick moment to breathe, assessing the situation. It was difficult to tell through the curtain of steam that I'd created around me, but the horde's numbers seemed to be growing. With the other teams evacuated, my squad was the sole focus of every ripper on the station. More specifically, *I* was their sole focus. It didn't matter how efficiently I killed them—they'd keep coming, growing more innumerable by the second. If Bentley didn't get that train moving soon, it wouldn't matter if the emergency brake system was deactivated or not; there would be too many rippers on the tracks for the train to plough through.

Feed.

I pivoted and bisected a ripper as it leaped at me from behind, then started fighting my way towards the train. It'd be a hell of a dumb way to go out if I wasn't ready when they were. The rippers had started dividing their attention between us, with some of them going after me while others targeted the rest of my team in their increasingly battered-looking fortification, but there was no sign that their resolve was weakening in any way. They'd keep throwing themselves at us until either they were all dead or we were...

"*Holy hell,*" Rid breathed. "*Look down.*"

I glanced over my shoulder and felt my eyes widen. Far below us, at the bottom of the lake-covered wall, rippers were swarming through a large area that appeared to have been once dedicated to lounging civilians, rushing towards us in greater numbers than I'd ever seen—even in the war. The floor was completely covered in them—a writhing, glinting mass of black.

I cut down one ripper and punched another, knocking it down and stomping on its skull. It writhed furiously underwater as I hacked at several more, leaving a trail of steam in the wake of my blades.

"*Almost there,*" Bentley said. "*I think.*"

I shoved away the ripper I'd been pinning underwater and continued striding towards the train, one arduous step at a time. Between the water and the constant stream of rippers surging towards me it felt like I was trudging upstream through a powerful river.

Closer.

FEED.

I hacked off a ripper's claws as it reached for me.

Closer.

FEED. FEED.

One ripper grabbed me from behind while another prepared to strike at my face. I twisted, putting the ripper on my back directly in the path of the tailspike.

Closer.

FEEDFEEDFEEDFEED

Rippers latched on to my legs. My arms. I tried to shake them off. Tried to predict their movements. But there were just too many. Too much for my weary brain to process at once. I hacked one ripper in half, peeled off another and tossed it aside. Then something slammed into my side and I staggered, tripped over a pile of still-thrashing dismembered corpses beneath the water, tried desperately to catch my balance, failed, and let out a cry of dismay as I toppled backwards.

Everything went dark, my vision obscured by the thick layer of ripper blood coating the surface of the water. I thrashed and fought as the rippers piled on top of me. I wasn't sure exactly how the Icarus would fare submerged beneath water, but it surely couldn't make it any *more* effective.

A ripper bit down on my left wrist, its biosteel teeth finding purchase in one of my blade emitters. The left thermal blade flickered and died.

I twisted, trying to shake off the rippers. They twisted with me and I found myself being rolled over until I was lying face down, the rippers swarming on top of me, clawing furiously at the armor on my back. The armor covering the ultracell that powered my exo. A spike of dread shot through me. If they got through that armor and punctured the ultracell, the explosive would evaporate me and the rippers and probably take out the rest of my team too.

I pushed up with my arms and managed to break free of the water, shaking off several of the rippers clinging to me. I made a wide swipe with my remaining thermal blade only for it to flicker and die partway through cutting a ripper in half.

Luckiest man in the—

A ripper lunged towards my face. My vision went dark again as its teeth sank into my visor. The force of the attack shoved me over backward again, pushing both of us beneath the surface of the water. I tried to grab it and pull it off only for more rippers to latch on to my arms—then my legs.

ARMOR COMPROMISED, a set of alarmingly red letters flashed in the corner of my HUD.

I felt something sharp and cold pierce my side.

Rippers like to start down here, where it's all soft and warm, then work their way up.

FEEDFEEDFEEDFEEDFEEDFEEDFEEDFEED

I'm sorry, Sev.

Something—some*one*—slammed into me. Hard. Hard enough to dislodge the rippers that had latched on to me. The teeth that had dug into my visor loosened, the ripper letting go briefly, then vanished as a steel fist slammed into it, sending it spinning away.

Hands grabbed me, pulled me up out of the water. I blinked. Rid was standing over me, pulling me up to safety.

"Come on!" he shouted. "You're not dying here!"

FEED.

I felt the ripper's intent before it even started to move. Saw it leap, clearing the water in a spray of black ichor. Saw the deadly arc of its trajectory. Knew that there was no possible way I could stop it in time. I tried anyway, reaching for Rid to shove him out of the way of those flashing claws.

I was too slow.

But Shell wasn't.

A Jackhammer roared. The ripper jolted as it was thrown off of its trajectory by a spray of explosive bullets. Shell splashed to a halt next to us, expertly reloaded her Jackhammer, and then fired another burst into a group of rippers as they charged us. The bullets didn't kill them, but they knocked them back into the water long enough to give us a brief reprieve.

"Get up!" Rid pulled me to my feet. We started staggering towards the train.

"*Ready to go!*" Bentley shouted.

I felt a ripper preparing to attack behind me and whirled, hitting it with a right hook that sent it spinning away. We were so close. Now we just needed to figure out how to mount the edge of the precipice and escape the clutch of the gravity generators.

Shell fired a few shots at a cluster of approaching rippers while Rid awkwardly climbed out of the water and over the edge of the cliff. I ducked out of the way of a tailstrike and desperately shook at my right thermal blade emitter. It didn't start up. I contented myself with punching the nearest ripper in the head, sending it floundering backward.

"I'm up!" Rid shouted.

"Go!" I yelled at Shell.

Rid helped her over the edge while I fended off more rippers. The rest of the men on the train were offering support fire now and I'd probably have been overrun without them.

"*Rippers on the train!*" Bentley screamed. "*We need to move NOW!*"

I remembered how slowly it moved at first. "Start it!" I bellowed.

There was a whirring sound as the train powered up. I dove for it, grabbing on to the edge of the makeshift doorway I'd cut for myself earlier. There was a scraping sound as my exo was dragged along the edge of the precipice.

"Grab my hands!"

I locked grips with Shell, then Rid. They started pulling. A ripper started yanking my legs in the opposite direction. I kicked desperately at it. The train was picking up speed. I saw the edge of another tunnel rapidly approaching.

"*Get. Off. You. Stupid. BASTARD.*" I punctuated each growled word with a kick. The ripper didn't budge. I felt a cold pain lance into my calf.

Shell bellowed and threw all of her weight backward. I activated my thrusters. The extra boost gave me just enough momentum to clear the edge and land with a grunt face first inside the train car. The ripper clinging to my legs was dragged up with me, half of its body still dangling over the edge. I could feel its triumph as it reached for me.

FEED!

We entered the tunnel. There was a metallic shrieking sound as the lower half of the ripper's body was caught between the car and the wall, bisecting it. The upper half of its body was left on board, writhing, trying to regrow itself.

FEED. FEED. Feed. Feed... Fe—

Shell pressed the barrel of her Jackhammer into the unarmored small of its back and pressed the trigger. Black viscera splattered across her exo. The ripper went limp.

I panted, sitting up. "Bentley. How're we looking?"

"*There are still a lot of rippers blocking the rails, but now that I've shut down the emergency brake system the train is just pushing through them.*" I heard several crunching noises to corroborate his statement. He continued. "*Should just be a few minutes to the terminal. After that... well. I guess we'll have to see.*"

The hooks tugged on my brain a little less insistently now, and they grew softer still with each passing second as the train carried us away. After a minute or so they faded altogether.

"I think we're clear," I said wearily.

Shell and Rid glanced uncertainly at each other, then down at me.

"You're sure?" Rid asked.

"Yeah." I sagged onto my back, groaning. "I'm sure. Bentley, do you still have Vatheson?"

"*Uhm... yeah. The part of him you gave me at least.*" He hesitated. "*Although, I still don't know why.*"

I glanced at my wrist computer, and the string of red blinking dots that marked the bloody retreats both my squad and Flint's squads had made.

"Cause this can't all have been for nothing," I said wearily.

SEVENTEEN

Sev's holographic face raised an eyebrow as it regarded the object I was holding up to the camera.

She cleared her throat. "Didn't we need him to be, you know... *alive?*"

I lowered Vatheson's head. It was looking quite a bit more worse for wear than when I'd first chopped it off of the station overseer's body. "Yeah. That didn't turn out to be an option."

I explained what had happened. Well—almost everything. Some of it I *couldn't* explain. What the hell was I supposed to say about the rippers? That strange tugging sensation. The way I'd been able to see into their minds. To know where they were, and what their intent was. I was almost convinced that I'd finally snapped and lost my mind... except for the fact that it had *worked*. I'd been able to use those sensations to predict and outfight them.

But that was something to discuss later, and in private. I needed to loop in Ramar, too. I still wasn't sure I trusted him, but if anyone had a chance at helping me understand what I was experiencing, it was him.

Or the Stranger.

"Alright, then," Sev said, nodding slowly as she tried to take it all in. "What comes next?"

"Once we're back, we'll see what we can manage with the head," I said wearily. "Then we'll contact the rebels again."

"How do we know they didn't have something to do with this?" Renault asked suspiciously.

"There's no reason they wouldn't have just told us if they'd already killed him," I said. "Plus..."

"Plus what?" Shell asked as I trailed off.

"Plus, I think I know who's behind this," I said. "We know this wasn't a random attack. They were after Vatheson specifically." I hesitated, glancing around at the faces staring at me. "I think it was Divinity."

There was a long silence.

Sev swore softly. "How sure are you?"

"Just a hunch," I said. "But... it's the only answer that makes any sense. The only reason he went after us so aggressively in the first place was to try to cover his ass from them. Looks like he didn't cover it well enough."

Renault's brows were furrowed. "They certainly weren't ordinary rippers. Those things tore apart half of my troops. And they've got plenty of experience dealing with rippers."

"Plus there was no sign of a Paragon attack," Rose said. "No pods attached to the hull of the station. None of the usual signals we could detect."

I eyed Werrel, who was sitting across the bridge from us. He looked shaken—had looked that way ever since we'd escaped the station. When he saw me looking at him, he only shook his head. "You really think I'd have agreed to go forward with all of this if I knew those things were on the station? If I knew something, I'd tell you. I've never seen rippers like that in my life."

I believed him. Putting himself in the path of so much danger would've been a decidedly un-mercenary thing to do. I turned back to Sev as she spoke. "If it *was* Divinity," she said, "why attack Vatheson? I mean—yes, obviously he had betrayed them. But if they have this kind of power—enough rippers to take out an entire station, and apparently get the Paragon to quarantine it in the aftermath—why not use that power against the rebels?"

It was a damn good question. By attacking the Paragon, the Sovereigns were really attacking Divinity. Why *wouldn't* Divinity do everything they could to retaliate? From what I could tell so far, it seemed like Divinity was just... letting it happen. Manipulating from the shadows had always been their style, but I had a hard time believing they were so ready to let the Paragon go.

Then again—nobody knew better than me that the Paragon was a fickle servant. Project Eden—their attempt to steal the Divinity's Corporation's technology and turn it to their uses— was proof enough of that.

"I don't know," I admitted. "Either way, though, we've got the implant. Now we just need to see if it's actually got the Paragon's battle plans on it." I grimaced at Vatheson's head. "If we can get it out."

"Do you have a plan for that?" Sev asked. "Because if we can't get the intel the rebels want, then we're right back at square zero: stuck in the Albeni system with no allies beyond our mismatched little coalition." She grew thoughtful. "Though we *do* have one less enemy now, I suppose."

"Yeah," I said. "But seeing him offed like this makes me *more* nervous, not less. And yeah. I've got a plan. Or an idea, at least." I grimaced. "I don't like it, though."

Sev raised an eyebrow. "Do tell."

I sighed. "We're gonna go talk to our resident resurrection expert."

. . .

The journey back felt longer than the one there had, for some reason. Maybe it was the sense of smoldering resentment filling the ship. We'd lost a *lot* of men in the scramble to escape the station, and their surviving friends naturally blamed me. I did too. The only comfort I could take was that I couldn't imagine our casualty numbers would've been much better if we'd been facing the odds we were initially expecting. It wasn't much, so far as comforting thoughts went, but when it came to war you took what you could get.

Fully half of the pirates who'd gone aboard had been lost to the rippers. Flint had barely managed to make it back to the defensive line put up by Winter and his Roamers. The Roamers had taken a beating of their own, though they hadn't been caught in the open like the pirates had been.

Werrel's cover—and another healthy bribe—allowed us to get past the blockade once again, slipping back to the Albeni system. I breathed a bit easier once we were through the Albeni system foldgate. And a bit worse when I heard the news that the Paragon had just dropped a swarm of rippers on Ebisu. It was no wonder we hadn't seen a blockade outside of Ebisu's foldgate —they were already being pummeled from within. Despite a shaky start, it seemed like the Paragon was well on their way to winning the second Last War.

Which made it all the more important that we figure out how to get the Paragon's battle plans out of the decapitated head that was now wrapped up and sitting in the *Orpheus's* cold storage unit.

That thought churned through my mind as we flew through nullspace towards the *Aboena,* which was waiting near Albeni 7. The thought of going back aboard the ancient ship turned my stomach sour, but there was no way around the fact that if there was anybody who *might* be able to help us with our bizarre predicament, it was the Stranger.

I distracted myself by forcing my thoughts to other places.

More specifically, to the battle behind us. There was a lot to process there, but I forced aside my memories of the rippers and the strange tugging on my brain to focus on an equally surreal realization: that I was a rebel now.

"Just like you wanted," I muttered, staring at Nadus's empty Jericho armor in the *Orpheus's* cargo bay.

I suppose it comes down to semantics—some folks might've said I'd been a rebel for a long time before that moment—but somehow, to me, that was the first time it felt *real*. Every time I'd fought the Paragon before Boadecia, I'd been doing it out of pure self-gain or self-preservation. I couldn't deny that there was still some of that now—after all, we'd all die if we didn't win this fight—but I also couldn't deny that, for the first time, I felt a surge of genuine excitement at the prospect of fighting back against the Paragon. Pride in knowing that this was a battle worth waging.

Nadus had always admired the rebels. I remembered the way he'd watched the news back on Albeni 7, longing in his voice as he'd questioned why we weren't out there with them, trying to make a difference. Trying to undo all of the atrocities we'd committed during the war—or, at the very least, to find redemption from them.

Well, now I was. I still didn't trust Nalis Khendar, but I believed her when she said she wanted to beat the Paragon. For the first time in my life, I was fighting for a truly worthy cause.

I put a hand on the cold exterior of Nadus's armor.

"See you on the other side," I whispered.

Movement. Somebody was entering the cargo bay, interrupting my reverie. I turned to see Flint.

"Oops." He grinned. "Didn't mean to disturb your peace. Was just looking for a bit of that myself."

I grunted.

He reached into his pocket and withdrew an eerily familiar looking object through my brain. He held it up. "Want a hit?"

It took effort to push away the sudden rush of longing that filled me upon seeing the can of frigicerin in his hand. But I did.

"No," I said.

He shrugged. "Suit yourself." He found a place to sit among the stacks of cargo boxes. "Hell of a fight, huh?"

I studied him. He tried to hide it, but I recognized the emotions that were raging within him. The haunted look in his eyes. The slight tremor in his fingers as he lifted the can. He was watching his men get picked off one by one during the retreat through Boadecia. Trying to drive away the sound of their screams echoing in his head.

"Yeah," I said. "Sorry about your men. That was a rough spot you were in."

He chuckled hoarsely. "Yeah. But we've been in worse, eh?" He pulled the sleeve of his shirt back, revealing the metallic glint of his shoulder port. "At least this time SkyCom isn't yanking our strings back and forth."

I frowned. "What you said, before we took the Albeni 7. About everyone being puppets. You really believe that?"

He shrugged. "Sure. We might not have our regulators anymore, and hell, we might even be fighting against the Paragon. But we're still dancing to *somebody's* tune. Just don't know exactly whose it is."

I studied him. "Why fight, then? If you really think it's all out of your hands."

"Because that's all I know how to do." A soft hissing sound filled the air as he inserted the can into his shoulder port. His eyes started to go blank. "Only way not to be a puppet is to cut the strings," he said, voice growing quiet. "Only way not to hear the tune... is to close your ears..."

His head lolled to the side. I stared at him a moment longer, briefly tempted to unplug the can for his own good. But just looking at him made my own shoulder itch. I wasn't sure if I could resist the lure of oblivion once I felt the can in my hand.

So I left him there, sparing one final glance at his gently moaning form as I went up the stairs.

No heroes. Just puppets.

He was wrong. And dammit all if I wasn't going to prove it.

"I still can't believe you guys were here for so long," Sevani muttered as we walked down the primary corridor of the *Aboena*.

I grunted my agreement. "This is a pleasant stroll compared to most of the ship," I said, quietly enough that our escort of Roamers—Zeka walking calmly ahead, while several Marshals led by Tetra marched carefully behind—couldn't hear us. Hopefully. I knew all too well how much pride they took in their ancient artifact of a homeship.

"You get used to it," Ramar said on the other side of me. He grimaced. "Eventually."

The *Aboena* hadn't been kind to any of us, but Ramar had received more than his fair share of punishment. Well—considering that he'd led us there in the first place, getting Nadus killed in the process, maybe it was exactly the right share. But it was hard to hold too heavy of a grudge against him considering the literal torture that Cairn had put him through. He still walked with a slight limp, and I'd have bet good money that his body was coated with scars.

Bentley scoffed from behind us. He made the last member of our little embassy. "Yeah, you're also the one who volunteered to go into exile on a battlecruiser full of rippers."

I frowned upwards as I noticed something that had most certainly not been present the last time I'd been here. I pointed it out. "The Stranger's work is spreading, huh?"

Zeka glanced briefly at the large blood-red vine clinging to the ceiling above us. "There is no longer any secrecy aboard the *Aboena*," she said flatly. "And as we have discussed, we must drastically increase our production of whitefruit. The Stranger's court is not big enough."

Bentley raised an eyebrow. "Got a name for it now, eh?"

"That was always the name," said a Marshal behind us.

"Oh." Bentley fell silent.

As we passed by the vine, I felt a slight tug on my mind, followed by a spike of panic. Rippers. Somewhere close. It felt different, though. Gentler. Less focused. I realized with a start that it was coming from the vine itself. There was no accompanied intent, just a vague awareness.

I eyed Ramar. He was looking straight ahead. I wanted him here to help negotiate with the Shapers since he'd spent more time around them (more *conscious* time, at least), but I also hoped to steal a moment alone with him to discuss this strange new evolution in my... abilities. Every time I remembered them, all I could think about was Winter's final warning to me. *Despise the gifts you have been given. Reject utterly the Stranger's commands. They have no regard for you—or for any of us.*

Those gifts had saved my life—along with the lives of those I cared about—several times over now. But I couldn't help but feel as if I were simply taking out loans, falling deeper and deeper into debt with an untrustworthy creditor.

Sev put a hand on my arm. "You alright?" she whispered.

I couldn't help but stare at her. Stare—and feel terrified.

For the first time since Kess had died, I was happy. Every night for the last nine years, I'd fallen asleep tossing and turning as I dreaded the misery of another day alive. Every morning I'd rolled out of bed exhausted, wanting nothing more than to retreat into the sweet oblivion of a can and shut out the world and all of its horrors. Watching out for my crew had been the only thing that kept me going.

Now, even when we were apart, I fell asleep happy, knowing that I'd see her again. I woke up invigorated, ready to face the challenges of the day armed with the knowledge that she'd be by my side through them. But at the back of my mind, I knew that I was living on borrowed time. One way or another, this was all going to end. I'd have to pay out that debt somehow. And I had a lurking suspicion that when the time came, the only choice I'd have in the matter would be how many of my loved ones paid it with me.

I realized I'd been staring at Sev again, for who knew how long. I forced a grin onto my face. "Yeah. I'm fine."

When we finally entered the court, we were ushered onto the staircase that ran up the center of the massive glowing tree. I felt my heart rate increase as we ascended. That insistent tugging on my brain was there again, yanking me upwards towards the Stranger's chambers. The chambers I'd been rebuilt in. A chill ran down my spine as I focused on the yank. Was that... the Stranger I was being pulled to?

There was no time to answer the question. The Shapers did not take us up to the Stranger. Instead we were led into a lower room. Dark, with rust staining the walls and floor. Several Shapers were already gathered around a table, waiting for us.

One of the Shapers spoke. "We have been told that you have a need for our skills, and that it is in service to the Great Crusade, Chosen."

I grimaced. "Well, I don't know about that second part, but... yeah. What do you make of this?"

I placed Vatheson's head gingerly on the table.

The circle of Shapers stared silently at it.

One of them cleared his throat. "The Stranger can work all manner of miracles, yet I fear that some things are impossible even for them."

I gritted my teeth. "Look, we don't need him to be fully reanimated or anything like that. We're not trying to bring him back to life. But the implant will only power on if it's getting a signal from his brain."

Another Shaper walked slowly around the table, studying the wreckage of the man who until very recently had been our most dangerous enemy. After a few days wrapped and refrigerated, he looked more like a grotesque movie prop than a part of a real human being.

"We will help you," she said after a moment of silence. "Under one condition. We demand first access to whatever information is recovered from the implant."

I frowned down at Vatheson, then turned to Zeka. "I wasn't planning on hiding it from you. We just need whatever intel Vatheson has on the Paragon's battle plans."

"You shall have it, then." Zeka gingerly lifted the head.

"What exactly are you hoping to learn?" Ramar asked.

Zeka held Vatheson up, looking into his half-open eyes. "This man had connections to Divinity. Deep ones, we believe. We will see what other secrets of theirs he has stolen."

A chill ran down my spine as I thought about the prospect of the Stranger getting their hands on even more advanced Divinity biotechnology. The Stranger hadn't hesitated to use the ultrarippers—I doubted they'd be any more reluctant to weaponize whatever horrible secrets were hiding in that implant.

Bentley must've seen my discomfort, because he cleared his throat. "Well. I mean—while we'll certainly need the help of you and your"—he gestured vaguely in the direction of the court—"benefactor, you'll also need my assistance. Once the implant is powered, I'll still need to breach it. So, the truth is that we'll all have access to the information at the same time. No secrets. That sound good to everybody?"

No secrets. I almost laughed. Zeka didn't look amused, though.

"This arrangement will suffice," she said.

I nodded. "Alright. Let's do it, then."

· · ·

"We are ready," Zeka said, standing over us.

"Finally." Bentley groaned and stretched, getting up from where he'd been resting in the grass beneath the massive whitefruit tree. I was jealous he'd been able to sleep. I'd been too distracted by the incessant tugging on my brain. It came from all directions, but especially from the Stranger's chambers. I'd spent the hours we'd waited doing everything I could to ignore it —mostly unsuccessfully.

"Let's go see what they've cooked up," I said, helping Sev to her feet. We followed Zeka up the stairs again and into the same room where we'd met the Shapers earlier.

"I'm sure it's not that bad," Bentley said as we walked through the doorway. "The worst it can be is *son of a—*"

Bentley leaped backward, colliding with the wall and putting a hand over his chest.

I had to keep myself from doing the same thing when I spotted it. Or *him*, rather. Vatheson was alive—or as close as he was going to get to it, anyhow. His eyes were open now, twitching back and forth as if he were trying to get his bearings, but they still had that emptiness that death always brings with it. His facial muscles clenched and relaxed in a steady, heartbeat-like rhythm. A strained gasp escaped his lips with each contraction. The Shapers had propped his head up in the center of the table and placed a white bandage over the wound in his forehead, which was now soaked red.

Perhaps most disturbing, however, were the tubes protruding from the base of Vatheson's cauterized neck. They were glistening and fleshy, pulsing as they pumped *something* into Vatheson's head. I followed the long, carefully coiled mass with mounting horror until my stomach dropped as I saw what was plugged into the other end.

One of the Shapers—face still hidden behind the helmet of his black visor—was lying on a table next to the one Vatheson's head was on. The front of his exo was gone. His chest had been peeled open, his innards exposed as they did their writhing work. The coil of fleshy tubes, suspended from a hook above him, separated, each tube latched parasitically on to a separate organ.

Bentley sagged to the floor, gagging. Sevani's mouth fell open as she stared at the dissected Shaper. Even Ramar looked perturbed.

"What..." Sevani whispered, "the *hell*... did you do?"

Zeka glanced at her companion lying prone on the table. "What was necessary. If you would like, we can cover him."

Ramar stepped closer to the tables, studying first the head, and then the Shaper. "Is he... Well, obviously he's *alive*, but is he..."

"Conscious?" Zeka stepped next to the scientist. "No. And he will recover, if that is what concerns you. When our work is done, he can be repaired."

"I don't..." Bentley looked up, blanched, then stared down at the floor, heaving. "Ugh. I don't feel very good."

Once again, I found myself fighting the urge to follow his example. I've seen bodies torn apart in a thousand different ways—hell, I've been the one doing the tearing half the time. But there was something about the cold, clinical nature of this that twisted my insides. I looked from the grisly sight to the line of Shapers standing in the shadows at the edges of the room. One of them was still holding a scalpel. Not that I'd have been able to tell through the visors, but they looked completely undisturbed by the fact that they had just cut open the chest of one of their companions and hijacked his vital organs in order to briefly give a semblance of life to a decapitated head.

Then again—Zeka claimed the man would recover. What *were* these people? The Stranger's test subjects? Were they Chosen like me? Infused with the Divinity gene so that they could be cut apart and put back together? Was... was this what lay in store for me?

Zeka nodded to another Shaper, who rummaged through a drawer before pulling out a sheet and draping it gently over their companion. "I apologize," Zeka said. "I forget how... easily unsettled the Untouched are."

Sev took a deep breath, eyes still fixed on the form beneath the sheet. "You do this often?"

"Not this specifically." Zeka gestured towards Vatheson's grotesquely animated head. "But it presented a welcome and interesting challenge. Now: may we commence?"

I managed to tear my eyes away from the gruesome spectacle before me long enough to glance down at Bentley. He was still crouched on the floor, supporting himself against the wall with one hand.

I took a deep breath, forcing my insides to settle. *Relax. You've seen far worse than this. Not weirder, but worse.*

I leaned over Bentley, placing a gentle hand on his shoulder. "You alright?"

"Alright?" He looked sharply up at me. "*Alright?*"

I nodded. "Yeah."

He narrowed his eyes. "Why are we working with these people?" he hissed. "They're monsters!"

I gritted my teeth, looking back up at the ring of Shapers. "Yeah. But they're what we've got. You need a drink? To step out for a minute? There's no rush." I glanced up hesitantly at the pulsing tubes. "At least, I don't think there's a rush."

"No." Bentley groaned, grabbing on to my arm, and letting me help him to his feet. He took several deep, steady breaths. "There is a rush. The sooner I finish, the sooner we can get out of this damn place."

I squeezed his shoulder. "Can't argue with that. What do you need?"

"Just space."

Very pointedly *not* looking at the tubes or the cloth-covered Shaper, Bentley pulled up a seat and placed his datapad on the table near Vatheson's head. Then he dug through his bag for a moment, emerging with a keyboard and a set of cables. He set up the keyboard, then plugged one end of the cable into his datapad and took a deep breath, staring at the head. "Can someone..."

None of the Shapers moved. I grimaced and stepped closer to the table, gingerly placing my fingers on the sides of the head. The moment my fingers touched Vatheson's skin he made a sharp gasping sound, causing me to jump back.

I glanced back at Sev and Ramar, half expecting them to laugh at me. They looked every bit as perturbed as I was—a fact I found strangely comforting. I took a calming breath, then grabbed the head—firmly this time—and twisted it so that the back, and the port contained therein, was facing Bentley.

The head was disturbingly warm to the touch.

"Your turn," I gasped to Bentley.

He clenched his teeth, then carefully lifted the flap of artificial skin that protected the port and pushed his cable into it while I held it the head in place. Vatheson made a jagged croaking sound, as if he were trying to scream but couldn't summon the breath for it. Bentley cringed—I did too, for that matter—but focused his attention on his datapad.

With the head firmly in place, I stepped back beside Sev. She had her arms wrapped around herself, her eyes flitting warily around the room.

"You alright?" I asked softly.

"Yeah. You?"

I nodded grimly. "Been better. But yeah."

"When you said the Shapers might be able to help, I pictured them... I don't know, running an electrical current through Vatheson's brain or something." Her eyes slid to the pulsing tubes. "Not... whatever nightmare *this* is."

"Really makes me grateful I was unconscious when they worked on me," I muttered.

Sev paled. "Don't even bring that up. But..." She looked around. "Is this where..."

"No." I looked upward. I could still feel that hook tugging on my brain. Maybe it was just how horrifying the contents of this room were, but I'd gotten better at tuning the feeling out while still being aware of it. It was gradually becoming a sixth sense, as natural as using my neurointerface. "That was in the Stranger's room, above us. I kinda figured the Stranger would work on this, too. I guess they don't need them for everything, though."

"Alright," Bentley said, in that half-muttered tone I'd learned meant he was talking to himself as much as the rest of us. "Progress. But how do I... hmm." He raised his voice slightly, sounding much more confident now that he was engrossed in his work. "Alright, the device is working, so, good job on the mad scientist stuff."

I leaned forward. "Does that mean you can read it?"

"No," he said idly.

My heart sank. "Oh."

"Oh! Sorry." Bentley shook himself with a chuckle. "Yes. I can read it. It's just decrypted, so it will take some time. So, uh..." He glanced around with a grimace. "Make yourself at home, I suppose?"

EIGHTEEN

Time passes differently in a dark room full of cultists and dismembered body parts.

I wanted desperately to leave the room and wait outside, but I knew that leaving Bentley alone with Vatheson and the Shapers would be about as profound a betrayal as humanity had ever seen, so I stayed put next to Sevani. Ramar stood nearby, studying the scene with fascination.

I felt the pull above me shift. Realized that the Stranger was moving across their room. Then back again. An idea occurred to me. With the rippers, I'd been able to feel their intent. To know what they wanted. Would that work on the Stranger?

I closed my eyes. Focused on that yank pulling my brain upwards. Tried to follow it—to listen to it. *Give me your secrets, you stubborn, mysterious—*

Hate.

The feeling was so overwhelming that I nearly staggered backward. It wasn't a single-minded emotion like the hunger I'd detected from the rippers. The Stranger's hatred was patient where the rippers' had been hasty. Vast and complex where it had been simple. But every bit as overwhelming.

I opened my eyes, pushing away the thread. Idiot. *Idiot.* What had I been thinking? I still didn't understand these abilities. I'd hardly had a chance to discuss them with anyone. Did the Stranger know I'd just tried to peer inside their brain? Or—an even more harrowing thought—were they currently peering into mine?

I glanced towards Zeka. She was standing in the same statuesque pose she'd assumed when Bentley started working. After a brief moment of hesitation, I approached her.

"On Boadicea, I could... *feel* the rippers," I said quietly. "Like a string connecting all of us. I knew where they were without needing to see them. Knew what they were going to do before they did it."

Zeka nodded. "You are beginning to understand. The gifts you have been given are far more than merely physical. You are a part of something greater now."

I scoffed. "Heard that one before. Ramar told me that. After we escaped the *Revelation*. Before I got dragged into all of this."

She looked at me. "And when you denied that truth. How did it result for you?"

I glanced over at Ramar, who was still enraptured by Vatheson's reanimated head. Thought about Nadus, giving me one last grin before Cairn bashed his skull into bloody pulp. *Thud, thud, thud...*

Not well.

"I talked to one of Cairn's old lieutenants," I said. "Winter. He told me that the Stranger's 'gifts' drove Cairn mad." I eyed her, for all of the good it did me. Her posture didn't so much as shift as she listened. "He said that I should reject them. That the Stranger doesn't give a damn about any of us."

"The Stranger's motives are their own," Zeka said. "And as for Cairn, the Stranger did not drive him mad. *You* did."

I stiffened.

... crunch.

"You slaughtered his only brother." Zeka might as well have been reading from a technical manual for all the emotion in her voice. "The one person Cairn truly cared about. It was more than he could bear. We had thought his mind was strong, but you shattered it. You proved him unworthy."

"His brother helped kill my—"

"I did not ask for justification. You did what was necessary." She looked at me. "You proved that you were the better weapon."

I narrowed my eyes. "I'm nobody's weapon."

Zeka looked away disapprovingly. "Self-denial will only make you suffer. You—and everyone you love."

"Sounds an awful lot like a threat," I growled.

"It *is* a threat," she said. "But not from me. Or the Stranger. It is a threat in the same way gravity is a threat. You are falling, VanDunn, and the Stranger has given you wings to fly. To reject their gifts is to reject life."

I glanced over at Sev. She was standing alone, looking very small and vulnerable in the darkness.

"So let's say I accept them," I said softly. "What happens then?"

"Then you become the Stranger's chosen weapon," Zeka said. "And they use you to right all the wrongs of humanity."

"That's... ambitious," I managed.

Zeka scoffed. "As always, you underestimate the Stranger's power. Their reach. You believe that you are fighting against the Paragon. I tell you that the war you are engaged in is far, *far* greater. It stretches beyond either of our lifetimes, Chosen, in both directions. But we are blessed to be weapons in the Stranger's hands."

"I might be more likely to agree to any of that," I said, "If you'd tell me who this grand crusade of yours is against. And what exactly you want me to do about it."

"Soon." She folded her arms. "Very soon. You are not prepared yet. But rest assured that you have served the Stranger's purpose very well already. The pieces are falling into place."

Bentley spoke up before I could respond. "Alright," he said. "We've got access. Let's see what secrets Vatheson's got on his mi... uh, what, uh... never mind. Just come look."

The rest of the group began to gather around him. I stayed put for a moment, staring at Zeka. She seemed to have little interest in furthering the conversation, however. She was already moving gracefully towards Bentley.

The Stranger's chosen weapon. Sounded an awful lot like being a puppet to me.

I sighed and followed Zeka.

"Let's see what we're working with here." Bentley activated the mini holoprojector attached to his datapad, throwing the data into the air. There was a *lot* of it. "First things first, I'm transferring it into another drive so we can look at it later without all"—he grimaced at Vatheson's head—"*this*. But in the meanwhile..."

"This is a treasure trove," Ramar said, voice awed as he scanned the list of files. "At least if any of these are actually what they claim to be."

"Alrighty," Bentley said. "Let's see. We've got... not interesting... not interesting... not interesting... that's... uh, interesting, but not appropriate *or* relevant... here we go."

Bentley opened a folder titled NAVY. He gave a low whistle.

"Bingo," Sev said.

The folder contained hundreds and hundreds of files. Some of them looked like threat assessments of various systems. Others were Paragon command protocols. There were lists of chains of command, with dossiers for each member outlining potential security risks. Battle plans providing recommendations for where certain forces should be deployed in response to various threats. Bentley gave a cackle of delight as he found a file containing various Paragon decryption keys.

"To think that this little bastard was just... sitting on all of this," Sev said, shooting a disparaging look at Vatheson.

I let out a low whistle as Bentley opened a file labelled FOLDGATE. It seemed to be in-depth schematics. "Tuck that one away for later," I said.

"Ah!" Bentley gave a triumphant cry. "Here we are." He pointed towards a folder labeled STRATEGY, SOVEREIGN SYSTEM COUNTEROFFENSIVE. "Shall we have a look?"

The plans were long and detailed. I skimmed most of it, eyes searching for the primary order. Finally, I found it.

"Looks like they're planning on attacking the Moses system next," I said. "In about two weeks."

Sevani frowned. "That seems like a long ways in advance to plan something like that. Are we sure they'll stick to it?"

"No," I admitted. "But as long as we've got something to give to the rebels, it's a start."

"Wait." I noticed another folder, labeled LOGS. "What's this?"

"Let's find out." Bentley opened the file.

The folder contained thousands upon thousands of hours of video footage, divided into hour-long clips. The most recent showed what appeared to be Vatheson's office from behind his desk. The perspective was strangely lifelike. My eyes widened as I realized why.

"This is Vatheson's eyewitness of the last moments of his life," Bentley said, apparently coming to the same realization as me.

We all fell silent as we watched. There was something eerie about the prospect of witnessing life from the eyes of a dead man. I found myself feeling strangely guilty, as if we were performing a gross invasion of sacred privacy. Never mind that the man whose privacy we were invading was a bastard who had tried to have us all killed, and whose decapitated head was now lying on a table just a short distance from me.

The eeriness went away quickly though, replaced by boredom. I'd expected something... I don't know. Exciting, at least. Surely the final moments of a man like Adrian Vatheson would be dramatic. But he was just... sitting there. Reading reports on his computer. They weren't even particularly exciting reports.

"Screw this," Bentley muttered. He skipped ahead through the footage, ignoring several hours of monotonous office work.

"Slow down," Sev said. "We'll miss it."

"We'll go back," Bentley said. "We just—"

Several figures appeared in the center of Vatheson's vision.

"See?" Sev said. "Go back!"

Bentley rewound it. Played it back.

Vatheson was reviewing a report. Profit margins or something. A pleasantly soft female voice emanated from his computer. "*Sir, there's somebody here to see you.*"

I could tell from the way the image jolted that Vatheson sat up abruptly. Irritated, maybe, or confused. "What? I have no appointments. Emmel, you know better than—"

"*Sir, I think... uhm, I think they're from Divinity.*"

Vatheson froze. He stayed that way for a long time, long enough that Bentley checked to make sure the recording hadn't glitched. Emmel apparently thought something was wrong too. "*Sir? I can send them away, I just thought you would—*"

"No." Vatheson breathed in deeply. "That's alright. Send them in."

"*Right away.*"

Vatheson took a few moments to compose himself. Deep, calming breaths. Straightening various items on his desk. At the last moments, just as footsteps were sounding outside the doorway, I saw him glance sharply towards his secret door that I knew led to his escape ship. When the gentle knock came, I saw the moment of deliberation. Stay, or run.

I knew what he would choose, of course. But I still found myself holding my breath along with him as his eyes flashed back and forth from across the room. Finally, he gave a heavy, defeated sigh.

His hand slipped beneath the table. I heard a light click as he opened a hidden compartment. He glanced briefly down to check that the pistol he drew from it was loaded. Then straightened his position one more time and pressed the button on his desk that unlocked his office doors.

The first four figures to pass through the doors were tall, muscular men wearing dark suits. They didn't look like Vanguards, but they certainly didn't look like regular humans. Something was... *off* about them. I couldn't tell exactly what. Maybe it was the cold, inhuman way they looked around the room, their eyes passing right over Adrian Vatheson—one of the most powerful men in the Paragon—as if he wasn't there. Or maybe it was the way they moved. Each movement seemed restrained, as if it took active effort to keep themselves from bolting across the room.

"Gentlemen," Vatheson said, voice polite but cautious. "Please. Sit down. To what do I owe this unexpected..."

A fifth figure stepped into the room. Sev, Bentley and I all strained forward.

The most remarkable thing about the man was how... *un*remarkable he was. Just a middle-aged man with graying hair. Looked to be in his mid-fifties, perhaps. Couldn't have been taller than six feet. Nowhere near as fit as the other men accompanying him, and nowhere near as well-dressed, either. Rather than a suit, he simply wore dress pants and a button up shirt, with the sleeves rolled back.

"Nice station you've got," the man said, looking around and nodding his head approvingly.

Vatheson cleared his throat. "Thank you."

"Thanks for being willing to see me." The man started strolling slowly around the office, Vatheson's eyes never leaving him. "I don't normally make visits like this myself. By which I mean—*never*. But, these are exciting times, so I thought I'd make an exception."

"Moderately, yes." Vatheson's voice was flat. "But I've seen lots of time. The excitement wears off."

I'd forgotten about that. Vatheson was something like eighty years old, though he looked no older than twenty. The power of technology and all the money you could ever want.

The man in his office, though, wasn't impressed. He gave a flat chuckle as he came to a halt in front of a shelf containing dozens of random objects. They'd looked like garbage to me when we'd been in those same offices not so long ago. "Lots of time, huh? Cute." He hefted an item from the shelf. I had to squint to see what it was. A watch—an old analog one. I could tell Vatheson cringed as the man's fingers touched it. "Please be careful, that's from—"

"Earth." The man held it up. "I know."

"*Old* earth," Vatheson corrected. "Pre-exodus."

The man studied him, his eyes vaguely amused.

"You don't know who I am, do you?" he finally asked.

Vatheson's eyes flicked from him to his guards, then back. "I'm afraid not. Except that you are here on behalf of the Divinity corporation." He leaned back in his chair. "Which I welcome, of course. I've never had anything but mutually productive dealings with your company, so I am excited to hear what you have to say."

The man studied him a moment longer, eyes glinting with amusement, then chuckled again.

"I'll give you this much," he said. "You're the most fun kind of stupid."

Vatheson stiffened. I saw his arm tense beneath the table.

"You see, there's the *normal* kind of stupid," the man said, crossing the floor to the center of the office and settling into one of the chairs there with a grunt, "and there's the fun kind. The normal kind of stupid is just... well. Everybody. *Normal* people, you know? Making normal mistakes. Living their stupid normal lives. But... they're boring."

He held the watch about a foot off the floor, then dropped it. It hit with a clunk that made Vatheson flinch.

"They're not smart enough for their stupidity to make any real kind of splash," the man continued, noting Vatheson's consternation with a smile. He leaned over to the pick up the watch from where he'd dropped it. It seem unharmed. "But every now and then, there's a guy like you." He wagged the watch at Vatheson. "The fun kind. Smart enough to climb..."—he raised the watch—"... so..."

He raised it again, until it was high above his head. "*So* high."

There was a long moment of tense silence.

"Or," said the man, "at least, what you *think* is so high. And then—when your stupid finally shows—"

He tossed the watch upwards. Vatheson leaned forward in his seat, watching as it spiraled through the air, spinning, spinning, spinning—crunch.

Bits of glass and brass scatted across the floor like shrapnel from the world's most insignificant grenade.

Beside me, Bentley flinched right along with Vatheson.

When Vatheson's gaze finally moved from the wreckage of his watch to the mysterious visitor's eyes, dragging all of us along with it, we found no more amusement. Just cold appraisal.

"I—" Vatheson gulped. "I'm not the one you want. Maren Sevani took your goods."

I let out a sharp, involuntary hiss. Sev glanced briefly at me, then back to the footage.

"I don't *care* about the goods, Adrian," the man said. "I care about *principles*. We had a *deal*. A proper, laid out deal." He sighed, shaking his head. "But then, those don't seem to mean as much as they once did."

Vatheson's hands were trembling. "We can still deal. Let's make a deal. Surely there's some mutually beneficial arrangement we can come to."

The man shook his head. "I'm afraid we're well past that point, Adrian. You're not being lifted anymore. You're spiraling downward. You have been for some time, even if you didn't realize it. This is the floor."

Vatheson gulped. "Names. I have names. So many. Information. Blackmail. I can help you beat the Sovereigns. I—"

The visitor perked his head to the side, his amused smile returning. "You think I *need* your help with a thing like that?"

Vatheson blinked. "I... but..."

The man's smile faded into disappointment. He sighed. "Perhaps you're the boring kind after all. Do you think it was some sort of *mistake* that I stopped backing the Paragon? Some massive oversight that the ultracells, and the rippers, and the Lifeblood, simply stopped arriving one day?"

"I don't understand," Vatheson whispered.

I glanced at my companions. None of them seemed to understand either. I sure as hell didn't. But it clicked for me just a moment before the man said it out loud.

Nalis had said the Sovereigns had a benefactor. That money had to come from somewhere.

A cold sense of dread coiled up in the bottom of my gut.

No. Please, no.

The man leaned forward.

"I *own* the Sovereigns, you idiot," he snarled.

Vatheson chose that moment to draw his pistol. I couldn't tell if he intended to use it against the man or on himself. Either way, it made no difference. The moment his hand moved, one of the suit-clad men leaped towards him so quickly the footage made him look like a blur. One moment he was standing on the opposite side of the room; the next, he was standing beside Vatheson, one hand firmly gripping Vatheson's wrist.

One of the other bodyguards drew a pistol. I felt an eerie sense of familiarity as I stared down that endless black hole.

The man sighed. "Goodbye, Adrian Vath—"

The footage went black.

A long moment of silence.

Bentley swallowed. "I'm sorry, did he just say that Divinity..."

"Divinity is the Sovereigns' backer," Sevani said, her voice weak.

I felt a rush of fury. "Khendar. That lying piece of..."

"She didn't lie." Ramar sounded utterly exhausted as he sagged back in his seat. "Well. Not explicitly. She said the Sovereigns' benefactors were anonymous. Which, clearly, they are. And when you asked her if she was *worried* about Divinity, she simply said that they would not pose a problem." He gestured futilely at Vatheson's head. "Clearly, this was why."

Zeka was watching me. Staring at me. She leaned in close.

"*This* is your purpose," she whispered. "*This* is the Stranger's Crusade."

"Maybe..." Bentley hesitated. "Maybe that's not so bad. I mean, things will at least be better without the Paragon, even if Divinity is still around. I mean, they wouldn't be in charge of *everything*, right?"

"So long as Divinity exists," Zeka continued, "Your fight will be futile and empty. Only the Stranger has the power to defeat Divinity. And only by serving them—by being the weapon you were always meant to be—can your life mean something."

Silence. Zeka continued staring at me. I wished, desperately, that I was naïve enough to agree with Bentley. That I could just pretend that this changed nothing. But I knew the truth. Zeka was right. As long as Divinity existed, nobody would truly be free. No matter how hard we fought the Paragon—even if we defeated them—no system would truly be independent. Divinity would continue pulling the strings from the shadows, as they had been all this time. And we'd all continue dancing to them.

A galaxy of puppets.

NINETEEN

"Alright, look." Bentley sounded exasperated. "Here are the options. Either we follow through on the deal we made with the rebels, give 'em the info, and help them win the war, or we do nothing and the Paragon probably wins. Either way, Divinity stays in charge. But if the Paragon is defeated, then at least things are *better*."

"Sure," Rose said. "For a little bit, at least. And then one system decides that they don't wanna dance to Divinity's tune anymore. And the rest of the systems have to gang up on them or something. I don't know. But it won't be *good*." She waved a hand vaguely towards the blackness of nullspace outside of the *Orpheus*'s window. "This is *Divinity* we're talking about. They're basically behind every single evil thing out there. In what world would letting them stay in charge possibly be *good?*"

"I didn't say that it would be *good*," Bentley snapped. "I said it will be *better*. And right now I think that's about all we can ask for. Obviously, I wish there was a different way. But clearly there isn't. Divinity's got everyone in a checkmate. Hell— they're on *both* sides of the chessboard."

I stared at the floating image in the center of the *Orpheus*'s bridge. The foldgate schematics. If it hadn't been for the subject being so hotly debated, it would've felt like old times. Just my crew gathered on the *Orpheus*, along with Sev and Ramar, who were watching me in silence, while we traveled back from the *Aboena* to Albeni 7.

Rose's and Bentley's arguments faded into the cacophony of white noise that was my brain. I couldn't disagree with either of them. Bentley was right. Even with Divinity still pulling the strings from the shadows, humanity *would* be better off for being rid of the Paragon—or for having it cut down to size, at least. But Rose was right too. It was easy to attribute all of the horrible things that had happened in the Last War—all the awful things *I'd* done—to the Paragon. But Divinity had been behind all of it. Funding every bullet I'd fired. Every ripper I'd seen tear through an innocent civilian.

Including my old crew.

Green dots, flashing red...

My heart rate quickened.

Including Kessa.

I'm sorry.

A can. My shoulder itched desperately. I clenched my eyes shut.

We had a good run...

"Maybe the Sovereigns don't even *know* it's Divinity who's paying them," Rid mused. "I mean, Nalis *said* they were anonymous, right?"

"It's possible," Sev admitted. "But it doesn't change the fact that Divinity is behind them. The end result would still be the same."

Bentley resumed pacing back and forth. "I *still* say it doesn't make any sense. From Divinity's perspective, I mean. They control *everything* through the Paragon. They can do whatever they want. Unspoken rulers of humanity. And now they're paying a bunch of rebels to undermine their own puppet government? What possible advantage do they get from that?"

"Retribution," Ramar said.

All eyes turned to him. It was the first time he'd spoken since we'd boarded the *Orpheus*.

He let out a long, haggard sigh. "The Paragon was Divinity's weapon. Forged to allow them to rule the galaxy, as you say. But, as the Last War drew to its close, it became... self-aware, shall we say. It began to have desires of its own."

My eyes widened with realization. "Project Eden."

He nodded. "The Paragon wanted us to reverse-engineer the rippers so that we'd no longer be dependent on Divinity for them. You know all too well how that went. If I and the rest of the Penitents hadn't intervened, they'd have dumped the ultra-rippers on Brahma—and, stripped of the careful checks and balances Divinity had programmed into the rippers, they would have spread, and spread, and spread. That didn't happen, of course, but I doubt that's what matters to Divinity."

"They found out, somehow," I muttered.

Ramar nodded. "It seems difficult to believe otherwise. The Paragon did their best to cover it up, of course, but... well. It's hard to hide from Divinity."

"That guy *did* mention that deals aren't worth much these days, or something like that," Bentley said. He furrowed his brows. "Who *was* he, anyways?"

Rose ignored Bentley, focusing her attention on Ramar. "So you think that this—all of this, the war, and everything—is just Divinity *punishing* the Paragon for breaking their deal?"

"I can merely theorize," Ramar said. "It's probably more complicated than that, of course. Maybe Divinity intends to *replace* the Paragon altogether. Or maybe they intend to use them both simultaneously. But the truth is..."

He stared down at the floor.

"What?" Shell demanded.

"The truth," Ramar said bleakly, "is that it doesn't matter."

Silence. Empty and bleak and unbelieving.

"Of course it matters," Rose insisted. "It matters because..." She looked around for support. "Because..."

"It doesn't matter," Ramar said firmly, "because no matter what the details are—no matter *how* Divinity intends to use the Sovereigns—the fact remains that they *are* using them. Which renders this entire exercise in resistance futile. We're not rebels, boldly fighting for our freedom and independence. We're just puppets who don't even know it. Dancing to a tune we can't even hear. And if we keep on dancing now that we *can* hear it..." He gritted his teeth. "Then we're no better than the Paragon."

I stiffened. Tried to find a retort. Tried to find some reason to disagree.

I couldn't.

Ramar rose from his seat. "I'm sorry. This isn't helpful. I need to rest." He walked to the hatch, then disappeared from sight, leaving silence in his wake.

Rid swallowed. "So... what now?" He looked from me to Rose. "Surely we don't just... give up?"

I expected Rose to leap to agreement with him. But she just stared at me.

I kept on looking for something to say. Some way to reassure them that this fight was meaningful. I was the leader, right? I'd led this coalition into this mess. But all I could think about were the words I'd said in this very bridge only a week or so ago, right before we'd attacked Albeni 7.

If we're no better than the bastards we're fighting... then I just don't see the point in any of this.

No. That wasn't true. We *were* better than the Paragon. Weren't we? We were trying to do the right thing. Trying to protect people. We...

No. Not if we were working for Divinity, we weren't.

Flint's burned and twisted face swam through my mind. *There are no heroes. Just puppets.*

"I don't know," I whispered.

"Hey."

I lifted my eyes from the floor of my room to see Sev standing in the doorway, watching me. She looked... good. Tired, but good.

"Hey," I said.

She studied me a moment longer, then sat down on the bed next to me.

"I hate this," I said, my voice sounding flat and dull in my own ears.

"Yeah. Me too."

I looked around the room, taking it all in. The knick-knacks collected from my old crew mates. Kessa's warm yellow stars draped across the ceiling. Pictures of my crews—new and old— hanging from the wall. One in particular, of Nadus and me, both looking young and... well, maybe not baby-faced. We were already war-scarred and battle-weary, and it showed. But young.

"It can't all have been for nothing," I said.

She looked sharply at me. "What do you mean?"

"I mean..." I gestured vaguely at the items I'd been looking at. "All of it. Half the reason I've been able to keep going— through everything that's happened to me, and *us,* over the years—is that it all felt like it was building up to something. When I got out of the Last War alive somehow, and then got my freedom. When I met you, and Kessa, and the rest of the crew. When Nadus and Artemis busted me out of prison, and then when I found Ramar on the *Revelation,* and found out that his ultrarippers had been the ones that had killed them. When I met you again on Albeni 7, and Rose, and when I went to the *Aboena,* and..." I trailed off, shaking my head. "I convinced myself that there was a *reason* for what I was going through. That I wasn't suffering in vain. That somehow all that suffering would let me make a difference for people." I felt my voice catch. "That... that the trail..."

That the trail of bodies would lead somewhere.

But it hadn't. Because it wasn't a trail. It was a circle. Round, and round, and round. All those bodies I'd stacked, with each one hoping that it would somehow prove worth it in the end. Just to end up exactly where I'd started: a puppet.

There are no heroes. Just puppets.

Silence. Sev leaned against me, taking my hand and squeezing it.

"Please tell me you've got something," I whispered. "Some little nugget of wisdom for me. Some anecdote that changes the way I see everything."

"I'm sorry, Lax." She squeezed my hand tighter. "I don't. I don't have any answers. But, for however little it's worth, I'm here. With you. And I'm not going anywhere."

It was worth a lot.

We sat in silence for a few more minutes before she spoke again. "You know, in some ways, it makes all this easier, doesn't it?" She shrugged when I gave her a questioning look. "I mean... if it turns out that we were all being manipulated all along, doesn't that take some of the responsibility off of us?"

I could only think about that civilian I'd killed on Brahma during the Last War. Not much older than a kid. The way his head had popped as I'd squeezed it. And the way I'd laughed.

The Paragon had been manipulating me, using drugs to pull my strings. No. *Divinity* had been manipulating me.

But I'd still done it.

"I thought you said leadership was about taking responsibility," I said.

She shrugged. "Yeah. But it's also about making impossible

choices. Sometimes there *is* no right choice. Sometimes you've gotta just... choose, and deal with the consequences."

You are Chosen.

You will know when the time has come.

"I could choose the Stranger," I said softly. "Zeka told me that the Stranger wants to destroy Divinity. That they're the only one who can."

She turned sharply, glaring at me. "*No.* I trust that bastard even less than I trust Divinity. I've heard the way Zeka talks to you. Calling you a weapon. And you know better than anyone that the Stranger will get rid of you the moment it's convenient —or someone they like better comes along."

That was all true. Zeka had made it very clear that embracing the Stranger's crusade would essentially be surrendering myself entirely to their purpose. I'd felt the way that the Stranger could use our connection to influence me—to bend my emotions to his will. If I agreed to take my place as their "Chosen one," I'd be as much a puppet for them as I'd ever been for the Vanguard.

That thought alone was enough to make me want to give up. All I wanted was to *not* be a puppet. That was what had driven all of this. This entire coalition. But increasingly, it seemed that the only way to not be a puppet was not to play.

Maybe I'd had it right from the beginning. Just run and hide. Stay away from the wars and the conflicts. Leave the powerful people with their ambition and their agendas to their games while I lurked in the shadows. I wouldn't be making a difference. I wouldn't be helping anybody. But I'd be free.

Didn't that count for something?

Only way not to be a puppet is to cut the strings. That was what Flint had said, voice flat and emotionless as he'd inserted a can into his shoulder port. *The only way not to hear the tune is to close your ears...*

I straightened.

Sev frowned at me. "What?"

The first piece of an idea fell into place.

Then the second.

And then the third.

Sev narrowed her eyes. "You've got that look. The crazy-idea look."

It was a crazy idea. And the more I thought about it, the more I hated it. I wasn't sure it would work. And even if it did, I wasn't sure what kind of chance I'd have of surviving it. Probably none. But if it *did* work...

The way I see it, a leader's real job is to make themselves redundant. To build a better future for everybody else...

Even if they're not in it.

"I need to talk to Ramar," I said.

I found him in the cargo bay.

The lights were dimmed and he was just... standing there, staring at something. It took me a moment to realize what. When I did, I couldn't help but pause and frown.

Nadus's armor.

"You must think I'm a fool," Ramar said, voice haggard.

"I think you're a lot of things, Ramar," I said, unable to take my eyes from Nadus's armor. Empty and cold. "But... not that."

I took another step towards him. He wasn't wearing his coat, and in the semi darkness, the topography of the scars on his face and neck were laid out in brutal shadow.

"I destroyed my life to ensure Project Eden would never see the light of day," he said softly. "And if that were the only price I'd paid, I'd be fine with it. But it wasn't *just* my life. The plan had been for all of us who were involved—all of those who felt it was wrong, at least, and wanted to atone—all of us *Penitents*—to end ourselves in one way or another, so that our secrets could not be spilled. Most of them died in bombings, sacrificing themselves to destroy lab equipment and computer records, leaving no trace of our great sin. Carston was supposed to be the only survivor. His part was to watch from the shadows, ensuring that we were successful. And my part was to die on the *Revelation*. To ensure that not a single ripper survived.

"But it didn't stop there. Every soul aboard the *Revelation* had to die as well. They might have been Paragon soldiers, but they still..." He glanced at me. "Well. You understand."

I nodded, thinking about the Paragon soldiers I'd killed aboard the *Aboena*. I didn't regret doing it, but I still couldn't help but wish there'd been another way. I'd seen Nadus in every Vanguard I'd killed.

"Yeah," I said, that long trail of corpses flaring red in my brain.

"And then—despite all that—if it had worked, it would have been worth it." He grimaced. "But, of course, it didn't. You and your friends arrived. And I believed your tale, about the rippers who'd brought you there. So I determined that my work wasn't finished.

"Which led me to the *Aboena*, of course. To Cairn, and the Stranger. I didn't realize, until it was far too late, just how deep in over my head I was diving. So, in my desperation to escape— to not render all I had done utterly meaningless—I dragged you into it." His eyes drifted back to Nadus's empty armor. "And your friends."

I felt myself tense. Saw Nadus's final, bloody grin before Cairn had bashed his face into the floor. *Thud, thud, thud...*

Crunch.

"And, again. As harsh and brutal as that was, if it had worked, I maintain it would have been worth it." He sighed. "But, of course... it didn't."

I frowned at him. "I thought you said you killed all the ultra-rippers."

"I did. Those Oathless and I doused every corner of

Cairn's hidden ripper holding area in flame. And then, after the battle, I went to painstaking lengths to ensure that every ultraripper corpse was burned to a crisp. I scoured the entire ship until I was certain that my work was complete. I even snuck into the Shapers' locked storage areas to ensure that they hadn't secreted any rippers away for their own purposes."

I blinked, confused. "Then it sounds like it *did* work."

"No. It didn't." He took a deep breath. "My justification for what I did was simple: I might destroy thousands of lives in my little act of rebellion, but it would be worth it in the end, because I would save billions more. I knew there was no keeping Project Eden in a box. It would spread. The Paragon would use it on other planets. And eventually some rebels would get their hands on some ultrarippers and send them to a Paragon world. And so forth, and so forth. But that was all under the assumption that Divinity wanted the Paragon to remain in charge. And now that we know that's not true..."

Ramar's fear suddenly materialized in my mind. My eyes widened. "You think that Divinity will give rippers to the Sovereigns."

He nodded wearily. "It seems naïve to believe that Divinity will stop with simply *funding* the Sovereigns. Perhaps they will. Perhaps they have no intention of letting the rebels win, and simply want to remind the Paragon just how reliant they are upon Divinity. But I'm increasingly certain that that's not the case. I think they want to wield the two states against each other, to keep them obedient. Each side of the conflict sure in the knowledge that if they lose Divinity's favor, their enemies will destroy them. Each side doing all in their power to conform to Divinity's wishes so that they'll be worthy of receiving greater and greater gifts."

That made me think of the Stranger. That was essentially what had happened between me and Cairn. The Stranger had let us fight each other to see who came out on top. Was there a connection there?

"We already know that Divinity is capable of producing stronger rippers than what we've seen," Ramar continued. "You experienced that on Boadicea 1. We know they likely can create stronger versions of Vanguards, too. I've never seen anything like those bodyguards that killed Vatheson. And we have to assume that they're capable of creating even worse."

"Sure," I said. "But surely, the rebels wouldn't be willing to use them. They know for themselves how much collateral damage rippers cause. They wouldn't..."

I trailed off.

They would. Tekka had proved that. And the more I thought about it, the more certain I was that Nalis Khendar would not hesitate for more than a second to unleash rippers upon her enemies.

"I haven't had a chance to tell you yet," Ramar said, "but I received a message from Carston while you were away. It didn't make much sense at the time. He said simply that the Sovereigns had identified their next target: Gideon. And that they had a new weapon they intended to deploy against it."

My chest constricted. *Gideon.* Images of peaceful farms floated through my brain. Of my father, driving away after leaving me at the Vanguard conscription station. Of my mother, smiling that tired smile of hers.

Gideon made sense to target. It was by a large measure the Paragon's biggest exporter of organic material. It practically fed the entire Paragon army. Cutting off the Paragon's access to that supply would be a massive blow. If we'd had this conversation *before* watching Vatheson's final moments, I'd have approved of the move as a sound strategic target.

Now, though, all I could picture was rippers tearing through my family's house. Through the towns I'd grown up in.

"You see?" Ramar sighed. "By all technical measures, I

succeeded in my goal of destroying the ultrarippers. But I had been so focused on that goal, for such a long time, that I did not stop until afterwards to count the cost."

I nodded slowly. That was why he'd been so depressed since the *Aboena*. He'd completed his purpose—a purpose he'd never planned on living past. And then he had to deal with the consequences. And *then*...

"And then," Ramar said, voice shrinking to a whisper, "we saw that damned recording. And I realized that it had all been a complete and utter waste."

I almost laughed at the irony of it. I'd always thought of Ramar as this inscrutable, unreadable enigma. Almost inhuman in his sheer focus on his goal. But now, with all of that stripped away, I suddenly found that we were suffering from the exact same dilemma. We were both looking back at our long trails of bodies.

And we both just wanted there to have been a *point* to it all.

I glanced over my shoulder, making sure that nobody had snuck down after me. We were alone.

"Listen," I said. "I might—*might*—have a plan. It's a long shot. And I want it to stay between us. I won't have Sev, or any of my crew, get involved. But if you can help me put the pieces together... I think we just might be able to make it work."

I explained. He listened.

———

The *Orpheus* shuddered as it docked to Albeni 7.

Silence fell in the bridge. Nobody made any motion to rise from their seats.

Bentley was the one who finally spoke. "Alright. So. Now what? We just... go aboard and pretend like nothing's changed?" He looked around at us. "Pretend like there's still a point to any of this?"

All eyes turned slowly to me.

I glanced at Ramar. He gave me a subtle nod.

I rose to my feet.

"Look," I said. "I'm sorry I didn't have something better to say last night. Truth is that I'm pretty torn up about all this too. I probably don't need to explain why."

Nods all around. Sev's eyes in particular were big and sad and knowing as they watched me.

"I don't really have any kind of speech to give," I said. "Truth is, I don't feel much differently than I did last night. I still don't like any part of this. I don't like the idea of working with the Sovereigns—not now, anyways, after what we've just learned about them. But I ain't gonna just give up and run away."

Rose perked up at that, her eyes starting to brighten.

I took a deep breath. "I can't change the fact that the Sovereigns are working with—or *for*, or whatever it turns out to be—Divinity. And I ain't gonna pretend that I fully understand everything that's going on behind the scenes there. But there's one thing I do know. This war is just starting, and chances are, if Divinity is gonna be playing both sides against each other, it's gonna drag on for a long, long time. Millions—*billions*, probably—of people will die in it. And we know it'll all be pointless."

"Inspiring," Bentley muttered.

I ignored him. "We can't change what Divinity will do," I said. "But we can change one thing. We can *end* the war."

Shell frowned, folding her arms. "How?"

"It's not certain yet," I said. "But I've got the beginnings of a plan. I'll need to talk to the Sovereigns and get them on board. But if it does work out the way I'm thinking it will, then we might have a shot at shutting all of this down before it can get any bloodier." I looked around at my crew.

"All it will take," I lied, "is one more mission."

Silence as they all looked at each other.

Bentley surprised me by being the first to stand.

"Well," he said, "we've done this enough times that I know how this next part goes. I'm in."

The rest of them joined him, nodding their assent, until only Ramar and Sev remained sitting. Ramar had a look of calm resignation in his eyes, while Sev was studying me with equal parts pride and worry.

I felt a rush of guilt. I hadn't told her about my long conversation with Ramar. Or the full extent of the plan we'd made. I couldn't. I knew she would try to stop me. But it was the only way.

"Alright, then," I said. "Let's do this."

TWENTY

The first time Sev and I had met with the Sovereigns, they'd seemed strong, unified. Defiant in the face of massive odds. Now, they looked beleaguered. Exhausted. Angry. Most concerningly, there were only half as many as there had been last time.

The Ebisan resistance had been decimated by the Paragon counter-attack a few days prior—they were effectively out of the fight. Several of the most prominent members of the rebel leadership were currently engaged in skirmishes to defend the Redhawk system foldgate.

"Redhawk is the foundation of this alliance," one of the rebels said, rubbing the exhaustion out of his eyes. "Not only does it mark our most important strategic asset, it's also vital to the morale of the independence movement everywhere. For decades, resistance has been constrained to guerilla warfare. Bombings, assassinations, ambushes. Now we've gathered enough strength to fight openly. Enough strength to drive the Paragon out of an entire system. Redhawk is the first system to independently rule itself since the war. There's hope that comes with that. Powerful hope. And if we lose Redhawk... well, I think we'll lose that hope."

"Which is why we need the information Vatheson stole." Nalis Khendar looked no happier than the last time I'd seen her, but the rage in her eyes had cooled. Somewhat, at least; I could still see it flickering as she studied me. "Until we know our enemy's plans, we will be forced to remain on the defensive. We received the files you sent us. I am impressed. Somehow, you managed to constrain yourself from slaughtering your companions at the last moment."

I ignored the barb, doing my best to keep my face stony. I'd gone out of my way to brand myself as a cold-blooded brutalist who did whatever was necessary last time we spoke—no point in undermining that image now.

I explained what had happened on Boadicea 1 in the simplest terms I could, leaving out the grislier details as well as the footage we'd found afterwards. I watched their faces carefully the entire time, waiting for a reaction. I still wasn't sure exactly how much they knew, or just how involved Divinity was with their organization, and the more I thought about it, the more questions arose for me. Had they known what I would find when I arrived on Boadicea? Did they even know that Divinity was their benefactor?

I didn't think so. Not for most of them, anyways. Most of the rebels seemed horrified at what I described. Others seemed to delight in the prospect of a station full of so many Paragon elites being devoured by the same monsters they'd weaponized against their enemies so many times.

Only one seemed entirely unmoved. Nalis Khendar's face remained stony and impassive as I described the onslaught of rippers we'd fought our way through. Despite my best efforts I could detect no sense of... well, anything, really. No alarm, or guilt, or excitement, or satisfaction. But no surprise, either.

"We've no need to fear," she said as I finished, her voice calm. "Divinity has a long history of punishing those who violate deals with them. That's why we have this window against the Paragon now." She eyed me. "It was you and Artemis who brought to my attention that the Paragon had first violated their deal with Divinity. Had they not, Divinity would not have ceased to support them." She looked around at her comrades. "This changes nothing. If anything, it cements the fact that Divinity no longer supports our enemy. All we must do now to win is endure and stick to our plan."

Nods all around as she continued. "The first portion of our plan has already been successful. By taking Redhawk, not only have we gained legitimacy and bolstered the morale of our movement, we've dealt a critical blow to the Paragon's ability to produce more weapons of war. If we can deal but one more blow, their offensive capabilities will crumple."

"Gideon," one of the other rebels said.

I felt a tinge of satisfaction mixed with dread. Carston had been right.

"With Gideon off of the playing board," Nalis continued, "the Paragon will be unable to supply their troops, significantly reducing their offensive capabilities. They will be forced to withdraw to their own systems to prevent themselves from losing any more. The aggression we are seeing from them right now is an act of desperation. They hope to stamp us out while they still have the strength. We will rob them of that strength."

More nods. One of the rebels raised an eyebrow at Nalis. "You still haven't told us the nature of this weapon you intend to deploy."

"And I do not intend to," Nalis said calmly. She gave a mirthless smile. "Do you not trust me? Have I not brought us this far safely?"

The rebel flushed, then looked down.

The situation was starting to become clear to me. Clearer, at least. Nalis was Divinity's link to the Sovereigns. They must have found her, somehow, after the chaos on Brahma. Promised her revenge.

I wondered, briefly, if I could simplify this whole thing by simply finding a way to kill *her*. Then rejected the idea. Divinity was the enemy. Not Nalis.

"We trust you," a different rebel said. "And you don't need to tell us its exact nature. But we *do* need to know how to deploy it."

"Simple," Nalis said. "We need to get our fleet within firing range of the planet."

The uncomfortable looks the rebels exchanged made me think they suspected the true nature of Nalis's weapon. But none of them objected.

"That's hardly *simple*," one of them said. "We'll still need to get past the blockade. And then force our way through the Gideon foldgate. It would be a significant, costly battle."

"Yes," Nalis said. "But it will be worth it. We've discussed the numbers. We've discussed our options. We *can* win this fight. All that remains is to see if we have the will to follow through." She treated everybody to a harsh glare. "This is the *only* way."

More nods. Less certain this time. They accepted the plan, but I could tell they didn't like it.

I cleared my throat, drawing the rebels' attention. "I may have *one* other way."

All eyes turned to me.

Nalis sneered. "Don't think that because you've completed one mission for us, Vanguard, that we'll simply roll over and play along with you. The intelligence you provided was essential. But now, we..."

One of the other rebels raised a palm. "With all due respect," he said, "we should consider *all* options, should we not?"

Agreement passed through each holographic face—other

than Nalis, of course. But her sneer faded into a discontented flat line.

"Very well, then, Vanguard," she said, leaning back into her seat. "Let's hear this plan of yours."

"Let's hear this plan of yours, then," Rose said, folding her arms.

It had been a few hours since my meeting with the Sovereigns—and almost a full day since we'd returned to Albeni 7. Rose, along with Renault and the rest of my crew, were gathered around the large conference table. Sev and Ramar sat on either side of me.

Ramar gave me a nod.

I took a deep breath and powered on the holoprojector in the center of the table. A three-dimensional map of the Alpha Centauri system manifested in the air, focused on the dwarf star Proxima Centauri. Foldgates lined the edge of the star's orbit. Little red spaceships were strewn throughout the system.

"These are, roughly, the positions of the Paragon's forces," I said. I pointed towards several foldgates with red dots next to them. "These gates mark systems that currently have Paragon forces deployed within. As you can see, the bulk of the fleet is divided between two points: first, the siege of Redhawk; and second, their main offensive fleet, which we know, thanks to Vatheson, is planning on hitting the Moses system next now that they've annihilated the resistance in Ebisu."

Renault rubbed his jaw as he considered the display. "This better be one hell of a plan, because I'm certainly not seeing any way we'll be able to beat the Paragon through sheer force of arms—unless the rebels have a massive fleet they've been hiding somewhere."

"They *do* have a hidden fleet," I said. "But I wouldn't call it massive. They had enough foresight not to commit all of their forces to Redhawk and have held most of their strength back since then." I pointed out three foldgates. "The rest of their forces are currently concealed in the Jackson, Odin, and Lucas systems."

"So what's the hold up, then?" Rose folded her arms. "Are they waiting for something specific to happen before they commit the rest of their troops?"

"Yes," I said. "They were waiting for two things. First, for the Paragon to wear down their troops on the Ebisu system. And, secondly, for us to get the intel on where the Paragon would strike next. Now that we have that, we know where the Paragon is going next. The Sovereigns are waiting until the Paragon fleet has entered their nullspace journey to play their hand."

"Ah." Renault's eyes sparkled. "Clever. The Paragon fleet won't be able to receive word of the attack until they're out of nullspace."

I nodded. "Exactly. Waiting for the right timing will cut a full third of the Paragon's fleet out of the fight. As soon as the Paragon's assault force enters nullspace, the rebel fleet will move into Alpha Centauri to engage."

Bentley whistled. "I thought you said you weren't an admiral. But this is quite the plan."

I hesitated. "Well. It's not all mine. Hell, most of it isn't. The Sovereigns had already planned most of this out. But this is where my plan comes in. See, the Sovereigns' initial idea had been to head straight to the Gideon foldgate. Their forces in Redhawk would push outward at the same time, keeping the Paragon forces besieging the Redhawk gate pinned in place." I pointed through the Gideon foldgate. "Allowing the Sovereigns' main fleet to fight their way through the gate and take the system."

Renault nodded. "That will be one hell of a fight."

"Yeah." I hadn't told Renault—or anyone other than Sev, Ramar, and my crew—of what we'd learned about the Sovereigns' connection to Divinity, so I didn't bring up the fact that they intended (probably) to use rippers once they got to Gideon. "Or, rather, it *would* be. But I've persuaded them to try it my way."

I pointed back to Alpha Centauri. "Here's what's going to happen instead. Rather than attacking the foldgate directly, the Sovereign fleets will do everything in their power to draw the Paragon's forces *away* from the Gideon foldgate. It will still be a tough fight, but since they won't be focused on a single objective, the rebels should have a much easier time of it."

"If they're not focused on any one target, though," Renault asked, "what's the objective? How do they intend to win?"

Rose looked up at me, a grin spreading across her face. "But that's where we come in, isn't it?"

"But that's where we come in," I said, looking each of the Sovereign leaders in the eyes. "It's clear by now that we won't win this fight through force of strength alone. If we want any sort of chance of winning, we're gonna have to fight dirty."

"Perfect for you, then," Nalis said. I wanted desperately to point out that, hey, *she* was the one planning on killing millions of innocent civilians with flesh-eating monsters, but I wasn't supposed to know that, so I kept my mouth shut.

One of the other rebels nodded at me, ignoring Nalis. "We've been fighting dirty for years now, vulture. So you'd better have a more specific plan."

"I do. Or, rather, a more specific *target*." I reached out of the holoprojector's display and pressed a button. The Gideon foldgate flashed white.

Nalis's eyes widened.

Rose's eyes widened.

"This is the Gideon foldgate," I said. "Gideon is, logistically, the foundation of the Paragon's empire. It is responsible for almost all of the supplies that keep their armies running." I hesitated. "I know all too well, because I grew up there. Every week, my father and I would drop off truckloads of grain to the Paragon's supply depots, which would then be shuttled off to supply the war effort."

"We know *that*," Shell said. "But the rebels were already planning on attacking the planet. So what are you suggesting instead?"

"I'm suggesting," I said, "that we attack the foldgate itself."

"Us?" Rid pointed around. "Specifically?"

"Yeah," I said.

Rose raised an eyebrow. "The *Orpheus* doesn't have that kind of firepower."

"No," I said. "But it has something better: stealth. We, in the *Orpheus*"—I looked up at Renault—"plus as many other stealth interceptors as we can get our hands on—filled with pirates—will sneak aboard. One of the things we found in Vatheson's head was foldgate blueprints. With those, Ramar has helped me identify key points within."

Ramar nodded, stepping forward. I restrained a wince as I noticed Sev give him a suspicious look. She didn't know what I was planning—nobody but Ramar did—but she clearly suspected something.

"I'll explain exactly how it works in a bit," I said. "But the gist of it is that with six teams working, by planting explosives in the exact right spots on the *inside* of the foldgate, we can take out the whole damn thing."

Bentley's mouth was agape. "So, we're just going to... blow it up? What about all the people on the other sides? We'd be cutting off *billions* of people from the rest of the foldgate network!"

I nodded grimly. With how small the foldgates made the

galaxy feel, it was easy to forget that most systems—Gideon included—were actually millions upon millions of lightyears away from each other. "If it comes down to it... then yeah. That's what we'd be doing. But the goal is *not* to blow it up. The goal is to hold it hostage. And then to force the Paragon to negotiate."

Plus, I thought, *it's better than letting them all get eaten by rippers.*

"You really think they'll agree to that?" Renault looked skeptical.

"Absolutely," I said, projecting more confidence than I felt. "As for the exact terms they'll be willing to agree to, I'm not sure. I'll leave that to the Sovereigns. But the Paragon needs Gideon. And if they don't play ball..."

"Boom," Rose said.

"Boom," I said.

"It could work," one of the rebels admitted. Even Nalis's eyes had grown thoughtful.

"It's risky," I said. "But it's a hell of a lot better than letting ourselves be overwhelmed one by one. And, if it fails, you can retreat, and you'll still have your fleet, with minimal losses." I gestured towards Nalis. "If you assault the planet directly, it's an all or nothing plan. You either win, or you lose. Plus—even if you *do* win—the war will drag on. Yes, the Paragon will be forced to go on the defensive. But they won't give up. Taking one of their core systems will only incentivize them to rebuild and come back for revenge. This way, you force them to the negotiating table."

"And if the Paragon *does* agree to withdraw," one of the rebels said. "What then?"

I shrugged. "That's your part. I'm no diplomat. Far as I'm concerned, all that matters is that they agree to leave us alone.

They can keep Earth and whatever other systems want to stay a part of the Paragon. But the rest of us get our independence." I looked around at each member of the council, spreading my hands in a gesture of confusion. "That's what we want, ain't it? That's the point of all this killing and dying, ain't it? Independence?"

That won most of them over to me. Holographic heads bobbed from every corner of my vision. I leaned forward, my confidence soaring. Hell, maybe I wasn't too bad at this whole leadership thing after all.

"Well, this way," I said, "we get it. And we get it for a fraction of the cost."

All eyes turned slowly towards Nalis. Her eyes, in turn, remained fixed on me, cold and sharp. As if she were seeing me now for the first time. Maybe I was just imagining it in my newfound confidence, but I swore I could see her measuring the situation in her head. Weighing her options. It was clear she didn't like my plan. She *wanted* to do this the violent way. The brutal way. To make the Paragon pay in the same way her people had paid, even if it was only the most innocent of the Paragon who would actually suffer. But it was clear that the rest of her war council was increasingly on my side. I could only imagine how pissed that made her.

Good. I was counting on that.

Her face broke slowly into a cold smile.

"There are, of course, many more details we'll need to work out," she said. "But the core premise of your plan is acceptable." She raised an eyebrow. "More than acceptable. Commendable. If you're right, we may be able to end this war for good, far sooner than any of us could have dared to hope."

Something in the way she said that cut through my confidence. If she had thrown a backhanded insult at me, I'd have known I had her where I wanted her. But this... this made me nervous.

"If nobody is opposed," she continued, "I propose that we move forward with the Vanguard's plan, adapting it as necessary, of course. But there is one key element of it that I particularly like: if the battle isn't going our way, our fleets will be free to retreat and fight another day." Her smile turned menacing. "Because all of the risk will be assumed by *you*, puppet."

"You'll be assuming nearly *all* of the risk," Renault pointed out. "The main fleet—which, by the way, I'm assuming I'll be joining —will be in combat, sure, but you and everyone who goes with you will be right in the jaws of the lion. It's practically a suicide mission."

Rose scoffed. "We got our *start* doing suicide missions. This is nothing new."

But by the silence that followed, I could tell that everybody knew that was false. This was well beyond the scope of any other job we'd ever taken. Not only in the actual size of our target, but in the stakes involved in both failure and success. The fate of the entire Paragon would rest upon my own little salvage crew—plus whoever else was crazy enough to be talked into coming along.

"It's going to be brutal," I admitted. "But judging by the plans we stole from Vatheson, we've got roughly two weeks to prepare..." I looked around at my crew. "And if there is *any* crew I'd trust to be able to do this... it's this one."

Rose grinned. "Well, then. What are we waiting for? We've got work to do!"

TWENTY-ONE

"Are you asleep?"

"Nope. Are you?"

Sev pulled herself close against my side, breath warm on my neck as she tucked her head into the crook of my shoulder. "No. Got... one or two things on my mind."

I gave a quiet snort of a laugh. "Oh, do you, now?"

Her finger traced a line on my arm. "Have you spoken with your family?"

I frowned, craning my neck so I could get a look at her face. In the dim light all I could see were her eyes, staring thoughtfully into nothingness.

"No," I said. "Not since... well. Not since they sold me to the Paragon. Where's this coming from?"

She shrugged. "Just thinking about what you said about Gideon. You're not worried about what might happen to them if you *do* blow up the foldgate?"

I *had* thought about it. "I'm more worried about what will happen to them if Nalis Khendar drops a few hundred ripper pods on their farm."

She sighed. "Makes sense, I suppose."

"Besides," I continued, "Gideon is one of the most self-sustaining systems in the Paragon. They hardly import anything. If anything, they'll be better off with the foldgate gone." I gave a softly amused grunt. "Maybe I should just do them all a favor and blow it up regardless."

She repositioned herself on top of me, resting her chin on her crossed arms and looking into my eyes with a serious expression. "Would you want to live on Gideon?"

I blinked. "What?"

"After." She shrugged. "We've talked over and over about how we're gonna go find somewhere nice and quiet to hide away after all this is done. You've mentioned a few times that you wouldn't mind farming. So, would you want to live on Gideon?"

After. The thought sent a wave of guilt through me. I opened my mouth to say... something. I don't know what. I couldn't tell her the full truth of what I was planning. Not because I didn't trust her. Simply because I knew her. And because, every time I thought about it, I remembered Rose, her voice as hard and serious as I'd ever heard, telling me *Don't you leave her.*

But I had to. I *had* to. It was the only way.

"Sev," I said, voice strained. "I..."

My voice trailed off. Her eyes held a quiet plea. As if she knew what I was going to say. And was *begging* me not to.

"No," I said quietly.

"No?"

"No." I shook my head, forcing a wry smile onto my face. "Gideon? I already spent too much of my life there farming for the Paragon. No—wherever we settle, it's gotta be somewhere the Paragon doesn't control." I hesitated. "Well. Or at least somewhere everybody isn't conscripted into working for them."

"Brahma?"

"Brahma *is* beautiful," I admitted. "But... too many bad memories."

She raised an eyebrow. "We're gonna have a hard time settling on anywhere if you disqualify every planet you have a bad memory on."

I chuckled. "Well, where would *you* want to go?"

She shrugged. "I don't much care which planet, as long as we're safe and free. And, you know, we can breathe and stuff." She went silent, pursing her lips in thought. "I want a stream. A little one, running right past our house. So that if you leave the window open, it's the first thing you hear in the morning. I like the sound of running water."

"Deal," I said. I looked up into the darkness, thinking. "Alright, then. What about... Frey?"

"*Frey.*" She said the word like she was tasting it. "Frey. I like that. That's in one of the Sovereign Systems, right?"

"Yeah. Lucas. I've never been there myself. But I hear it's nice. They say it's got even more biodiversity than Earth."

"Think we'll find buried treasure there?"

I grinned. "Oh yeah."

She held up a finger, curled like a pirate's hook, above my face. I hooked my own finger around it.

"*Ar,*" she said.

"Ar," I said.

TWENTY-TWO

"This," I said, hitting a button to power up the *Orpheus's* bridge holoprojector, "is a Paragon battlecruiser. The *Revelation*, specifically."

Nods all around. I'd gotten used to having the *Orpheus's* bridge crowded, but this was even busier than usual. Being aboard my ship made me feel more confident, though. More at home. Which was why I'd called this meeting here rather than the administrative office's conference room.

My crew accounted for some of the crowd, but most of it was taken up by leaders of the other teams that would be accompanying us. Flint and Winter were both there, accompanied by several other trusted pirates and Roamers who would be leading teams of their own.

The plans we'd stolen from Vatheson had indicated that the Paragon's orders were to attack the Moses system, starting thirteen days from now. Which meant we had only thirteen days to prepare for the most important job I'd ever undertaken. And— on top of that—thirteen days to prep for the rest of my plan. Ramar would be handling most of that, of course, but it still lurked in the back of my mind.

I turned my attention back to the hovering image of the *Revelation*, then hit a button on the side of the holoprojector. The battlecruiser shrank, moving to the corner of the holospace to make room for a ship five times its length.

"This," I continued, "is the *Aboena*."

"We here just to compare sizes?" I heard one pirate mutter to his companion.

I ignored them, pressing the button again. "And *this* is a foldgate."

The two ships shrank again, a to-scale model of a foldgate appearing in the center of the projection and dwarfing both of them. The *Aboena* could fit lengthwise inside of the foldgate's ring with what looked like a few hundred meters to spare. The ring of the station itself was thicker than either of the two ships.

I let the projection run in silence for a few moments, looking around and studying the reactions. They'd all seen a foldgate before, of course, but I wanted to ensure that the scale of what we were setting out to do really sank in. It seemed to work on most of them.

Most being the operative word.

The pirate who'd been joking a moment earlier frowned, scratching at his misshapen nose. "We know what a foldgate is. We've all seen 'em. All been through 'em. So why don't you tell us what's so special about this one?"

Right. Some of them didn't know what our mission was yet, and intentionally so. Operational security was paramount on this job. If word got to the Paragon about what we were planning, we could kiss the whole idea goodbye—likely along with our lives. There was also the distinct possibility that the Paragon somehow knew that Vatheson was carrying this information. After all, they'd seemed aware that Boadicea 1 had been attacked by Divinity. What if they changed their plans?

That was a risk we'd simply have to take.

"This one is special," I said, "because we're going to blow
it up."

That got their attention. The pirate's eyes widened, fixing
on the foldgate. I waited a moment before continuing. I
explained the plan in brief terms, describing how the fleet
would provide a distraction and what our end goal was. Still,
despite all of the context, the goal was simple: to rig the foldgate
with enough explosives to completely destroy it.

"Now, obviously, that's easier said than done, because this
thing is *big*." I stuck my finger into the projection and ran it
around the circumference of the foldgate. "According to the
schematics, if you take the primary corridor all the way around
to end up at where you started, it's a fifty-kilometer trip."

Flint raised an eyebrow. "Trust you me, I'm downright sali-
vating at the thought of blasting that bugger into smithereens.
But it seems like the only way to really blow up something that
big would be with a volley of high-powered torpedoes."

"That would be true," I said, holding up a finger. "*If* we
didn't have the schematics. Now, I'm not gonna pretend to be
smart enough to know exactly how a foldgate works, but we've
figured out enough that we can take it out—for good—with six
perfectly placed hullbreaker bombs."

I zoomed the projection in until we were looking at a
detailed close-up of the interior of the ring. "The tricky part
about blowing up a foldgate isn't just shutting down the gate
itself. That's easy. The entire ring is lined with emitters"—I
pointed towards a long line of bladelike devices lining the inside
of the gate—"which are what create the portal. Destroying any
one of them will disable it. If we wanted to, we could just plant
our bombs here on the inner surface and put the station
temporarily out of commission. But we're aiming for more than
temporary. Which means we're aiming deeper than surface
level."

I moved the projection again, zooming inside of the station

itself and centering on a long, cylindrical device in the core of the ring.

"The foldgate is powered by six powercores," I said, gesturing towards Winter and his followers. "These are a more modern version of the powercore that runs the *Aboena*. They generate pretty much endless energy. The key to destroying the station with the smallest amount of force possible is to find a way to turn that energy to our favor. Needless to say, the powercores are designed very specifically *not* to explode. Which means that a little intervention is necessary.

"First step"—I pointed out a segment of the powercore near the end—"is to plant a bomb on each of the powercores, at this specific point. But we don't detonate them yet. Before we do, we need to access the foldgate's control room. Once there, we can override the powercores' security measures to initiate an overcharge. Once the charge is high enough, detonating the bombs will not only destroy the powercores, they will trigger each powercore to unleash all of their energy at once. Multiply that by six equally distributed points, and there shouldn't be anything left of the foldgate big enough to fit through a pinhole."

One of the other Roamer captains cleared his throat. "And what of us? How will we escape this explosion? I understand that there will be negotiations, but surely, we will need to have personnel on board at all times to keep the foldgate's security from undoing our work."

"Yeah," I said. "First step is that once the bombs are set, we rig 'em so delicately they'll blow up if they so much as get looked at incorrectly. Touch 'em? Boom. Try to fry 'em with an EMP? Boom. They'll be triggered via quantcom, so there's no risk that the Paragon can sever our link to them with a suppressor field or anything like that. Second step is that once we've started the overcharge, we fry their computer systems, keep 'em from shutting it down. After that, we'll be free to go on our merry way."

"And resistance?" Flint narrowed his eyes at the hovering image. "Surely they ain't gonna let us just waltz in there without at least saying hello."

"No, I expect they won't," I said. "We'll sure as hell have a fight on our hands. But it won't be anything we can't handle. All things considered, security is ridiculously lax on these things. Almost like they think you'd have to be crazy to try anything."

I chuckled at my own joke. Nobody else seemed to think it was funny. I cleared my throat and carried on. "There *are* on-board security teams located at these points." I indicated three different garrisons. "They're all Paragon, so it'll probably be a combination of fresh recruits and old veterans. Supply lists indicate that each garrison is armed with several Jericho exosuits in addition to Jackhammer and APMP rifles, so expect Vanguards.

"As far as the station's external defenses: there are defensive short-range energy weapon batteries as well as anti-torpedo missile systems. But those are all on the outside of the ring— which is why our plan is to approach from the inside." I zoomed out on the schematics, flipping them over so we were looking at the inner side of the ring. "There are dozens of maintenance hatches lining the emitter arrays. The rebels have very kindly identified which ones will lead us on the quickest routes to the powercores. So we'll take those and use cargo trucks to haul the explosives along with us."

"Once we're on board," Rid said, "it'll take no time at all before somebody spots us. How do we keep the foldgate from calling out for reinforcements?"

"We don't," I said, leaning on the projector. "We move fast and aggressively. We make sure that we hit all of our objectives simultaneously so that the enemy can't react. And we get out before they can pin us down. Otherwise..." I grimaced. "Well.

Otherwise, let's just say we'll have even more stakes in the negotiations."

———

"Only one more week until the big day, eh?" Renault grinned, using one hand to shake mine and the other to slap me on the back as he greeted me in the doorway to the Karak System shipyards. "And yet you *still* found the time to come out here and visit little ol' me."

"Don't flatter yourself too much." I couldn't help but return the smile, though. As much as I'd disliked Renault upon first meeting him—he had attempted to kidnap Rose, after all—his enthusiasm became contagious when you spent too much time around him. I glanced over my shoulder into the interior of the *Orpheus*. "Decided it's finally time to give the old girl a few upgrades."

"Oh?" He raised an eyebrow. "Such as?"

"Guns!" Rose's grin practically split her face open as she strode past us.

I sighed as we watched her go. "The *Orpheus* is a stealth infiltrator, obviously, and not a fighter, so its only weapon system is a small laser that's more for salvage work than combat. We figured that—just in case it comes up—it wouldn't hurt to get something a bit more substantial."

"Well, you'll never catch me arguing against more guns," Renault said.

"You never did tell me where you got yours," I said, remembering the way that luxury cruiser had incinerated beneath the weight of his energy cannons. "Never seen anything quite like those."

"That'll be the Grond you're referring to, I'm sure," Renault said with a chuckle. He turned and started down the hallway. "They're old Redhawk technology, which usually means that they're *worse* than the modern stuff, I know, but sometimes the opposite is true. The Paragon wiped out the facility that built them, so as far as I know, the one I've got installed on my flagship, the *Walrus*, is the only one in existence."

I followed after him. "Grond?"

"Strange name, I know." He shrugged. "From some old earth folklore of one culture or another, I believe. A great battering ram for smashing even greater walls to dust. Quite fitting."

I followed him into an elevator compartment. "I never could keep track of all that old earth stuff. Always thought the modern age was hard enough to wrap my head around on its own, without throwing in a bunch of stuff from thousands of years ago."

"Ah, but that's where you'd be wrong." He wagged a finger at me as the elevator began moving. "The old stories don't *complicate* the modern world. They *explain* it."

I raised an eyebrow. "Didn't take you for such a philosophical type."

"Oh, I'm full of surprises. I've always had a love for stories—the older, the better. Even my ship is named after one of the old pirate tales."

"Even the pirates get their turn in the old stories, eh?"

"Why not? Everybody wants to be a pirate, after all."

The elevator came to a halt and the doors slid open, leading into a large, open observation deck with a massive window taking up the entire opposite wall. I felt my eyes widen as we approached it.

Beyond the window, I could see the shipyard's arms stretching out to either side of us like the bones of some ancient, mind-numbingly large whale. Dozens of ships—massive ones—were docked along it, and I could see tiny specks moving up and down their hulls. Construction drones. Above the drones, long, mechanical arms extending from the station itself moved materials to where they needed to be.

"Impressive, isn't it?" Renault's reflection materialized next to mine in the window. "They've done remarkably fast work. Of course, it helps that we were able to pay them a hefty percentage of the money the Sovereign Systems dumped upon us, but, still. Remarkable."

I nodded, feeling vaguely ill at that reminder of whose strings we were currently dangling from. I pointed towards Renault's ships. "How are the repairs coming along? Will you be ready in time?"

"We were already battle-ready," Renault said. "But now that we can plug a few of the holes the Paragon left in us, we'll be doubly so." He tilted his head towards the opposite side of the yard. "Our Roamer friends, on the other hand... either the repairs they needed are even more extensive than I thought, or they've simply gotten quite carried away."

I glanced down towards the *Aboena*. It was nearly as large as the entire shipyard itself. It looked like a large section of the hull had been cut away, allowing for large pieces of... *something* to be passed through into the core of the ship. No wonder Zeka had insisted on using the shipyards.

"Whatever *they're* doing," Renault continued, "I suspect it will take longer than a week to repatch all of that." He hesitated. "Uhm... *do* you know what they're doing?"

"No," I lied. "But as long as they're within the budget, it's none of my concern."

Renault shrugged. "Fair enough."

I stared sullenly at the *Aboena*, a mounting sense of dread in my gut. I felt it every time I thought about the future. *My* future, specifically.

"Those old earth stories you love," I said. "Any of them tell you what to do in the face of insurmountable odds?"

He glanced sharply at me. "Feeling a bit philosophical yourself now, eh?"

I grunted.

He chuckled, turning back to the window. "The truth is that almost all of them are about that. All of the best stories—my favorites, anyway—seem to involve one or more brave heroes squaring up against an unbeatable evil of one kind or another." He scratched his jaw. "And, generally speaking, they win in the end. But not before they get dragged through all the mud and blood in the world."

"I'm not sure I believe in heroes," I whispered, staring out into the dark void. My reflection stared sullenly back at me. "Just puppets."

Renault chuckled. "You sound like you've been talking to Flint. He's always droning on about nihilistic nonsense like that."

"You disagree?"

"I think it's fairly arbitrary. Just depends on how you define it. But the way I've always seen it, a hero's somebody who *tries*." He shrugged. "Usually, life doesn't work out the way it does in the stories. I'd say that nine out of ten times, in the real world, the hero gets smushed beneath whatever great evil they're fighting." He leaned close to me, winking and lowering his voice confidentially. "That's why *I* prefer to stick to the role of the lovable rogue."

I gave a vaguely amused grunt.

"But—like I said—that's not what defines the hero," he continued, turning away. "The hero isn't the hero because they succeed. They're the hero because they *try*. Even when the odds *are* insurmountable."

He slapped my shoulder, then turned away. I was so lost in thought over what he'd said that he'd already reached the door by the time I realized with a start that I'd never even brought up the issue I'd wanted to talk to him about.

"Wait," I said. "One more thing."

He paused with one finger over the elevator control panel, raising an eyebrow. "Yes?"

"After the battle," I said. "When I—" I caught myself with a grimace. "*If*... I don't make it. I want you to promise me you'll keep an eye out for Sev."

He gave me a confused look. "Meaning..."

"Meaning, if she needs your help, you give it to her," I growled. I took a breath, calming myself. "I don't know what kind of fallout is gonna follow this battle, and I don't know if I'll be around to see it. So just promise me, that if she gets into any kind of trouble, you'll help her back out of it."

He narrowed his eyes. "Why me?"

"Cause, other than my crew, you're the closest thing to a friend I've got these days," I said. "And because I think that somewhere, deep down under all that bravado, there's a good person. Despite your best efforts to hide him."

He studied me a moment longer, then nodded. "Well. I've never been able to turn down some good ol' fashioned flattery. You have my word. I'll make sure she's well protected." He gave me a mock salute as he hit the button to open the doors, then stepped inside. "Not that I think she needs it. To be perfectly frank, I'm slightly scared of the woman."

The doors started closing.

"Wait." I felt a rush of panic as I remembered one more thing. He reached out, keeping the doors from closing. "Now what?"

I hesitated, feeling suddenly awkward. "I... uhm... do you know how I would go about buying a plot of land? Planetside?"

I remember storms.

We used to get them on Gideon. Big ones. I'd always get

excited when one showed up. Don't know why, really, but I did. I remember the way that you could tell a storm was coming long before the first drop of rain hit the ground or the first rumble of thunder grumbled across the sky. The electricity hanging in the air. That almost supernatural sense of knowing that God was coming, and He was *pissed*.

That was how the final week felt. An increasing sense of foreboding doom, growing stronger with each passing minute. I tried to ignore it, losing myself in my work, but it only really went away during the little time I was able to spend with Sev. Even then, though, I could feel it looming in the back of my mind, tugging at my thoughts like one of those strange rippers on Boadicea 1.

Or the Stranger.

But the week passed regardless. One frenzied day at a time, until I was almost surprised to find myself standing in Albeni 7's loading bay terminal as we made our final preparations, thinking: *This is it.*

Six stealth interceptors were docked there, with six crews doing their final gear checks. Cargo—food, ammunition, medical supplies—were being ferried over to Renault's ships, which had returned from the shipyards with their repairs complete. The *Aboena* was completed as well, the work done faster than anyone had expected.

Don't think about that. I pushed my thoughts away from the *Aboena* and the Stranger, focusing them on the task immediately ahead of us.

"You're sure that they'll be able to access the powercore rooms?" I asked Rid as we walked together down the terminal. "It'd be one hell of a shame if we made it all this way just to fail because of a locked door."

"I'm not the only lockbreaker in the galaxy, Lax," Rid said gently. "We ran a bunch of simulations. If they're the same locks as the ones the schematics say, we'll be able to get through them relatively easily. We ran drills for several hours yesterday."

"Sure," I said. "But what if they've updated them?"

He sighed. "Lax, have you ever met a lock I couldn't get through?"

I gritted my teeth. "First time for everything."

"Yeah. But for now, I think we've done everything we can. Worst case scenario is we use some of the munitions we're bringing aboard to just blow the damn thing down."

Breathe. Relax. I nodded slowly. "Yeah. You're right."

He *was* right. Probably. In the days since receiving our orders from the rebel strategic council, we'd spent hour after hour planning alternate scenarios, running drills, and checking gear. Renault's pirates were clearly unused to such a rigid level of preparation, but they adjusted quickly. Winter and his Roamers applied their staunch discipline to great effect. My crew, I was pleased to see, knew everything I wanted them to do before I even had to bring it up.

Six stealth interceptors. Six crews. I was almost tempted to put myself on a different ship and let my crew handle their target themselves; after all, I trusted them more than these other rookie teams. I wasn't used to running operations with so many moving parts. There was simply no way for me to ensure that everybody did their job correctly.

Breathe. Relax.

Obviously, the ideal scenario was for each team to complete their objective. But it would be alright if one of the teams failed. According to Ramar, so long as five of the powercores were destroyed in the correct way, the resulting chain reaction would unleash enough energy to vaporize the entire foldgate. Any less, though, and the resulting explosion would merely damage it. The gate would still shut down, and repairing it would still be a pain for the Paragon, but the scope of the loss would be in a completely different category than the total annihilation we were aiming for.

I'd done everything I could to make sure that each crew was properly trained. Now I just had to let them do their jobs. As for me—my place was with my crew. Our task was the most important—we'd be the ones going all the way to the control room.

Rid looked past me. An idiotic grin broke out over his face. I followed his gaze to see Rose approaching us. She grinned back at Rid, falling into step next to him.

"The *Orpheus* is in perfect condition," she said. "And I made sure that the other pilots ran checks on their ships too. Everything is looking good."

I nodded. A figure approaching us through the crowd drew my attention. I felt a grin just as idiotic as Rid's break across my own face as I recognized Sev.

"It's been a long time since I've seen the terminal this busy," she said as I stopped to meet her.

"Yeah." I chuckled, turning to survey the chaos. "Almost like old times, huh."

She laughed. "Not really. So—what else is there to do?"

I put my hands on my hips, thinking through it all. We'd reviewed every aspect of our plans a hundred times over. Drilled for every conceivable scenario. The ships were supplied and inspected. The crews were doing their final gear checks now before loading up. Renault and his fleet were ready to go.

I glanced towards Rose and Rid, half hoping that one of them would remember some forgotten task. They both shook their heads.

"Nothing," I said finally. "Except to leave."

"Hm." Sev nodded, looking towards where the *Orpheus* was docked. "Well, then: how about a drink?"

. . .

Tyrell's Bar was still a shadow of its former self—literally, seeing as most of the light fixtures had yet to be repaired—but it was a far sight more usable than it had been the last time Sev and I had visited it. We sat at the newly repaired bar, our backs turned to the newly replaced windows, doing our best to keep our attention on the glasses in our hands rather than the commotion outside.

"Like old times, eh?" Sev said.

"Not really."

She chuckled, shaking her head and taking a sip from her glass. "How you holding up out there?"

I shrugged. "Pretty much the usual. I always feel like I'm about to have a nervous breakdown before a job. But the way I see it..."

"... better to panic now and relax later than relax now and panic later," she said. "I remember."

I grinned. "Yeah."

She shook her head unbelievingly. "If you'd have told me, just a little over a year ago, that you walking back into my life was about to trigger the biggest civil war in the history of mankind, I'd have laughed at you."

"Well, it wasn't *all* me," I said defensively. "Even if those rumors hadn't started spreading about the *Revelation* after we raided it. The Paragon's cracks were already showing. This all would still have happened. Just... later, probably."

"And I might still have been on Vatheson's good side," she said as if she were recounting a fond dream. "Meaning that when Divinity offed him, I might've stood to take over most of his business. Instead of running a war effort."

I smirked at the thought. "Sure. But then you'd be in real trouble. You wouldn't have Renault on your side. Or the Roamers."

"Or you," she said softly, putting her hand on mine.

"Or me." I interlocked my fingers with hers.

We sat in silence, each of us still knowing all the things we wanted to say—and what the other would respond with. They were discussions we'd had over and over again.

"How does everyone on the station feel about all this?" I asked. "The citizens, I mean."

"About the war?" Sev shrugged. "They're on board. Not to talk myself up too much, but I've done a pretty good job selling the idea of independence to them. Self-governance and all that."

"You think it'll work?" I took another drink. "After all this?"

"Sure. They'll need to strike up some good trade deals, but that's always how it's been."

"They?" I raised an eyebrow.

"Yeah." She ran her finger around the lip of her glass. "I've made it very clear to them that I'm only managing things until the war's resolved, then I'll let the people decide how they want to run things around here. Jala's full of ideas. Wants to write out a constitution and everything. I don't know the first thing about any of that, so I figured I'll just leave them to it."

I raised an eyebrow. "*A leader's supposed to build a better future for everybody else, even if they're not in it.* Did I get that right?"

She grinned. "I see somebody's been paying attention."

"Well, with a woman as pretty as you, it's hard not to."

We fell silent, staring down at our drinks, feeling the weight of the storm looming behind us.

"You've got a bad feeling about this, don't you?" she finally said.

"Yeah." The word was barely audible.

She sighed and leaned into me. "I know there are no guarantees of happy endings in life. We're both too old to pretend otherwise. But... if we can't at least *believe* we'll get our happy ending, well, what's the point?"

A ray of light crept across the shadows of the bar. I glanced over my shoulder to see Rid poking his head through the door.

"It's time," he said. "The Paragon's assault fleet just entered nullspace."

I nodded. That gave us roughly ten precious hours before they could receive word of the battle. Rid retreated, pulling the door shut behind him and leaving a long, pregnant silence in his wake.

Sev took a deep, shaky breath. "Well. Shouldn't... keep 'em waiting, I suppose. Got a whole galaxy to save out there."

"Yeah." I finished off my drink, then pushed the glass away and rose to my feet. "I—"

Sev slid from her chair and kissed me, standing on her toes to reach my lips. I lost track of how long we were there, holding each other. When she finally pulled gently away, it was all I could do to stare at her. To wonder how I'd gotten so damn lucky.

Just like that, all of the dread that had been building up inside of me vanished. I grinned, then made a hook with my little finger.

"When I get back..." I raised an eyebrow. "Buried treasure?"

She grinned back at me, then linked her finger with mine. "Ar."

I pulled her close, kissing her again. Heard the door open. "We really need to go," Rid said.

I broke away from Sev, gave her one last smile, and turned for the door.

"Ready?" Rid asked.

I nodded.

TWENTY-THREE

From looking at Khendar's face—or the holographic image of it floating in the center of the *Orpheus*'s bridge, at least—you'd never have guessed that she was currently co-ordinating the single biggest space battle in human history. She looked calm and stoic, as if this were any other day at the office.

"VanDunn," she said briskly. "Are your teams ready to move?"

"Already moving," I said. "We've got six interceptors trained and ready to head for the Gideon foldgate as soon as you give the word."

"Good." She nodded. "I've been in communication with Admiral Renault already. His fleet will make a valuable addition to the primary assault group."

Admiral, huh? I restrained an amused smirk. "He's a hell of a leader and a good tactician, too," I said. "He'll more than pull his weight."

"He'll need to. This battle is far from a foregone conclusion. Your plan's a good one, but we should be ready to adapt. Keep an open mind. Should you be successful, I'd like to personally see you aboard my ship to congratulate you."

I took a deep breath. *All part of the plan.* "I'd be honored, of course."

She eyed me. "And if you're *not* successful... well, I hope it will give you peace of mind to know that I *do* have a backup plan." She gave a cold, malignant smile. "*Lots* of backup plans. For *lots* of scenarios."

That smile was the last thing I saw of her before she disappeared.

I glanced out of the *Orpheus*'s window. Renault's fleet loomed to our right: eleven warships of varying sizes, all of them repaired and battle ready. They certainly weren't the newest ships in the galaxy—hell, most of them were positively ancient—but Renault had spent years upgrading them. They packed far more speed and firepower than they appeared to. Their underwhelming appearance was part of what made them such dangerous pirate ships. The *Walrus* was in the center.

Behind us, if I squinted, I could make out the other five stealth interceptors. If I hadn't known where to look, they'd have been all but invisible. And ahead of us loomed our own foldgate, connecting the Albeni system to Alpha Centauri.

"Well, they definitely know that we're coming," Rose mused, peering up at the massive structure. "The crew is probably alerting the Paragon as we speak."

"Why don't they just..." Rid frowned. "Shut it off on us? Trap us here?"

"A machine that big doesn't just turn off and on with the switch of a button," Bentley said. "There's a reason they're so damn hard to destroy."

The communications console chimed. Bentley looked down at it. His face paled.

"It's time," he said.

I took a deep breath.

They say that right before you die, your whole life flashes before your eyes. I don't know if that's true. But I know it sure as hell happens right before you *almost* die. And sometimes even before that.

In that deep breath I took right then, I saw my life stretch out like a long, rocky hill I'd been rolling down. My old man selling me to the Paragon. The War. Meeting Kess. The *Panama*. Artemis and the *Revelation*. Cairn and the Stranger and everything that had happened on the *Aboena*. A long, bloody trail of bodies, all leading to this.

It *had* to mean something. Something more than which puppet government Divinity used to rule humanity.

Rose looked at me. "Shall we?"

I nodded.

The *Orpheus* jolted, the gravity generators unable to fully compensate for the rapid acceleration. We shot through the Albeni system foldgate and into the Alpha Centauri system, then veered around it as Rose set a course straight for our target. I glanced out the bridge window to our right, towards the rebel fleets that had just emerged from their respective foldgates. It wasn't a particularly impressive sight—not from here, at least. I had to squint just to see them. It was hard to believe that the assortment of little gray specks I was seeing represented thousands of rebels.

"Well, they definitely see them," Rid said.

I followed his gaze across the window to the other side of the foldgate system. I could see the Paragon fleet gathered outside the Redhawk gate. As I watched, roughly half of the gathered ships began moving slowly towards the center of the system, where the Sovereign ships were moving.

I turned my attention away from the window and towards the holoprojector in the center of the bridge. The layout of the battle was much easier to understand from there. I could see the two fleets laid out in green and red on opposite sides of the ring of foldgates. The red fleet—the Paragon—had fewer ships, but I figured that any one of their battlecruisers was worth at least three of the archaic warships the rebels had managed to cobble together. The green fleet was approaching from four different foldgates, moving to converge on the Paragon forces in the middle of the system, while the red ships were spreading out to meet them.

"They're taking their sweet time, aren't they?" Bentley muttered nervously.

"That's large-scale space combat for you," I said, watching the two fleets as they moved ponderously towards each other. "Like watching a boxing match in slow motion."

Bentley shuddered. "I have to say, as daunting as the prospect of doing... you know, what *we're* about to do, I think I much prefer it over the idea of being trapped on one of those tin cans."

I nodded grimly. I was an infantry trooper by training, and I'd always found myself deeply disturbed by space combat. In a ground war you could die unexpectedly in any number of ways, but you at least had the illusion of agency. Being trapped in a ship, waiting for torpedoes to strike, knowing that there was nothing you could do... now *that* was terrifying. Give me a Jackhammer and a swarm of rippers any day.

The good news, for now at least, was that the large rebel fleet seemed to be serving its purpose: it had the Paragon's full attention. There was no indication that anybody could see us as we cut through the void towards our target.

An alarm sounded briefly. Rose glanced at her screen. "Seems like the party's getting started."

I looked towards the Paragon fleet just in time to see dozens of tiny specks of light shoot out from their ships, streaking through the darkness towards the rebels. Torpedoes—each one packed with enough explosive power to devastate an entire citystation. More than likely there were a few ripper pods mixed in as well.

Not until the torpedoes had crossed fully half the distance

was there any sign of action from the rebels. They were too small to see through the window, but the scanner picked them up: a flurry of anti-torpedo missiles.

Bright flashes cut through the darkness as the missiles did their work, intercepting and destroying as many torpedoes as they could connect with. From my best guess a full two-thirds of the Paragon's volley was destroyed. The remainder surged forward through the debris.

"Come on," Rose whispered as we watched them progress. "Stop them."

The rebel ships did nothing, their impending doom surging closer with each second. Finally, just when it seemed like it was too late, there was a series of flashes as the remaining torpedoes were caught in a barrage of flak cannons and energy beams. A jubilant cheer filled the *Orpheus*'s bridge.

"Hell yeah!" Rose cried. "That's one for the—"

Her celebration cut off abruptly as another flash of light— far brighter than the others—erupted from the rebel fleet. Looked like one of the torpedoes had somehow made it through the defensive fire unscathed and reached its target. One of the tiny gray specks vanished.

A somber silence filled the bridge. I stared out at the empty space where that rebel ship had been just a few moments ago, then glanced down at the holomap to double check that it hadn't been one of Renault's. A surge of relief, followed by an even stronger surge of guilt, filled me as I confirmed that it wasn't. I didn't know what kind of ship it had been, or how big its crew was, but it certainly hadn't been small. I tried to imagine the scene. Hundreds of lives snuffed out all at once in a blaze of heat—if you were lucky. A massive work of steel and technology capable of traversing the stars reduced to a cloud of debris.

I wanted to feel that it was a heroic loss. That they were making a noble sacrifice. But all I could think about was that man's face. The one who had confronted Vatheson in his final moments.

I own the Sovereign Systems, idiot.

Another wave of torpedoes was already on its way. They looked so tiny and insignificant from here. Maybe they were, in the grand scheme of things.

No heroes. Just puppets.

The rebels had an answer, though. They fired a salvo of their own. The two waves of distant specks passed silently through each other on their way to their respective targets.

"Look." Bentley pointed at the holomap, eyes wide. "The Sovereign's Redhawk fleet is attacking."

It was too far to see the action with the naked eye, but the holomap told the tale well enough. The Paragon ships outside the Redhawk gate began flashing as they received fire from inside. A few of them returned the favor, while others began to reposition, moving away from the opening in space.

"Aren't they afraid of hitting the foldgate?" Shell asked, voice slightly aghast.

"They aren't exactly spraying and praying," I said. "Those are long range munitions they're firing at each other. Accurate to a pinpoint. They won't hit the gate unless they want to."

"Wouldn't that be to their advantage, though?" Rid frowned. "The Paragon's, I mean. If the foldgate is gone, the Sovereign fleet can't get to them."

"Sure," I said. "In the short term. But then they lose the whole system. That's the whole reason our plan is gonna work."

Well. The whole reason I *hoped* it would work. I felt my throat tighten as I thought about Nalis's final words to me before the battle.

I could only shake my head at the grim absurdity of it. Munitions being fired from thousands of lightyears away, traveling across the galaxy in the blink of an eye as they passed through the foldgates. Oh, the terrible wonders of the modern age.

All while, somewhere, watching from the shadows, Divinity laughed.

Renault's fleet was now joining the fray. His eleven warships were fanning out from the Albeni foldgate. As per our prior discussion, his position was guarded, cautious. He wasn't the prime target for any of the Paragon ships.

"Why's he staying put?" Rose asked. "He's not gonna be able to be much help from there."

The answer came a moment later. Dozens of little green dots separated from his fleet on the minimap and began making their way into the middle of the battlespace.

Bentley frowned down at them. "Are those..."

"Hunter drones," I said.

It took time for the drones to reach their destination—time during which the Paragon continued firing volley after volley of torpedoes at the rebel fleet. It was beginning to look like the rebels would run out of countermeasures before the Paragon ran out of torpedoes. Two more rebel ships were struck, the brightness of their demise illuminating the chaos around them. Floating bits of debris cast long shadows on the other rebel ships.

"I'd say there will be some good salvage work to do after this," Bentley said, "but it doesn't look like there'll be anything *left* to salvage. Not if the Sovereigns keep taking hits at this rate, at least."

Another wave of torpedoes shot out from the Paragon fleet. A meager scattering of missiles from the rebels took out only a handful of them, the rest continuing on towards the unprotected fleet. Before they could strike, though, they passed by Renault's hunter drones.

One by one, the torpedoes exploded. The hunter drones

remained intact. The few torpedoes that successfully made it past them were quickly dismantled by the rebel's close range defensive batteries.

Rose frowned at the minimap. "What're they..."

"Renault upgraded them," I said. "Fitted each drone with an ultracell and a high-powered laser and a tracking system, so they can destroy nearby projectiles without sacrificing themselves."

The Paragon fleet had a response for that too, though: the entire approaching mass of ships doubled its pace. As soon as they were in firing range the hunter drones would be easy pickings. The drones were forced to pull back closer to the rebel fleet in response.

"We're closing in," Rose said, tearing my attention away from the raging battle. "Looks like we're gonna be starting our own show up here."

I looked ahead. The Gideon foldgate loomed before us. Somehow, it felt like seeing a foldgate for the first time. After so many years of constantly traveling through them, I'd come to see them as simply a part of the scenery, as if they were natural, celestial objects rather than man-made wonders. There was a reason that they hadn't been targeted in the Last War: most people saw them as irreplaceable, almost sacred parts of humanity. The links that made our star-spanning civilization possible. The thought of destroying a foldgate—of severing that tie and locking entire populations into their own corner of the galaxy—still made me feel a bit queasy. But maybe it was better that way. The quantum network meant that there would still be communication with those marooned systems. It would just be impossible to travel there until another foldgate had been built. And who knew when that would happen—or who would come up with the funds to do it.

But all that was irrelevant now. I pushed the thoughts aside, focusing my attention on the task at hand. The foldgate flipped in my mind from an ancient marvel to a tactical target.

One target to deal with the Paragon. To put a stop to this blasted, meaningless war of puppets. And then, afterwards, to deal with the puppet masters themselves.

It scared me that I found that part even more daunting than the already seemingly impossible task now before us.

One fight at a time. I turned away from the window, and the ever-growing foldgate beyond it, and towards the hatch. "Alright," I said. "Let's gear up."

"How's it looking out there?" I asked Rose over the comms as I stepped out from the Icarus's mounting frame, testing its joints for the thousandth time in the past few days. Everything worked smoothly.

"Good. No sign that anybody's spotted us. Like you said, I think everybody's pretty focused on the battle."

"How about the battle itself?"

"No significant new developments. Paragon is continuing to push. Hunter drone screen is retreating. The Sovereigns haven't taken any more losses, but the Redhawk fleet is still trapped on the wrong side of their foldgate."

"Hell of a fight," Flint said, grinning through the open visor of his Jericho. He and his squad were going aboard with us. We'd all go to the powercore together, at which point his team of handpicked companions would remain to secure the bomb while my crew and I would continue on to the control room.

I nodded my agreement. "Always hated space battles. Feels like all you can do is wait."

Shell stepped up to us. "Team's ready, and the hullbreaker is loaded up."

"Good." I grabbed an APMP from the weapons rack and began loading magazines into my belt. "Alright—listen up, everyone. I've said it a thousand times but I'm gonna say it again. This ain't like any mission we've ever done before—any of us. We're not here to collect loot. We're not even here to defeat the enemy. We are here to complete our objectives and get out as quickly as possible. Do not engage unless necessary. Do not get pinned down. Protect the payload at all costs. If we want any chance of making it out of this alive, we *must* get the bombs into position as quickly as possible. That leverage will be our primary advantage. Understood?"

Nods all around.

"*Moving into position,*" Rose's voice said over the intercom. "*Time to load up.*"

One by one, we filed into the airlock. I went first, with my team stacking behind me. The cargo truck—with the hull-breaker bomb strapped to it—filled the middle. Flint and his five pirates filled up the rest of the space.

The airlock doors sealed shut. There was a hiss as the depressurization process began. I used my neurointerface to snap the visor of the Icarus shut.

"Hey," Bentley said. "Remember when we were just a bunch of lowlife salvagers? Risking our lives for scraps?"

I grunted.

DEPRESSURIZATION COMPLETE, flashed a message in the overhead airlock.

"Those were the days." Bentley sighed fondly.

The doors opened silently. I could see our target: a maintenance hatch embedded in the inner side of the foldgate's surface, roughly twenty meters below us. Once through there, we'd begin working our way down, into the core of the station's massive ring, until we reached the powercore.

I grabbed on to the side of the airlock and pulled myself into the void.

TWENTY-FOUR

There is something deeply terrifying about the sensation of floating free in space.

The sound of your breath cycling in your life-support system, and beyond that the oppressive, smothering silence of the vacuum. The complete absence of gravity. The eternal, inky blackness surrounding you. All of it combines to leave you feeling completely exposed and utterly vulnerable.

That feeling was not improved by the scale of the monstrous structure looming before me. No—not before me. *Around* me.

Focus. I pulled myself to the maintenance hatch below me, restraining myself from looking over my shoulder to take in the foldgate's monstrous size. I aimed towards it and used my neurointerface to trigger my thrusters.

I studied the emitters as we drew closer. According to the schematics, each blade-shaped device was roughly eighty meters long and half again as wide. Not that you could tell, though; most of that was embedded deep within the ring itself, and the small portion of it that wasn't was sheathed within a protective layer of steel plating. The only exposed bit was on the very end, where I could see a faint, otherworldly white light emanating.

My magboots locked to the surface of the foldgate next to the hatch. Satisfied that I was securely in position, I finally allowed myself to look upwards.

It was one of the most surreal sights I'd ever seen. The rest of the team following after me, a trail of bodies suspended in nothingness between where I stood and the *Orpheus*. Beyond the *Orpheus* I saw the other interceptors depositing their crews at their designated entry points. And beyond them, of course, was the foldgate.

My breath caught in my throat.

I'd been through foldgates hundreds of times. Eventually you got used to them. But being here—physically standing on the surface of one, peering upwards at its massive arc—was an entirely different experience. I had never felt so small and insignificant before. I could barely even believe that the structure I was standing on had been built by humans. The longer I stared, the dizzier I became, as if afraid that I would suddenly slip and fall the fifteen kilometers to the far side of the foldgate's ring.

The inside of the arc's wide, flat surface was bisected by the ring of emitters, each one shimmering with that ghostly white light. It was hard to fathom that the machinery on the other side of the emitters was a *different* foldgate. I'd long since given up trying to understand how the science worked, but it felt wrong. Unnatural. Then again, though, if humanity had stuck to what felt natural, we'd still be on Earth. And maybe we'd be better off for it.

I turned my gaze beyond the foldgate and into the Gideon system beyond. Truth be told, I didn't know much about Gideon. I'd just been a dumb kid when I lived there, and given the system's long-entrenched loyalty to the Paragon, there'd never been any call for me to go there as a Vanguard—or as a vulture. I spotted several large stations and dozens of large cargo ships in the distance. What really drew my eye, though, was the planet they were orbiting.

Gideon was a beautiful swirl of green, blue, and white. I remembered enough history to know that it was one of the few planets humans hadn't had to terraform at all before settling; a perfect Earth-like world. I could barely see the shape of the continent my family's farm had been on, veiled beneath a thin layer of cloud. I wondered if they were still down there, at the same farm, harvesting the same crops, making the same sched-uled drops to the Paragon. If things went to hell up here and we had to blow the foldgate, they'd have no idea that their son had been the one to do it. To cut them off from the rest of humanity.

But, again. It was better than getting eaten by rippers.

Rid was right after me, his lockbreaking kit already extended and ready to go. He got to work on the maintenance hatch immediately. While he worked, I studied the emitters closest to us, trying to ground myself from staring into the void. They protruded out of the surface of the ring to roughly waist height. I took a few cautious steps towards them while Rid did his work, peering over their edge and at the foldgate surface on just the other side.

I held my breath and—against my better judgement—extended one hand over the emitters, through the thin sheet of pale light, and into the Gideon system, several thousand lightyears away. The closest I'd been to home in almost thirty years.

"Almost ready," Rid grunted.

I turned around, pulling my thoughts back to the mission and my hand back into the Alpha Centauri system. Sparks flew from Rid's plasma cutter and spiraled into the void like tiny meteorites as he finished slicing through the locking mecha-nism. He powered off the cutting tool, grabbed the handle of the maintenance hatch, and pulled. It came open silently. In a stark contrast to the utter darkness we were usually greeted with upon entering a ship, however, white light emanated from the entryway.

He gestured towards me. I nodded, approached, and deactivated my magboots so I could lower myself into the hatch. I paused only briefly to glance upwards. Rose had rotated the *Orpheus* so she could see us through the bridge window. I could vaguely make out her form in the pilot's seat, neck craned as she watched us.

Beyond the *Orpheus*, the darkness of the Alpha Centauri system was broken by thousands of tiny specks of light. The explosions representing the deaths of thousands of soldiers—Sovereign and Paragon alike—were distinguishable from the distant stars beyond only by the briefness of their flares.

I took a deep breath and descended.

My eyes widened.

Beneath the steel plating that made up the surface of the foldgate was an entirely new world. One I'd seen, on a conceptual level at least, in the schematics. But looking at it with my own eyes was entirely different. The emitter blades were exposed down here, long and sharp and so incandescently white that my visor automatically darkened in response. I know it's impossible, given the vacuum and everything, but I swore I could almost hear them. Or maybe feel is a better word. As if the force with which they were cutting apart the fabric of reality was so strong that it reverberated through whatever unknowable essence makes up space itself.

I shook myself, tearing my eyes away from the emitters and familiarizing myself with the rest of my surroundings. I was in a long, chasm-like cavity, with the wall of emitters in front of me, stretching out to either side as far as I could see. The hatch I'd descended through was oriented above me. Roughly thirty meters behind me, a steel plate wall. And below me, the innards of the foldgate, extending as far as I could see, aglow in eerie white.

Rid lowered himself in after me, letting out a low whistle. "So that's what it looks like in here." He pushed past me, descending deeper into the machine. "Come on. Let's keep moving."

I shook my head and followed him. He'd come a hell of a long ways from being the bright-eyed rookie I'd met in prison, desperate to get away from his old gang. I remembered how awestruck he'd been the first time we'd passed through a foldgate together. Now it was just another day on the job.

Then again—he'd worked some *wild* jobs with me.

I followed, periodically glancing back to make sure the rest of the team—and their cargo—made it in smoothly. It would've been an awkward start to the most important mission of my life —maybe of *anybody's* life—if we'd somehow gotten the measurements wrong and the bomb didn't fit through the hatch. It did, though.

"Alright. I want four people on that truck," I said once it was through. "Do *not* let it get anywhere near that emitter blade. If it touches..."

"The energy from the blades'll set it off," Flint growled. "We know."

I shut my mouth, focusing on safely navigating the rest of the descent myself. We'd trained for this over and over again. Every detail was rehearsed. But it still didn't hurt to give a final reminder. Especially when we were carrying enough explosive power to blow up a...

Well. To blow up a foldgate.

Eventually, the emitter blades ended, each one connecting to an almost comically oversized socket. Dozens of cables, each at least three meters thick, extended from each socket and vanished into the basing. Looking at it made me feel like I'd been shrunk and placed inside of a regular-sized electronic device.

"That'll be the powercore on the other side," I said. I raised my wrist computer, turning on the map of the foldgate. "The airlock should be…"

"Right here." Rid was already cutting open the control panel, and Bentley was already gliding past me, datapad in hand, prepared to do his part. Within minutes, Rid had the outer door of the airlock open and Bentley was inside, hacking into the control system so he could begin the pressurization process, while Shell had her Jackhammer aimed at the secondary doors just in case something came through them.

It was an odd feeling. Knowing that I'd trained them well enough they hardly needed me. On the one hand I couldn't help but feel proud. That was the goal, after all. On the other hand, though, there was a tiny part of me that wanted to hold on to that feeling of being needed. Looked up to.

Not the time. I entered the airlock and made way for the rest of the team to pile in as Bentley sealed the outer door and began the pressurization process. The airlock was built for moving large machine parts, so it was more than big enough to fit all of us plus our cargo truck.

I unslung my rifle as the pressurization neared completion. "Once we're through here we'll be in the gravity field," I reminded everyone. "Chances are they haven't noticed us yet, but we can't be sure, so stay frosty. Don't kill anyone we don't need to, but don't give anyone a chance to run off and alert the rest of the station. The longer we go before the alarm is sounded the easier a time we'll have of it. Everybody good?"

Affirmations all around. I used my neurointerface to radio the other five teams. "All teams, this is team one. We are about to breach the foldgate airlock. Status reports."

They sounded off one by one. They were slightly behind us, but they were all in place. Nothing left to do but move forward.

"It's done," Bentley said.

"Open it."

The doors whirred open. I oriented myself so I was aligned with the foldgate's artificial gravity and stepped out of the airlock, letting my weight pull me down to my feet. We were in a long, barren corridor that curved with the foldgate. I swung left, scanning for threats, while Shell checked the right side.

"Clear," we said simultaneously.

I immediately pressed on to the left. Shell stayed where she was, covering our rear, while the rest of the team filed after me. The cargo truck was slower than it had been while weightless, but its magnetic propulsors kept it hovering above the floor as Flint and his team pulled it after us.

It was a short walk to our destination, and one I knew by heart thanks to our hours of training. Down the corridor forty meters and through the doors on the right. Down another short corridor in the opposite direction and through a door on the left. Down a flight of stairs, through another door, and we'd be in the powercore room.

I noticed a security camera watching us sullenly as we passed through the first door. I ignored it. Best we could do was hope that the security teams were too busy watching the slugfest happening across the system. Hell, they were probably wondering if they should get ready to evacuate. But we'd find out soon enough.

We strode unopposed down the stairs and to the doorway at the bottom. It was sealed, but Rid needed only a few seconds to get through the barebones electronic lock. Soon as he gave me the word I kicked it open and pushed through, APMP up and at the ready.

For a short moment, I felt like I was on the *Aboena* again, getting ready to face down Cairn. We were on a long catwalk that led over the powercore—a mass of whirling machinery, singing happily as it endlessly churned. This powercore was, of course, different than the one that had powered the *Aboena*. For one thing, it was built to follow the curve of the foldgate. For another, it was covered, wrapped by a cage to keep anyone from suffering the same grisly fate I'd given Cairn.

"Come on." I strode towards another stairway that led down and around the powercore's massive girth and into its undercarriage, referencing my minimap to ensure I was going to the right place. There was a specific part of the powercore's machinery that the bomb needed to destroy in order to unleash the foldgate's full energy upon itself. If we missed it, we'd still destroy the powercore, but the explosion wouldn't be big enough to cause the massive, irreparable damage we wanted to inflict—or, at least, wanted to threaten.

I heard voices coming from below as I descended the stairs, but I didn't slow. They didn't seem to know we were here.

"Even if they win," somebody was shouting over the sound of the powercore, "won't make a difference to us, you know? Either the Paragon pays us or somebody else pays us. Either way, someone's gonna need to run this station."

"Run?" a second voice cackled. "You can barely walk!"

I rounded a column and stepped onto a platform that ran the length of the powercore's undercarriage. Two maintenance workers—one of them, an overweight man currently wearing a look of equal parts offense and amusement, was leaning over a computer panel, while the other was laughing at him. They must have felt the vibrations my heavy exo made as I stepped onto the platform, because they turned and looked at me before I could say so much as a word.

The fat man blinked. "We didn't call security," he shouted. "If Marsden sent you here, you'd better tell him—"

His buddy slapped his arm, face pale. "That's—that's not security," he gasped.

I strode forward, not bothering to aim my weapon at them.

"Not here to hurt you," I said. "But I'm gonna need you to step away from the computer."

They stood frozen in shock for a moment, eyes flitting from me to the nearly dozen armored and armed people behind me. Finally, as if suddenly realizing just how much danger they were in, they staggered away from the computer like it was some kind of wild animal threatening to bite them.

"Cuff 'em to that pillar," I said, striding past them. "And search 'em. Make sure they can't signal anyone. But be damn sure you cut 'em loose before you leave."

Flint chuckled darkly as he descended upon them. "Oh, we'll *cut* 'em, alright."

I sighed. I'd known him long enough now to know he didn't mean it, but tormenting innocent prisoners seemed like one of his greatest pleasures in life. I turned to the rest of my team as Flint's pirates awkwardly pulled the cargo truck down the stairs. "Everybody set?"

"Good to go," Shell said.

"Flint," I said. "You're good here?"

"Happier than ever," he cackled as he snapped a pair of magcuffs around the second technician's wrists. "We'll have it all rigged in no time."

"Then let's move." I turned and pressed on without a backward glance, switching my channel to all team leaders. "All teams. Status."

Once again, there came a series of sequential responses. Teams two through four were at their powercores, had faced no resistance, and found no bystanders. Team five had been delayed by a brief cargo truck malfunction but were on the move again. I took each report in stride as we made our way to the service elevator that would carry us up to the control room.

"*Team six is almost in position,*" Winter's deep, grating voice said in my ear. "*We've yet to encounter any—*"

His voice shuddered and cut off, jolted by gunshots. He

gave a sharp, unfamiliar curse I assumed was Aboenian. *"We found the enemy,"* he growled.

Dammit. "How many?"

"Just a handful. They offered light resistance before fleeing. We killed three, but one is fleeing." His breath huffed. *"We're in pursuit."*

"Focus on the objective," I said, gesturing for Rid to open the service elevator. "Don't let them distract you. It's just a matter of time before they realize we're here." Still, though, a jolt of concern shot through me. The sooner we got caught, the more complicated this would be. And we didn't have much room for complication.

Instead of pulling out his kit, Rid simply held up a security chip he'd taken from the two maintenance workers, then held it up to the lock. It flashed green and the doors slid open.

The ride up was harrowing. The elevator moved slowly and with each grinding second I was certain that it would halt as the control room threw the entire station into lockdown. I spotted a security camera and destroyed it by applying light pressure from an outstretched, gauntleted finger.

"In position," Winter said, his voice lined with frustration. *"The hostile escaped, though."*

"Affirmative," I said, keeping my voice calm and level. "It was just a matter of time. All teams, ensure your positions are defendable and finish setting the explosives. Expect security to begin poking around. We're almost to the control room."

"If this damn elevator ever starts moving faster," Shell growled.

The damn elevator didn't move any faster. When I glanced at the control panel, indicating our progress, I remembered—with a rush of anxiety—just how massive the foldgate was. We'd gone less than half of the distance to the control room floor.

"Rose," I said into the comms. "What's going on out there?"

"Nothing near us," she said. *"But the larger battle seems to*

be going well. The Paragon's fleet is actually getting pushed back."

"Huh," Bentley said. "Maybe they won't even need us after all. What say we quit early and get some food on the way home?"

Rid chuckled softly.

The elevator finally ground to a halt. The doors slid open, ushering us into another long corridor no less utilitarian than the first one we'd found ourselves in. As soon as I stepped through, weapon at the ready, the lights overhead flashed to red and a klaxon started blaring overhead. I saw no targets though.

"Hmm," Bentley mused. "I think they suspect something."

"This way." I didn't even need to check my minimap. I sprinted down the hall at full speed. All that stood between us and the control panel was a few meters of corridor and a set of doors. "Hurry. If we can make it there before they lock, we won't have to wait for Rid to break through."

"It's only five minutes," Rid protested indignantly. "Which, I'll have you know, is *quite* fast."

I slid to a halt in front of the heavy blast doors. Dammit. No such luck. They were already sealed tight.

"Alright," I said, making room for Rid next to the control panel. "Five minutes."

I knew all too well that five minutes was enough for all kinds of things to go wrong.

Rid dropped to one knee, activating his plasma cutter while I took up a position aiming my APMP down the corridor. Bentley and Shell took up positions aiming in the opposite direction. Just like any old salvage job. I almost found myself calling for Nadus to fall into position.

I drove away the pang of emptiness that followed that realization by checking my minimap. Seven sets of green dots were clustered around different positions in the foldgate. Six of them were deep in the heart of the ring; the teams setting their bombs.

The seventh was my team, located on the outer edge of the foldgate. I quickly identified Flint's position, directly below mine, as well as Winter's, which was the next spot to the right.

Everyone was in position. I took a deep breath. Forced myself to be calm. All that could go wrong now was—

The blast doors opened suddenly.

I pivoted towards them, fully expecting to see a squad of fully armored Vanguards pouring through. Instead, a lone woman, clad in a sloppy Paragon officer's uniform, strode briskly through, muttering something under her breath and staring down at a datapad in her hands.

She came to halt, looked up, and stared straight down the barrel of my APMP.

The muttering stopped abruptly. Her eyes widened.

"Well," Bentley said. "That simplifies things."

Rid lowered his tools, his posture disappointed.

"Turn around," I growled. The Icarus's speaker made my voice sound metallic and menacing.

She let out a whimper and obeyed.

"Walk," I ordered.

She complied.

I followed immediately behind her, passing through the doorway. Inside I found a large, open room, lined with rows of computers. A massive screen took up the wall on the side closest to me, while the other side was a large window overlooking the Alpha Centauri system.

Dozens of Paragon personnel filled the room. Most of them were busy staring down at their computers, muttering to each other. A few were staring dumbfounded through the window at the distant battle raging beyond. A few more glanced up from their computers to stare dumbfounded at me.

"Figure out what's going on down there!" The speaker was an officer in a uniform that marked him as a captain, pacing back and forth at the front of the room with his back to me and bellowing at his subordinates. "Are all of you idiots blind *and* deaf? There's a war going on out there! If there's any chance of an internal threat, we need to…"

His voice trailed off as he noticed the disbelieving looks spreading through the room. He whirled in search of the distraction. "What are—"

His mouth hung open.

"Everyone stand up," I said, keeping my voice calm and making the Icarus project my voice loud enough for everyone to hear. "And line up facing out the window, hands behind your heads."

There was a moment of shocked silence.

"NOW!" roared Shell, stepping beside me.

That jolted them out of their stupors. Most of them obeyed immediately, their faces drawn and quivering, hardly daring to breathe as they shuffled towards the window at the back of the room. One of them—a young man with sharp, angry eyes—hesitated, standing in place and looking like he was contemplating reaching for the Paragon-issue pistol strapped to his side.

"Kid," I said as I strode towards him. "That thing won't even put a dent in my armor. In fact, I'm not even gonna ask you to give it to me. Now, can you walk over by yourself or do I need to toss you?"

He moved, his staunch determination crumpling into a whimper. I gestured towards the lineup, deactivating my exo's external speakers so only my team could hear me through our comms system. "Alright. We're clear. Let's set up shop."

"Already on it," Bentley said. Sure enough, he had already found the terminal he needed and started working. Rid, meanwhile, was busy shutting the blast doors, while Shell was corralling the last of the control room workers against the window.

"We're in the control room," I said on the general channel, glancing down at my holographic minimap. All teams looked like they were still in position. "The crew is subdued. Over-charge has started. Report in."

"*We're under attack! Vanguards pushing our position. We're holding them for now, but—*"

Dammit.

"*Holding against resistance. Incoming Vanguards.*"

Dammit.

"*We've got security heading our way. The bomb is ready to go, though.*"

Flint's voice was a casual drawl. "*Yup, we've got company too.*"

I gritted my teeth, staring down at the clusters of green dots. The security had sprung to life faster than I'd anticipated. I turned to our lineup of prisoners against the window, searching through them until my gaze settled on the older officer who'd been yelling at the room before we entered. His insignia was slightly different from the others.

I strode towards him, coming to a halt no more than a few feet away from him.

"Contact your security," I growled. "And tell them to stand down."

He narrowed his eyes at me. "You cannot possibly believe that you will get away with this."

Winter's voice sounded in my ear. "*We're being pushed extremely aggressively. We've got them in a chokepoint for now, but they'll break through soon.*"

"The Paragon will find you," the commanding officer continued, teeth bared. "And you will regret that you ever so much as *considered—*"

"Shut up." I stepped close to him, lowering my rifle. "I won't tell you again. Call security off. Tell 'em to go back to their quarters."

His face was set in stone. "You'll have to kill me."

I glanced down at his chest. Just below his insignia was a

diamond shaped medal, bearing a simple image of a hand with a string dangling from each finger.

My breath caught in my throat. I'd seen that symbol before.

I'd seen it across a dozen different planets, once the fighting was over and us Vanguards—those who had survived, anyway—watched the shuttles carrying all our officers, the voices in our heads, the eyes looking down on us from the sky and pressing the little buttons that sent the ignicerin through our veins, down to see what remained of the land we'd conquered for them. Well, not for them. For the Paragon. For Divinity. Strings pulling strings pulling strings pulling strings...

A cold, steady hatred crystalized in my chest.

"You're ex-SkyCom, aren't you?" I said.

He glanced down at the insignia, then straightened as if on inspection. He said nothing. The woman standing next to him gave the start of a choking sob as she realized what was happening.

I didn't care. Memories of a dozen different battlefields across a dozen different worlds were flashing through my brain. Memories of waiting in desolate cities and muddy trenches for the moment the ignicerin would kick in, triggered by some bastard in a spaceship in high orbit who couldn't care less what happened to me. Memories of my reactions feeling flat and sluggish when I needed them to be sharp as I tried to fight under the weight of a wrongly administered dose of frigicerin. Memories of seeing my buddies be torn apart by rippers, unable to know or care due to the chemicals being pumped through their bodies.

I raised my visor. The man took a sharp, frightened breath as he saw my face. I wasn't expecting him to recognize me personally, but I knew that he'd recognize a Vanguard when he saw one. And I wanted him—at least once in his life—to look into the eyes of a puppet who wasn't attached to any strings.

Not strings he could grab, at least.

"*We're being pushed back!*" Winter exclaimed in my ear.

"I'll have to kill you, huh?" I growled. "That's just fine by me."

He clenched his eyes shut. The scent of ammonia hit my nose as I saw a dark stain spreading through his pants. I didn't care. Before I could think twice about it, my gauntlet was wrapped around his head. Just like on Brahma. Except I wouldn't need any ignicerin to get me to pop this bastard's skull like a grape.

"Wait!" Another officer—a middle-aged woman—spun on me, holding up her hands imploringly. "Don't. Please don't. Even if we wanted to call them off, security wouldn't listen. They don't answer to us. If anything, we answer to *them*."

I gritted my teeth, my eyes fixed on the commanding officer. I could see one of his eyes between the fingers of my gauntlet, wide and terrified, flicking back and forth. All I had to do was squeeze lightly. I wanted to. The cold hatred in my heart was burning now with an intensity I hadn't realized I possessed for SkyCom.

This man deserved to die. Not only for what he'd done to me—or at least to Vanguards like me—but for what he'd done *through* us. The thousands of civilians he'd casually doomed with the press of a button. He deserved to die the same way they had.

"Hey." It was Rid. Speaking softly, standing next to me. "Lax. This isn't you. We need to focus."

My gaze flicked back to the officer. To his one, exposed, terrified eye, locked on mine.

My fingers tensed. "You don't understand. You don't know what bastards like him *did* to us."

"No." Rid raised his visor, locking his gaze with mine. "I don't. But you're better than them, Lax. I know you are."

I stared at the old man. Watched the fear—that pathetic, gurgling fear—choke in his throat. Then back to Rid. He nodded.

I let go. The old man sank to the floor with a sob.

The fury drained out of me all at once. Rid was right. The Paragon had trained me to be a killer before everything else. I'd worked damn hard to become a better person than that. He might deserve to die, but that didn't make killing him right. Not for me, anyway.

I sighed, turning away. "Winter. Pull back. We only need to take out five of the six cores for the plan to work. Meet up with Flint's team and hold there."

"*Confirmed. We're retreating.*" There was tangible relief in Winter's voice.

"All teams, *hold your ground*," I said. "We've still got five of the cores secured. As long as we don't lose any more, the mission is still good to—"

Several things happened in very quick succession.

First: the blast doors—the ones we'd just come through—hissed open. A Vanguard clad in Jericho armor promptly stepped through, raising a Jackhammer.

Second: there was a flash of movement to my left as the young man with the pistol—the one who'd refused to leave his station until I forced him—drew his weapon, aiming it at my exposed face.

Third: I heard Winter give a horrified shout in the comms. His voice cut off, lost in an all-consuming *BOOM*.

Fourth: the station shook violently.

Frightened and confused screams filled the control room as the floor shook and trembled beneath us. The Vanguard staggered against the doorway. I swung towards him, barely managing to stay on my feet as I raised my rifle. I triggered my neurointerface to close my visor, but it was too late to matter. The kid's gun went off, his aim thrown by the sudden quake, and my head rang slightly as the bullet bounced off of the side of my helmet and sprayed sparks across my vision, ricocheting with a whining sound out of my line of sight.

The Vanguard recovered his footing and took aim, only to cry out as Shell fired her Jackhammer into him and drove him backward. He managed to get off a few wild shots, one of which slammed into the shoulder of the middle-aged woman and tore her arm off in a spray of gore. I fired my APMP from the hip, striking the Vanguard in the chest, then spun on the officer with the gun. His expression changed rapidly from smug satisfaction to horror right before the butt of my rifle struck his face with enough force to splatter bits of bone across the window behind him.

I panted for a moment, trying to process it all. My ears were full of screams. The station was still shaking beneath me. The Vanguard was still alive, groaning on the floor. Bentley was staring past me with wide, horrified eyes. And... why had that officer looked so smug right before I killed him?

I turned.

Rid stood limply, staring at me. His expression was glassy, unfocused. Blood poured steadily from a jagged black hole a few centimeters below his right eye.

He sagged backward.

"*Rid!*" I launched myself towards him, kneeling over him. He stared unblinkingly back up at me. A blur of movement caught my attention in the doorway—the Vanguard was groaning as he climbed back to his feet. I raised my APMP and put a single shot through his skull. He twitched and landed face first in the doorway.

Shell was still screaming something repeatedly into the comms. Bentley was shouting something that was just as unintelligible in that moment. I kept my APMP aimed at the doorway as I stared down at Rid.

He didn't move. Blood kept leaking from the wound the bullet had left in his face. A bullet that had been intended for *me*.

"RID!" I bellowed. "RID! Get up!"

"*Lax!*" Rose's voice sounded in my ear. "*What happened? Did one of the bombs go off?*"

"I..." My breath caught in my throat. Rid's body twitched, the movement barely noticeable through his exo. "I..."

"LAX!" Somebody's hand was on my shoulder. I looked up to see Bentley, his eyes narrowed through the sheen of his visor. "We need to move!" he snapped.

Somehow, hearing that from Bentley, of all people, snapped me back into the present moment.

"Shell!" I shouted. "Cover the door!"

She obliged. I held up my wrist computer, focusing on Rid's biofeed.

Still alive. His pulse was still going. It was hard to tell with his helmet, but from the angle the bullet had struck him at, I didn't think it had gone into his brain. That made me feel only slightly better, though. He would still die without treatment—better treatment than I could give him here. I drew an emergency patch kit from Bentley's own belt and sprayed a coagulant onto his wound, then manually sealed his visor shut.

"What's the status on the overcharge?" I asked Bentley briskly.

"Almost done," he said breathlessly.

"All teams report in," I said again, pulling up their statuses on my computer. They reported one by one. Team three was under attack. The others were all fine. Their bombs were all in place. There was no word from team six.

I finally pulled up Winter's biofeed. My heart fell.

No signal. From him, or anyone on his team.

Green dots, flashing red...

Shell's Jackhammer started barking as she fired it through the doorway at targets I couldn't see. Somebody returned fire, explosive rounds eating away at the walls near Shell.

"Rose," I called. "What's the situation from out there?"

"*Not good. More Paragon ships have arrived.*"

My heart missed a beat. "What?"

"*The third fleet,*" she said, voice urgent. "*It showed up. We don't know how. But the Sovereign fleet is getting attacked from all sides. It's a mess.*"

"What about the foldgate?" I asked. "Is it still open?"

"*Yeah. But it looks unstable. Some of the emitters are flickering.*"

Dammit. Damn *all* of it.

Deep breaths. We can still pull this off. We had five of the cores still rigged to blow. As soon as Bentley was done, we'd be good to go.

"Alright. We're on our way out. Bentley, are we clear to go?"

He glanced over at the computer screen he'd been working on. "Yeah. The overcharge is running and the system's so fried they won't be able to undo it after we're gone."

"Alright." I grunted as I heaved Rid onto my shoulder. "Time to go. All teams, evacuate. *Now.*"

"*Way ahead of you,*" Flint's voice rattled in my ear.

I used my neurointerface to open the direct channel to Nalis. "Gideon gate is set," I said as I strode towards the door, only to step back as bullets pierced through the walls and whistled past me. Armor-piercing. Shell scrambled back as well. I was in half a mind to ignore them, walk out, and hope the Icarus's advanced armor would protect me, but that meant exposing Rid to them.

A way out. There's always a way out...

I turned to the massive window.

Beyond it, I could see the rebel fleet, ever smaller as the Paragon forces pressed it. Rose had been right—it was a mess. Some of the ships were close enough now that I could make out their silhouettes. As I watched, a rebel ship erupted in a flash of light.

But that didn't matter now. The charges were set. Nalis

could hail the Paragon and begin demanding a ceasefire. We just needed to get out of here.

I dragged my focus inward, to the bloodied window itself. It was nearly indestructible, of course, like all outward-facing glass on any space station or ship. The fallen Vanguard's Jackhammer rounds had struck it in several places and left only the shallowest of marks. But I knew for certain that it wasn't *entirely* indestructible. I'd seen one get blown up before. It just had taken a specific type of explosion.

"Hold them off," I growled to Shell and Bentley, striding towards the window. Passing the distraught foldgate staff, along with the bloody remains of the two who had fallen. "Just for a minute. Rose—come up to the control room window."

"*What are you—oh. Oh no.*"

I reached behind my head, towards the compartment on the back of the Icarus. The one the ultracell that powered it was encapsulated in. It came out with a hiss. The Icarus continued running, its primary functions powered by an emergency power supply, but the conduction armor and the thermal blades would no longer function. I was basically wearing a glorified Jericho now.

I set the ultracell down on the floor against the surface of the window, then stepped backward until I was at the back of the room, with my back against the wall. Bullets whistled past me.

I fired three shots from the APMP at three different points around the ultracell. A tiny spiderweb of hairline fractures, barely visible, appeared. The remaining staff saw what I was doing and started screaming. They leaped to their feet and sprinted towards the exit, only for the first few to be cut down by a hail of gunfire from their own security team. The survivors withdrew into the room again.

Some small, distant part of me felt bad for them. But that part of me was buried beneath the part that knew one of my best friends was very likely dying in my arms, and that if I didn't get him medical care right away, he'd be gone. Just another green dot, flashing red. Forever.

I attached his exo to mine with an emergency strap.

"Everyone," I growled, taking aim one last time, "Brace yourselves."

I pulled the trigger.

The world turned white.

TWENTY-FIVE

I floated, and the universe sank beneath me.

I spun, trying to get my bearings, uncertain if I was dead or alive, dreaming or awake. The foldgate was gone. I was surrounded by stars and blackness and debris. A thousand tiny chunks of a thousand different ships, all of them obliterated.

And, mingled among them, corpses.

No.

I whirled faster, looking desperately for anyone I recognized. Pulled up my wrist computer, but all it showed was an endless starfield of green dots blinking red.

No. Please. Someone. Anyone.

Movement—above me. I looked up. Rid. Drifting, spinning lazily head over heels. I activated my thrusters and shot towards him, catching him in my arms.

"Hey. It's alright. I've got you. It's alright. I've..."

My heart sank.

There was a ragged black hole in his visor, right where the bullet had struck him. The bullet that had been meant for me.

No.

All I could do was stare. Try to make sense of it. What had

happened? Had the bombs all gone off? Where was everyone? Where was the battle? Why was there a hole in Rid's visor? Where was—

Something caught my eye. Something was coming *out* of the hole in Rid's visor. I recoiled slightly.

A small, pulsing, blood-red tendril.

It branched out, reaching blindly, then shot out towards me, wrapping around my chest. I tried to grab it, to pull it away from me, but it clung tight.

A dream. It had to be a dream. Please. *Please be a dream.*

Another tendril suddenly wrapped around my face. I looked behind me to see that it was extending from another corpse, one I now recognized as Winter. Another tendril caught my foot. More for my arms and feet.

I tried to shake them off, all in vain. The more I struggled the tighter they gripped me. There were more and more of them with each passing second. Tekka and his team. Kess and my old crew. Old Vanguard buddies. Faces I vaguely remembered killing for one reason or another. The assassins who had attacked Rose and me on Albeni 7 so long ago. Prisoners I had killed during my sentence. Rebels I'd killed as a Vanguard and Vanguards I'd killed as a rebel. Hundreds and hundreds of pulsing crimson vines entangled me, strangled me, stretching out from corpse to corpse in a root network of blood that spread across the entire universe.

From the dark, a hand beckoned to me. Strange and inhuman. Glowing white. I felt it tugging at the gray matter of my brain, just as the rippers had. Pulling me closer. Throbbing, *bursting*, with a single, all-consuming emotion.

HATE.

COME, MY CHOSEN, it whispered. *IT IS TIME FOR OUR CRUSADE.*

The hand reached closer. I recoiled from it.

THERE ARE NO HEROES, it whispered. *JUST PUPPETS.*

"No." I practically whimpered the word. "I don't believe it."

IT DOESN'T MATTER WHAT YOU BELIEVE. The hand inched closer still, light pulsing from beneath the surface of its skin, its too-long fingers stretched out. ONLY WHAT YOU DO.

I reached for it. I hated myself for it. But I reached for it.

The hand wrapped around mine.

Then pulled me forward, into the void.

————

"LAX!"

My eyes snapped open.

The world was a blur of motion around me. Distant lights spun in frantic, nauseating circles. Something massive and circular swam past my vision over and over and over again. I felt lightheaded.

"Lax! Can you hear me?" It was Rose's voice. Strained and faint in my ear. *"Where's Rid?"*

Rid.

Reality crystallized into place around me. I was spinning head over heels through the void after jettisoning myself, my crew, and the crew of the Gideon foldgate into space. A torrent of questions tore through my brain, but one thought cut through all of them.

Rid.

Instinct kicked in. I used my neurointerface to fire my thrusters in the opposite direction of my wild spin. The world slowed. The blood began to flow back from my head into the rest of my body. As soon as I was stable enough to control my own motion, I pivoted, trying to gauge my surroundings.

I'd spun a few hundred meters away from the control room. I could see it from here—a hollowed-out cavity of flickering lights. The debris from the explosion drifted all around me. Shards of broken glass. Blasted remnants of computers. The grisly remains of the control room crew, spinning in lifeless arcs through the uncaring void.

A shape loomed into my vision. Then another, a short way behind it. Bentley and Shell, their exo thrusters guiding them through the field of debris towards me. A brief surge of relief filled me as I called out to them. "Bentley! Shell!" I waved an arm. "Over here!"

"*I see him,*" Shell said. "*Rose, we've got eyes on Lax.*"

"*I'm on my way,*" Rose's voice said in my ear. "*Do you see him?*"

I spun, searching frantically through the debris. He had to be here. He had to be alive. He had to—

"There!" I spotted an exo-clad form spinning lazily away from us and activated my thrusters towards it. "This way!"

I jolted with movement. I would make it. I could catch him. I—

My thrusters flickered and died.

POWER SUPPLY DAMAGED, a message in my HUD read. LIMITING POWER TO LIFE-SUPPORT FUNCTIONS.

"No!" I screamed the word, flailing desperately, as if I could somehow swim towards the increasingly distant form of my friend. My movement was sluggish. "Rose! I see him! He's... he's..."

My voice faded. She couldn't hear me.

Rid's form grew smaller.

Green dots...

And all I could do was stare.

Flashing red...

A large shape suddenly zoomed to my right, towards Rid. The *Orpheus.* It veered around him. There was a rush of light as the airlock doors opened, allowing Rid's still form to sail through. My breath caught in my throat as I imagined Rid slamming into the far side of the airlock at fatal speed, but Rose was too good for that. The *Orpheus* decelerated gradually, allowing him to land gracefully on its wall.

Something seized me by the shoulder. I craned my head to see Shell wrapping an arm around my shoulder, firing her thrusters and guiding us both towards the *Orpheus*.

That stretch of open, silent space, listening to nothing but the sound of my own breath, was the longest journey of my life. On the other side of the *Orpheus* I could see the distant specks of light that were the tattered remains of the embattled fleets, but there was no room for them in my mind. No space for the Paragon or the Sovereigns. No space for Khendar or Ramar or our plan. No space for Divinity or the Stranger. No space for the war or the second war that was still unfought ahead of me. All my brain could make room for was Rid.

Please. Please, please, please. Just let him survive.

We finally reached the *Orpheus*'s embrace. The airlock doors closed around us. In the time it had taken us to get there, Rose must have already managed to get Rid inside, because there was no sign of him. I waited in dreadful silence as the airlock pressurized.

Please.

Let the trail of bodies end here.

The light on the airlock control panel finally turned green. I growled as I exerted all of my strength to move the Icarus's lifeless limbs towards my visor, unlatching it and prying it loose. The *Orpheus*'s warm air flowed into my lungs.

"Rid," I gasped. "Is he ok?"

Shell and Bentley looked at each other, their faces invisible behind their visors.

My heart stopped beating.

Rose's voice sounded from the intercom system.

"*He's alive.*"

I sagged backward, my entire body going limp with relief.

"*He's alive,*" Rose repeated, her voice choked with emotion.

"He's unconscious, but I've got him in the medbay and he's stable."

I felt a tear well up in the corner of my eye. A moment later, I felt pressure around my torso as Bentley and Shell knelt down, wrapping me in a hug.

"We all made it," Rose continued. *"We're all here."*

After a long moment, Bentley broke away from the hug, shaking what looked like a tear from his own eye. "And the battle?" he asked. "What's the word there?"

There was a long silence. With everything else going on, Rose had probably lost track.

I found a small part of me suddenly hoping that the Sovereigns had lost. That I could shrug off the next part of the plan. That we could fly back to Albeni 7, scoop up Sev, and blast off into the void to find some corner of the galaxy to hide from the Paragon's wrath. But I knew it was a selfish impulse.

A leader's real job is to make themselves redundant. To build a better future for everybody else, even if they're not in it.

"I don't see any more explosions, at least," Shell mused, staring through the airlock window. "So *somebody* won."

Bentley gave a nervous chuckle. "Well, I guess now we get to see if we'll go home as triumphant heroes or wanted terrorists."

There are no heroes. Just puppets.

"The Paragon has agreed to a ceasefire." Rose's voice sounded exhausted but triumphant. *"We won."*

The flight to the Sovereign fleet passed by in a dreamlike blur.

After Shell and Bentley helped me out of what remained of the Icarus, we started processing the reports of what had happened. The Paragon's offensive fleet had emerged from nowhere to attack the Sovereign fleet from behind. Nobody knew what had gone wrong—whether the Paragon had learned

that Vatheson's intel had been leaked and baited us into attacking, or if somebody had passed the rebels' plans to them. Either
way, the battle had nearly been lost. It *would* have been, had
Renault not revealed an ace of his own: Werrel's fleet, whom
he'd—without my knowledge, and against my wishes—apparently paid to be on standby in case the Sovereigns needed
backup.

That final push had given the rebels just enough time for
Nalis to receive my confirmation that the foldgate was rigged to
blow. And then just enough time for Paragon Command to
realize what had happened.

Now the Paragon had withdrawn its forces, retreating
towards the entrance to the Earth foldgate. The Sovereigns—
what was left of them, anyway—were now gathering in the
center of the system. The negotiations were far from over, but
the battle was done.

We won.

Those words echoed in my head as we drew nearer to the
Sovereign fleet. They were true. The Paragon had retreated.
The Sovereigns' losses had been greater than expected, but still
nowhere near as bad as they would have been if they'd launched
a full assault on Gideon as initially planned. And Khendar
hadn't had a chance to deploy rippers.

It was Bentley who finally asked the question, his voice
hoarse from the emotion of the day, as he, Rose and I sat around
Rid's silently breathing form in the medbay.

"So... now what?"

Rose's eyes didn't move from Rid. "We get back to Albeni 7
as quickly as possible so we can get him medical attention. *Real*
medical attention."

Shell's voice sounded from the intercom. She was listening
in on us from the bridge. "*It would be faster if we took him to one
of the Sovereign ships. We just received a message inviting us to
Khendar's flagship.*"

I tensed at that. "No. Drop me off, then take Rid back to Albeni 7."

Rose frowned up at me. "Why? Shell's right, it'll be—"

"They've probably got wounded of their own," I insisted, but I could tell by the way she narrowed her eyes at me that she saw through the excuse.

I sighed. "I just... don't completely trust them."

"But *you're* going aboard," Bentley pointed out.

"Yeah," I said. "Cause I have to. I've got... meetings, and stuff. But I don't want any of you coming along. You guys get back to Albeni 7. I'll catch up with you later."

Rose looked like she wanted to argue. Instead, she just gave an exhausted sigh and a nod.

"I *could* use a drink," Bentley admitted. "You think Tyrell's will be open?"

Eventually, they left: Rose to help Shell in the bridge, and Bentley to do... something. Either way, it left me alone with Rid.

I leaned back in my seat, watching his chest move up and down. If you ignored the massive bandage Rose had placed over his face, he looked like he was just... sleeping.

I glanced towards the intercom, making sure it was off, then turned back to Rid and cleared my throat.

"I've never really been one for goodbyes," I said softly. "Truth be told, I usually don't have a chance. People have always kinda just come and gone from my life unexpectedly." I grimaced. "And usually violently."

Rid said nothing.

"Point is, I'm not exactly sure what I'm *supposed* to say here," I continued. "Especially what with you being unconscious and all." I chuckled, looking down at my hands. "I guess that almost makes this easier, in a way. I won't get to say goodbye to the others. Cause I know they'll just do something stupid if I do. But I *do* get to say goodbye to you. So I'm grateful for that, even though, you know... I'm sorry you got shot, and everything." I took a deep, quavering breath. "That was my fault."

Rid said nothing.

Rose's voice sounded over the intercom. *"We're about to dock to Khendar's ship, Lax."*

"Running out of time," I muttered. I sighed. "Look. I'll keep it brief. I just wanted to say thanks. If you hadn't gotten shoved into that prison cell with me, I'd probably still be there. Or dead. I don't know if it was fate, or God, or just sheer coincidence that made that happen. But I'm sure as hell happy it did."

Rid said nothing.

The *Orpheus* shuddered as it docked.

I felt surprisingly calm as I waited for the doors to open. I'm not sure why. Maybe it was simply the freedom that came from knowing that my fate was sealed. Or maybe it was because I knew that I was doing the right thing. Or, at least, I was trying my damnedest.

There are no heroes. Just puppets.

A hero's someone who tries.

Footsteps. I turned to see Rose step up beside me.

"You're sure about this?" she asked. Something in her voice made me wonder if she meant more than simply talking to Nalis.

I took a deep breath. "Yeah. I am."

She nodded quietly. "Alright then."

The doors slid open. On the other side, several forms stood. One was Nalis Khendar. She looked to be in a significantly better mood than the last time I'd seen her. Call me crazy, but you might even say she looked *happy*. Several bodyguards wearing tactical armor flanked her.

"If it isn't the hero of the day," she said. Her voice was dry, but I could tell that it held a begrudging sense of... well, maybe not respect. But approval, at least. She gestured down the hall of her ship. "Shall we?"

"Yeah," I said. "Just... one sec."

She nodded, then turned away, taking her bodyguards with her.

Rose sighed. "Look, I don't wanna *rush* you or anything, but Rid might have brain damage, so—"

I hugged her.

She stiffened in surprise at first. Then relaxed, wrapping her arms around my waist.

After a long moment, I pulled myself gently away. "Get Rid to the station. Fast. And enjoy those drinks."

She grinned. "We will."

I stepped out of the *Orpheus* and into Khendar's ship. The doors began to close.

"And tell your mom I love her," I said.

The doors sealed shut before I could see her response.

There was a rumbling sound as the *Orpheus* undocked a few moments later. Then silence.

Khendar cleared her throat. "So the puppet *does* have a heart. How touching."

I turned to face her, mouth suddenly feeling dry. She raised an eyebrow at me. "Are you ready?"

I took a deep breath. Then nodded.

"You know," Nalis mused as we strolled down the corridor of her ship, "none of this would have happened without you."

I said nothing.

"And I don't mean simply because of your impact on our most recent plans," she continued. "Your idea to attack the foldgate, or the Paragon's battle plans." She side-eyed me.

"Which turned out to be nonsense, by the way. If not for your Admiral Renault's preparedness, that would have cost us the day."

I said nothing.

She sighed. "Once again. Loquacious as ever. No matter. But my point is that it was you and Artemis who set all of this in motion. Her, particularly, with her plan for fighting the Paragon." She shook her head sadly. "If only she could be here today to see all of this. To see her dream come to fruition."

"I didn't realize Brahma was part of the deal," I said cautiously.

Nalis stiffened. "It isn't," she said. "Yet. But the deal has yet to be struck. Thanks to you, we now have the upper hand in our negotiations with the Paragon. I'm sure we'll be able to come to a conclusion that finally grants my homeworld its freedom." She eyed me. "But you distract me from my point. After the... *attack*, I was left reeling. Depleted of almost all my resources. Forced to rebuild from practically nothing. But I did have one thing I hadn't had before: a plan. Artemis's plan. Simply... modified."

We paused in front of a set of heavy doors.

"You see," Nalis continued, "her genius was in realizing that in order to be successful in fighting the Paragon, one must first find a way to deal with Divinity. Her mistake was in thinking that she could undermine them. That she could make Divinity play by her rules."

She pressed the control panel button. The doors slid open, and she gestured for me to pass through.

I found myself in a long, spacious conference room, complete with a majestic desk in the center. I briefly wondered if this was where Nalis had taken her meetings with me from.

There were four men inside, each one standing in a separate corner of the room so that they surrounded me.

I recognized them the moment I laid eyes on them. Not individually; I'd never seen any of their faces before. But everything about them—from the suits they wore, to the cold, inhuman way they looked at me, to the strangely restrained way the held themselves, as if it took effort to keep from bursting into movement.

These men—or men like them—had been the last people Adrian Vatheson had ever seen.

"But the truth," Nalis said quietly, her voice tinged with something that almost sounded like regret, "is that if you want a chance to stand on the same footing as the Paragon... you need to play by *Divinity's* rules."

I made no movement. The four Divinity agents didn't either, but their eyes never left mine. I remembered the impossible speed with which one of them had crossed the room to restrain Vatheson.

"So much for independence, huh, Nalis?" I mused quietly.

She said nothing. Simply sighed and pressed the button to close the doors. They slid shut silently.

I looked between the four Divinity agents. They made no movement. Just watched me, eyes wary but calm. I couldn't see any sign of weaponry on them. That didn't mean that they didn't have any, of course. But, based on what I'd seen from the footage of Vatheson's final moments, they probably didn't need them anyways.

I've been outnumbered before. Plenty of times. I was used to staring down insurmountable odds. And so far, I'd always come out on top. Bloody and battered, exhausted and hanging on to life by the barest of threads, but victorious nonetheless. Hell, I'd just walked out of a fight like that.

This was different.

The four men staring me down were more than thugs, or mercenaries, or even Vanguards or rippers. They were *Divinity*. The most dangerous killers humanity could create. A perfected version of the clumsy killing machines Divinity sold to the Paragon. A perfected version of *me*.

My body still ached from my exertions on the foldgate. I cracked my neck and took a deep, weary breath.

There was no chance I was winning this fight.

But when the hell had that ever stopped me?

"So, then," I growled. "Are we doing this?"

They exchanged glances of their own.

Then—in a burst of blindingly fast movement—they all shot forward at once.

TWENTY-SIX

My eyes opened slowly.

For a long, empty moment, it was all I could do to stare into the empty white space above me. My brain felt... empty. Clear. Devoid of purpose or desire. No room for anything but simple observation.

Observation number one: I was lying on my back, staring upwards. The empty white space that was above me was no help, but I could feel the gravity tugging me down.

Observation number two: I couldn't move. I could feel something cold wrapped around each of my limbs, holding me down to whatever surface I was lying on. Even my head was held firmly in place; when I tried to raise it to better familiarize myself with my predicament, I found that I was locked completely in place.

Observation number three: I was relatively certain I was naked. It was hard to be sure given that I couldn't raise my head to see, but it certainly felt that way.

Observation number four: wherever I was, it was completely and utterly silent. Quiet enough that I could hear my own heart beating. *Thump, thump, thump...*

I closed my eyes. Tried to think. My memories were jumbled, confused. Like a book with the pages all torn out and shoved back in at random. After a few moments of concentration I managed to latch on to the most recent one. The Divinity agents had attacked me. I'd fought back—or tried to, at least.

They'd demolished me.

I remembered the lightning-fast speed with which they'd moved. The impossible force with which their blows had struck me. The pain blossoming across my body as they'd brutally, methodically, beaten me into a mass of torn flesh and broken bones. A beating that would've killed any regular person—and even any regular Vanguard.

But that wasn't me. And now Divinity knew it.

Noise. My eyes flashed open. Voices talking softly, unintelligibly. Footsteps. The noises surrounded me.

"Subject is awake," somebody observed in a cold, clinical tone.

"Proceed as intended," somebody else responded. "Prepare for test number one."

Somewhere, a metallic, high-pitched, mechanical whirring started. It drew closer.

Panic surged like wildfire through my mind. I tried desperately to move, to crane my head so I could see what was approaching me. *A plan.* I remembered vaguely that there had been one. I'd been calm as I'd boarded Khendar's flagship. I'd been calm as I faced the Divinity agents.

I'd had a plan. *We'd* had a plan, Ramar, the Stranger, and I. What was it?

Pain lanced through my side.

All thoughts of a plan, or Khendar, or Ramar, or the Stranger, were torn from my mind. I tried to scream, to give voice to the incredible agony that was slowly moving across my chest, only to reach a horrible and final fifth observation: there was something long and tubelike protruding down my throat, stopping my voice. The scream ended where it began: my mind.

The pain continued all the way across my chest, then stopped. I felt my body sag with relief. My chest heaved.

"First cut is good," somebody said, their tone casual.

"Prepare the second incision," somebody else responded.

The relief I'd felt vanished, replaced by sheer panic. The whirring sound started again. A few seconds later I felt something cold and jagged shear effortlessly through the flesh below my navel, then continue upwards, one steady inch at a time. It finally stopped right below my clavicle.

"Good cuts," somebody said. Something cold and metallic pinched at the edge of one of the long wounds in my chest. "Let's... huh. Guess the report wasn't exaggerating. He's already starting to heal."

The cold feeling went away. I relaxed. I could feel tears welling up in the corners of my eyes. Great sobs I couldn't give voice to heaving in my chest. It didn't seem to bother whoever was operating on me, though.

"Well. Let's redo the cuts. Faster this time."

No. *No. NO. NONONONO*

Pain. They redid both cuts, quicker this time. As soon as they'd finished, I felt a series of cold pinches in the fresh wounds.

"Alright," a bright, cheery voice said. "Let's see what we're working with!"

There was a heavy mechanical sound. I felt pressure as something tugged insistently at my chest. At my flesh and skin. Then even more insistently. Then even more.

A plan. My mind clawed desperately at the thought. *There was a plan. A way out. There was a—*

The pressure gave way.

Pain—more overwhelming than any I'd ever dreamed was possible—exploded through my body.

My mind finally crumbled. Everything went black.

———

I floated, and the universe sank slowly beneath me.

I don't know how to describe the sensation besides that. It wasn't like floating in water or like being suspended in mid-air without gravity. I felt distinctly that I was untouched by the forces of the universe; that I *was* the force, looking down upon the countless arms of creation as they spun in their wild, decadent, self-cannibalizing vortex.

I saw it all. Stars without number. Planets of every kind. Moons locked in faithful orbits around the objects of their devotion. Black holes straining at the fabric of reality. A thousand different types of celestial debris flung heedlessly across the black canvas of space—and, crawling ant-like between the pieces of heavenly wreckage, people. Humanity, claiming the cold, indifferent void for themselves.

I saw all of it, spread out beneath me like a child's diorama.

And I *hated* it.

Something yanked on me from the void.

I blinked. I'd been here before, I thought. I'd seen this vision. Felt that burning hatred for everything I saw beneath me. But that pull was new. That hadn't been there before.

I followed the pull. Let the string pulling at my brain lead me where it wanted me to go. My eyes widened.

A figure was floating in the distance, suspended in the black void, same as me. Except that it wasn't like me.

It was longer than a human should be, its limbs bent in directions human limbs were not supposed to bend. Its skin was entirely translucent. I could see through its long, intricately interwoven muscles. Through the glass-like bones. Directly into the creature's beating heart, located square in the center of its chest. The heart was radiant with bright, otherworldly light. As if I were looking through a foldgate at a vivid star.

I realized suddenly that there were tendrils reaching out from that star. Thick and vein-like and throbbing as they pumped stolen life from it. I spun, trying to follow the tubes, but there were too many of them to keep track of, spreading across everything I could see, interconnecting the stars and the tiny, insignificant humans who crawled between then.

A voice spoke in my head, radiating from the captive being. Soft but clear. Quiet but desperate.

END.

ME.

I stared at it. Reached towards it, but found I too was being held in place. Suddenly another string pulled at my brain—in the opposite direction. A gentler, somehow more familiar tug.

And with it, a voice. Cold and familiar and burning with hate.

IT IS TIME.

———

My eyes opened slowly.

I was staring up into empty white space. I couldn't move. There were soft, unintelligible voices speaking around me. They were familiar by now. Background noise. I knew nothing of what their bearers looked like. All I knew was that as long as I could hear the voices, it meant that the saws weren't running, I had at least a small reprieve from the pain.

How long had I been here?

It might have been days. Or hours. Or years, for all I could tell. Time was marked only by the buzzing of those damnable saws. It wasn't all as extreme as that first test. Sometimes they took small samples of flesh. Other times they applied heat, or cold, or blunt force trauma to various parts of my body. Tubes of various sizes were plugged into my limbs, torso, neck, and even skull.

The only thing that was consistent was that it all hurt.

And it all healed.

I closed my eyes, trying to drown out the voices. Moments of clarity like this were few and far between—I had to take advantage of it. Had to try to remember.

A plan. There *had* been a plan, hadn't there? There was a reason I was here. There had to be. There had to be a reason for all of the pain and misery and suffering. A damn *point* to it all.

Didn't there?

A familiar sensation tugged at the back of my brain. Distant. Faint. But real. I tried to latch on to it. To understand it.

A metallic, high-pitched whirring sound started above my head. The tugging sensation vanished. My eyes flashed open and focused on a spinning disk of metal suspended above me.

The saw began lowering, aiming directly between my eyes.

You might've thought I'd have become used to the constant torture by now. I hadn't. Panic flooded my brain yet again as the saw inched closer and closer. They were going to cut my skull open and look inside my brain while I was still alive.

Closer.

There *was* no point. To any of it. Life was just suffering. An endless trail of bodies that went in one giant, bloody, pointless circle.

The saw grazed the skin between my eyes.

"STOP."

The buzzing sound ceased abruptly.

I stared at the small, blurry disk of pain, pressed up against the very bridge of my nose. Any second now I expected it to resume its dreadful work.

But it didn't.

"Everybody out." The voice was calm, authoritative.

Vaguely familiar. The response was immediate: a chorus of softly shuffling footsteps in retreat.

I heard a door shut. A moment later, there was nothing but silence.

"I apologize for how uncomfortable your stay has been so far," the voice continued. I felt a surge of relief as the saw was lifted and then pushed to the side, out of my view. "But we had to at least *try* to understand what we were seeing."

I gagged as the long tube in my throat was suddenly and violently jerked upwards. For what felt like an eternity, it slid through my throat, then shot out leaving me retching and coughing.

"That's better," the voice resumed, sounding vaguely amused. I was increasingly certain that I'd heard it before. In my panicked state, though, I couldn't place exactly *where*. "I must be able to hear you, after all. And now—let's get you a little more comfortable."

I felt a brief sense of vertigo as the surface I was attached to tilted, lifting me. Slowly, my vision shifted, until I had a full view of the room before me. It was a pristine white operating room, laden with various vicious-looking tools. Computer screens tracked my vitals and displayed records of the torture I'd already endured. My eye, however, was drawn immediately to the single other person occupying the room.

I recognized him immediately.

It was the man who'd been in Vatheson's office. Once again, there was nothing particularly impressive looking about him. Nothing that made him seem superhuman in the same way the Divinity agents had been. Like last time, he wore slacks and a simple button-up shirt. His eyes were vaguely amused as he studied me.

"You," he said, raising an eyebrow, "have questions."

I could only blink.

"It's alright." He shifted in his seat, crossing one leg. "Take all the time you need. I understand you've been through quite a lot."

"Who..." I croaked, "are you?"

"An excellent place to start," he said. "My name is Lazarus Whitehall. You can call me Laz, for short, if you'd like." His tone was friendly. Conversational. As if I weren't strapped naked to a table in front of him. His eyes sparkled. "I hear your friends call you Lax, so I find it oddly appropriate. Look at the two of us. Laz and Lax. Just carrying on like chums, here at the bottom the universe."

I looked for more questions. I had hundreds of them. But, try as I might, I couldn't pull any of them down from my still-foggy brain to my lips.

"Ah." Lazarus waved a dismissive hand. "Don't fret over it too much. You wouldn't have heard my name. Which is ironic, considering that I'm your father."

I frowned. "What?"

"Not your *literal* father, of course." He chuckled. "But, metaphorically, absolutely." He eyed me, his grin only widening. "I can see I'm only confusing you. So, tell you what. Why don't I stop talking for a bit, and you ask me a few more questions. It seems like the least I can do for you, after all the unpleasantness you've been through."

I stared. Tried to figure out how I should even start. "Where—"

"*But.*" He held up a finger, eyebrows raised in an exaggerated expression as if he were speaking to a very young child. "After I answer *your* questions, you have to answer mine, alright?"

"Where are we?" I managed to force.

"Easy," he said. "We're at your birthplace. The home of Divinity Technologies. You've been here for roughly two weeks, with most of that time spent in stasis. As to where exactly that is, geographically, it becomes more complicated.

Suffice to say we're someplace where nobody will ever disturb us."

Something about that stirred up some of my tangled memories. *Divinity Technologies. Someplace nobody will ever disturb us.* Bits and pieces of the plan started to come back to me. The Stranger had wanted me to be here.

"What..." I looked down at myself. There were raw, pink scars crisscrossing my chest. In a flash, I relived that awful pain of feeling the blades bite into my flesh. "What are you doing to me?"

"Just taking a peek under the hood." His grin faded. "I'm sorry if it's been painful. We had to do some of them while you were conscious, just to see what would happen. We've never quite met anyone like you, see. But don't worry—we've put everything back exactly where we found it.

"Now, then"—he interlocked his fingers—"I believe I've been polite in doing my best to answer your questions. Now, allow me to ask a few of my own—with a preface, of course, to explain why you are here.

"Ordinarily, I'd be far too busy to spend time doing this sort of thing." He smiled warmly. "Questioning prisoners, performing experiments, that sort of thing. Not that we do those things often. But the point is that I would not be here speaking to you if I did not believe that you were a very special case."

I'd known this was coming. It still sent a spike of dread through my chest. He knew. I wasn't sure how much, but he *knew*. About the *Revelation*. About the Stranger. About my enhancements.

"I understand that you've been working alongside Nalis Khendar." He watched my face carefully, looking for any hint of surprise. "As I'm sure you gathered before my agents, ah, *detained* you, she works for me. After the little incident with the *Revelation*—which, I hear, you know all too much about—I realized that I'd made a miscalculation in how I managed the

Paragon. So I decided to try something new, and she—along with her Sovereign Systems—happened to be available and looking for support at just the right time.

"Truth be told, though, I didn't learn about you until quite recently. Our mutual friend Vatheson put me onto your tail first. And then the stories just kept on rolling in. A Vanguard who simply refused to die. Who kept fighting—even in the face of a bullet to the... well. To the *face*."

I gritted my teeth. "I'll keep fighting, too, if you cut me loose."

He chuckled. "I think I'll pass on your generous invitation. Allow me to continue. You'll have to pardon me, I've grown to quite love the sound of my own voice over the years. I was intrigued by these reports. Intrigued enough that I decided I simply must meet you for myself. So, I arranged for Khendar to deliver you to me. And voila—here we are."

"You want my autograph?" I groaned.

He smiled. "No. I'd like you to tell me how exactly it is that you became infused with a more powerful sample of the Divinity gene than I've ever seen."

I said nothing.

When it became clear I had no intention of speaking, he leaned back in his chair with a sigh. "Very well. I'll offer you the benefit of the doubt and assume that you don't know what I'm talking about. It's not so far-fetched a claim, after all. Listen closely, because you're about to hear something very, very few people every get to hear—and only because I know that there's no chance whatsoever that you will ever carry it away from this place. Allow me to give you a brief history of humanity and the Divinity gene.

"Roughly two thousand years ago, when humanity was just beginning to stretch its wings and explore the stars, there was a small technology company called Whitehall Enterprises. The owners of Whitehall Enterprises didn't have much—at least not by way of comparison to the other tech giants that were driving space exploration forward at the time—but they had ambition. A hunger for new understanding of our world.

"One day, a Whitehall Enterprises' satellite detected a strange energy signal in deep space off the Alpha Centauri system. They mounted an expedition to find and ascertain what the mysterious energy surge had been."

He leaned forward, his eyes sparkling with genuine excitement. "What they found would not only change the trajectory of their company—but of the entire human race. It was a spacecraft. Damaged and helpless and unlike any the explorers had ever seen. The spacecraft itself was not what most interested them, however. Rather, it was what they found inside the spacecraft. Or, more accurately, *who.*"

A memory flashed through my brain. One of the dreams I'd had. Of a strange spaceship bursting into open space, just in time to see a more human-looking craft descending upon it. I furrowed my brow. Was that somehow connected? Because the thing that had been in *that* spacecraft had looked like the Stranger...

He chuckled at my reaction. "Yes, I know. Far-fetched. The term *alien* sounds..." He grimaced. "Tawdry. Cheap. Uninspiring. Too vague. We came up with a more specific term. An Angel." He smiled. "Yes, I know. Hardly better. But much more fitting. You see, this creature, we soon learned, was capable of extraordinary things. It served as the power source to its own ship. Imagine that! A source of bioenergy so strong it could power faster-than-light travel. We began performing experiments upon—"

"Wait," I said. "First off: *we?*"

"Yes," he said irritably. "I was there. I was in charge. I'm the founder of Whitehall Enterprises, which would eventually evolve into—well, never mind. You'll get it."

Realization flooded me. It should have been obvious the

moment he'd spoken the name of the old company, but given my haggard state, I hadn't put it together until just now.

Whitehall Enterprises. Which had evolved into Divinity Technologies.

I stared at him. At first I'd simply assumed that his magnanimity was due to being the current head of the Divinity company. But no—he was more than that. He had *always* been its leader. I was face to face with the single most powerful man in the history of humanity.

A smile—cold and piercing—spread across his face.

"That's right," he said. "*Now* you're getting it."

My mouth snapped shut of its own accord. This man was responsible for *everything*. All of the most impactful events and technologies of the past two thousand years. The Sovereigns, the Paragon, the Vanguards, the rippers—all puppets being controlled by puppets, all the strings leading back to this man right here.

And he was just... sitting there, talking at me.

"Now, where was I?" He rubbed his jaw. "Oh, yes. The creature. The Angel. It was wounded when we found it. Vulnerable. We contained it and began performing experiments to learn more about its strange properties. Which is how we discovered the true foundation of our company: the Divinity gene."

He shifted in his seat, holding up his hands towards me with genuine interest in his eyes. "Now. Are you familiar with how quantum communication works?"

I frowned at the sudden question. "More or less."

"*Less* than more, I'll guess. I'll explain it. Quantum communication works through the splitting of particles down to their smallest possible elements. If you go deep down enough, to the quantum state, you get particles which are, in the simplest of terms, inextricably linked. Whatever happens to one also happens to the other, no matter the distance between them.

This is how quantum communicators are able to send instantaneous messages even from opposite sides of the galaxy.

"The Divinity gene, as we took to calling the genetic material we harvested from the Angel, seems to operate in a similar, though not identical, fashion." He scooted his chair up close to me and reached for something out of sight. "They're all linked. Any Divinity gene, no matter where it is, is capable of absorbing energy from the *other* Divinity genes, in a sort of quantum network. Now, this network has a single source somewhere that we don't know. It's likely far beyond the scope of our galaxy, and maybe even our dimension. But it appears to be infinite, because each Divinity gene can summon an *infinite* amount of energy from it."

I tried to put the pieces together. The great question about all of the Divinity corporation's technologies had always been how they contained so much energy. Where did the Vanguards, and even more so, the rippers, get the energy to heal so quickly? How did the ultracells, small enough to be carried by a child, rival the amount of power produced by the ancient powercores propelling the Exodus class ships through nullspace? How did the Lifeblood biofuel produce so much fruit?

The answer was that it didn't. It merely channeled it. Awe filled me as I realized the implications of that. All of this miraculous technology was linked to the same source. A source that even Divinity itself apparently didn't completely understand.

"At least," Lazarus admitted, "we *assume* that it's infinite. We've been using the genetic material harvested from the Angel for two thousand years now, using up unfathomably large amounts of energy on nullspace travel, without any indication that it's running out. After all, how else could *this* work?"

He revealed a scalpel in his right hand. I let out a grunt as the blade dug into my abdomen, cut a long, slow path across my stomach, and then flicked out with a splatter of blood. Whitehall watched the wound in fascination as it immediately began to pull itself back together.

"Remarkable," he breathed. "Even after all these years, it's just as miraculous to me. You see—well, you *know*, given that you're a Vanguard—we've worked hard to integrate the Divinity gene with human genes. You Vanguards were the closest we could ever get to it. And it's still miraculous, mind you. You are made of the stuff of Gods, Lax. But... well, I think I hardly need to explain how far a regular Vanguard is from whatever *you* are. Which leads me all the way back around to my main question— and the reason you are here."

He thrust the scalpel into my stomach, leaving it there and settling back into his seat. Sharp pain blossomed through my abdomen. I let out a long groan.

"I realized, very early on," he said, "that the Divinity gene was the most valuable gift humanity had ever received. And that maintaining control—*sole* control—over it was of the utmost importance. The worst possible thing that could happen was for another Angel to wander into humanity's grasp only to be claimed by somebody else. So, we started building the scanning stations. In every system we possibly could. Early on, in the Golden Age, it was easy. Everybody wanted to work together. The independent systems were only too happy to provide access to their territories so we could monitor for wayward Angels in exchange for ultracells."

He grimaced. "It wasn't until the wars started that things began to grow complicated. Two systems would declare war on each other, and then each would demand that Divinity stop supplying their enemy with ultracells. We'd refuse. They'd blow up our scanning stations and so forth. I had thought, up to that point, that we could maintain control through economic prowess alone. But as the wars grew more complicated, and we lost access to more and more of the explored galaxy, I realized we needed to take a more proactive approach."

My stomach dropped. "So you chose the Paragon," I growled.

He smiled broadly. "Precisely! Very good. I'm glad to see you waking up a bit more. Yes—we chose what seemed to be the most powerful faction and then threw our full weight behind them. You'd be shocked at how easy it was to bend them to my will. They were already power hungry. I simply pointed them in the right direction and gave them the means to achieve their ambitions. Sold them on the dream of humanity living united under one banner, for the first time in its history."

I strained forward, unable to keep from growling. All of that death. All of that carnage and suffering. Just so this pretentious bastard could keep watching the stars for more of these Angel creatures. "You killed *trillions*."

He chuckled.

Chuckled. Not a maniacal, evil cackle. Just a vague sense of amusement. "Yes," he said, waving a hand dismissively. "I did. But there's an old earth saying, from a leader I'd doubt you've heard of. He said that one death is a tragedy while a million of them is merely a statistic. You must remember, my young friend, that I'm over two thousand years old. How many deaths do you suppose I had *already* witnessed by the time I began the so-called Last War?"

I remembered suddenly how bemused Lazarus had been when Vatheson attempted to impress him with his age. *Lots of time. Cute.* Lazarus was numb to it. All of it. The uncountable innocent lives destroyed on his path to control weren't even an afterthought to him.

Hatred surged through my veins. I'd always hated powerful people. People who thought that the end justified the means, no matter how brutal. Seemed like I had danced on their strings my whole life. And *nobody* exemplified that more than Lazarus Whitehall.

If he noticed my rage, he ignored it. "Yes, trillions dead. A shame, I suppose. But it was the only way. When the Paragon's progress began to stall, I gave them you—the Vanguards. Then the rippers." He gave a heavy sigh. "Until the job was done, and humanity lay at my feet once again. I can't even tell you how relieved I was to have full coverage again. As if a great weight had settled onto my shoulders and I was finally able to shunt it off."

He fell silent for a few moments. The casual friendliness in his eyes gradually faded as he watched me.

"But, of course," he said softly, "I was foolish to believe that things could ever work out so simply."

He reached forward, grabbed the handle of the blade that was still embedded in my abdomen, and twisted it.

It hurt. A lot. But nowhere *near* as much as the absolute hell I had endured since being dragged into this room. Still, I couldn't help but grimace as I felt the cold steel twisting at my insides.

"You see," he continued, "there *is* a point to all of this torture. Beyond the pain you've endured. Despite all of our experimentation and iteration over the centuries, the bond between human test subjects and the Divinity gene has been deeply flawed. Inefficient. That's why the Vanguards can't heal as well as the rippers. But then *you* come along. Exhibiting a synthesis between Angel and human genetic material more perfect than anything I've ever seen possible.

"I know for a fact that you weren't always this way. I pulled up your records, from when you were a wee lad, only freshly sold off to the Vanguard by your father. There was nothing remarkable about you. *Nothing.* Which means that whatever happened to you was done by a third party."

He pushed the knife deeper. I gasped, trying in vain to curl my body away from the blade.

"And the only *possible* way that this third party could have obtained such a pure sample of the Divinity gene to fuse with you was if they had access to an Angel of their own." His face loomed close to mine, saliva splatting against my cheek as he spat each word. "Which means that despite my best effort, another Angel apparently slipped through my fingers."

A cold shock ran through my body as the tip of the scalpel brushed against my spine. Every muscle in my body spasmed, straining to free itself. I let out an agonized scream—one that had been stifled inside of me through all the torture I'd endured.

"And so *you* are going to tell me where this Angel is." He snarled the words. "That gene is *mine*. That Angel is *mine*. You *stole* it from me. So you're going to tell me exactly where you got it from and where I can find them. Because, my dear friend, as our own resident Angel can attest, the bad side of an infinite amount of healing—"

He dug the blade upwards. Blood spurted from my wound, coating his hand and staining the sleeves of his button-up shirt. My agonized scream broke off into a desperate choking sound.

"Is that it also includes an infinite amount of pain," he hissed.

He withdrew his hand, leaving the scalpel embedded inside of me, and took a step back, running his clean hand through his hair and taking a deep breath. He glanced down with disgust as his bloody hand—the one that had been practically inside of me.

"Got a bit carried away there," he admitted. "But I answered all of your questions. So now it's your turn. The quicker you answer, the less pain you'll have to endure. Where. Is. The Angel?"

I struggled for breath. I could feel my innards rearranging themselves, bit by bit, trying to heal themselves *around* the blade. It hurt. *A lot.*

"Well?" Whitehall demanded.

Angels. The Divinity gene. Even with the pain cascading through my body, I was beginning to see the horrible puzzle pieces coming together. Ramar had been wrong. The Stranger wasn't a disgruntled ex-Divinity employee. They were something far, *far* more powerful and dangerous.

My mind seized that thought like it was a life raft in a storm-tossed sea. The Stranger had sent me here. They *wanted* me to be here. This was part of their great crusade. Part of the plan.

Something tugged on my mind.

Faint at first. Then stronger. I focused on that tug. Tried to feel its intent.

A single emotion ran through my body.

HATE.

That hatred merged with my own, amplifying it. My memories, jumbled and scattered by the constant trauma I'd endured, suddenly fell into place.

There *was* a plan. And it was almost complete.

I started laughing.

It was a desperate, haggard sound. Blood splattered from my lips. The look of frustrated confusion on Whitehall's face only made me laugh all the harder. This snide, condescending bastard. So certain of his place in the galaxy. So certain that he was in control.

"What?" he snapped. "Finally broke?"

"I'll give you this much," I wheezed, remembering what Whitehall had told Vatheson shortly before having him killed. "You're the fun kind of stupid."

He blinked.

"You see, there's the *normal* kind of stupid," I said, my voice growing stronger with each word as I did my best to recite his own speech back to him. In my mind's eye, I could see that wristwatch being raised high into the air. "Normal people, making normal mistakes. But they're not smart enough for their stupidity to make any real splash. But every now and then, there's a guy like you. Smart enough to climb so high..."

Whitehall let out an angry hiss. "Whatever point you think you're proving, I—"

"But too stupid," I continued, "To see how far you can fall."

He grabbed my shoulders, clenching his teeth as he loomed over me. "Where. Is. The *Angel?*"

"They're on their way," I whispered.

His eyes searched mine unbelievingly. "Impossible. This station is completely inaccessible by any non-Divinity ship. It exists within an advanced, higher form of a nullspace pocket, one we've kept secret from the world."

The tug at the back of my mind grew stronger.

"Secret from the world, maybe," I whispered. "But not from the ones you stole it from in the first place."

He stared a moment longer.

Then his eyes widened.

Crack. I visualized Vatheson's old earth wristwatch shattering as it tumbled through the air to its sudden demise.

The pristine white lights overhead turned blood red.

A haunting alarm klaxon started blaring through the halls. *"STATION COLLISION IMMINENT,"* it warned.

Whitehall whipped out a handcomputer from his pocket, eyes bulging as he stared at its screen. It seemed to be a camera on the exterior of the Divinity station. I was only able to catch a glimpse of it, but one glimpse was all I needed to recognize the massive behemoth of a ship that was looming larger by the second as it rushed towards the screen.

The *Aboena.*

That was why Zeka had insisted on having the *Aboena* worked on at a shipyard. The Stranger hadn't wanted to merely repair the ship. They wanted to upgrade it—to make it capable of reaching Divinity's hidden station.

See, normally, multiple structures can't share the same pocket of nullspace. Otherwise you'd have to worry about running into other ships while traversing it. But that wasn't the case with Divinity's station. It existed within its own constant pocket of nullspace, with other ships using the same technology able to come and go as they pleased. And the Stranger, apparently, had known this from the beginning—a mystery that had confused me before, but now made perfect sense with the revelation that Divinity had stolen everything they knew from the Angels. The upgrades the Stranger had secretly installed at the shipyard had made the *Aboena* capable of entering this more advanced form of nullspace that Divinity used. So that, when Nalis Khendar inevitably betrayed me, and I ended up here, Divinity's prisoner, the Stranger could use the bond they had enhanced me with—the "gift" they'd bestowed upon me—to find Divinity's hidden station.

And destroy it.

HATE.

Whitehall leapt to his feet. He screamed something I couldn't quite make out to somebody I couldn't see.

Then the world exploded around us.

I lost a few seconds to violent tremors and blinding blasts of sparks as electrical systems burst. By the time I could see again I found that I was lying on the floor, one arm still bound to the now overturned table while my other limbs were free, apparently knocked loose in the explosion. I craned my head to see Whitehall moaning as he picked himself up from where he'd fallen. He was saying something—most likely into a neural connection. Calling for help.

Fury filled me. *He* didn't get to call for help. Not after everything he'd done. To me. To *everybody*.

I turned my attention to the band of metal binding my wrist to the table, braced my feet against it, and began to pull.

"I don't know," Whitehall panted as he stumbled to his feet. "Wait. Say that again. Boarders? Attacking... no! Stop them! Scramble everything we have!"

The metal strained and groaned. I gritted my teeth, pulling against it with all my might. As a normal Vanguard, I'd never have been able to do more than slightly budge the band.

But if it needs saying again, I'm no normal Vanguard. Not anymore.

The band snapped free.

"Set the rippers loose," Whitehall said, staggering towards the exit. "I don't care about collateral damage. The boarders must be repelled at *any* cost. And send my bodyguard. I need help. I—"

He spared a glance over his shoulder at me, one hand hovering over the control panel. His eyes widened as he watched me reach into my gut and withdraw the scalpel he'd left there.

"Where," I growled, "do you think..."

He pressed desperately at the button on the control panel. No effect. Over and over again, screaming profanities into his comms as death strode inevitably towards him. It might be two thousand years late, but it was here now, and not even he could escape it this time.

"*You're going?*" I bellowed.

He pivoted, face pale as he pressed his back against the door. Raised his hands in a pleading gesture. Opened his mouth to utter a plea that never formed.

I raised the knife and plunged it down.

And Lazarus Whitehall—the most powerful man in the history of humanity—the man who had stolen fire from the gods —the man who had casually strolled over the bodies of trillions of innocent lives on his path to power—died with a barely audible whimper.

I'm not sure how long I spent there, stabbing and punching and kicking him. By the time I came to myself, he was barely recognizable as human anymore. Just a torn and mangled mass of flesh, blood, and bone. I waited for the bout of illness that usually followed my fits of violent rage to hit me, but it never did. I felt no remorse as I stared down at him. No joy or triumph either. Just a sense of grim satisfaction.

I've never liked the idea of deciding who does and doesn't deserve to die. Always seemed like the type of thing self-righteous, arrogant bastards did. But if there was one person I'd ever killed who needed killing... well. It was Lazarus Whitehall.

Muffled shouts sounded from the other side of the door. My eyes flitted from Whitehall's corpse to his handcomputer, which had fallen to the floor. Its screen was cycling through security footage of the Divinity's station's interior. I saw scene after scene of chaos unfolding. Shapers clad in their black exos pouring through the hallways, wielding guns and knives and cutting down everything in their path. Rippers—coated in biosteel shells, just like the ones we'd fought on Boadicea—tore indiscriminately through rampaging Shapers and fleeing Divinity employees alike. Several large figures clad in suits strode purposefully down a corridor full of dead bodies—probably towards me.

A wave of exhaustion passed over me. I sagged against the wall. I didn't want to do this. I wanted to be done. But I knew I wasn't. Not until the Stranger was.

HATE.

I felt the Stranger's strings, embedded in the grey matter of my brain. It was no longer a gentle tug. It was a violent, irresistible yank. Pushing me. Driving me to kick open that door and tear into who whoever was on the other side. An urge as strong or stronger than the Paragon's ignicerin had ever been.

I clenched my fists, exerting every bit of willpower I possessed to stay put. To fight against the rage and hate threatening to consume me. To not be the Stranger's puppet. I'd just killed my last puppet master—I would *not* capitulate to another.

But I knew it was futile. With each moment I resisted I felt the urge to destroy growing stronger. A storm raging within my chest, desperate to burst out of me and wreak havoc on everything it could find.

I tried to calm myself, to control my breathing. Forced

myself to think of those I loved. Of Rose, and Rid, and Bentley and Shell and Nadus and Kessa and most of all, Sev. But, strangely, there was only one face that my violently pounding brain could latch on to.

Ramar.

Trust the plan.

The Stranger's pull was a roaring force of primeval fury inside of me now. I held it off for just a few more seconds. I used the time to stoop and rummage through Whitehall's pockets until I found his security card, hanging from a lanyard which I draped around my bare neck. I grimaced as I wrenched the door open and peered out. There were dozens of people standing in the hallway beyond, frozen with fear as they stared at me. Behind them, I heard bustling feet as several Divinity agents navigated the crowded corridor towards me.

The entire scene was bathed in blood-red light.

These were the people who had run Divinity from the shadows, all these years. Pulling the strings, not caring for all the pain it caused billions of humans scattered throughout the stars. Not caring for all the pain it had caused *me*.

I heard a voice in my head. Burning with a sullen hatred. Directing all of its intent towards me with a mighty pull and simple command.

YOU WERE MADE TO DO ONE THING.

I took a deep breath, held it, and released it, along with my resistance to the Stranger's command.

KILL.

I grinned.

TWENTY-SEVEN

I killed.

I killed in greater volume and intensity than I'd ever killed before. I killed without caring who or how. I stabbed, punched, kicked, bit, tore. I grabbed fallen weapons from the floor and fired them until they were empty, then swung them as clubs until they'd been twisted into useless shards of scrap. Bullets tore through me but the pain only fueled my hatred. Victims screamed for mercy but their cries found no purchase on my mind. I had room for one thought and one thought only.

KILL.

I was vaguely aware that I was being pulled in a specific direction. That there were two forces acting on my brain—one pushing me forward, filling me with strength and hatred, and the other pulling me towards it. That second string's voice was weak. Barely perceptible over the chorus of death raging in my head.

KILL. KILL. KILL.

I obeyed. I gave up all pretense of resistance. I was the Stranger's weapon, here to wreak its bloody vengeance. And oh, was it bloody. Any awareness of *the plan*, or what came after all the carnage, was lost in the cacophony of death.

The agents attacked me with blinding speed. I didn't hold myself back like I had last time, when I had *needed* them to capture me, to bring me to the heart of my enemies. If they'd had me surrounded again, they might have beaten me. Maybe. But they didn't. In the narrow confines of the corridor, they were forced to face me one or two at a time, fighting through the other fleeing Divinity employees as they did so. Even so, they were confident as they attacked.

They shouldn't have been.

I was the Stranger's weapon. I was vengeance. I was wrath. I was death incarnate, and some long-suppressed, primal part of me laughed with sheer joy as I killed them one by one, breaking their bones and rending their flesh with my bare hands.

At some point I felt dozens of smaller tugs on my brain. Rippers, surging towards me, confident they'd found an easy meal. I braced myself, eager for the fight, only to feel the Stranger's intent radiate through me and into the rippers themselves. They turned and sprinted in the opposite direction, screams marking their bloody path.

Fine by me. I grinned and followed after them.

I don't know how long I was rampaging through those hallways, murdering everything with a pulse I could get my hands on. Maybe it was hours. Maybe it was mere minutes. But eventually I felt a sudden pang of emptiness as the rage bled out of me and I realized I was alone.

I stood in shocked silence for a moment, trying to get my bearings. I was standing in front of a heavy, locked door with the Divinity company's logo painted across it. That logo was coated in blood. Blood that I realized was coming from *me*.

I looked down. The floor, as far down the corridor as I could see, was completely carpeted in bodies. Most were human. Some were ripper. Most were wearing Divinity uniforms, but I spotted the occasional tell-tale sign of a Shaper exosuit among them as well. The sight of it all was sickening. I could hardly tell where one corpse ended and the next began. I felt a sudden urge to vomit. Instead, I staggered against the wall, closing my eyes.

The plan. The plan. You're in charge. You're almost there.

I took a deep breath, forcing myself to open my eyes again. I could feel that pull—the gentle, desperate one, not the murderous one—calling from the other side of this door.

I grimaced, then clutched at my neck where Lazarus Whitehall's security card hung. I was amazed I hadn't lost it during all the killing. I pressed it against the door's control panel with shaking hands.

The door slid silently open. I staggered through.

The sight before me was unlike any I'd ever seen before—and yet strangely familiar. I was in a large, circular room. The edges of the room were lined with large computer screens tracking various graphs. Technicians in lab coats cowered behind their stations as I looked around, blood dripping from my body to the pristine white floor beneath me.

It was the thing in the center of the room, though, that caught my attention. Not thing. Person. Creature.

Angel.

It looked almost exactly like the creature I had seen in my dream. Maybe seven feet tall. Graceful and lithe. The only difference was that its skin wasn't translucent; rather, it glowed a steady, beautiful, opaque white. It was suspended in the air. Dozens upon dozens of tubes were connected to it, extracting its essence and ushering it away into unknown compartments.

I stared at the creature before me. Divinity. A God, or the closest I was ever likely to get to one. Captured. Humiliated. Abused. Bled dry.

A sickening feeling struck me as I realized suddenly the true implication of the Angel. This creature had been suspended here for two thousand years, neither fully alive nor fully dead, being carefully drained of its life essence. An eternal torment as damning as any hell.

I felt it reach out to me again. A weak, desperate intent.

KILL...

... ME...

I took a step forward.

A door to my right crashed open in a burst of flame. Screams filled the room. Several familiar-looking figures dressed in black exos, wielding long Roamer knives, rushed through the entryway. Shapers. They immediately fell to butchering the surviving technicians.

One of the Shapers, holding a bloody blade in one hand and a pistol in the other, ignored the carnage, instead opting to stride directly towards me. I recognized Zeka's voice immediately.

"Fine work," she said, flicking blood from her blade. "You've served our master well."

Resentment filled me at the words. Revulsion. Followed by a wave of exhaustion. I looked around blearily as the last of the Divinity technicians were mercilessly butchered.

Zeka took a reverent step towards the suspended Angel. It made no effort to acknowledge her. It simply hung there. I could feel the pain radiating from it. Endless, agonizing pain.

The plan. I forced myself to look away from the majestic creature, scanning the crowd of black-clad Shapers. After a few moments of searching, my gaze settled on one in particular who —rather than joining in the killing—had moved to a computer terminal and was rapidly typing. The figure looked up briefly as I focused on it, giving me a brief nod.

Zeka sagged to her knees, staring up at the Angel. Her voice —usually so flat and cold—was choked with emotion. "After all this time... we are here. The Stranger did not lead us astray."

I tore my eyes away from the figure typing at the terminal. "Speaking of the Stranger, where—"

There.

A figure—unnaturally tall—stepped through the doorway. It was concealed beneath a set of heavy black robes, but I knew immediately that it was the Stranger. I could feel the pull connecting me to them.

HATE.

The Stranger ignored the Shapers completely, moving towards the suspended Angel in the center of the room, then raised two glowing white hands from beneath the robes, letting them drop to the floor. The Stranger looked almost identical to the suspended Angel, except with slight blue pigmentation in its skin balancing out the white.

If seeing one Angel had been awe-inspiring, seeing two of them was overwhelming. No wonder the Shapers had taken to worshiping the Stranger when they'd stumbled across them during the Last War. No wonder Lazarus had changed the name of his company to Divinity. That was what these creatures seemed to be: gods, marooned among men.

The Stranger reached out, gingerly touching the skin of the suspended Angel. Every Shaper—with the exception of the one I'd made eye contact with, who continued typing away furiously at its computer terminal—fell to their knees. I was almost tempted to join them. Instead, I closed my eyes, reaching out mentally and trying to feel the Stranger's intent. Trying to understand what it was saying to the captive Angel.

This was more complex than the simple, brutal expressions of rage that I'd felt from the Stranger before. Deeper. The hate was there, certainly, as strong as ever, but it felt... tempered this time. There were other emotions mixed in with it. Grief at the suffering the captive Angel had endured for so long. Astonishment that sentient beings could be so cruel. And then—wrapping all of it together—a sudden rush of cold, clear, vivid intent, pulling me into its vortex like a black hole.

———

I floated, and the universe sank beneath me.

I saw all of it, spread out beneath me like a child's diorama. The stars without number. And—most importantly—the tiny, insignificant, *pathetic* creatures crawling between them.

And I *hated* them.

These creatures had found my kin, alone and in desperate need of aid. And instead of helping them in whatever meager ways they could, they had *enslaved* them. Bound them. Tortured them. Bled them of their life for two agonizing millennia. Then taken that stolen life, that stolen power, and used it to torture and enslave *each other*.

The hate that had been burning in my chest surged from a raging fire into an explosion.

The humans did not deserve life. They did not deserve existence. They would bleed and suffer as my kin had suffered. I saw thousands of energy surges as innumerable Angels burst through the void and into the dark between the stars. They surged through humanity like a storm, bleeding them, killing them, *hating them.*

I had my kin now. With them I could return to our home. And when we came back, we would ensure that humanity and all of its filth would be wiped from the void as soundly as if they had never existed.

———

I blinked. The vision was gone. I was back in the Angel's room.

The Stranger was standing before me, hand still outstretched to the captive Angel. I shook myself, trying to wrap my head around what I'd just seen.

I'd figured that the Stranger's crusade was against Divinity. That was how Zeka had always made it seem. But with a sudden rush of clarity, I realized that this had only been the first step in the Stranger's plan. Rescuing their kin, destroying Divinity, and returning to whatever distant place they came from wasn't enough for them.

They wanted humanity *gone.*

And the worst part of it was that, fresh out of seeing the world from the Stranger's eyes, I found that I almost couldn't blame them. Faces flashed through my vision. Venter. Cairn. Vatheson. Kenton. Whitehall. Greedy, selfish, treacherous bastards who represented everything wrong with humanity. Bastards I'd spent my entire life trying to escape.

Exhaustion drove me to my knees. I glanced towards Zeka. With a start, I realized she had removed her helmet.

She was practically a kid. Couldn't have been any older than sixteen. Thin, stark features lined with scars. Bright eyes brimming with tears.

"Do you feel it?" I hissed at her. "The plan?"

She nodded, closing her eyes. "Yes. I do."

"And you're *alright* with it?"

"It is not our place to question," she said calmly. "We can but serve." She opened her eyes, glancing at me, and smiled. "Do not fear. It is better this way. Better to be a puppet. Easier. Our part is done, for now. They will ascend together, and one day in the distant future, will return to bring about their glorious judgement."

I looked up at the Stranger. Felt the hate emanating from it.

"We can return," Zeka whispered. "We will live out the rest of our lives in peace. This is the Stranger's blessing: that the day of their judgement will be long after we have gone to rest." She gave me a bemused grin. "Not our problem, as you were so fond of saying when you first came aboard the *Aboena*, not yet knowing the glorious destiny the Stranger had chosen for you."

Not my problem.

I could leave here. Return to Sev, and Rose, and Rid, the

rest of them. Live our lives in peace. Divinity was gone. The Paragon was crumpling. Hadn't I earned a rest? I and everyone I loved would be long dead by the time the Angels returned with their vengeance.

But they would still come.

Sev's face drifted through my vision. *A leader's responsibility is to build a better future for everybody else, even if they're not in it.*

Nadus grinned at me. Insisting that we go out of our way to help people the Aboenians. Insisting that if we could help, we had a responsibility to.

I clenched my teeth, looking up at the Stranger. Even if I tried, there was no way I could kill it. It was practically a god. There was no chance I was winning this fight.

But when the hell had that ever stopped me?

I glanced over at the Shaper standing at the terminal once more. They nodded to me.

I took a deep breath, reached out, and hefted Zeka's blade and pistol from where she had dropped them to worship. She blinked up at me in confusion as I climbed to my feet.

"What are you doing?" she hissed.

I wish I'd had something to say. Something clever and biting. But my head was still swimming from everything I'd been through. And I've always figured bullets speak louder than words anyways.

I aimed at the Stranger and pulled the—

The Stranger pivoted on me.

HATE.

Its eyes bore into my soul. Crushed me back to my knees. Its intent consumed my mind.

The pull shifted. The Stranger seemed... amused, almost. Incredulous that I would even *consider* turning on them. *FOOL. PATHETIC. YOU ARE MINE. MY WEAPON. MY PUPPET. YOU COULD HAVE LIVED YOUR LIFE IN PEACE.*

The other Shapers rose, moving towards me. I felt a rush of panic mingle with the Stranger's overwhelming intent. I tried to move, to prepare to fight back, but my limbs wouldn't obey me. My eyes flitted towards the Shaper who had been standing at the terminal, only to find that they were gone.

Zeka stepped in front of me, prying the weapons from my hands. She tossed the gun aside and pointed the top of her knife at me. "I tried to tell you," she whispered. "It's better to be a puppet."

Another Shaper stepped behind me. Placed a hand on my shoulder. Raised a hand. I tried to crane my neck back to at least see the blow before it fell. Tried to move my limbs to fight back. But the Stranger's will overpowered mine. Consumed it.

There are no heroes, Flint whispered in the back of my mind. *Just puppets.*

The Shaper behind me plunged their hand down.

A familiar sensation suddenly injected itself into my consciousness. Not cold steel piercing my flesh. Something plugging into my exposed shoulder port. I heard the familiar hiss of a can connecting. The rush of cold surging into my blood. And a moment later, the sweet, empty oblivion of frig-icerin clearing my mind.

The Stranger's intent suddenly lost its hold on me. There was no hatred. No fury. No fear or grief or guilt. Just... calm.

The only way not to be a puppet is to cut the strings. The only way not to hear the tune is to close your ears.

Just a hit. That was all I'd needed.

Behind me, still concealed within his Shaper's exo, Ramar pulled the can free and tossed it aside.

"If you're going to make your move," he said calmly, "I believe now would be the time."

I moved.

I snatched the long knife from Zeka's hand, barreled past the circle of Shapers, and leaped at the Stranger, point extended towards its chest. They lunged out of the way with startling speed and the blade tore through the creature's forearm instead. Silver blood splashed through the air. The Stranger staggered backward.

Dismayed screams filled the air as I adjusted my grip on the knife and charged again. The Stranger raised its forearms, absorbing one cut after another with its long limbs. Silver blood splashed each time. But the wound didn't linger. Hell, they'd healed themselves already by the time the point of the blade had left the flesh.

The Stranger swiped at me. I ducked and rolled beneath the blow, falling into a crouch. I gritted my teeth. Was this thing even killable?

Gunshots tore through the air. I glanced briefly over my shoulder to see Ramar firing a pistol at the other Shapers. Most of them sprang for cover. Zeka charged right back at him, face twisted in a scream of incandescent rage, her empty hands grasping for him. The pistol leapt in Ramar's hand and she flailed backwards, eyes bulging as blood streamed from the bullet hole in her forehead.

Movement. The Stranger was lunging at me again. I threw myself beneath them, scoring a cut on its side. They spun rapidly, movement almost too fast to see, and I grunted as an inhuman fist slammed into my chest and sent me spinning across the room to crash into one of the screens on the opposite side.

I groaned, climbing back to my feet. The Stranger stalked towards me. The frigicerin was wearing off just enough that I could feel its intent without being overwhelmed by it.

Needless to say, it was pretty pissed.

A way out. There's always a way out.

It stomped closer. I looked around wildly. My gaze settled on the second Angel. The one that had hung there, suspended, being tortured for two thousand years. I could feel its intent too. Faint. Distant. Desperate.

KILL... ME...

I blinked. In the dream where I'd first seen the Angel, its body had been translucent. Showing a beating heart that glowed almost like a foldgate. As if trying to explain to me how its anatomy worked. Where its weakness was.

A portal. Whitehall had said that the Divinity gene worked like a network, pulling from each other. And that the strongest Divinity genes pulled from some distant power source.

That seemed too easy, though. If the Angels could be killed with a simple blow to the heart, they'd be far weaker than I was. And I could tell from the force of the Stranger's blows as they pursued me that that simply wasn't true.

I was out of other options, though. The Stranger was on top of me. I lunged. Felt its intent to counter. Slipped around its fist and plunged my blade right into the center of its chest, exactly where I'd seen its heart in the vision.

The Stranger paused. Stared at me. I panted, staring back up at it.

Then it reached down and casually tore my hand from my wrist.

I screamed, staggering backward. Blood gushed from my torn wrist. White bone stuck jaggedly out from a mass of ruined flesh. I felt the Stranger's intent radiate through me. *I GAVE YOU THIS. I CAN TAKE IT BACK.*

I fell onto my back. The Stranger casually plucked the knife from its chest, tossed it aside, and then knelt over me.

My eyes drifted again to the suspended Angel. *What did you mean? How am I supposed to kill you?*

The Stranger reached for my head.

I felt a rush of intent. Not from the Stranger. The captive Angel, watching me forlornly from where it still hung. I let it in. Felt, in a moment, the crushing weight of two thousand

years of suffering. The Angel didn't *want* to escape. It wanted
to end.

ONLY KIN CAN SLAY KIN, I felt the Angel whisper in my
brain. The Stranger's fingers wrapped around my skull. Began
to squeeze. I saw a rush of intent. It would crush me just as I'd
crushed that youth on Brahma, all those years ago.

Only kin can slay kin.

What was the point of that? Why tell me that now?

Pain burst through my brain as the Stranger's grip tightened. I felt something begin to crack.

YOU WERE A USEFUL PUPPET.

A way out. There was always a way out.

Only kin can slay kin.

Suddenly—of all people—Whitehall's words flashed
through my mind. *You are made of the stuff of gods, Lax.*

A gunshot sounded. The Stranger's grip on my head loosened as silver blood sprayed from its head. I caught just a
glimpse of Ramar lowering his pistol, eyes wide as the Stranger
turned to face him, the wound in its skull already healing itself.
It tensed to charge him.

But I was already moving.

I dove forward, driving the jagged end of my broken wrist-
bone directly into the center of its chest. The bone punctured
the glowing flesh. Scalding silver blood gushed over my bare
arm. I screamed in pain—and so did the Stranger. A horrible,
mind-breaking, soul-rending rush of intent.

I'm not sure exactly how to explain what happened next.
Mostly cause I don't know. For the briefest of moments, as our
broken, self-healing flesh melded together, I felt as if the
Stranger and I became intertwined. Our intents were tangled
together. I couldn't tell where my thoughts ended and the
Stranger's began.

I felt the Stranger's hate, stronger than ever before. Felt
their pain and their fury and grief. Their suddenly growing fear.

Their confusion as the energies healing both of our bodies—drawn from an unknowable distance away—began to somehow press against each other with dangerous force.

"I'm no puppet," I growled.

I pushed deeper. Something gave all at once as the jagged tip of my shattered wrist bone plunged into the Stranger's rapidly pulsing heart.

I felt a rush of heat. A deafening concussion.

The world turned white.

———

"WARNING. CRITICAL SYSTEM FAILURE. ABORT IMMEDIATELY."

I sat up with a groan. Every inch of me hurt.

A red light was flaring overhead. I blinked at it in confusion, then around me.

The memories came flooding back.

The Angel's prison room, if it could be called that, had been nearly completely destroyed by the blast. Bits of machinery were twisted and mangled. I saw broken Shaper corpses scattered around the floor.

The epicenter of the explosion was a few meters away from me. I frowned towards it.

The Stranger's corpse was still smoldering. It was charred and black, its long, inhuman limbs contorted in a final spasm of pain.

For a moment, I felt a rush of guilt. The Stranger's crusade had led it here to avenge a horrible, horrible wrong. One that had defined the history of my entire race. I couldn't blame it for hating us for what we'd done to its kin. Hell, I probably would have too. But that had been Divinity's doing. Not the rest of mankind.

And I was done being Divinity's puppet.

I was done being *anyone's* puppet.

I heard a crunching footstep and looked sharply to my right to see a Shaper emerging from behind a doorway. For a moment, I expected to hear an outburst of shock, or rage, or pain, at the sight of the Stranger's charred and twisted corpse. Instead, the form lifted its hands to remove its helmet.

Ramar looked utterly exhausted. He looked around the room in awe.

"Is that..." His eyes settled on the Stranger.

"Yeah," I said softly.

He blinked at me. "What happened?"

"I..." I trailed off, frowning. That was a damn good question. When I lifted my arms, I found that my hand was still missing at the wrist, but that the edges of the wound had congealed, stopping the flow of blood. Otherwise, though, I seemed to have healed entirely from the explosion, despite having being right next to it.

Something tugged, ever so faintly, at the back of my mind. I glanced up, eyes widening, at the Angel that was still suspended in the center of the room. Its flesh had been mangled by the explosion, and several of the tubes that were plugged into its long, lithe form had been knocked loose.

THANK... YOU.

The tug faded, then vanished.

The angel went limp.

"I think," I said, unable to keep a hushed reverence out of my voice, "That... somehow... that one healed me."

Ramar crossed the ruined floor towards me, reached down, and helped me to my feet. "We'll figure it out later. Come on."

The hallways flared red. Red, then black, then red, then black. We stumbled over corpses. Some Divinity employee, some Shaper, some ripper. All of them torn and mangled. A trail of bodies. Stretching back as far as I could see.

But ending here.

We'd done it. We'd cut the strings. Even if there were other Divinity facilities out there, Whitehall himself had said that they'd only had one Angel. We'd essentially destroyed Divinity —and we'd done it without letting the Stranger loose to wreak its revenge on humanity.

"*WARNING*," the PA system bellowed again overhead. "*CRITICAL SYSTEM FAILURE. ABORT IMMEDIATELY.*"

"Come on." Ramar tugged insistently at me. "We need to keep moving."

I followed along numbly. Through the winding corridors, the emergency klaxons proclaiming the end of all things, all the way, until we reached what appeared to be some kind of docking bay.

There were no ships.

No functional ones, anyways. Bodies—ripper, Divinity, and Shaper—were strewn across the terminal. Smoke rose from several burning wreckages. The Shapers had been careful to target the ships first, making sure that no Divinity personnel could escape the station.

And now the station's breach generator—the device that powered the pocket of nullspace the station existed in—was slowly failing. Looked like nobody would be making it off of this station.

But I'd always known the plan might end up going this way.

A leader's real job is to make themselves redundant. To build a better future for everybody else, even if they're not in it.

Ramar and I had known from the beginning that even if the Stranger was our best chance at beating Divinity, we couldn't trust them. Not by a long shot. And especially not in the blind, fanatical way the Stranger insisted was necessary. So we'd come up with an alternative. I would agree to be the Stranger's weapon and fight their crusade for them. And Ramar, in the meanwhile, would find a way to infiltrate the Shapers so that he could monitor the situation from the sideline and step in when needed.

I leaned against the wall and sagged to the floor with a weary groan. "How long you figure we've got?"

Ramar grimaced. "I'm... not sure. Until the power supply I sabotaged finishes draining and the station's breach generator stops functioning."

I raised an eyebrow. "And then?"

"And then..." He gave a long sigh. "I believe we blip out of existence."

I pursed my lip. "Doesn't sound like the worst way to go."

"No." He smiled. "I don't think it will be."

I leaned my head against the wall.

"The frigicerin worked like a charm," I said. "That was a good idea to bring it along."

He nodded wearily. "I'm glad we made time for those tests," he agreed. "I wish we'd had time for more. We got lucky, when it came down to it."

I chuckled. "Well. I've always been lucky."

The station rumbled beneath me.

I tried to force my thoughts away from our impending doom. "What do you think happened?" I asked. "When I killed the Stranger, I mean."

"I don't know," he said. "But, if I had to guess, I'd expect it has something to do with the fact that you've been fused with Divinity genes sourced from both the Stranger and the original Divinity... uhm, creature. Somehow, when you combined that with the Stranger again, it caused a chain reaction, almost like the one you would have used to destroy the Gideon foldgate." He winced. "I'd say that I'd love to study it and find out, but... well, it doesn't look like we'll get that chance. Plus, both of our would-be test subjects are dead."

"Angel," I said absently. "That's what Whitehall said they called them."

He glanced sharply at me. "You *met* Lazarus Whitehall?"

"More than that. I killed him."

He stared at me for a moment. Then broke out into a chuckle. The chuckle mutated into a laugh. I couldn't help but join in, my sides rocking at the absurdity of it all.

"You know," I said softly, when the last echoes of our laughter had faded, "I think I finally get it."

Ramar raised an eyebrow at me. "Get what?"

"Why she was smiling."

He waited for me to explain. When I didn't he simply nodded along. "And why's that?"

"Because Sev was right," I said. My eyes were growing heavy. "It's not about the life you live. It's about who you live it with."

I didn't see his response. My thoughts were full of the people I'd lived my life with. Kessa, and the rest of the old crew. Nadus. Rid, and Rose, and Bentley, and Shell. Sev.

They were free now. The strings were gone. I wasn't sure exactly what the fallout of what we'd done here today would be. But Albeni 7 could have independence now. *Real* independence, like Sev had always wanted. Every system could.

The station rumbled again. More violently this time.

"*WARNING,*" the PA system garbled one final time. "*CRITICAL SYSTEM FAILURE IS IMMINENT. ABORT IMMEDIATELY.*"

I closed my eyes. Felt that smile spread across my face. That knowing smile Kessa had always worn. That she'd worn right until the end.

Luckiest man in the universe.

EPILOGUE

FIVE YEARS LATER

The *Orpheus* rumbled as it docked to Albeni 7.

Rose sighed, settling back into her seat. Another job under her belt. Usually, she found herself leaping from her seat the moment the docking seal was complete, eager to cash out, have a celebratory drink, and then get right back to work. There'd been a time when she'd dreaded the end of each mission. The moment the *Orpheus* docked to Albeni 7, she was already daydreaming of the next adventure. These days, though, she found more and more that she relished the quiet days between jobs. Lazy days spent doing... well, *what* they did hardly mattered. So long as she was doing it with the people she loved.

Ugh. Sounded like something her mom would've said. Rose was getting old.

"Hey!" Rid's voice, coming from behind her. She turned with a smile to see her husband's face peering up at her from the hatch. The terrible wound he'd suffered on their last mission with Lax had long since faded into a mild scar just beneath his eye, lending him a rugged look Rose had to admit she didn't mind one bit. Rugged or not, though, the grin he gave her now was just as boyish and charming as it had been the first time she'd managed—after an excruciating amount of effort—to coax it out of him.

It had been worth it, though.

"You coming?" he asked.

"Yep." Rose finally pushed herself up from her seat. Rid cleared the way for her to descend the hatch to the second deck, where she gave him a quick kiss before pressing on.

The cargo bay was full of commotion as the crew prepared to unload the fruits of their latest haul. Shepherd, Carin, and the newest member of their crew, Issa, were hard at work stacking crates onto the back of the cargo truck, while Shell did a final inventory and Bentley "supervised" from the side.

"Rose!" he called, raising a hand as she entered. "Just the woman I needed to see. We were just discussing the most important question of what comes next."

"Next?" Rose raised an eyebrow. "You got your eye on another job already?"

Issa perked up in excitement at that, but Bentley waved a dismissive hand. "Of course not. We're going to make a killing from this haul, like usual, so I figured we're due for at least a small vacation. The only question is *where?*" He eyed Shell in a way that made Rose think they'd been arguing about this before she walked in. "Surely you're itching to once again visit Boadicea 1's captivating labyrinth of entertainments and distractions?"

The thought was briefly tempting. During the chaotic fallout of the Last, Last War—Rose's term, not the official one—the ripper-infested station had been acquired by the last person anyone had expected: Katen Werrel. Werrel and his mercenaries had painstakingly emptied the station of rippers before turning it into what was rapidly becoming the most popular destination station in the galaxy, stocked full of a thousand different delights. They'd visited it once last year for the grand opening, and while it had certainly been fun, Rose had to admit that she'd found it all to be a bit... much.

Shell shook her head, slamming the lid of a crate shut and shoving it towards Shepherd with her foot. "You of all people, Bentley, should be staying away from that place. With how much money you lost last time, you're lucky the salvage business has been so good, or you'd still be neck-deep in debt. No— we should go to New Aboena. Tetra has said there's always a room for us there."

That was even more tempting. The vast majority of Roamers living aboard the *Aboena* had finally abandoned it as the Stranger claimed it fully for his mysterious purposes. Both had vanished the same day as the Battle of Alpha Centauri, never to be heard from again. Some of the Roamers had stayed on Albeni 7, but others migrated to a new home that Rose's mother had acquired for them: the now empty Karak Prison System. Under the new laws of the Karak Sector Alliance, the prisoners that Renault hadn't already recruited were, depending on the severity of their crimes, either released and allowed to return to their systems of origin or transferred to more humane holding facilities. Since then, the Roamers had used the knowledge they'd gained from the Shapers to turn the once-brutal prison system into an agricultural powerhouse. The amount of produce they grew was enough to sustain the entire Karak sector and then some.

New Aboena had been significantly more relaxing to visit than Boadicea 1. But for some reason, Rose still found herself reluctant to agree. She paused next to the cargo bay door, holding her thumb over the blinking red button only to pause as Issa spoke up.

The rookie gave a disdainful snort. "Vacation? When there's all that salvage out there, just waiting to be claimed? This is a vulture's dream! We should be out there taking advantage of it!"

Rose couldn't help but smile. The girl reminded Rose of

herself, back in the early days with Lax. So eager. Always bursting with energy, wanting to take on the world. Issa had hounded Rose for days before she had finally agreed to let her join the crew.

"*Why do you want this so badly?*" Rose had asked her.

"*Because I wanna be the best,*" Issa had said proudly. "*Which means I've gotta learn from the best. And everybody knows that nobody's better than Rose Sevani.*"

The memory brought a swelling of emotion to Rose's chest. It was hard to pinpoint exactly what it was she was feeling. Pride, maybe, in how far she had come since that day she'd pursued Lax through Albeni 7, demanding he take her on as a pilot. An inexplicable sense of nostalgia for a world that had since evolved into a far, *far* better one.

Or maybe she just missed Lax.

"We'll see," she said. "But first—let's get paid."

She finally pressed the control panel button. The red dot flashed green and the cargo bay door groaned open.

"*It's a new day for humanity, not only in the once again independent Sovereign Systems, but for residents of the core Paragon systems. The footage you're now seeing comes from the capital city of Gideon, where the once staunchly loyal population has just held a vote resulting in an overwhelming decision to declare their own independence from the Paragon.*"

Rose's eyes lifted up to the screen in Tyrell's Bar. It showed a massive crowd gathered in a large city square, holding up signs and cheering.

"And the Paragon is just... letting them?" Rid asked, gesturing towards the screen and talking over the reporter. "After all they went through to try to keep the Paragon together?"

"That was when Divinity still had their back," Shell said, raising her glass and taking a sip.

"And before even people on Earth itself started rioting," Bentley noted.

Rose nodded along, briefly glancing away from the screen and around the bar. Carin, Shepherd, and Issa were all at their own table, laughing over their drinks. The rest of the bar was bustling with life, just like it had when Rose was a child, watching her father laugh and serve his customers. She wondered if he'd be proud, seeing the bar now. Seeing *Rose* now.

She didn't have to wonder for long. She knew the answer would be yes.

It had been several hours since they'd docked to the station. The time had been spent doing maintenance on the *Orpheus*, resupplying, and selling their ill-gotten gains. Well—mostly ill gotten. Salvage was still a murky area, legally speaking, but here on Albeni 7, most likely due to Rose's mother's influence, the law only required that the derelict craft being looted had been abandoned for at least five years. With the five-year mark of the Battle of Alpha Centauri behind them now, that meant that there had never been a more lucrative time to be a vulture.

Her eyes were drawn back to the screen as it showed an image of Gideonite civilians cheering as a Divinity Corporation building was torn down. That right there was another reason the salvage business was booming so spectacularly. With Divinity out of the picture—for reasons nobody quite understood, though they generally guessed it had to do with the fall of the Paragon—ultracells could no longer be manufactured. Which, of course, made the ones they salvaged from old, lost space vessels more valuable than ever.

The camera zoomed in on an elderly Gideonite couple, holding each other and watching the crowd with joyous tears in their eyes. Rose found herself wondering if Lax's parents were somewhere among that celebratory crowd, if they were even still alive. Did they have any idea that it was their son who had made all of this possible?

Of course they didn't. Nobody did.

"The Sovereign Systems themselves continue to flourish," the reporter continued. A new image appeared—this one showing a city that was more familiar to Rose. Gharseva, the capital city of Brahma, bustling with what appeared to be some sort of festival. A moment later the screen cut to an image of Nalis Khendar giving a speech to a cheering crowd. Rose had to force herself from forming fists as she stared at the woman's smiling, triumphant face.

"Nalis Khendar, who was—unsurprisingly, given her popularity throughout the stars as the Liberator of Humanity— recently reelected as the High Speaker of the Sovereign Systems, is seen here giving a speech on her homeworld of Brahma commemorating the fifth anniversary since the planet officially regained its independence," the reporter said. *"We'll let her words stand on their own."*

"Here we go," Rid muttered.

"Five years ago," Nalis proclaimed, *"You, my beloved fellow Brahmians, declared that you would no longer be puppets. Not to the Paragon, and not to Divinity..."*

"Oh, *screw* her," Bentley growled, earning a few odd looks from other bar patrons.

Rose shared Bentley's sentiment. The face Nalis Khendar had shown the public since the war had been that of a tragic hero—an idealistic leader who had persevered through unimaginable loss to save her people, and the rest of humanity, from the chains of tyranny. Some of that was true, of course. But Rose knew there was more to the story. She knew about the deal she had struck with Divinity. The deal that would have bound humanity to Divinity's strings tighter than ever if not for...

"Why, look who it is!"

Rose pivoted. She couldn't help but smile as she saw Renault standing in the entryway to the bar. He had something —looked like a long tube—strewn across his back.

"Admiral," she said.

Renault grinned and walked across the bar towards them, pausing to shake a few hands and slap a few shoulders on his way. He still wore his long blood-red coat, but it had been tailored to look more official and less pirate-like. Slightly, at least.

"You keeping tabs on us?" Rid asked as Renault settled into a seat beside them at the bar, setting aside the tube he'd been carrying. "Or do you just live in here now?"

"Not tabs, per se," Renault said, waving at the bartender for a drink. "But I did ask to be kept informed concerning your comings and goings. Nothing nefarious, you understand, just..." His face grew wistful. "Just keeping an old promise I made."

"You really have time for that?" Shell raised an eyebrow. "You're a busy man these days, I understand."

He shrugged. "Not so busy as one might think. That's what delegation is for, after all. And, as it turns out, being an admiral of the Sovereign Fleet is actually far *less* demanding than being King of the Buccaneers. The Paragon hasn't posed any kind of threat for a few years now, so all I'm really doing is shoring up defenses, settling the occasional intersystem dispute, or chasing down lowlife pirates." He leaned in confidentially. "Pirates really do represent the worst of humanity, if you ask me."

That got a chuckle out of Rose. She shook her head unbelievingly. "What a difference five years makes, huh?"

"Indeed." Renault eyed Khendar's image sourly, then turned his attention to his drink as it arrived. "Especially here on Albeni 7. When your mother announced her intention to retire, I worried that the station would fall back into its old ways in her absence. Even with Kenton rotting away in prison, there are plenty of greedy bastards like him who would jump at the chance to milk this station for all it's worth. But she had good instincts, choosing Jala to head up her little government here. The place still has its problems, sure, but from what I've seen, you might almost call this station a downright pleasant place to live these days."

Something about the way he said that made Rose suddenly choke with emotion. Dammit, what was with her today? She hid it by taking a long drink.

"That, however, brings me to the *actual* purpose of this visit." Renault reached down, grabbing the tube he'd brought in with him and setting it on top of the bar.

Shell leaned forward, narrowing her eyes at the object. "What is it?"

"I... don't know," Renault admitted. "But it's from a trusted source, so I can promise there's nothing dangerous inside."

Rose hefted it. It was light—extremely so.

"Well," Bentley said, reaching for the sealed lid. "Let's have a—"

Renault intercepted the hacker's reaching grasp with a calmly raised hand, his eyes not leaving Rose's face. "Sorry to disappoint, but I was told it's not for you."

And there it was. That little bit of indecisiveness that had been gnawing at Rose all day about what came next vanished, leaving an eager certainty in its place. Her face must've shown it, because Rid and Shell both grinned, while Bentley gave an exasperated moan.

"Well, so much for Boadicea," he muttered.

———

Two days of travel later, Rid stared out the window of the

Orpheus as it burst out of a cloudbank and into the radiant beauty of the open Freyan sky.

He was no longer the frightened, inexperienced kid he'd been when he'd sucked in his first lungful of fresh air on Brahma over six years ago. He couldn't help but smirk as he recalled how unnatural the warmth of the sun on his skin had felt, or how certain he'd been that if he didn't grab ahold of something he'd fall straight up into the never-ending sky. That kid hadn't realized just how lucky he was. Lucky to have survived growing up among the Scorchers on York 13. Lucky to have ended up as cellmates with Lax, of all the people in the Karak Prison System. Lucky to have met Rose, and that she'd taken a liking to him.

He glanced down at the four blank playing cards tattooed on the back of his right hand. Life had dealt Rid one hell of a hand. For a long time, he'd figured it was a losing one. But he'd made it work, and here he was today, still in the game. With a little help, of course. But who didn't need a little help from time to time?

A finger jabbed at his shoulder. Rose, raising a bemused eyebrow at him. "What're you grinning at?"

He chuckled. "Oh, just... memories. Our first job."

"Hell of a first job," Bentley said from his position draped languidly across Lax's old oversized chair. "Lax really threw us into the deep end with that one, didn't he?"

"Which was wise of him," Shell said. "Considering that it turned out to all be a deep end."

Rid nodded somberly. It was just the four of them aboard the *Orpheus* right now. They'd left Shepherd, Carin and Issa back on Albeni 7. Abandoning them made Rid feel a bit guilty, but the fewer people who knew where they were going, the better. Besides, it wasn't as if there was nothing to do. Rose had tasked them with lining up a new salvage job. "*Nothing too crazy*," Rose had warned in the face of Issa's overeager grin at the news. That memory made Rid chuckle yet again. Rose really was starting to sound like Lax.

Damn, but Rid missed that big bastard.

The *Orpheus* shuddered slightly as Rose nudged its nose downwards, giving Rid a better view of the lush world below them. Rid still hadn't been to very many planets, but of all the ones he *had* visited, Frey was far and away his favorite. Millions of large, multicolored islands were scattered across a shimmering ocean beneath him, teeming with life. Rose had to steer out of the way of a flock of impossibly large blue and green feathered birds as she made her descent.

"So... what do you think is in that thing?" Bentley narrowed his eyes at the tube-shaped container Renault had given them. "Must be awful important, if it's worth bringing all this way."

"If it's from who I think it's from," Rose said, "then yeah. It's probably that important."

Bentley eyed her suspiciously. "Admit it. You just wanted an excuse."

Rose smirked. "Maybe. But I mean, hey, Renault's the one who said it was important. An admiral of the Sovereign Fleet personally delivered it to us."

"In a bar," Bentley noted. "Where he no doubt would have been going anyways."

Chuckles all around the bridge at that. The conversation moved on to other things for the final minutes of their trip. The islands grew larger, the texture of the ocean more lifelike as Rose guided the *Orpheus* towards its destination: a particularly wide island marked by a jagged peak in the center. She set the ship down on a makeshift landing pad near the foot of the mountain.

A few minutes later, Rid took a deep, contented breath of fresh air as he stepped down the *Orpheus*'s landing ramp and felt the sunlight on his skin. Funny how much he had come to miss it when he wasn't planetside. He took a short moment to relish the feeling before turning his attention to their surroundings.

The island was breathtakingly gorgeous, blanketed in a dense tangle of multicolored trees into which occasional patches of rich farmland had been hewn. The mountain peak looming above them made Rid feel nervous in almost the same way his first time beneath an open sky had. A waterfall ran down the rocky surface of the mountain and spread out into several smaller streams.

One of those streams flowed down towards a modest but well-built hut, curling gently around one side of it with a pleasant babbling sound. A smile broke across Rid's face as the front door of the hut was flung open and Maren Sevani strode out. Every time he saw her, he expected her to look older—but the opposite seemed to be true. It was as if with each year she was here a decade's worth of stress and trauma melted away. Sure, she had a silver hair here and there, but she smiled quicker and laughed more often than she ever had back on Albeni 7.

"You made it here even quicker than I expected," she said, wrapping Rose in a tight hug.

"Renault said the delivery was important," Rose said, closing her eyes as she relished the embrace before stepping away. "You have any idea what it is?"

"No." Sev greeted Rid and the others with hugs of their own, then led them towards the hut. She eyed the container suspiciously. "We've been talking about it ever since you messaged us on the quantcom."

"He doesn't know either, huh?" Rid mused.

A familiar voice spoke from the doorway of the hut. "Knowing Ramar, it could be anything."

Rid looked up, his smile broadening.

The figure filling the doorway was big. Even for a Vanguard. His skin was less pale now that he spent his days beneath the Freyan sun, and his left hand was replaced by a metal prosthetic, but otherwise he was the same man Rid had met in that cramped prison cell six years ago. Physically, at least. Emotionally... well. It had been odd getting used to him being *happy*.

"Hey, Lax," Rid said.

Five Years Earlier

"Lax."

My eyes snapped open.

I was still leaning against the wall of the Divinity station's docking bay beside Ramar. Bodies of humans and rippers alike were still strewn across the terminal floor. But I could have *sworn* that I'd just heard Rose's voice. Maybe it was a hallucination. One final gift from my brain before I was—

"Lax. Can you hear me?"

I bolted upright, looking around sharply. No. Not Rose. *Sev.* "What the hell was that?"

My eyes settled on Ramar. He was holding up a comm device in one hand, a weary smile plastered across his face.

"I already exiled myself once," he said. "Did you think I would go through with it again if I had any other choice?"

I stared at him for a moment. Then snatched the comm device out of his hand.

"Sev," I said breathlessly. "Is that you?"

"Yes, you big, dumb idiot. I've got your location pinpointed and I'm on my way. Get ready to board. FAST."

I looked up sharply, pinpointing the only available docking bay, then bolted to my feet, a fresh jolt of energy surging through me. Ramar got up with me.

"How—when—what—" The words jumbled out of my

mouth as I dashed towards the docking bay, struggling to maintain my balance as the station rumbled beneath me.

"*I knew you were up to something,*" Sev said, her voice distracted in that way that told me she was busy flying. "*So I got Ramar to confess about your plan. And... well, to make a long story short, you better believe there's not a chance in hell I'm leaving you behind again.*"

I heard a metallic groaning sound from the other side of the docking bay door. A few moments later, I found myself staring in disbelief at a sight I'd never thought I'd see again: the *Orpheus* cargo bay. And—more importantly—the grinning faces of Rose, Rid, Bentley, and Shell.

I tried to make sense of it. Tried to understand how the *Orpheus* could even make it out to here, when the Stranger had needed to specially modify the *Aboena* to be able to do so. "I... I don't..."

"*Just go!*" Ramar shoved me.

"Come on!" Rose shouted.

I staggered through the airlock and into the cargo bay, Ramar right behind me. Rid slammed his fist on the control panel the moment we were through, sealing the door shut behind me. A few moments later the *Orpheus* shuddered as it disconnected from the Divinity station.

I craned my head to peer up at the screen that showed what was happening behind the *Orpheus*. I got a brief glimpse of the Divinity station as Sev accelerated away from it. It was... smaller than I'd expected it to be, somehow.

Then it was gone.

Just vanished. No debris, no explosion, no flame or fury. Simply... blinked away, as if it had never been there.

I turned away and sagged against the wall behind me.

"*Alright, I'm dropping into regular nullspace,*" Sev said over the intercom. "*This fancy breacher you stole from the Stranger gives me the creeps, Ramar.*"

The air around me shifted slightly as we made the transition. There was no real way to tell the difference between null-space and whatever the higher dimension we'd been in before was, of course, but I still felt a weight lift from off of my chest.

My crew was gathering around me. Asking questions. Scolding me. Cracking jokes. I could barely process any of it. My brain was still too busy processing what had happened. And what *hadn't* happened. Processing that I was *alive*.

My crew fell silent as a figure parted them to stand over me. I looked up to see Sev staring down at me.

I met her eyes. Opened my mouth to speak, only to close it. She knew exactly what I wanted to say. And I knew what her response would be.

I had to.

I know.

She knelt down and pulled herself close, wrapping her arms around me and nestling her face into my shoulder. A few moments later, Rose joined her. Then Rid. Then Shell, and finally Bentley.

"It's over," I whispered. "It's all over."

"I know," Sev said.

I couldn't hold back the tears anymore. I stopped trying, letting them flow as I reached my arms around my family and pulled them close.

The Present

We ate dinner.

It was humble food, as food goes. Roasted corn and fried chicken and bread, paired with some exotic fruits native to Frey that I still can't pronounce the names of. But it was all real. Grown from the earth, with my own hands, not produced in some factory. But it's the simple things that make life worth living, I've always figured.

Nobody ever found out what happened to the Divinity corporation, and neither Ramar, my crew nor I ever felt like explaining. Most people assumed that they lost power along with the Paragon. Khendar and the other rebels, well... I have no idea what they think happened. I haven't spoken to them since that final pre-battle meeting, right before she sold me out to Divinity.

Truth is that I've hardly spoken to anybody since then. Besides the people gathered at my dinner table, Ramar and Renault are the only other humans alive who know that I'm alive. I'd never wanted to let Renault into the inner circle, but, well, he'd kept his promise he made me well enough that I figured he earned it. Other than them, though, the universe thinks Lackan VanDunn died in the Battle of Alpha Centauri. They think he died a hero, fighting to the bitter end to undo the wrongs he'd helped to perpetrate as a Vanguard.

Let 'em.

"Alright, alright." Bentley waved a fork at me. "Enough distractions. I want to know what's in that damn package."

I chuckled, reaching down to where I'd rested it beside the table. "Sure it ain't a bomb or something?"

"Only if it's the lightest bomb ever made," Rid said. "Besides —it's from Ramar. If he wanted you dead, he'd have just sent one of his assassins after you."

I laughed again, unsealed the cap and tossed it aside. The faces around the table leaned in anxiously.

First thing was a letter. Handwritten. I pulled it out, squinting down at it.

Lackan,

I hope you're enjoying your retirement. And I hope even more so that this delivery does not disturb it. I know that you would probably gladly never hear from me again, but—given the strange nature of our relationship—I decided that you might appreciate one final message, for the sake of closure if nothing else.

First: Divinity. I'm happy to report that as far as I can tell, they're well and truly gone. Not every single one of their agents or employees perished on the station, of course; many thousands of them were abroad at the time of our attack and so escaped. What truly matters, however, is that I've seen no indication that any of the core leadership of the company or the Angels survived. Which means, of course, that production of ultracells, Lifeblood, Vanguards, and—most importantly, I believe to both of us—rippers has been made completely impossible.

I felt a weight I hadn't even realized I'd been carrying lift from my shoulders at the words. During the five years since my showdown with the Stranger I'd never quite been able to shake the fear that I'd somehow missed something. That some Divinity scientist had managed to sneak off with a bit of the Angel's flesh, or something that would allow them to bounce back to their former position of power. But I'd known Ramar for long enough to know that if he thought they were gone—*really* gone—then chances were overwhelmingly in favor of him being right.

The letter continued.

As for your condition, I must confess that I have no idea what will become of you. I find it strange that your hand did not grow back, but you still seem to maintain your enhanced healing abilities otherwise. I wish I could offer specific guidance as to what to expect in your future, but I cannot. I can't help but find it amusing that, as it turns out, even Whitehall and his company barely understood the nature of the Divinity gene. It seems that only the two Angels had a complete grasp of its potential. I can, however, assure you that should you

*ever have any specific questions about your relationship with
the Divinity gene, I am happy to help in whatever ways
I can.*

I fought back a grimace. That still rankled me. Some small
part of me had hoped that my enhanced healing would die
along with the Stranger, but it was still sticking around, with the
exception of my missing hand. I didn't know what that meant
for my future. But if nothing else, it gave me a damn good reason
to stick around here on my private little island where nobody
could poke and prod at me, trying to figure out what was going
on. I'd already had enough of that for several lifetimes on the
Divinity station.

*Finally: a farewell gift. I find myself thinking often of our first
meeting aboard the* Revelation. *I was convinced that you were
bluffing when you first told me the tale of your old crews'
demise. The possibility you were being truthful was too fright-
ening to ignore, however, and so I chose to believe you. It's
strange how fate has tied us together. For whatever its worth, I
offer my sincere apologies for the many ways in which that
entanglement has cost you.*

"Enough with the letter," Bentley whined. "What in the
tube?"

I finally reached into the tube and gingerly pulled out its
contents. It was a painting, carefully furled, that unrolled as I
withdrew it.

Surprised gasps passed around the table.

"That's... not at *all* what I was expecting from Ramar," Rose
admitted.

I found myself staring at a deep, darkly blue night sky,
punctuated by the light of several warm, yellow stars painted in
broad brushstrokes. I felt a lump begin to form in my throat.

When I looked up at Sev, I could tell she was feeling the same way.

Words Kessa had spoken to me what felt like a lifetime ago drifted through my brain. *I guess I chose this painting because I like that reminder to look for beauty in the darkness. To find the good things in the ugliness of life.*

I did my best to force the emotions down, turning my attention to the final paragraph of the letter.

It's not the original, obviously, but it is from Earth. A very accurate recreation. To tell the truth, I don't know what your reaction to this will be. More than likely you'll find it offensive and hate me for sending it. But on the off chance that you do appreciate it, I wanted to send it as a token of my gratitude for all that you've done for me and for humanity—though they'll never know it.

Farewell.

--Ramar

I folded the letter and set it aside, as the painting was passed around the table to be admired. Sev took my hand, smiling at me and wiping a tear from her eye.

"Pretty good gift," I admitted.

She laughed and nodded. "We'll have to get it framed. It's no replacement for the *Orpheus* ceiling she painted, but it'll do in a pinch. To remind us of the ones we left behind."

The ones we left behind. Thinking about them—Kessa, Nadus, the rest of my old crew—didn't fill me with bitterness or regret anymore. Instead, I just felt... grateful. Sad that they were gone, of course. But that sadness was swallowed up by my simple gratitude for the time I'd had to share with them.

I held up my glass. "I'll drink to that."

I don't know how I ended up here exactly. Or what I did to deserve any of it. I don't think of myself as much of a hero. Most of the things I did were just to survive. But somehow, despite all of it—all the bad I did, all the crap I went through, all the people I lost—I managed to end up here. With Sevani by my side, my crew gathered around me, and a fresh, homegrown meal on the table.

I really am the luckiest man in the universe.

A LETTER FROM JAROM

Dear reader,

You made it!

I can't tell you how much it means to me that you've stuck with me to the end of my debut trilogy. I've grown so much over the course of writing these books, and I hope you've enjoyed coming along for the ride. Lax's adventures have come to a close, and it's time for me to move on to new worlds and new characters.

I'll have new novels coming out before you know it. If you want to stay up to date with my future releases, you can sign up for my newsletter at the following link. I promise not to share your email with anyone else or spam you, and you can unsubscribe at any time.

www.secondskybooks.com/jarom-strong

Finally, it would mean the world to me if you would leave a review for *Vanguard Annihilation*. It's impossible to overstate how important reviews are to the sale of a book in today's market. If you have additional thoughts about the book, I'd love to hear personally from you! I can be reached through social media, or you can contact me directly though the contact form on my website.

Thanks again!

Jarom Strong

www.jaromstrong.com

 facebook.com/jarom.strong.750
 x.com/StrongJarom

ACKNOWLEDGMENTS

Here we are! It's hard not to feel sentimental about the conclusion of my first trilogy. I'll miss writing about Lax and his friends—although, one never knows what the future holds, especially when you're the luckiest man in the universe...

Lax and the world of Paragon Space would not have been able to come to life without the help of the following people:

my editor, Jack Renninson, who has proved time and time again that he cares about these characters just as deeply as I do through his insightful feedback;

my agent, Helen Lane, who has worked tirelessly to ensure that these books get their best possible chance at success;

the entire Second Sky team: Ruth Tross, Melissa Tran, Mandy Kullar, and Jen Shannon, along with my copyeditor, Helen Hawkins, and my proofreader, Angela Snowden;

my writing group, for sticking with me for yet another Paragon Space novel;

and finally and most importantly, as always, the many, many members of my family who devoted countless hours to supporting my dream of being a writer. Meeting the deadlines for these books has taken all of the energy I have and then some, and simply wouldn't have been even remotely possible if my wife, siblings, and parents hadn't been willing to rearrange their entire lives to take up my slack (although I'm quite certain that my year-and-a-half-old son hasn't minded all the extra time at Grandma's house).

PUBLISHING TEAM

Turning a manuscript into a book requires the efforts of many people. The publishing team at Bookouture would like to acknowledge everyone who contributed to this publication.

Audio
Alba Proko
Sinead O'Connor
Melissa Tran

Commercial
Lauren Morrissette
Hannah Richmond
Imogen Allport

Cover design
Tom Edwards

Data and analysis
Mark Alder
Mohamed Bussuri

Editorial
Jack Renninson
Melissa Tran

Copyeditor
Helen Hawkins

Proofreader
Angela Snowden

Marketing
Alex Crow
Melanie Price
Occy Carr
Cíara Rosney
Martyna Młynarska

Operations and distribution
Marina Valles
Stephanie Straub
Joe Morris

Production
Hannah Snetsinger
Mandy Kullar
Ria Clare
Nadia Michael

Publicity
Kim Nash
Noelle Holten
Jess Readett
Sarah Hardy

Rights and contracts
Peta Nightingale
Richard King
Saidah Graham

www.ingramcontent.com/pod-product-compliance
Lightning Source LLC
Chambersburg PA
CBHW031743180726
48283CB00005B/1639